Lumaworld

Lumaworld

Book 3 of the Colorworld Series

Rachel E Kelly

Edited by Jamie Walton

Published by Rachel E Kelly, Williston, North Dakota, USA

Published by Rachel E Kelly, Williston, North Dakota, USA.
Web Site: http://colorworldbooks.com

ISBN-13: 978-1500757762

Cover Photograph by Richard J Heeks

Cover Design by Beth Weatherly

To Wednesday, June 18th, 2014.

Acknowledgements

This series… I can't really express here what it felt like to want to quit something so badly but to be driven forward by a will not your own. I'd like to think Wendy does a pretty good job of it in these pages, however. Few things have gone "right" for me in the six months prior to the release of Lumaworld, but as Wendy has taught me, all the absolutely necessary things do. And every part of a journey is necessary to who you become by the end. So if you are someone who has interacted with me at all in the last six months, you played a part, and you have my thanks for being exactly who you are.

I began to make a list here of all the angels who have been part of my life recently, who have carried my family, who have carried me, but the list grew excessively long before I'd ever finished it. I have shed tears of gratitude with your names on them. Many times. Every small act was just as necessary as the big acts. I didn't feel right only listing some of them based on the scope of their help. If you have done a kindness to me, in any measure, you know who you are. I love you more than words, and may that goodness be heaped upon your head in return. You cannot fathom how much I have needed you.

That said, I need to give a shout out to a few people involved directly in production of this work. These people have made Colorworld their endeavor, too. They have invested their time and talents. They own a part of this series, and their name belongs here:

Bradley L Kelly, my Felicity Smoak. Most readers can't fathom how much goes on behind the scenes in book production. Were it not for my husband, you would not have this book. You wouldn't know about it. And you wouldn't have all the amazing art and extra content available at conventions and on my website. There would be no author signings or podcasts or awesome reviews. No Twitter and no Facebook. No sweet YouTube commercials and no 2015 Tour. How many people can say the love of their life quit their job and risked everything to dedicate every waking moment to making sure a few heartfelt words on a page were seen by the rest of the world? I can. Because mine did.

Tiffany Dawn Thornton, advisor, copy editor, tour companion, and the very first Wendy cosplayer :-) The best angels are not floating, glowing personages. They are people who care more than any reasonable person would. Tiffany is one of those people.

Tiana Matson, videographer, YouTube advisor.

Richard J Heeks, over-achieving camera genius.

Beth Weatherly, dedicated friend and cover designer.

My God, who left me love notes when I needed them most and sent angels when I could not take one more step on my own.

And many thanks to:

The C.S. Lewis Company for use of the epigraph quote from:
THE GREAT DIVORCE by C.S. Lewis copyright © C.S. Lewis Pte. Ltd. 1946.

My copy editors: Tiffany Dawn Thornton, Heather N. Burns, & Marie Zimmerly.

And finally. To readers. Do you know the power you wield? It is the power to immortalize. In the words of Bastille's Poet, "I have written you down, now you will live forever. And all the world will read you and you will live forever. In eyes not yet created, on tongues that are not born. I have written you down, now you will live forever."

The Lord said we were gods. How long could ye bear to look on the greatness of your own soul and the eternal reality of her choice?

-C. S. Lewis, The Great Divorce

Part I

"*How* long are you two going to keep this up?" Ezra asks, scrunching his nose at his tiny plastic cup of watered-down apple juice. The continental breakfast at the hotel leaves a lot to be desired.

I reach for Gabriel's wrist and pretend to check the time on his watch. "About ten more minutes." I steal a glance at Gabriel who is buttering his toast and smiling faintly. We both know that wasn't what Ezra meant, but messing with him is fun.

"Ten minutes?" Ezra asks. "Really? What's the plan?" He stuffs a piece of waffle in his mouth and looks at me excitedly.

I cross my arms over the table casually and look at Gabriel. "Then we have a date with a romantic stroll out to the pier. Digging our toes in the sand. Rolling our jeans up and doing a little wading…"

Ezra stops chewing abruptly. "I *meant* how long is this honeymoon in which you drag me and Kaylen along for the ride going to last?"

"Oh," I reply and sit back in my chair as if the idea hadn't occurred to me. I look over at Gabriel. "This is a honeymoon? Can't be much of one if my brother and adopted sister are here, can it? Maybe we should think about taking a real one."

"Absolutely," says Gabriel, expertly tossing his plastic knife into a nearby trashcan. "We've barely been married, yet we're already parents, having to watch these two boyos all the time. Could it be any *less* like a honeymoon?"

"Boyos? What the…? *Watch* us? You know what… Nevermind," Ezra garbles through a huge mouthful. "You guys are running around from place to place, seeing the sights and then holing yourselves up in your room. We barely see you. *That* is exactly like a honeymoon."

Gabriel watches Ezra with a lip curled in distaste. "Your manners are nefarious. Ladies don't like to see men stuff their faces and then talk through it."

Kaylen leans forward over her magazine and giggles. A lock of her thick, dark brown hair escapes the clip haphazardly holding it back and she reaches her hand up to tuck it behind her ear. At the same time, the page turns, seemingly by itself, but I know she has used her telekinesis. I glance around automatically to see if she was spotted, but we're nearly alone. In my mind's eye

I see her standing beside me, hurling cars at armed men in a parking deck only a couple weeks ago. I know it was necessary, but sometimes Kaylen's power frightens me.

"Ladies also like to be able to understand the language you're speaking," says Ezra, forking another bite into his mouth and chewing obnoxiously. "What kind of word is *nefarious* anyway? And *boyo*? Do I even want to *know* what that means?"

"It doesn't really matter *what* you say if they can't hear you over your oral digestive sounds," Gabriel replies. "Really, Kaylee, how do you put up with this? It's positively boorish."

"He saves his Neanderthal side just for you, Gabe," Kaylen says.

"Did you say something, Kaylen?" Ezra says loudly, cupping his ear and leaning Kaylen's direction. "I couldn't hear you over the prose prima donna's ego inflating."

"Prose prima donna?" I laugh. "Good one, Ezra."

Even Gabriel smiles, unperturbed by the gibe. Those two go at it all the time, usually for show. "Indeed, Ezra. You obviously *do* have rudimentary language skills; you simply choose not to exercise them. Why is that? Afraid women will think you're too much of a nerd? Don't worry, it's not your language that's the problem. It's your unhealthy devotion to spandex-clad Barbie dolls. Wonder Woman can't possibly get anything practical done in an outfit like that, you know."

"Ooookay," I say, holding up my hands. "You two are on a roll so this could go on all morning. But like I said, I have plans later. So break it up."

"You didn't answer my question," Ezra points out, mopping up the syrup on his plate with his last forkful.

"I know," I reply. "And we aren't planning on ignoring the rest of the world forever. And a couple weeks is hardly excessive."

"Your sister is right," Gabriel says, sipping his glass of orange juice. "Don't fret, Ezra. We have plans for you two."

"Well thank the light of the Green Lantern," says Ezra with exaggerated relief. "Because I am sick of the inside of a hotel room. Plus, I do want to graduate from high school before I'm thirty."

"Oh please, you've been by the pool and in the hot tub practically every day," I say. "Geez, are teenagers always this dramatic and whiny?"

"So I've heard," Gabriel replies. "They are always discomfited about something, no matter how good things are."

"Good?" asks Ezra, incredulously. "Switching between the same two outfits because we can't go back to get our things or someone will shoot us. Living in a hotel room." He counts the items off on his fingers. "Paying a million dollars to a cab every time we want to go somewhere—that is, if you even *let* us go. Then there's being homeless. Hotels are only great when you know you live somewhere you can go back to. And no comic books."

"Ohhhh, I see. It's really just the comic books, Gabriel," I say. "I should have known that was the real complaint. I guess we should give him a weekly comic book budget and he'll be happy indefinitely."

"If he gets a comic book budget then I get a riding budget," says Kaylen, looking up from her magazine. "I haven't been on a horse in months, and I heard there's a barn nearby…"

Gabriel laughs. "It might have appeared that way this last week, but we aren't made of money. Someone around here is going to have to get a job at some point if anyone is going to have any kind of budget."

"Okay, what *is* the plan?" Ezra asks again.

"We're working on it," I say. "Contrary to what you think, we haven't been taking pictures in front of the Golden Gate Bridge and going whale watching. Reentering society when people are hunting you down takes time. Dan, Gabriel's dad, has been helping us out with that."

We've been in communication with Dan for about a week now. He said Robert was close-lipped for the most part, but vehement that he has no intention of abducting me—not that *that* means anything. When Dan tried to get more information, Robert refused, saying he would speak only to *me*. He said there are things I have a right to know that shouldn't go through a third party. It's starting to sound like a Louise repeat the way Robert is demanding my audience and waving information in my face.

"Oh yeah, your Dad's a lawyer, right?" Kaylen says. "What did he say? Did he talk to Robert?"

"He says we need to be careful," Gabriel replies. "What worries him the most is that Robert was unfazed by threats of legal action—he didn't even bring his own lawyer into it. That means Robert has a way to take Wendy without repercussions."

That's the truth. Robert's business in surveillance software would allow him access to any technology he wants, and he has enough money that he can buy his way out of anything. Dan has been helping us out with cash because it's more important than ever to keep ourselves untraceable. And Robert's ability? I'm amazed he hasn't found us already... I've kind of been freaking out about it, scanning the perimeter all the time whenever we're away from the hotel.

"Robert's bottomless resources are going to make this impossible," Ezra points out, mirroring my thoughts.

"Money makes you overconfident," Gabriel says. "Our plan is to keep Robert close, prohibiting him from acting openly against us. We'll arrange a meeting with him in a public place, make a show of trust or some such story. Things were always easier with Robert when he believed we trusted him. We need to get that illusion back so he doesn't feel the need to hide Wendy away somewhere. Meanwhile we'll expose whatever it is he's up to. It'll work out. You'll see."

"And when does this grand plan happen?" Ezra asks skeptically.

"First things first," Gabriel replies. "Tomorrow we're headed back to Monterey to my apartment so we can breeze in and pick up a few things. Then we're going to LA where we're going to work out a more detailed plan." He downs the rest of his small cup of orange juice. I haven't seen him eat anything but one piece of toast and juice. Where is his usual appetite? As I take stock of that fact, I notice that his breathing seems a little off, too. Is he getting a cold?

"LA?" I ask. "You worked something out?" We've been trying to figure out a more permanent housing situation, and even though Dan is more than willing to foot the cost until we can become contributing members of society again, it's virtually impossible to not leave a paper trail and Dan isn't versed on the illegalities necessary to accomplish that.

"I spoke to my dad this morning while you were in the shower," Gabriel explains. "He's been talking to my brother. Mike knows someone who can do what we need. My brother has been picking up quite a few odd skills and people the last few years. He'll have something lined up for us when we get there."

"Skills?" I ask. "What does your brother do anyway?"

"He's a personal trainer. He has a very exclusive client list—celebrities and other wealthy individuals. I've never met any of his clients, but I suppose you meet all kinds of people with all kinds of skills when you deal with that sort." A hint of disapproval colors Gabriel's words.

Interesting, I think, remembering Mike and his extremely muscular physique. *So the Hispanic Harlequin cover model spends his days with sweaty supermodels and drug lords.* Okay, so maybe not. But I can totally imagine it anyway and it would explain how the guy can get us a place that won't be traceable. He sounds like the bad boy version of Gabriel—resourceful in *other* ways.

"Today though, Wendy and I are going to laze about," Gabriel says, standing up and holding out a hand to me. "Tomorrow we'll get back to our adult lives—full of responsibility and annoying teenagers. You two stay out of trouble."

"Well in that case, Kaylen and I will go hang out by the pool, once again, and avoid annoying adults who don't realize they actually *are* adults," quips Ezra, giving us an impudent smile.

"A capital idea," Gabriel says, pulling me along with him. Then over his shoulder, "And I mean it, stay out of trouble!"

Ezra grumbles something about prying brothers-in-law and Kaylen laughs.

Gabriel leads us down the empty hall as I take off one of my gloves to test the texture of his hand in mine. I've felt it plenty of times since the day I finally found the courage to risk touching him, but it hasn't gotten old.

"I've been meaning to tell you," Gabriel says, "this new development in your wardrobe is adorable."

I look down at my clothes, which today consist of tights underneath shorts. I wear ballet flats because they're safer than flip-flops around people. "It was purely strategic," I explain. "When we were separated and it was summertime I hated that I couldn't safely wear shorts. Kaylen suggested I wear tights under shorts and skirts. I did it a few times and liked it, but it wasn't really appropriate for work. But when we planned to escape Robert, tights were more space-efficient than bringing jeans so I bought a bunch. We planned to be south where it would really be too hot for jeans most of the time anyway. So I have all these tights now and two pairs of shorts. We're kind of low on wardrobe options."

"Well I like it. It makes you look your age and it also gives you a flair of individuality, especially with the gloves. It embraces your handicap rather than having your handicap hide under layers. I especially like the pink tights you wore yesterday."

"My age?" I ask. "You *like* me to look eight years younger than you?"

We turn a corner into the hall our room is on, and all of a sudden Gabriel stops, pushing me gently toward the wall. "I want you to look like exactly who you are. Which is a twenty year-old woman whose skin can sometimes be lethal. I want what you wear to be exactly you, not a stifled you. Those jeans and long-sleeved shirts you wore after I met you were the guilty and oppressed you. This looks like a woman who is comfortable in her own skin." He walks me backward into the wall. "The confidence you exude these days is intoxicating." He sweeps my hair in front of my shoulder and then grasps my face in his hands, looking into my eyes for a long moment, his intentions becoming more obvious in his emotions. He leans forward, resting his forehead gently against mine, his breaths heavy. I want to kiss him, but Gabriel likes to take his time with such moments—even spontaneous ones like this. But I tease him anyway, putting my bare hand on his skin just under the edge of his shirt and moving upward which elicits a low, almost inaudible groan from him.

After a while of building tension, he whispers, "May I kiss you, Wendy?"

I smile. He asked that same thing before he kissed my lips for the first time, and he has asked it every time since. I love it, not just the veneration I hear in his voice, but his emotions as he speaks. When Gabriel kisses my mouth, he puts his whole self into it. There is no such thing as a peck on my lips. Only my forehead or cheek or palm get such treatment. A kiss on the mouth is an occasion each time, and each time he is… humbled that I say yes. I can't get over the novelty of it or over feeling practically worshipped when he touches me with so much esteem. I can't get over Gabriel's devotion to putting the depth of his soul into everything he does. I am convinced, without an ounce of platitude, that I am the luckiest woman alive.

"What would you do if I said no?" I whisper back.

That surprises him—I have always said yes. But he recovers and answers, "I would thank you."

"Thank me? Why?" I ask, bringing my mouth very close to his, tempting him.

His need to kiss me builds, but he doesn't move his lips any closer to mine. "Because the absence of your lips gives me an opportunity to more accurately remember the times I could not touch them. Strangely, I miss those times."

"Really?" I ask, pulling away enough to see his eyes.

"Yes. I loved wanting you that badly."

A shiver moves through me at the ripple of desire we share. "Mr. Dumas, do you keep a book under the mattress titled *Things to Say to Drive Your Wife Wild*?"

He tilts his head at me slightly. "No. I just say what I feel."

"I know," I sigh, tucking my head into his chest and inhaling, slightly jarred by his smell. It's... not quite right. And his breathing is a little tight. He *must* be getting sick, and apparently I can now smell it.

Ignoring it, I continue, "What you feel already communicates to me so clearly that I think I don't even *need* your words, but then you speak and... it turns my heart inside out. It's kind of painful and awesome at the same time. Emodar is like overindulgence with someone like you. You're like chocolate ice cream with brownies and chocolate fudge all over it. If love could be measured in calories, I'd be obese by now."

He puts his arms around me, his cheek against my head. "Good. I won't have you sampling any other ice cream flavors."

I roll my eyes. "Like *that's* possible. I think you've spiked my ice cream with something. I'm an addict. This can't be healthy."

He chuckles, gleeful. "My plan is working perfectly."

"I'm warning you, you're spoiling me. I've had more chocolate ice cream in the little time we've been together than most people get their whole lives. I think you might be upsetting some kind of balance. And pretty soon I'll be useless, fat and happy on my proverbial couch."

"Hmm, then you can never ever escape," he murmurs into my hair.

I reach up and twine my hands behind his neck. I find his lips with mine and close my eyes, releasing an audible sigh as his arms tighten around me, his lips pressing more firmly to mine. "Yes, you can kiss me," I whisper. "And this time I'd like all the toppings."

***

Gabriel holds the door to the shop open for me. Realizing where we are, I laugh and shoot him a raised eyebrow as I walk in. We just finished eating lunch at a tiny bistro downtown, and then Gabriel led me to this place, an ice cream shop, for dessert. Admittedly, we both have ice cream toppings on the brain. When I asked for all of them while kissing him in the hallway of the hotel, I knew I was being suggestive, but Gabriel took my request seriously. He suggested the colorworld was excellent scenery for an intimate interlude—something I have been begging him to try with me.

A little over a week ago we discovered that I could channel people into the colorworld with me when they touch my skin. So

7

far, Gabriel, Kaylen, and Ezra are the only ones to have seen it. They are the only people safe from my lethal touch that I know of so far. As if giving people my ability to see isn't incredible all by itself, we also found that I channel every other ability I have as well. That means anyone who touches me can share my enhanced senses and also my ability to feel the emotions of those around me. Gabriel has finally gotten his wish to be able to share my emotions like I do his. The catch is that this new skill to share my abilities only works while we are in the colorworld.

And that's why I've wanted to make love to him in the colorworld all this time. Imagining sharing emotions and being able to experience each other's souls so profoundly while sharing our physical bodies sounded like love making on every level all at the same time. Gabriel, however, was hesitant, not because he didn't want to, but because, in true Gabriel style, he didn't want to rush through what was already an entirely new intimate level for us.

"El Cielo, Wendy," Gabriel had said. "I'm already fully consumed by you when we're together. Let's at least get this new physical relationship of ours out of the wrapper before we start upgrading."

"Whatever you say," I had replied. "But you can only live in the moment so long. Life still goes on even if you're standing still. I swear if you get hit by a bus tomorrow without having exalted our sexual experience in the colorworld, it's your loss."

I had expected Gabriel to make me wait longer than he did, but I think because we're nearing the end of this honeymoon period and are about to be faced with possible danger, he wanted to end it with a bang.

It was a bang alright. Maybe more like an entire fireworks display. I hold my bottom lip in my teeth as my thoughts wander back to the memory of having him sense my feelings so accurately and respond perfectly—our souls in complete sync as well as our bodies. It was beyond what I had imagined. I choose a cup size for my ice cream and assess the available flavors. I'm kind of ticked at Gabriel for waiting so long. To think we could have been experiencing what we did *today* for days now... It's like driving around a Honda when you've had a Ferrari in the driveway the whole time.

Settling on sugar-free chocolate—to appease my now more temperamental diabetes—I start scooping toppings, casting an eye at Gabriel who has been on top of his own cloud this whole time, stealing small smiles at me and touching my hand whenever he's close enough.

Gosh, we are so disgusting. Thank goodness Ezra isn't around.

Once we both have our bowls and are sitting down in a corner, Gabriel reaches for my hand again. Instead, I take my glove off and channel us into the colorworld. I can do it so quickly now that it takes nothing more than blinking my eyes and willing myself to go there. We've been meaning to look at other people in the colorworld more, and this is the perfect opportunity.

His attention immediately moves to where our hands are joined. Where our skin meets, our life forces become one—or at least appear to. Gabriel has been continually intrigued by that fact, and aside from this morning's activities, he has spent most of his time in the colorworld watching the interaction.

"Do you think that the reason people are affected negatively only when I touch their skin is because our life forces merge like this?" I ask, the thought just occurring to me.

"Sounds logical," Gabriel replies, and then he yawns. His emotions are subdued, confirming his fatigue.

"You're awfully tired lately," I say, remembering how Gabriel has napped almost every day in the last two weeks since our reunion. I don't recall him sleeping so much before our separation—which was a couple of months long.

"So it would appear. I think I'm making up for so many sleepless nights I endured while you were gone." His attention moves to a mother holding her small child by the hand in order to keep him from running around the shop. "See that?" he says in a low voice. "It looks like their life forces bond in the same way, but look at their light... Fascinating!"

He's right. Where the mother's hand joins the child's, their life forces meld like Gabriel's and mine. But the interesting part is that the child's light is brighter than the mother's overall; where their hands meet, however, that light blends so that you can't tell which strands are whose.

I used to have a lot of trouble seeing the difference between the brightness of people's souls, but I can now tell easily. The colorworld has taken on sharper, more defined edges, and the lights that were once so blinding, are easy to handle. That I *am* improving my skills on a regular basis is certain. It used to frighten me; I imagined that my death-touch would become more lethal one day. But now I'm more curious. How is my ability improving?

9

"I still say there is some difference in the merging of strands when *you* touch people," Gabriel ponders as his eyes move over the different souls milling around the room.

"I agree," I say. I release Gabriel's hand but keep close enough to him to stay in the colorworld. I look at our life forces side-by-side, touching, but not merging, noting the difference between our souls. Then, while watching my left hand, I touch him with my right.

"What?" he says excitedly, knowing I'm watching what happens as our skin meets. He can only see the effect after the fact.

I do this several more times, touching him and letting him go while watching the different parts of my life force that I can see: my arm, my leg, my foot. I want to see what happens to my light as I touch him. Gabriel is jumping inside, but I make him wait until I've come to a definite conclusion.

"Now that's something," I say finally, grasping his hand once more.

I take a bite of ice cream with my free hand.

Gabriel's eyes are boring into me. "What?!" he says, unable to contain his curiosity. "What did you see?"

I chuckle at his impatience. "The light of our souls merge entirely. Not just around where our skin meets like we see in other people."

"Perfect!" Gabriel breathes. "So *that's* why you can be lethal sometimes. Merging unequal life forces! It's exactly as I said! Some people can't handle your wattage because you channel *all* of your light at once rather than a portion!"

I nod, contemplating telling him the *other* part of my discovery, which is that Gabriel's soul is brighter than mine on its own. I can only tell when we aren't touching. That's how I know we share light entirely. When I touch him, our life force brightness appears to be equal; I can't tell the difference between us.

"Intriguing," Gabriel gushes, off on a two hundred mile-an-hour train of thought. But then he looks at me. "I wonder how bright a person has to be to endure your skin? How much brighter are you than me?"

"What makes you think *I'm* brighter?"

He gives me a dry look. "Wendy, don't josh with me. You said our light is the same when we touch, which means one of us is brighter than the other normally. Tell me. How much brighter are you?"

It's at that moment that I determine I won't tell him. It's not that I'm ashamed that he has more light than me. In fact, it doesn't surprise me in the least. I know how good he is; the past two weeks have been more eye-opening about Gabriel's character than ever. I can't believe I never noticed before. Or maybe I can. I spent a lot of time before being obsessed with my lethal condition. But in the past two weeks I've seen the man do things like let everyone ahead of him in line at the store (literally everyone), order an extra sandwich at a restaurant to give to the homeless guy we saw on the way in (despite the fact that we don't have anything to spare), clean up trash along the beach while we were taking a walk, and tip our waitress exorbitantly when he learned she was a single mom—which he only learned because he chose to take an interest in the woman's life. And Gabriel does these things naturally, without thinking. I've learned a *lot* about him in the past two weeks that I didn't know, and all because I finally started paying attention.

"I'm not telling," I say decidedly.

"What! Really? Why not?"

"Because then we're going to have a pointless conversation in which we try to convince the other person of all their merits. And then it will end up being some kind of competition to see who can come up with more good things. There's no point in telling you. It serves no purpose."

He slumps in the bench, pouting. "No purpose," he murmurs, stabbing his melting ice cream with his spoon. "The woman wants to figure out how her death-touch works but won't share the most *basic* data that would give us a starting point."

"Excuse me," I say indignantly. "I *do* know about data, Mr. Know-it-all, which is why I have a theory."

He looks up, eyes wide. "You have a theory? Heavens, woman, you've been holding out on me!"

"For what? Like the last five minutes?" I say, rolling my eyes. "Anyway, the theory is that my ability has been improving regularly because my light has been increasing."

Gabriel pauses with his spoon in his mouth as he moves into analysis of my words. After several pensive moments, he pulls the spoon out of his mouth and says, "Hijo de un sacerdote casto. That's bloody brilliant, Wendy. So… does that mean your ability decreases when you touch me—since you're passing some of your light to me as we equalize?"

I roll my eyes again, grateful Gabriel has no way of finding out, because he has to touch me to even *see* the colorworld, which means to him our light will always appear equal. "I'm not going to say *what* my ability does when you touch me. I'm only going to say that it *does* change."

He scowls at me but continues to ponder. Meanwhile, I marvel over the discovery myself. My ability definitely increases when I touch Gabriel, not a lot, but it does. It's subtle enough that I've never noticed that the ceaseless fluctuating of colors in the colorworld becomes a little more manageable when I touch him. And the lights have slightly less glare. Even in the visible world, now that I'm paying attention, my senses benefit.

If Gabriel can boost my ability when he touches me—and I know I'm sharing his light—then that means light is what powers an ability. And if my abilities have been improving on their own all these months—as I know they have—then the only explanation is that *my* light is increasing. And if Gabriel's rudimentary explanation that goodness equates light is true—which I think it is—then I've been improving myself as a person somehow. After all I've been through, and all the growth I've seen, this is very comforting. I've been moving in a positive direction, not a negative one, and my actions have visible proof in the colorworld.

Something else hits me at that moment. I turn to Gabriel to say what I'm thinking, but I swear we've come to the same conclusion at the same time.

"Carl," I say at the same time that Gabriel says, "Dina."

"That's why they lost their abilities," I breathe, remembering that both of them inexplicably lost their abilities at some point and that both of them had misplaced ethics.

"They lost the light to power them," Gabriel finishes.

2

*A*fter driving around Gabriel's apartment complex in Monterey to be sure we aren't being watched, Gabriel, Ezra, Kaylen, and I pull into the parking lot around noon. We roll down the windows and everyone is silent while I listen. I close my eyes and stretch my awareness out to the sounds beyond.

I hear a few conversations, none of which concern me, and none of the voices are ones I recognize. After a few minutes I open my eyes. "I think it's clear."

"Off we go, then," says Gabriel, unbuckling his seatbelt and opening his door. We all follow suit, looking around for anything suspicious—although I have no idea what that might be. I keep my ears tuned in, but the closer we get to our apartment, the more relieved I become.

When we get to the door, I search out the sounds within. "Not even a heartbeat in there," I say.

Gabriel puts his key in the lock and turns. He swings the door open slowly, and when everyone pauses like they expect an attack I brush past them. "Oh geez. I already told you there was no one in here. The ears don't lie," I say, pointing to them.

Gabriel chuckles and follows behind me. The place has been disturbed. Papers are spread out on the coffee table. Glancing over them, Gabriel says they are from the filing cabinet in the other room.

I sit on the couch and inhale deeply. "I smell Louise. And Carl. They've both been here. Recently."

"Geez, Wen, you're like a bloodhound," says Ezra as I lean down and pick up a long white hair from the carpet—more proof of Louise's presence. "I think you should start a private investigator service when all this is over," he adds, looking at the hair between my fingers and then at the off-white carpet that would make seeing the white hair near-impossible for normal human eyes.

"You memorized what Louise smells like?" asks Kaylen, wrinkling her nose in repulsion.

"Sure," I reply, "It triggers all of my unpleasant memories of her. It's people who don't leave much of an impression whose scents I don't really recognize or even notice."

I don't like that Louise has been here at all; it puts me on edge. "Let's do this," I say, hopping back up to go to the bedroom.

"Louise somehow managed to get in without damaging the lock. Chances are she'll come back. Let's grab some stuff and get out of here."

I grab a suitcase from the closet of my room—the room I stayed in before Gabriel's and my two-month separation. There aren't many clothes in the closet. The majority of my things are still at Robert's house. I was only married to Gabriel for two weeks before our separation, and I never got around to moving everything out of my uncle's house.

The memories of those tumultuous two weeks are more vivid as I stand in this room. I think I can actually smell the despair here. The latch I installed on the door to keep Gabriel out is still there. I think I can even draw up the precise sadness I felt as I screwed it into the door. The place is permeated with it. I wonder if the room looks different in the colorworld.

"Gabriel?" I call.

After a moment, I feel his presence behind me.

"I want to see if it looks different here," I say. "Because it *feels* different, you know?" Not waiting for his reply, I channel us into the colorworld.

He relaxes in agreement, and we both scan the room. If we weren't already looking for a difference, given the history here, we wouldn't notice the lackluster quality of one place on the floor where I laid many a night by myself, furious and afraid and sad over my unsure situation with Gabriel when I couldn't touch him. Without looking, we also wouldn't notice the door latch. In the colorworld, objects have always appeared lit from within, but something occurs to me as I stare.

"Gabriel," I say. "The colors have darkened. Darker colors don't reflect as much light."

"You're right," he says, equally captivated. "It's obvious looking at that section of floor right there." He points to a spot next to the wall. "It's a definite shade or two darker in hue than the rest of the carpet."

"So… inanimate objects don't actually have their own light. They just *reflect* whatever is around them."

"But obviously their structure can be changed to reflect less. As you said, the result is a darker color."

I never paid attention to which colors were darker before, but probably because the color of inanimate objects fluctuates so much in the colorworld that a patch of darker carpet wouldn't readily capture my attention. I guess the colorworld only reveals its secrets when you're looking for them.

My gaze strays to the bookshelf where Gabriel keeps his collection of books and music. One CD is a cheery pink, a brighter hue by far than surrounding CDs. The title is Sir Mix-A-Lot. I crack a smile as I recall the day he rapped *Baby Got Back* to my rear end.

"See the bookshelf?" I say, pointing. "It's bright yellow, except the top shelf. That's brighter lemon yellow. Same shelf as your favorite books."

"I do tend to shower my books with good feeling," says Gabriel.

"Do you think…?" I muse.

"Emotions affect inanimate objects?" offers Gabriel.

"Yeah."

"Perhaps it has something to do with that energy vapor." Gabriel has seen the vapor-like substance that pours off of everything. It can only be seen in complete darkness or at sunset. And I've seen it gather around a person when their emotions are especially intense. "I wonder if it's the presence or absence of that vapor that permeates surrounding objects, affecting their makeup and corresponding color," he says.

"I bet so."

Gabriel sighs in sadness then as he looks around the room. "I must have memorized four hundred books while you were away. It was the only thing that kept the despair at bay when I wasn't at work."

"*Four hundred?*" I ask, incredulous. Gabriel doesn't exaggerate. If he said he memorized four hundred books in under two months, then he did. "Gabriel, that's insane."

"That ability you manifested in me came in exceptionally handy. You provided the balm to my wounds even when you weren't around." He wraps his arms more fully around me.

I knew the ability I gave him was impressive, but that's absurd. I do the math in my head. I was gone for around two months. Sixty days. That would mean he memorized somewhere between six and seven books every single day. *And* he went to work? His ability to accurately and nearly instantaneously count strands of hair or cars in a parking lot alone is ridiculous, but this is equally mind-blowing. Frightening even, because *I* managed to stimulate that kind of ability.

"What is that bombilation?" says Gabriel all of a sudden.

"Bombilation?" I ask, amused. "Seriously, Gabriel, do you have to try hard to think of these words, or do they come to you naturally?"

"Oh I come across words that I really like the sound of and keep on the lookout for opportunities to try them out," he replies.

"And by bombilation, you mean?"

"Humming, droning, murmuring, vibration. A quiet but insistent sound."

"Oh!" I say. "You mean the voices in the colorworld!"

He listens for a moment. "Yes, you're right. I didn't catch that right away."

"Neither did I at first. It's some kind of foreign language, right?"

"Indeed. A rather beautiful one. Sort of like the repetitive cadence of Latin and the barely guttural yet unpredictable sound of Hebrew."

"So you don't recognize it?"

"No. It has quite a few unique sound combinations I've never heard before. And I've heard nearly every language out there at one time or another. Plus, it sounds like many voices speaking at once, further complicating my ability to isolate the sounds into patterns. I don't think there is any way for me translate it amid the roar. Curious... I wonder if there *is* a way to isolate one voice..."

"Wait. Are you saying you can translate a language you don't know simply by hearing one person speak it?"

"Oh yes. It's the easiest way to learn."

I turn around to face him. "You're joking."

He shakes his head. "The spoken word is more than just words. It's rising and falling, pausing, enunciating, arrangement, tone. It's more sound than syntax. It's music. If you throw in body language, it becomes musical theater. And music is universal. People communicate verbally with so much more than words. The words themselves translate themselves."

I gape at him. What more am I going to learn about him that blows me away like this? "You've always been able to learn a language like that?"

"No. Communication doesn't come overnight to anyone. I had to learn verbal skills like any other child—though I'd say it was accelerated compared to others. The more people I heard speak, the faster I got at mastering new languages. I've perfected my methods over the years, and the more languages I learn, the more easily I learn new ones. It's a compounding effect."

"How many languages *do* you know?"

"That depends on your definition of 'know.' Some languages I can only speak. Some I can read, speak, and write.

Some I only know on a rudimentary level—meaning I've only spent enough time learning them to know the most frequently used words and grammar. Some I've only ever encountered in written form. I have very little skill with those."

"Uhhh, nevermind then," I say and then start pulling clothes out of the closet again. "My question then, is why, when I asked you on the compound what your abilities were, you never mentioned that you're some kind of walking Rosetta stone?"

"I suppose it's because I never thought about it in the same way I do my other abilities. Counting, for instance, has never required work. Neither has character memorization. But deciphering languages is a skill I've been perfecting for years. I realize I have an abnormal proficiency, but I've also invested a lot of time in improving the way I learn until a lot of how I do it is automatic. It only *seems* beyond normal now. But it wasn't free like my other abilities. And as far as I can tell, hypno-touch hasn't done anything to improve it." He wheezes at the end and breaks into a coughing fit.

"Huh," I say, turning. "I guess I really can smell sickness. You alright?"

He nods as he recovers. "Yes. I think I'll go finish packing, unless you need something else?"

"A catalog of your many bizarre talents so I can have it for quick reference?" I grin, folding a shirt and putting it in my suitcase.

"Oh damn," I hear Ezra exclaim from the living room before Gabriel can answer.

"Ezra?" I call. "What's up?"

"That boy and his language..." Gabriel mumbles. "Like sister, like brother, apparently."

"Carl's here," Ezra replies loudly.

3

Coming to an abrupt stop in the living room, I glare at my father, Carl, who stands beside the open front door. For a moment I pointlessly try to remember who came inside the apartment last. Whoever it was must have forgotten to lock the door behind us. The good news is Carl appears to be alone and unarmed. So far.

"What do *you* want?" Ezra demands, hands on hips. Gabriel, meanwhile, moves to stand slightly in front of me. Kaylen has her fists clenched, her face hardened. This is the first time since Carl's betrayal that she has seen him—her adoptive father who is also *my* biological father. He adopted Kaylen after I disappeared as a child in hopes of making her into another me, someone capable of seeing the colorworld.

Carl's eyes move over each person in our group, finally coming to rest on me. "Wendy. Where have you been?"

I laugh at what is, at face value, a typical fatherly question to ask—as if I've been out past curfew. Coming from Carl, though, it's totally wrong and out of place. "Dad, I'm sorry. I lost track of time," I say apologetically. "Please don't ground me. I won't do it again."

Ezra sniggers.

The corner of Carl's mouth twitches, and after several seconds he says, "No phone privileges for a month."

Oh my gosh. Carl just made a joke.

Amazing how much that freaks me out. I think it's due to the sudden and unexpected twinge of familial connection in this most bizarre moment.

One big dysfunctional family.

"I'm sorry I barged in on you like this," Carl says, exhaling, that small moment of humor taking his guard down and making the moment even stranger. Even his shoulders slump a little. "I just wanted to check on you myself. Robert wouldn't tell me a thing and you've not been around."

He's sorry to *barge in?* Carl might think of this as a familial reunion, but I'm not buying it. I put my hands on my hips. "*Check* on me? Or did you mean check to see if I was alone so you could throw me in an unmarked van and make me disappear?"

Gabriel backs up closer to me, nervous. He reaches back and touches my arm, seemingly to check that I'm still here and not in said unmarked vehicle on the way to nowhere. "I think you need to leave, Carl," he says.

Carl's eyes zoom right in on Gabriel's hand on me and I know what he's seeing: Gabriel's *skin* on mine. After several beats, he looks back up to my face. "You're touching him... How did you figure... It was an accident? Have you... *showed him?*"

I stare back at him, unsure of what to say, *if* I should say anything at all.

Ezra scoffs. "Nobody here is going to tell you *anything*. So why don't you turn around and go back where you came from."

Carl stares at my face for a while, trying to read me I think. Then he turns to Kaylen. "Are you alright? I've missed you."

Kaylen's knuckles turn white as she flexes them harder. "I'm fine," she says sharply. "What do you want?"

Carl's grey eyes tighten a little, and at that moment Gabriel breaks into a coughing fit again, this one more violent than the one only minutes ago in the bedroom.

Carl moves his attention to Gabriel, appearing fascinated by the noise. His eyes roam over Gabriel's face, and then the rest of his body.

I put my hand on Gabriel's back. "Carl, either tell me why you're here or get the hell out. We've got things to do. And they don't involve you."

But Carl is fastened on Gabriel whose hacking finally comes to a close. "Things to do? Is he... ill?"

"That's usually what coughing means, dumbass," Ezra says, crossing his arms.

"Carl, state your purpose," Gabriel wheezes.

Still Carl doesn't move. His eyes dart among us again, assessing. Gabriel puts a protective arm around me and a faint iron smell hits me: blood. I look over at him but see none. The scent is faint but I'm sure that's what it is. And Gabriel's breathing sounds like a freight train now. The man needs a heavy dose of cough syrup and a nap.

Carl appears to be thinking, his eyebrows pinched together as he looks at the floor. His hands are clasped behind his back. "I suppose it's possible," he says softly to himself. "Such a short time though... But we never got to see how much stronger they would be... That means it would be quicker." He nods to himself. "Makes sense." He looks up at us and says confidently, "Wendy, you should take him to a hospital if he's sick."

What is he rambling about? "A hospital? What are you, a germ-o-phobe?"

"I don't need a hospital" Gabriel protests. "Just more sleep. Carl, *why are you here?*"

I can't translate Carl's expression: parted lips, relaxed jaw, raised eyebrows, slightly tilted head. I have no idea what he's thinking.

"If you haven't brought a cavalry," I say, "what is it you're trying to accomplish?"

"To help you," he replies. "And it looks like I am just in time."

"Just in time for what? And what could I possibly need your help with?"

Carl nods at Gabriel. "Him. Wendy, if you haven't taken him to a hospital yet, you need to *now.*"

I glance at Gabriel's somewhat bewildered face, and the smell of blood hits me more strongly. It's definitely coming from Gabriel. "Did you cut yourself?" I ask him.

He gives me a confused, questioning look. "Cut myself?"

"I'm trying to help you," Carl repeats. "Do I look like I'm here to take you? Do you see anyone else? Hear anyone else? I came here on my own. I've been waiting for you."

"Waiting for me?" I ask, inhaling deeply so I can figure out where the blood smell is coming from on Gabriel while maintaining an eye on the doorway for anyone else Carl might have brought. "That's supposed to make me feel better about you standing in my living room uninvited?"

"You didn't leave me much choice," Carl replies. "You took up residence with Robert, and my brother wouldn't even let me send my own daughter a postcard. The only hope I had to talk to you was to wait for you to return here."

"Why would I care about anything you have to say?" On tip toes and inhaling close to Gabriel's face, I finally determine the source of the blood: his breath. The only explanation for that is that he's coughing it up. I don't know if it's his throat or his lungs, but it's coming from inside him. And if that's true, that's a lot more serious than a cold.

"Are you hacking up blood?" I demand, my attention fully on Gabriel.

"I don't think so…" Gabriel says, confused. "Why?"

"I smell it on you."

"Wendy," Carl says, more demand in his voice. "You smell blood on his breath? I told you he needs a hospital. You ought to listen to me for once."

I snap my attention to Carl now. He sounds as if he has been *expecting* this. "You!" I hiss. I shrug off Gabriel's arm. "Carl... Tell me what you know. What's wrong with him?"

Confusion all around. Nobody understands what I'm talking about. But Carl does. I can see it in his eyes.

"You can fix him," he urges.

"*Fix* him?" I shrill, taking a step toward Carl, who retreats. "Fix *what*?"

"His life force," Carl says almost haughtily as if he has done me a favor. "You thought you had it all figured out, didn't you? I tried to help you, offered to train you. You could know everything I do by now, but you can't stand getting help from anyone, can you? I'm a doctor, Wendy. *And* a skilled energy therapy practitioner. My knowledge far exceeds yours. You need to accept that."

I care only about two of his words: *life force.* Realization crashes down on me. I flinch from the weight of it and grab Gabriel's arm for balance as I stare at Carl, appalled. *Please let me be wrong...*

"Oh please no," Kaylen whispers. Her hand goes over her mouth. She's close enough to me that I can tell she has gone to the same place as me: the old files in Robert's office. They catalogued people with incredible abilities manifested by something called visuo-touch... And then the bizarre, terminal illnesses that followed soon after...

Gabriel has incredible abilities, one in particular that was manifested by hypno-touch and astronomically improved when *I* performed hypno-touch on him. We were just talking about it— his ability to memorize books in minutes.

"Visuo-touch," I breathe, reeling as I realize what it is. Visuo—sight. *Sight*-touch. Energy medicine done while *seeing.* And the only thing I can think of *seeing* is the colorworld. Something Carl can also see—or at least *could.* Those weren't Robert's files. Those were *Carl's.* "Oh *no*," I say, my voice catching into a sob as I remember the *sound.* That horrible, gut-wrenching sound I heard whenever I did the hypno-touch hand movements Louise taught me. It never sounded that bad when *Louise* did them. Just me. And there was only ever one person I did full-fledged hypno-touch on: Gabriel.

"Where did you hear that word?" Carl demands. "What do you know?"

I'd all but forgotten Carl until he spoke, and now I whirl on him. "You!" I fume. "*You* manifested abilities in people twenty years ago back when you still had your ability! And they died from it, didn't they?"

Carl doesn't answer me, but his eyes are wide, his mouth slightly open. I bet he didn't realize I knew about that. If he did, I can't imagine he would brave showing his face alone like this.

"You bastard!" I seethe. And then I lunge for him.

I don't get very far. Someone catches me. Gabriel. He locks his arms around me. "Shh," he says near my ear. "Wendy, calm down."

But I won't calm down. I glare at Carl with murder in my eyes. I want to get my hands on him like I want air. If he survives, then that means I'm wrong. If he dies, well... then he obviously deserves it. "You bastard!" I shriek again, pushing against Gabriel's arms. Carl retreats a step, and I can tell by the look on his face that I'm right. "You did this! You knew what would happen, didn't you?! You had to! You had to know... And you let me do it anyway! And that's why you're here, isn't it? You came to see if he was dead yet!"

Carl backs up again. He is entirely through the door now.

"Carl, I hate you," I spit, scrambling to free myself from Gabriel. "You are a lying, murdering, son of a bitch. And you deserve to die for what you've done." Saying the words doesn't satisfy my rage. The need to cut him as deeply as the wound I feel right now, overwhelms me. Then I remember something else, something that will accomplish exactly that. "You killed her, didn't you?" I say, sneering. "My biological mother? You loved her didn't you? But you killed her just like you did all those people. Because you ruin everything you love. You don't know how to do anything else."

Carl's face slackens and pales.

"That's right," I say nastily, no longer struggling in Gabriel's grasp, consumed by vindictive pleasure at the pain I see written all over Carl's ugly face. "How does that *feel*, Carl? The guilt? It's like fire in your brain, isn't it? You walk around, waiting for an exhale that never comes. Like being buried alive but never dying. Suffocating, isn't it, Carl? Remembering what you did to her? Nothing you *ever* do will make up for it, you know that, right? She probably hates you, wherever she is."

Carl shakes his head, takes another step back, his back now against the door jamb. "You don't know what you're saying," he says barely above a whisper.

"Yes I do," I say, my eyes never straying from his face. "That's why you're such a sorry piece of crap now. Never got past it, did you?"

His eyes flash in anger. "You know nothing. This is more than me or you. More than Gina. She understood that."

I laugh mirthlessly. "Keep telling yourself that," I sneer, tossing my head to get my hair out of my face since Gabriel is holding my arms. "Tell me, Carl. What would my *dear mother* say if she knew how you turned out? What you did to me after I was born—giving me diabetes so you could screw around with my life force? If she doesn't hate you for killing her, she surely hates you for what you've done to me..." I tilt my head. "Unless... unless she was just as sadistic as you. Yes, that makes more sense. Who else would choose to be with someone like you but someone as vile as you are?"

Carl's hands have balled into fists. "Stop it!" he yells. "You will *not* speak of your mother that way!"

My eyes narrow. "Oh yeah? And you're going to stop me? Come on then, Dad. I *dare* you. Let's see how you hold up to me torturing your mind like you did her body. But I promise, you'll die much quicker than she did—not really fair if you ask me."

"Wendy," Gabriel rumbles soothingly in my ear. "Don't do this. You're better than this."

But I'm *not* better. I want Carl dead. He and Louise made me kill Gabriel, encouraged it, pushed it. What Carl did to manipulate me into hurting the man I love is sadistic. Worse than if he'd held a gun to Gabriel's head himself and pulled the trigger. No, killing Gabriel himself wasn't enough. He had *me* be the weapon. He used me against my own husband. He needs to die.

"How could you do this?" Kaylen says then. "You knew who Wendy was when she came to the compound. You knew what she could do, what would happen if she did hypno-touch, but you let her do it anyway. And on Gabe? *Everyone* knew how she felt about him then. You knew how she would feel because you'd done the same thing to the woman you loved... How could you do that knowing how she'd suffer? How?" A lamp and a chair lift off the floor by themselves then and I can see the fire building behind Kaylen's eyes.

Fury at Carl consumes me once more, fire in my bones not letting me remain still in Gabriel's arms. I make a leap for Carl again, almost making it. But once again Gabriel reaches me before I can get far, holding my arms. "I hate you, you evil bastard. *I hate you!*" I say, leaning toward him, infusing my words with as much venom as I can.

And with that, Carl backs through the doorway, turns, and retreats.

"Run, you son of a bitch!" I yell. "Run before I get my hands on you. And don't EVER show me your face again, because obviously Gabriel won't be here to save you!"

I collapse in Gabriel's arms, my heaving fury turning into sobs as the realization of what I have done to Gabriel replays in my head. "*No,*" I beg. "No, no, no," I say over and over, not knowing who I'm pleading with. I cling to Gabriel; I beg no one and everyone that I can be wrong. Gabriel sinks to the floor with me, holding me close, remaining silent as he tries to comfort me through his own shock.

"We don't know Gabe's sick like that..." I hear Ezra say over the sound of my crying. "The people in those files took *years* to get sick."

"Didn't you hear him?" Kaylen says, her voice dead. "Even *he* thought it was weird. That's what he was mumbling about. But he must have figured out why it might be happening more quickly with Gabe, because he said it made sense. And besides, if he isn't that sick now, he *will* be."

"This can't be happening," Ezra says. "It can't. Not after everything..."

"I should have done something," Kaylen says. "I should have stopped him before he could leave. The man doesn't deserve freedom."

"Stopped him and done what?" Ezra says. "Tied him to a tree? What good would that do?"

"I don't know!" Kaylen yells, her voice cracking. "I should have known... All those years, why did I never know?" And then I hear her cries join my own.

My tears wet Gabriel's shirt. I'm going to lose him. I'm going to lose him by my own hand. Guilt and self-loathing rack my already exhausted body in waves. I sob louder, desperate as I pull at Gabriel as if by so doing I can keep him with me and stave off the inevitable.

"It's early, right?" I say, coming up for air, searching Gabriel's face. "We don't even know what's wrong with you, do we?" But there was not a single case in those files that hinted at survival—except for the one with diabetes. But I'd be willing to bet that guy is dead, too. In fact, I remember being horrified by how quickly the diseases progressed as if they were fed disease Miracle-Grow. Even diabetes is lethal under the worst conditions.

Gabriel remains silent. I don't know what he's thinking. I dissolve in tears again because anguish is too loud in my own head, my body too consumed. I've killed him. I don't even have a diagnosis yet, but it doesn't matter. One way or another he's going to die in too short a time, just like the people in those files. A horrible, violently ill death.

"I'm sorry," I choke out once I find a portion of my voice again. "I'm so sorry."

"You were hurt and in shock. You don't have anything to be sorry for," Gabriel says, his voice surprising me with the tiny threads of comfort it weaves in me.

I don't know what he's talking about at first, but then I realize he thinks I'm apologizing for acting like a revenge-crazed psycho with Carl. I am sorry for a lot of things in my life, but that is not something I'm sorry for. If regret over it is in my future, I don't see a hint of it yet.

Rage rises up within me just *thinking* about that awful excuse for a human. But Gabriel squeezes me tighter, reminding me of his presence, reminding me of the apology I made that he mistook. I was apologizing for killing him, but the thought that I might be to blame for that in even the smallest way didn't enter his head. To be reminded of how Gabriel's heart works in this way, to never dwell on blame unless it's his own, fills me with a montage of memories reminding me of the innumerable qualities I love and admire about him. And he will live too short a life to properly share them with me or anyone else.

I sob so loudly that I don't hear anything else over the sound. I have never felt such sorrow. Not even when Elena died. I didn't know her like I know Gabriel. There were no memory triggers that caused me to miss her. There was only helpless love, and then debilitating guilt over her missing out on a life. Afterward... years of numb indifference.

With Gabriel there are thousands of moments to mourn and they all hit me at once. He has changed me from the inside out, and I no longer see the world the same because of him. Numbness isn't possible when the person is as vital to your soul as Gabriel is to mine.

4

*O*bligatory smile back in place, the nurse looks up. No eye contact though, which aggravates me. Not as much as her cutesy frog-patterned scrubs though. "How long has this cough been going on?" she says with rehearsed interest.

"Probably a couple of weeks," Gabriel replies pleasantly. " But it's been worse in the last two days."

A couple of weeks? Am I deaf or something?

"Is it a dry cough or a wet cough?" she asks as her fingers tick across the keys of her laptop.

"Of course it's a wet cough," I snap. "Blood is wet, isn't it?"

"Ah, what Wendy means to say is yes, it is wet." Gabriel gives me an exasperated look but I glare at him and cross my arms.

Okay, so I suppose there could be blood but no mucus, but we already told the girl up front what exactly is happening.

The nurse doesn't acknowledge my annoyance, and she continues to ask all kinds of questions about possible allergies and medications, finally getting to the part about his breathing and bodily functions. Then she asks about his appetite.

"I haven't had much of an appetite, to be honest. I supposed I was getting the flu," Gabriel says.

"He had nothing but orange juice, a piece of toast, a half-portion sandwich, and two bites of pasta yesterday. This morning he ate a banana," I supply. "And he normally eats like a horse."

"Fatigue?" she asks.

"Yes," he replies. "It seems to have increased, although I can't say when it started. There were several weeks there of being especially stressed—I attributed my tiredness to that."

"He's been taking midday naps nearly every day for the past two weeks," I add.

"Any chest pain?" she asks, head down, intent on her screen.

I look at Gabriel. He better not have been having chest pain and not told me.

"Not unless I breathe deeply. But that's only been since this morning. And it's very faint," Gabriel replies, honestly from what I can tell.

Froggy-top girl records that, and then takes a throat swab.

When she's done, she says, "Okay, the doctor will be in to see you shortly. You're lucky. It's very slow today."

Lucky? I want to scream at her. Hacking up blood is not *lucky.* A doctor showing up quickly is not *lucky.* It's merely convenient—and entirely *unlucky* since, by all accounts, Gabriel shouldn't be having to see a doctor in the first place.

"Thank you," says Gabriel, flashing her a smile.

When she leaves, I turn to Gabriel and say, "Why have I not noticed your cough until today? Two weeks? Why didn't you say something sooner? And chest pain? How long were you going to go before you got *that* checked out?"

"It was only a little congestion, hardly worth mentioning. Now come here and stop getting so worked up. I did my best to ensure you didn't maul the nurse, but I can only imagine what you'll do to the doctor once he or she arrives. Probably flog them... You'd better stay behind me in that case," he says, his eyes laughing.

I know he's trying to bug me on purpose, to get my mind off the situation, and I bite, wanting equally as much to escape it. The ride over here in the car was stifling with everyone's anxious emotions drowning me. "I'm getting a little hot in here," I say, fanning myself with a gloved hand. "You know what happens when I get hot. The gloves come off, literally. I can't help myself then. I might end up touching him if he rubs me the wrong way."

I bite the fingertip of one of my gloves and start pulling with my teeth.

Gabriel grabs me around the waist from where he sits and lifts me into his lap. "There will be no removal of clothes here, young lady. Those hands are mine. Besides, stripping isn't appropriate in public places."

I giggle, feigning a struggle to get away from him. "Yes, I think the doctor will find it very erotic if my hands are exposed. I might be kicked out for indecent exposure."

Gabriel holds me against him with strong arms and nuzzles my neck, placing a kiss below my ear.

"No fair," I breathe, squirming. "No kissing allowed. If I can't strip, then you definitely can't be allowed to do that."

Gabriel kisses my neck again and I stop struggling, unable to fight against the surge of pleasure his kisses there always bring. Not long after I touched Gabriel for the first time, I noticed a magnetism, like Velcro between our skin. That magnetism increases between us now. I think the desperation I've been clinging to since we saw Carl only a few hours ago in our apartment is fueling my hunger for him.

"I will prevent your uncivil behavior by any means necessary," he breathes into my neck. "Con mi propio comportamiento incívico."

"This emergency room cubicle has absolutely *no* privacy," I complain, lacing my fingers behind his neck and bringing my lips tantalizingly close to his. "Nothing but sheets on hooks. How do they expect patients to pass the time?"

"We might have had better accommodations if we'd gone to the urgent care like I suggested," Gabriel says, running his hand suggestively the length of my back.

I sit back and roll my eyes. "Even if I *had* agreed to that plan, there wouldn't have been an urgent care to go to. It's Sunday. Or did you forget?"

His brow furrows. "No, I didn't. But urgent cares aren't open on Sunday? Why? People don't have urgent, non-emergency issues on Sundays?"

I look at him in disbelief. "Of course they do. But they figure if you have an urgent issue that can't wait until Monday, you ought to go to the emergency room. Everyone knows that."

"Not *everyone*. If you've never had an occasion to go to an urgent care, why would you ever bother with knowing their hours?"

"You've never been to an urgent care?"

He shakes his head and then pushes a lock of my hair behind my ear. "I can't stand medical establishments so I avoid them at all costs. Most people foolishly panic at even the most minor immune system responses because they don't understand basic human physiology. Furthermore, I don't get sick much, and the last time I saw a doctor for more than a routine physical was when I was still a minor and my mother forced me to go."

I think about that a moment. Clearly, Gabriel has been in model health his whole life to have made it to the age of 27 without ever being ill enough for medical intervention. It's hard for me to imagine since I've been a regular visitor to doctors since the age of four because of my diabetes. I also routinely inject myself with insulin—something that requires physician approval to get. The advances of modern medicine are ingrained in my life every day. I can never stray too far from society without worrying about how I'll get insulin. In fact, that was something I've fretted over constantly since we've been living off the grid. Dan keeps assuring me that he'll take care of getting me what I need. But someone like Gabriel... he can go and do whatever he wants without thinking. It's times like this that I realize how diabetes screws with my life.

As my thoughts go back to Gabriel, I lament again that I've put him in this position. He's been so healthy his whole life, and now he will likely be facing... I don't want to think of all the grotesque possibilities. In the car on the way here, he started listing off all the curable conditions that have bloody sputum as a symptom. But I didn't care. Gabriel has something more than untreated Bronchitis and I didn't appreciate his attempts to placate me. Carl was not surprised by Gabriel being sick in the least. He expected it even—though apparently not this soon. Which begs a question.

"Why do you think you got sick so much sooner after... after what I did to you than the people in those files did from Carl?" I ask.

Gabriel frowns at me. "Wendy, we've been over this. We don't know anything yet. We don't know how ill I am, whether it is anything to be upset about. We don't know if what you did is the same as what Carl did to those people. We don't know for sure that Carl was the one behind the deaths of those people in Robert's files. Why are you so eager to jump to the worst conclusions?"

I hop up from his lap and collapse on the partially upright adjustable exam table instead. "Gabriel, if you can decide to act on a theory about how my ability works with so little evidence just because it *makes sense,* then I can choose to believe a theory that *also* makes sense that has *overwhelming* evidence. I'm preparing for the worst."

He heaves a sigh. "When you put it that way, it's logical. Carl certainly didn't say anything to dispute your accusations. He was taken off-guard by what ensued though. I wonder what his original intent was for showing up? Clearly he wasn't expecting me to be sick already, so he must have had a reason other than warning me to see a doctor."

I hadn't thought about that. Why *did* Carl come there? I experience the first stirring of regret for how I handled things with him, but only because I might have missed out on getting information from him that might have helped me.

"Whatever his reasons, I guess I totally screwed them up," I say, playing with the button that adjusts the table.

Gabriel stands up and comes to sit next to me. "We'll get through this, Wendy," he says, putting an arm around me.

Dead or alive? I think to myself as a stab of sadness pierces my heart.

"Is this your first time in an emergency room then?" I ask, wanting to change the subject.

He chuckles at that. "Heavens no. My brother and I used to compete to see who could rack up the most ER visits."

I'm about to ask how many he racked up and why he wanted to if he hates hospitals, but footsteps approaching capture my attention. The curtain parts and an Asian woman appears. Dressed in a long white coat, the doctor is short and petite with her hair held back in a ponytail. She looks really young, and I wonder how long she's been in practice. She looks like she still belongs in medical school.

"Hello, Mr. and Mrs. Dumas," she says pleasantly. She pronounces the 'as' on the end of our name incorrectly, making it sound like Dumuss. Even so, I have never been addressed by my married name, and I like it.

It warms me to her. I smile and say, "Hello. How are you?"

After my less-than-polite treatment of the nurse, Gabriel is moved to suspicion at my cordial greeting.

"I'm well, thank you," she says. "I'm Dr. Ryang." She looks at Gabriel. "So coughing up blood, I hear? That doesn't sound so good. You haven't been using any illegal substances, ingesting any chemicals, have you?"

I'm surprised that she jumped right into things, but I like her style.

Gabriel smiles. "I've never ingested an illegal substance in my life. And I haven't tried any chemicals since I was ten and my brother dared me to drink anti-freeze."

"Anti-freeze?" I ask, astounded. "Isn't that stuff massively toxic?"

"Well yes, Love, but it warranted a trip to the ER, and I told you my brother and I had a competition going," says Gabriel. "It put me well above my brother in terms of points that summer and I ended up winning."

"But—you could have died!" I exclaim.

"Oh dejar de ser dramática. I did my research. I only ingested one with propylene glycol instead of ethylene glycol or methanol. It's far less toxic. And I only had about half a teaspoon. And right after, I had my mother take me to the hospital. No harm done. Of course she wasn't too happy about it. She made me scrub the kitchen floor every day for a week, but she didn't realize my brother had to do all my chores for me for an entire semester of school because I won. So really, it was just my brother that suffered." He chuckles at the memory.

I stare at him with my mouth open. "You *researched* what type of poisonous substance to ingest?"

Dr. Ryang chuckles. "I hope you've matured since then and don't make anti-freeze part of your Friday happy hour."

"Of course not. And I don't drink at all, actually," says Gabriel proudly.

I'd never noticed that Gabriel doesn't drink... I assumed he abstained for my benefit since I'm not yet twenty-one. I don't know why I'm analyzing it now. Or why I'm interrogating him about something that happened years ago. Babbling through my stress maybe?

"Have you had a fever?" Dr. Ryang asks.

"Not that I'm aware of."

"You've had a TB test?"

"Yes, negative, but that was years ago."

"Are you on any medications?"

"No."

Dr. Ryang pauses for a moment, thinking, before saying, "If it's an infection in your lungs or airway, you should have had a fever at some point. And most infections go on for a long time before you start coughing up blood. Not that a lack of fever rules it out, but we'll run some tests. Your throat swab didn't reveal anything bacterial, but it could be viral."

Or it could be cancer. She didn't mention it, but why would she? He's a 27 year-old nonsmoker in excellent physical condition. I'd bring it up myself, but since I like her, I'll let her do her job and rule out all the easy things. Despite believing that Gabriel has something ghastly, I'm still afraid to jump in with both feet. I'd give anything for it to be a bad case of pneumonia or something.

After recording some information on the tablet she brought with her, Dr. Ryang says, "I'm going to listen to your chest now, if you could sit here." She indicates where I'm sitting. I take the cue to move out of the way, standing behind Gabriel who takes my place, closing my eyes and listening to hear what the doctor hears.

She doesn't know it, but I can probably hear his chest sounds better than she can with her stethoscope. His heart thuds evenly, but his breaths are short with the tiniest whistle, which I haven't heard before now.

When Dr. Ryang is done, she frowns. "Before now, when was the last time you were ill?"

"Probably several months ago," says Gabriel, taking in her reaction.

I hold my breath as I await her response.

She shakes her head, wrapping her stethoscope back over her neck "I'm going order a chest X-ray. I don't like the sound of things."

Gabriel exhales a long breath, lacing his hands in his lap as I struggle to get my heart under control. The doctor is definitely alarmed, but I don't know how much it should upset me yet. "What exactly are you hearing?" Gabriel asks.

"Fluid," she replies. "I'm leaning toward an infection of some kind that's gone untreated, and I'm mostly concerned about that fluid accumulating too quickly. We'll get that X-ray to determine the extent of it, but we're probably going to admit you for monitoring."

My face blanches and it gets colder as the blood leaves it. I wrap my arms around my middle and wish I had a wall instead of some stupid curtain partition to lean against. This is bad. This is just as bad as I imagined, except now it's real. I had hoped that by imagining the worst-case, it wouldn't come as such a debilitating shock when the worst-case turned out to be true. But I must have been holding out a lot more hope than I wanted to admit.

Gabriel and the doctor have an exchange about the process from here, but I barely hear. I keep picturing Carl's face as I accused him of killing my mother, Gina. I knew that look. I've seen it in the mirror before—back when I was consumed with guilt over my daughter, Elena, who I had at sixteen and put up for adoption. She died two months after she was placed.

I bet, like me with Gabriel, Carl had no idea what he was capable of doing—what he *did* do to Gina—until it was too late. And I have followed in his footsteps precisely. I am repeating his life in exactness, oblivious to the consequences of my actions until it's too late. Oh God, don't let me become him…

Fear ices through me instead of the anger and sadness of earlier. There are too many similarities between Carl and me for comfort. The things he has done… I want to say I am not capable, but I doubt that's true. Didn't I want to murder him only hours ago? I would have made a real effort, too, were it not for Gabriel stopping me.

I put a hand over my mouth, disgusted at how easily I felt justified in seeking retribution against Carl—even if it was temporary. It was still real. For a few moments, I reveled in imagining the life leaving Carl's eyes, without stopping to look ahead at the person I would be afterward. The desire for his destruction came far too easily. And I think it was because I easily saw myself in Carl. We are both motivated by guilt, and both of us have unwittingly sought penance in self-destructive ways. Carl has simply lived longer and thus had more time to evolve his methods into hurting *other* people since he has already destroyed himself. I know I've held myself to impossible standards of absolution before. I think I still do. And I think this time it revolves around Gabriel and my responsibility for him being in the hospital right now.

"Wendy." Gabriel's voice breaks through my thoughts and I look up to see him standing in front of me. He reaches for my hands. "Are you alright?" he says gently, his eyes pinched in concern.

The softness of his emotions wears away the sharp edges of my shame. I recognize the moment for what it is: a crossroads that will either have me following Carl or clearing a new path.

"I'm as good as can be expected," I say, squeezing his hands. "Just in shock. That's all."

He observes my face for several more moments before saying, "As am I. Do you need anything from me?"

I think about that. I don't need anything that can be picked up at a store, but I *do* need things. And Gabriel loves to *do*.

"I need you to keep being you," I say. "Determined. Stubborn. Unrelenting. I need you to not accept excuses from me. Don't let me become someone I don't want to be."

He cups my cheek in his hand. "I can do that. And it starts with you telling me where all that came from."

I exhale heavily. "I wasn't sorry earlier for trying to kill Carl. But I'm sorry now. It scares me that I wanted to."

He smiles mildly. "Wendy, I don't blame you. If our situations were reversed and *you* were the one possibly dying and Carl let it happen, I would have the same instinct. It was that much stronger for you because he happened to be right in front of you when you found out what he'd allowed to happen."

I throw my arms around Gabriel and close my eyes, memorizing the way his body fits against mine so I can conjure it at will. Because he's about to spend a lot of time at a hospital, I'm sure of it.

"Gabriel."

"Yes, Love?" he whispers.

"Your life force is brighter than mine. Not the other way around."

He fluctuates between curiosity and disbelief. I expect a denial, but then he says, "Why are you telling me that?"

"I—" I start. I actually have no idea why I told him that. "I'm not sure. It just seemed like something you should hear right now."

He kisses my forehead. "I did need to hear it."

"You did?"

He nods slowly, running his hands from my shoulders down my arms, looking bashful. "I know I've been downplaying what might be happening with me. I suppose I just hate the possibility of having to leave you after everything we've been through. Knowing the very real possibility exists, I've been racked with guilt over having spent the majority of our time as a couple tormenting you. I'd like you to have more good memories of me than bad, and I may be running out of time to turn the scale. It's had me tormenting myself. To know that my light can at least attest that I'm not the awful monster I imagine is comforting, indeed."

The morbidity of his words smarts. He has all but accepted exactly what I have—that he is sick. Terminally so. And he changed his mind so suddenly... That means Gabriel sees as much evidence as I do—probably even more that hasn't occurred to me yet. "Oh Gabriel," I say, placing my hand over his cheek. "I'm sorry. I should have realized how you were feeling. I've had guilt of my own. I guess that's why I didn't pick it up from you specifically."

"Guilt over Carl?"

I shake my head. "Over hurting you. However innocently, it was my hand that caused this. I allowed myself to be manipulated by Louise even though I didn't like it, and the price is far more than I imagined. But I *should* have imagined it. I should have listened—literally—to my instincts."

Before he can answer I hold up a hand, "Just let it go. I know you don't blame me. And I'll get past it. But I can't help the guilt. I'm only human. Just as you are. We screw up."

He smiles at me lovingly. "That we do." He brushes the back of his hand across my cheek. "That we do."

5

"Call me before you go *anywhere*," I add, grabbing Ezra's arm before he can get into the cab. "And don't forget to call as soon as you get to the hotel—Let me know your room number so I can check on you."

"Wen. I got it. We've been doing this covert thing for two weeks now," Ezra says. "I know the drill."

I give him a wan smile. "Sorry. I know."

Kaylen puts her hand on my shoulder before getting in with Ezra. Her eyes—and her emotions—are heavy with concern. "Don't worry," she says, "we'll be fine. Call us when you guys find something out."

"I will," I reply. "But remember we're not in San Francisco anymore. Don't go anywhere if you can help it."

She's about to ask me something, but changes her mind and kisses me on the cheek. "See you soon." Then she gets into the cab. I shut the door behind her and wrap my arms around myself to block out the wind as I wait for the cab to drive away. I left my jacket inside the hospital with Gabriel and it's a chilly November day in Salinas, a town just north of Monterey where Robert lives.

I think I managed Kaylen and Ezra okay. I told them Gabriel has been admitted for overnight observation and why, but I made sure that they knew I wasn't falling apart. I gave them money for the cab and for meals and did my best to put them at ease. I've done this before though. The last few months of my mom's life, I committed myself to being Ezra's rock. Now I have not only Ezra, but Kaylen and Gabriel as well.

It's a bit more difficult this time around, however, because I endure their turmoil all at once and I can't escape it if they're nearby. But I deal with it by occupying my mind with plans. One of those plans is Robert. I'm going to give him the audience he asked for. I'm not sure how or when yet. Right now Gabriel needs me more.

I turn and walk back through the automatic doors into the hospital. Inside, the air has gained weight. I stop in the middle of the entryway, imagining what the colorworld must look like here. Hospitals are not happy places for the most part. The colorworld probably reflects that.

When I reach the room where I left Gabriel—we finally got a consultation room with walls instead of a curtained cubicle—I find him sitting on the exam table, his arms crossed tightly, his socked feet dangling. He's wearing a hospital gown now.

His head pops up when he hears my footsteps. He's scowling. "Wendy, look what they did to me."

I give the diamond-patterned gown a once-over. "What? Not your color?" I lean against the door jamb with my hands tucked behind me, trying not to conjure memories of my mom in a hospital gown and what she looked like in it at the end.

His eyes narrow. "Who cares what color it is. The problem is it's not clothing. It's a glorified sheet. Evidently pants are too complicated for someone like me to handle in my condition. But tell me, do I *look* like an invalid that can't manage getting my own pants down in the loo?"

I chuckle and cross my ankles. "I'm pretty sure it's for *their* ease, not yours."

"Oh yes, that's what the nurse told me. But that's even sillier. I'm the patient, aren't I? Which makes me the customer. And this customer is *not* happy with the service. Does my comfort not matter? As if being in a hospital isn't upsetting enough, I have to concern myself with *their* ease?"

I walk over to him and put my arms around him, laying my head against his chest. "You sure are off to a fine start."

He relaxes into me—though it's more like him holding me since he's higher up. "I despise hospitals," Gabriel grumbles.

A nurse appears then, a wheelchair next to her.

"What is *that* for?" Gabriel demands before the woman can say anything.

"I'm going to wheel you down to radiology," she replies with a pleasant smile. "And then I'll take you to your room."

"No need," he says. "I'm perfectly capable of walking there on my own."

"It's policy," she replies.

"How about you bring me your policy book. I'd like to see for myself," he says.

She looks at him in bewilderment for several moments. So do I.

"Mr. Dumas," she says finally. "I'm just trying to do my job."

"I simply asked to see your policy book," he replies. "That isn't a statement of whether or not you're doing your job. I'm sure you've been instructed to do as you say. But I want to be sure your superiors have given you proper instruction about these so-called policies. I don't appreciate being treated like a shut-in. I walked into this emergency room without any trouble. I can certainly navigate my way to your radiology department in like manner. If it is indeed policy, I'd like to lodge a formal complaint. I want to be sure I have your policies straight before I do that."

Now she's really stunned. Even I'm taken aback by how obstinate he's being.

He looks back at her expectantly.

"Gabriel," I interject, grabbing his arm and tugging to get him to stand up. "She doesn't have time to go hunt down a policy book. Just sit in the damn thing so we can get this over with."

Resisting my tugs, he looks at me, aghast. "Really, Wendy. A simple, 'Please, Gabriel, forgo your policy book request for now so we can hurry this along' would suffice without the filthy language."

I roll my eyes. "Sometimes it gets the job done faster. Now, are you going to let the nurse push you or do I need to use more filthy language to convey my point?"

He finally allows me to pull him to his feet, but he gives me a sullen look before moping his way to the chair in the most un-Gabriel-like manner I've ever seen. The man is acting like a complete child.

He plops ungracefully into the chair, crosses his arms, his elbows resting on the chair arms. He refuses to look at me. He looks up at the nurse though with an insincere smile. "I expect that policy book within the hour."

"No you don't," I order him. "Now behave for the nurses and doctors or I'll call your mother and tell her what's going on."

He jerks his head around to look at me, eyes wide. "You wouldn't!"

I give him a smug smile and cross my arms. "Don't act like a baby and I won't have to."

The nurse, who has been waiting nervously, glances at me with a mixture of amusement and relief. I shoot her a reassuring grin and she turns him around and pushes him out. I walk behind her, listening to Gabriel mutter in Spanish. And then I think he starts speaking Russian. And then another language I don't recognize. And I'm reminded again of his astounding abilities and the fact that one of them, the one that I gave him, is likely killing him. And then my steps slow to a death march.

***

"Good evening, Mr. Dumas," the short, stocky doctor says as soon as he breezes into Gabriel's assigned room. We've not had to wait long, which puts me instantly on guard. I know from experience that bad news comes quick and good news comes slow.

"Hello," Gabriel says somewhat exhaustedly, perched on the very edge of his bed. He's been sitting on it like that the whole time, as if it's unsanitary or not fit to carry weight. But at least he's on the bed and not the chair like he was earlier. That took a lot of coaxing and threats. "I take it you've brought us some news?"

The doctor nods, tucking a file under his arm. "I just saw your X-ray. You've got some fluid in your lungs. We'll medicate you for that. See if we can't help you get some of that out. But I want to monitor you overnight still, to be sure it doesn't accumulate." The man isn't close enough for me to read, so I lock my eyes on his face from where I sit in the chair by the now-darkened window.

"Unfortunately, it also shows a mass in your left lung," the doctor continues, his tone apologetic. "I've already got you scheduled for a CT and MRI first thing tomorrow morning so we can get a better look at it."

A mass in your left lung...

The words constrict my lungs as I repeat them over in my head. Remember to breathe. Look at Gabriel. He's looking at the doctor, stunned.

"Anything else you can tell us at this point?" Gabriel asks when he finds words.

"Tests should tell us a lot more," the doctor replies. "And a biopsy of the mass. In the meantime, we need to keep an eye on you to be sure that fluid doesn't build up further."

Gabriel exhales resignedly. "Thank you."

"Any other questions I can answer?" the doctor says with practiced patience.

"Not until we know more," Gabriel replies.

Once the doctor leaves, I stand up to sit next to Gabriel. This is all happening so fast... It's ironic since the unknown—this moment—is exactly what we've both been dreading.

I remove one glove to hold his hand but we don't yet look at each other, lost in our own thoughts. There isn't really anything to be said. There's just... this moment. But this one is different than most. I'm vacant. Of words. Of action. Of understanding. Images and words float around in my head without order. We're creatures of reaction. Things happen and we react. But sometimes things happen and we don't know *how* to react. Sure, I've been here before: a hospital with someone I love who has just gotten terrible news. But I don't know how to react when that person is Gabriel, or when the reasons behind his suffering lie with what I did to him only a few months ago on a hypno-touch table with Louise breathing down my neck. Or when our relationship has only just begun to be the beautiful thing that it is. Given what I know about Robert's files, and the aggressive nature of the diseases those people endured, I don't know how much hope to have. I don't know what my expectation should be.

I need to know more. I need to see Robert.

"Are you alright?" Gabriel says, breaking the silence first.

I look over to find his eyes for a moment, but my attention is pulled downward to our hands.

"It's gone," I say, releasing and squeezing his hand a little to test it.

"What is?"

"The magnetism. Between our skin. It's gone."

"Just now?" he asks.

"I'm not sure," I say, thinking back on the last twenty-four hours. "I think maybe it's been fading today. I haven't noticed until now. Other things to think about I guess…"

He squeezes my hand harder. "Maybe it's affected by your state," he offers.

I shrug. I don't really care.

"So it's cancer," I say, testing out the words.

"We don't know that," Gabriel says. "Let's not speculate."

"Why? If it's not cancer, it's something equally terrible and you know it."

He rubs the back of his neck with his free hand and I can tell he agrees with me. He just doesn't *want* to agree with me. "Okay. So it's something terrible. Now what?"

I look down at the grey floor tiles for a moment. "I don't know. I just don't want to pretend that it isn't something terrible."

"Mr. Gabe," a voice says and we both look up to see a nurse standing in the room, her arms full of… medical things. "I need to start your IV and monitors now. I've got orders to draw more blood, and a deal is a deal," she says brightly. It's Sophia. She was the nurse on duty for this floor when we arrived in Gabriel's room. Deciding to try charm instead of mulishness, Gabriel managed to persuade her to let him stay 'unadorned' as he called it, at least until the doctor arrived with news. He and Sophia now have camaraderie already.

Gabriel nods without complaint, scoots back on the bed. "I never back out on a promise, Sophia. Go ahead and have your way with me. I imagine before this is done, I'll have a lot more to complain about than a few wires and an IV pole."

My shoulders slump as I push myself to my feet to get out of the way. I hate this.

"Want something to eat?" I ask Gabriel even though I'm not sure if *I* can eat. "I haven't eaten much since this morning and I think we missed dinner."

"Yes, Miss Wendy, you did," Sophia says, unwinding an IV line and affixing the bag to the hook on the pole next to his bed. "We have a cafeteria on the second floor though. It should be open for another hour."

Watching her work fills me with waves of déjà vu. And then my eyes brim with tears, which I wipe quickly away.

"Heavens, you're right," Gabriel says, not noticing me, more concerned with watching what Sophia is doing. "My appetite seems to be permanently amputated. Go ahead and get something. I'm not particularly hungry but I suppose I should eat." He looks at me now and tries for a smile. My eyes must be a little red because the curves of his mouth falter immediately. He reaches out for me.

"I'll be right back," Sophia says once she finishes with the IV bags. "Don't go anywhere Mr. Gabe."

"Wouldn't dream of it," Gabriel says, as she turns to dash out of the room for something.

I step forward and take his hand. "I'm fine," I whisper. "A memory just hit me. That's all."

"I don't know what to say," he says quietly, his voice bearing the notes of his helplessness. His eyes rest on mine for several beats as he wordlessly communicates the depth of that feeling to me. He knows I hear him. "Gads, I would do anything to put a smile on your face right now," he breathes.

I put my hand on his cheek. "I'm sorry. I thought I would be better at this than I am."

He tilts his head in confused indignation. "Better? At what? This situation? Don't be absurd. What are you apologizing for? *Feeling?*"

"I guess not," I reply, my hand falling. "I just don't want you to spend your energy trying to make *me* feel better and stressing out when you can't. I should be able to hold my own. I don't want to be a burden."

He grimaces at me. "Are you barmy? I'm the one with lungs on the fritz, wearing an easy-access accoutrement, being wheeled about in an armchair, and you think *you're* the burden?"

"Easy-access accoutrement?" I giggle, unable to help myself but not wanting to anyway. Gabriel's natural persona, as usual, has a grounding effect on me. And after that terrible news, I long to be close to him. I lean into him, pulling off a glove. "Hmm," I say, reaching for the fold of his gown to find his well-defined abdomen beneath. I snake my arm around the skin of his waist, and tug him to stand up. "There may be benefits to such things after all," I breathe, caressing the length of his back under his gown. "They do lend *ease* to *other* things, you know."

Taken by surprise for only a moment, Gabriel's hand finds my waist and he grips me tightly. "The woman knows how to look on the bright side, doesn't she?" His hand moves down to my butt. But the mischievous glint in his eye softens after a moment and he says, "There it is. The smile I was looking for. Who knew all this indignity would be the source of it."

"Hey you two!" Sophia's voice interrupts our moment. "There will be none of that," she scolds, carrying a tray into the room and setting it down with a clatter on the bed table. It has the needle for Gabriel's IV, among other things. "This is a hospital, not a honeymoon suite."

"Says *she*," Gabriel mumbles in my ear, squeezing my behind again when Sophia is out of eyeshot. Then he plops down on the bed again, bringing his legs up like a good patient and shaking out the thin blanket over himself. "El cielo, Sophia. How do you expect me to want to get better if you take the fun out of everything?"

"Fun," Sophia snorts, reaching for his arm so she can prep it for the IV. "I'm not fun?" she grumbles, rubbing the skin on the top of his hand a little too roughly with an alcohol pad. "I break policy for you even though I *knew* the doctor would chew me out for it, and you think I'm not *fun*? What do I need to do, Mr. Gabe? Bring a karaoke machine in here and perform *Girls Just Wanna Have Fun* for you?"

Gabriel chuckles and I smile. "You're right, Sophia," he says repentantly. "You are indeed, the most fun person I've encountered in this establishment—aside from my wife, of course. You have my apology. And for the remainder of your shift, I promise to use discretion so as not to incur further reprimand from your supervisors."

She eyes him, not missing the 'remainder of your shift' qualifier. "I'll be sure to warn the night nurse," she says, jabbing the top of his hand with the needle.

"She's got you pegged," I say. "And I think she brought my appetite back. I'll go check out the cafeteria."

"And I'll eagerly await your return," Gabriel says, gazing at me adoringly as I snag my purse from the chair and turn to go.

I sigh as I imagine that this is a scene that's going to start repeating regularly.

***

Digging my cell phone out of my bag once I reach the cafeteria, I find a seat and dial the hotel so I can update Kaylen and Ezra. I had considered putting it off until tomorrow when we'll have a lot more information, but I know better. Putting off the conversation doesn't make it any easier. Meanwhile, they'll be waiting by the phone, which is more torturous than hearing devastating news. I won't do that to Kaylen and Ezra.

"Hello?" says Kaylen's voice in my ear.

"It's me."

"Wendy, hi," she says, relieved but apprehensive.

"I don't have much news," I say. "But I wanted to let you know what we *do* know." I grit my teeth a moment to compose myself. "The X-ray shows fluid in his lungs and a mass on his left lung. That's all we know so far, but he's having more tests tomorrow morning."

"Oh Wendy," she says, her voice catching. I fiddle with the zipper of my purse. I think I lost my appetite again. "Anything I can do?"

I don't know why people ask that. What do they expect you to reply? People asked me that over and over when my mom was sick. "I don't know," I say, using the same reply I did then. It's honest, but it's not needy. It's strong, but not too strong. And it says everything.

I hear her breaths over the phone, and I'm glad I can't feel her right now. "Ezra's okay?" I ask, surprised I don't hear him in the background.

"Yeah. He's in the shower."

"Oh," I say. "You'll let him know?"

"Of course."

More silence.

"I should know more tomorrow," I say, though I don't know why. I all but said that already.

"How's Gabe doing with that fluid in his lungs? Has the coughing gotten worse?"

"No. they gave him a cough suppressant. He's fine. He's kept himself busy by giving the nurses a hard time. I heard the ER nurse warn the floor nurse about him when we got up to his room. He's already making a reputation for himself." Humor. That's what you do when you want to keep the conversation from getting awkward. Gosh, I hate these phone calls.

"I'm sure he is," Kaylen replies.

"Well I'm in the cafeteria to pick up some dinner for Gabriel. I'll call you tomorrow, okay?"

"Um. Okay." I taste frustration at the end of her words and in the empty silence on the line as I wait for her to say goodbye.

"You guys be careful," I say to wrap it up since she's apparently not going to.

"Wendy, wait," Kaylen blurts. "That's it?"

"I told you I didn't know much."

"No. I mean, what are you planning to do?"

That was unexpected. "What do you mean?"

"I thought we all understood what was going on—how Gabe got sick and who was responsible," she says in a rush. "But ever since we took Gabe to the ER you've acted like whatever is wrong with him just *happened* and now you go along with it like you would Joe down the street. Whatever is wrong with Gabe isn't *normal*, Wendy. I thought you knew that, but you're telling me about X-rays and tests and how Gabe is treating the nurses instead of telling me what your plan is. Do you even have one?"

My lips part in surprise, I'm not quite sure how to respond. I do have plans—or the beginnings of plans—in the back of my mind. I just haven't had a whole lot of time to spend on them yet.

"I think we need to go see Robert," Kaylen says when I don't speak. "He has had the files all this time. Even though they were Carl's, he must know something about them. What if there is already a solution to this thing? The files are over twenty years old."

"I was planning on it," I say, impressed with the consideration Kaylen has already put into this. This is also the first time I've heard Kaylen refer to her adopted father—my biological father—by his first name.

"You were?" she asks. "When?"

"I hadn't pinned anything down yet," I reply. "Give me a break, Kaylen. It's day one. I'm still getting past the shock."

"Oh... sorry," Kaylen replies, somewhat sheepishly. "I worried because you hadn't said anything at all."

"Admittedly, I wasn't planning on mentioning it. I was planning on just *doing* it."

"Alone?" she asks, surprised.

"Well, yeah. No reason to put more than just me in danger. I figured I'd call him up and meet him somewhere public."

Several beats of silence pass and then she says, "Wendy, did you forget I'm a telekinetic?"

"No, I... Oh... Yeah, I guess bringing you with me would be safer, huh?"

She laughs mirthlessly. "You think? Why would you consider going by yourself when you don't have to?"

"I don't know," I say, thinking. "I guess because you and Ezra are minors. And I don't want you getting hurt. And Gabriel's obviously going to be stuck in a hospital for a while so he can't go... Didn't occur to me, I guess."

"*Minors?*" she says incredulously. "You're worried about underage *laws*? You can kill people with your skin sometimes, practically read people's minds, and see people's souls. I can down a skyscraper or disarm anyone around me at will, Gabe can count crazy stuff and memorize books and speak all kinds of languages, and Ezra can... do crazy hard math problems. The law hasn't done anything for *us* the last couple weeks. Together we took down at least twenty well-trained, armed men in a shopping mall. You need to stop expecting to do everything yourself."

I slump. When she puts it that way, I have no idea why I'm treating her and Ezra like helpless kids. "I think it's because of how responsible I feel," I tell her. "Gabriel is sick because of something *I* did. It's my job to fix it, you know?"

"Wendy..." Kaylen says quietly. In her voice I hear the strain of sadness. "I'm an orphan. You and Gabe and Ezra became my family when you didn't owe me anything. Because of it, I owe you *everything*. I want to contribute to helping the people I love. I want to make it up to you any way I can. I know you don't expect it, but it matters to me. I don't want you dragging me along for the ride. It makes me feel like... like I don't belong with you."

My heart sinks. "Kaylen, I had no idea you felt that way." My gosh, do I underestimate this girl constantly. "I'm sorry. It never occurred to me you'd have trouble feeling like you belong, because as far as I'm concerned, you did from day one."

"Great," she sighs. "And now I'm making you feel bad. I didn't mean to do that. I only mean I want to help and I want you to let me help."

"Alright. Let's drop it then. You feel bad. I feel bad. Everyone feels bad around here. So let's move ahead and start acting like the family we are."

"I'm game. So you'll let me go with you to see Robert?"

"Yes. But just you and me. Gabriel can't for obvious reasons. And if we get into a tight spot, more bodies will just be a liability. So that means Ezra doesn't need to be there either."

"I'm with you. But you know Gabe will freak out if you leave him behind."

"Which is why I'm going to do it while he's getting his scans done," I reply, happy to be occupying myself with plans. "It should keep him busy for a few hours."

"What about Ezra? He's not going to be happy."

She's right about that, but I can't think of a good lie to tell Ezra for why Kaylen and I will both be going on an errand together early tomorrow morning.

"I guess we'll have to tell him the truth," I say. "He's smart enough to realize that having him with us won't be helpful. And besides, someone's got to stay behind who knows what we're doing in case something happens. So you two come to the hospital in the morning and Ezra will stay here while you and I go. He'll be here when Gabriel gets back from his tests and tell him where we are. By then it will be too late for him to do something dumb like come after us."

"Okay, what time?" she asks, her voice revealing definite excitement. I'm also climbing my way out of despair at the prospect before us.

"Gabriel is scheduled at eight-thirty. Show up then. The nurse will have already taken him over."

"Perfect. See you then."

6

"*Wendy*," a voice whispers from nearby. Someone shakes me, and I turn over groggily on the futon to find Kaylen's face, her thick dark hair braided over her right shoulder, her porcelain cheeks slightly flushed. A thrill revives me—her anticipation.

I sit up, look around. Ezra is perched on the edge of Gabriel's bed, which is empty.

"He was gone when we got here," Ezra says, guessing at my question. "There's a note though." He holds up a piece of paper. "Says he's left for his tests. He didn't want to wake you."

Ezra crosses his arms then, his jaw clamped and I know exactly what's on his mind: my visit to Robert.

"Perfect," I say, looking around for my shoes. "Then I don't have to figure out how to not lie to him."

After putting on my shoes, I sit up, my side aching from leaning over. I rub it absentmindedly. I must have pulled something yesterday morning when I was sobbing on the floor of the apartment. Looking up, I don't need emodar to read Ezra's expression. "Wen—" he starts.

"You want to come," I say. "I know. But you can't. You know it, too. Someone needs to stay here, and that person is you. Would you rather I take you and leave Kaylen?"

"No, but—"

I hold up a hand. "It's done, Ezra. But it's going to be fine. I promise."

"You can't promise that."

I grab my purse off the floor and wade through it for an elastic for my hair. "Robert isn't going to hurt us."

"You don't know that either."

"I do. Because I know something about Robert that you don't. That nobody does."

Ezra's hands fall to the bed on either side of him. "What?"

"Robert has the brightest soul I have ever seen."

Ezra's brow furrows. "What? I thought we believed life force light equated goodness somehow, so..."

I twist my unruly hair back into a messy bun and secure it. "We did. We do. I think we might be wrong about Robert."

"Wrong? He had us chased down to Del Monte Mall. Kaylen had to throw cars at his guys to take out their numbers. We've been on the run from him for weeks. Where is the mistake?"

"In assuming that those were Robert's guys. They could just as easily have been Carl's. And we already know those files in Robert's office were really Carl's. There could be any number of explanations for why Robert has had them all this time."

"We don't actually *know* that," Ezra points out. "Carl just didn't argue with it when you accused him of it."

I roll my eyes, shrugging into my jacket. "Get with it, Ezra. I know that's a *possibility,* but it doesn't jive with what we know about Robert, what I have *seen* with my own eyes."

"But you saw his life force before we ever suspected him. You've had that information all this time and I never heard you say we might be wrong about Robert. Why now all of a sudden? Is it really because of Carl?"

I hesitate. "Mostly... yeah... But also because... I guess I finally believe what I see in the colorworld. Now that I finally accept what light means there, how it affects us, how *we* affect *it,* everything makes sense. And if everything makes sense and I

46

believe it, then I must be wrong about Robert. There's no way for him to have that kind of light if he's bad. If he's bad, it upends *everything* we think we know about the colorworld. And I'm not willing to accept that's true."

Ezra crosses his arms again. "So why have you not told anyone about Robert's light until now?"

I exhale heavily. "I didn't tell you about life force light differences when I found out because it would have supported Gabriel's theory. And I didn't want you ganging up on me at the time. And since then... well there was the whole Del Monte Mall business and all those damning files... I hadn't accepted the theory yet."

"Didn't accept the theory?" Ezra asks, confused. "I thought the theory was why you ended up touching Gabe."

"Maybe partly," I say, searching for a way to express what I want. "But mostly I touched him because..." I look at Ezra as I tug my purse strap up higher on my shoulder. "Because I had to. It's a long story that you can ask me about another time. But we need to get going."

Ezra throws his hands up. "Fine. What do I tell Gabe when he gets here and starts yelling at me in Swahili?"

"Exactly what I just told you," I say, linking my arm with Kaylen's.

"Yeah, that'll go over well," Ezra grumbles as we walk to the door.

"We'll be back," I say over my shoulder.

"Wow," Kaylen says as we head for the elevator. "Robert's bright, huh? After my da—, I mean, Carl, came by, I started to wonder if we didn't have all the facts on Robert, but it sounds like... we could be *way* off. Brightest you've ever *seen?* Really? That means he's like... a saint, right?"

I shrug and press the down button. "I don't have a ton of experience with noting the differences in people's life forces so I'm not sure how common Robert's level of light is. It's only recently I've been able to pick up on the differences more easily. All I know is that when we lived with him, he was the only person at the time whose light was easy to distinguish from others'. I didn't need to compare him side-by-side with someone else to know he was brighter."

"Well I hope you're right and we really are wrong about him," Kaylen says, stepping into the elevator. "We need to be. For Gabe's sake. He can't be treated if we're on the run."

"Amen to that. But you know, if he's got full surveillance out for us, Robert will know we've popped back on the grid. It's kind of impossible to get medical help as a nameless person. We're in the system now. We even paid the ER copay with a credit card. But I've not seen hide or hair of anyone coming down on us."

"Good point," she says. "It probably was Carl then, at Del Monte. He knows Gabe is sick now. I wonder what his next move will be?"

"Carl has proven that the thing he's best at is sitting on the sidelines and observing while other people do the dirty work." I turn to Kaylen. "I think you didn't know about this side of him growing up because he's not actually the brain behind the heinous crimes. I think Louise is. Not that he's excused. I think he never protested what Louise was doing because it meant he got what he wanted without getting his own hands dirty. I think he's probably gentler than we think. And his heart was broken when my mother died. He hasn't had anyone around to pick up the pieces. I can see and feel emotion in him. With Louise I never really could. So I don't think you should feel bad about being blind to what he was."

Kaylen thinks about that, her brows knit together, her hands braced behind her on the elevator bar. But she doesn't comment. The elevator dings open and we step out. "Thanks for doing this with me, Kaylen," I say as we walk toward the exit doors. "I don't know what it is about you, but you have a way of making me look at things differently. Even without meaning to sometimes. Like the insight into Carl; I just came up with that. I like having you around."

"Funny. I've thought the same thing about you," she replies.

***

At Robert's office, we learn that Lacey, his assistant, has been instructed to connect us to him immediately should we show up. He's not in the office so she calls him. Once she hands the phone to me, I say, "I hope you're nearby because we need to talk."

"I agree. I'm actually just getting back from San Francisco. I should be there in about half an hour. Can you wait?" Robert asks, a note of insistence in his voice. I also don't think I've ever heard him speak so fast.

"Yes. But we need to meet somewhere public. Know what I mean?" I say. Bright light or not, it's clear Robert has lied to me.

"Of course. You want to meet at end of the pier, downtown? It's south of Cannery Row. Should be plenty of people there. Thirty minutes. Okay?"

"You got it," I reply, and then we hang up.

Having nowhere else to go, Kaylen and I arrive at the wharf early. Lots of people are out and about, but few linger at the end of the

48

pier, probably because the chilly wind is more unrelenting out here. The briny scent of it invigorates my senses though, and I swallow it in gulps. The knots of emotion I've been accumulating loosen a little. A quiver moves through my chest as my thoughts shift to Gabriel. Now that I'm away from the hospital setting, I feel the need to prepare myself for what lies ahead; his tests this morning are probably only the beginning of the endless cycle of waiting and enduring. I know it too well, and anticipating it settles a new cloud of exhaustion over me. We've yet to get an actual diagnosis, but I'm oddly resigned to the fact that whatever it is, it's as bad as any of those illnesses outlined in Robert's files. It's terminal. And it's going to kill him if I can't do something about it.

"Do you think Carl was lying when he said you can fix Gabe's life force?" Kaylen asks as if reading my mind. It's no surprise though, that we'd be thinking of the same thing.

"I'm hoping Robert knows something about that," I sigh. "Otherwise we'll be tracking Carl down... Gosh, if I never see Louise again it will be too soon."

Kaylen's face turns steely and her hands grip the railing. But she remains quiet. We both do for a while as we gaze out at the ocean. But I look without seeing, caught up in the quiet background turmoil in my stomach that catches up to me now that I'm sitting still. I've staved off crying since that first time yesterday, but I think it's because I've had something to do. Things to look forward to like logistics, getting a diagnosis, and talking to Robert—even if they aren't pleasant things. I desperately hope I don't come to a point where I have nothing to do but wait. Even now I'm on the edge of collapsing in misery. And misery has been too frequent in my life.

How long is this chronic desolation going to last? Surely I've had my fair share of it already. I think I deserve a bit longer than a two week reprieve. I know better than to dwell on unfairness, but I can't help it. It results in anger, which is easier to stomach than heartache. I'll take it.

I turn around to take a quick scan of the pier, and then I check my phone for the time, which is passing excruciatingly slow. With nothing else to do, I spend some time listening in on other conversations that mingle with the sound of the waves lapping at the beach and pier.

Most of the voices are uninteresting, but I linger on two of them because they sound like they could be brother and sister, and it's funny to listen to them bicker. They're about fifty yards away and moving in my direction at a slow pace as they argue about what time the restaurant they had planned to go to was supposed to open. The woman claims the restaurant changed their breakfast times, and the man claims the woman is mistaken: they start serving brunch at nine-thirty and it's always been that way. When their argument comes to a stalemate, they stop about twenty yards away and lean over the side of the pier, waiting, I guess, for the restaurant to open.

The woman says, "I wish the water wasn't so murky. You can't see a thing."

"It's pollution," the man replies authoritatively. "The water wasn't this murky fifty years ago."

"You don't know that," says the woman. "Last I checked, you weren't an environmentalist."

"Neither are you," the man says, propping a foot on the lower rung of the railing.

"I'm a doctor. Which makes me more qualified than a community college economics teacher."

"Oooh, burn," the man says. "I shape the minds of the next generation, and you stare at women's lady parts all day. How does that make you more qualified than me?"

The woman's face is the only one I can see from this angle and she scrunches up her nose as she punches his arm—not softly. "*Burn?* How old are you?" It's a valid question. The man looks to be in his early forties. But I guess if he's junior college professor, he probably has a ton of current slang in his repertoire.

"Old enough to know that the ocean is polluted," he says.

"Of course it's polluted," she says with exaggerated patience. "Everything is. But I read an article the other day that said the ocean is something like three hundred million trillion gallons of water. The amount of pollution it would take to dirty that much water to the point of actually *seeing* it is a lot more than people have been churning out since the industrial revolution."

"A million trillion? Did you just make that number up?" he asks.

She props her elbow on the railing. "Shut up. I didn't make it up. It's a trillion multiplied by three hundred billion. Octillion or something? I don't know," she says eyeing him expectantly. "Why are you being so difficult?"

"Sorry," he says—not apologetically—fluffing his slightly greying light brown hair as if he's trying to get it to stand up. "If I don't eat breakfast by nine, I get hyperglycemic. It makes me moody."

What an idiot, I think to myself. Not only is this guy obstinate on purpose, but he's also unintelligent. What he *means* is *hypo*glycemic.

She snorts. "Hyperglycemic, huh? Do you even know what that means?"

I smile. Go, Dr. Lady Parts.

"You're just changing the subject because you know not only am I right about the restaurant, but I'm right about seeing ocean pollution," he says.

Seeming used to the man's disagreeable nature, the woman smiles indulgently but condescendingly—a look I wish I knew how to pull off as effectively as she does. "Well, Professor, what you're seeing in the ocean is silt, otherwise known as dirt. And there is a whole lot more dirt in the ocean than pollution. Even if the ocean has a million tons of pollution in it, you'd hardly notice, not with pollution getting spread evenly throughout."

"You don't think a million tons of pollution is a lot?" the man asks, either not getting it or attempting to sidetrack her because she's making a good case.

"Not compared to three hundred million trillion gallons. You can't even picture that much water, can you? That's why it seems like a lot of pollution to you."

"No. I cannot picture a million trillion since it's not an actual number."

Oh my gosh. Please smack him.

She ignores his obnoxious persistence, continuing her lecture, "Water is a solvent. It can break anything down over time. Anything that goes in it will eventually be dissolved so well you would never know it's there. Picture it. Two-thirds of the earth. Millions of estuaries that feed into rivers and then into streams that are partly fed by underground water sources. It's all connected like one big vascular network, pumping whatever gets deposited throughout the whole system. The laws of dissolution guarantee it. At this point in history, pollution is still negligible."

"And now you're advocating water pollution?" he prods.

She rolls her eyes. "Remind me why I put up with you?"

I'd like the answer to that question myself. The woman is trying to have an intelligent conversation, and the man spends the entire time pushing her buttons. Ugh. This is why I don't eavesdrop unless necessary. People talk about meaningless drivel ninety-nine percent of the time. And the other one percent, like the woman's point about the layout of the earth's water system, clash with ignorance like that man. Gosh, it's not fair that people should be allowed to go on wasting their time being total jerks when people like Gabriel are faced with an early death. He never wastes *any* moment.

"There he is." Kaylen's voice breaks through my thoughts.

I turn my attention to where she's looking. Robert's goatee is a bit shorter than the last time I saw him, and the silver peppered through his dark hair stands out next to the light grey suit he's wearing. The suit itself is a bit more casual than I'm used to seeing on him and he has no tie on. I guess he travels dressed down.

I scan the surrounding people as he approaches but don't see any indication that he came with anyone. There are so few people out this morning. Even Dr. Lady Parts and Professor Econ have headed back to the boardwalk. "I think it's clear," I mumble to Kaylen.

Robert doesn't smile, but he doesn't frown either. Instead he looks a bit exhausted and stressed.

"Kaylen. Wendy," he says when he reaches us. "I'm *very* relieved to see you."

"Robert," I acknowledge.

"What can you tell us?" Kaylen asks.

Without hesitation, Robert replies, "That I have lied to you. From the first day we met."

7

"*D*o you mind if I stand closer?" Robert asks. "I would like you to be able to gauge my honesty... if you like?" He holds up his hands in submission.

"Suit yourself," I say, though I scoot closer to Kaylen and eye him.

Robert moves to stand adjacent to us, fingers laced together and resting atop the wooden railing. At only four feet away, it's strange to have him in my personal space like this since he spent so many months at a distance. He looks out over the water, mooring his wayward thoughts before he speaks, like always. Pushing past Kaylen's apprehension, I hone in on his emotions more closely. Well-being moves over me, a result of finding comfort in Robert's mind being the same as I remember: quiet and steady, his mental movement tedious and lengthy, but subtly nuanced like the tale of Moby-Dick. I don't know why I always think of that story when he's around. I don't even think I finished the book. But it has become my nickname for Robert. He's nervous, but sad mostly. It's a sadness drawn across time, one he knows well I think.

He shakes his head absentmindedly. "I've been thinking about this for days, you know—how to start?" He glances over at me. "You'd think I'd have it rehearsed by now, but... I've spent so much time worrying how you'll react to it because you are so much like Carl, and what I am about to tell you destroyed him." He hesitates. "We know each other so little... That's my own fault, but protecting the lies prevented me from really getting to know you. I might have gotten over my own misgivings anyway, but your mother asked me not to tell you, and as I told you before, I trusted her judgment and rights as your mother."

"And now?" I ask, shifting my weight, not quite comfortable enough to lounge against the railing.

"Now I think she underestimated you—what you were capable of handling. She was so adamant. When she was first diagnosed with cancer, she contacted me and reiterated that when she passed, I was not to tell you any of this. She said you needed to believe—" He stops, looking down at the planks and back up to my face. "I'm getting ahead of myself. I'll get to the whys of her decision in a moment. But I just want you to know that she lied to you, *we* lied to you, because sometimes ignorance is bliss. And she wanted nothing but bliss for you. She believed you *deserved* less burdens, which is why she committed herself so fully to it."

Sadly, I remember the person I was at that time my mom was diagnosed. It's no wonder my mom didn't think I could handle any more stress, not when I was already handling my life so poorly. "Alright," I say. "I can accept that. But now things are different. What about the files? I assume Dan told you we saw them."

Robert nods. "I realize how that must have looked. They are old files, from individuals who manifested abilities over fifteen years ago. What you don't know is that your father performed the energy touch on all of them."

"Yes, I know," I say.

Robert furrows his brow. "You do? How?"

"Carl paid me a visit yesterday," I say darkly. "He didn't admit it outright, but I guessed it."

"You guessed it? But— nevermind. I obviously don't know how much you know already."

"Pretend I don't know anything. Everything I think I know at this point is pretty much an educated guess."

He nods again before beginning in his halting, careful cadence. "Your father was the most powerful energy-touch practitioner at the time, and it was only through him that people manifested such powerful abilities—more powerful than anything Louise has been able to do since. He called his method visuo-touch." Robert sighs and shifts his feet. "The result, unfortunately, was that the people died shortly after discovering their new talents. I don't know why, but I think there's something about manipulating a life force that isn't natural. It sets things out of balance."

I slump against the railing, my assumptions now confirmed, and it's heavy. I really didn't want it to be true. The disappointment makes my eyes sting. Kaylen, too, trembles and releases a shuddering sigh.

She puts a comforting hand on my back, and after a moment, says, "If Wendy can do the same thing as Carl, and that thing is a death sentence, why do Louise and Carl want her?"

"He wants her to finish what he started," Robert replies. "I think he believes you can figure out a way around problem, Wendy. Probably because your ability exceeds his... There is so much I don't know. I'm sorry."

"That's what he wants alright..." I say quietly, mostly to myself. I have no idea if I believe I can. The colorworld is mystery wrapped in speculation. Just when I learn something about it, it opens up a whole new lot of questions. People imagine that seeing souls would automatically answer all the hard questions about life, but it has done nothing but screw up mine. And Carl's, too. Why didn't he drop this years ago? Especially when he lost his ability (which I am almost positive he did). Or even when my mother died? No wonder Robert worried about me.

Racked with regret, Robert continues, "I really didn't know Gina was your real mother. I didn't know much about her at all, actually. During the time he was with her, Carl was consumed with his work, and mine was rocketing. When you told me Gina was your biological mother, I remembered her from the files and realized what must have happened. Carl did visuo-touch on her and she died. Shortly after that, Carl came and told me they were losing clients to awful maladies: cancer primarily. But also genetic illness. Inherited disorders that normally kill babies and children were cropping up in adults as if their very DNA had mutated. I remember one man in particular who had Tay-Sachs. That should have killed him before the age of five but he developed it out of the blue at thirty."

Robert rubs his head as if to expunge the memory. His feeling of powerlessness has increased, and I watch him, still waiting to see where this is going and trying so hard not to imagine what Gabriel's visuo-touch-induced hell will be like.

"He sent me their files—the ones you found—to impress me with the urgency of the situation. You wouldn't believe how quickly they died. If it was cancer, the best case scenario was a few months after diagnosis. Their bodies didn't respond well to any kind of treatment. And there was nothing about their biology that showed why this was. But it was clear that what Carl was doing was killing people. So Carl asked me for money. He needed to fund his research so he could help the ones that were still alive. He knew they'd only have a few years before illness would strike, so I gave Carl a million dollars of seed money."

Kaylen and I figure it out at the same time, but she says it first, "The million dollars you gave him funded a lot more than life-saving research, didn't it?"

"Yes," he replies. "And he has managed to turn it into many millions more. I suspect they must have had someone then capable of predicting stock trends or something. When I gave it to him, I had no idea what was really going on. I had no idea he was *still* practicing. I mean... why *would* he? It was Leena who told me. She came to me right after Carl had supposedly died, bringing

Wendy with her." Robert looks at me with insistent eyes. "I had no reason to think you weren't Leena's daughter, but I think Gina would have appreciated what Leena did. Leena gave up everything to take you away from Carl. Everything she might have become or done with her life was put aside the day she came to me, terrified because Carl had performed his visuo-touch on *you* when you were barely past infancy. She had figured out what was happening and feared the same would happen to you."

Reeling from residual disgust of that, he has covered his eyes with his hands. He wipes down his face like the sweat of exertion has gathered there. "Leena never wanted you to know any of this. It was over, she said. If you were fated to die at a young age she would rather you didn't look toward your future with foreboding. I agreed, and we parted ways, but I kept in touch with her, protected you from both Louise and Carl who were intent on finding you. As I told you before, Leena didn't want me near you because it would have led Louise to you. But she was also afraid I would tell you something, and that I would want to run tests on you, try to keep you healthy. I did at first. I tried to tell her that if we were on alert, when you were stricken ill we might have a chance at fighting whatever it was. She said that was no life for you. Instead she devoted herself to giving you a good life, helping you find and explore your passions. She was... trying to accomplish your bucket list without you knowing, I suppose."

Oh Mom... A wash of sadness moves over me several times, each wave more sorrowful than the last. So much of my mother makes sense now. I've held on to a corner of resentment for her because I felt she had stunted me, made me selfish by giving me the illusion that what I wanted was the only thing that mattered. She lavished me with attention, with opportunity, with encouragement. I was so mad at her for not telling me to keep Elena. I wanted her so bad and my mom pushed me to give her up when all I wanted was to hang on to this new part of me that had me smitten from the first ultrasound. But my mom knew about sacrifice—she'd been doing it since she took me from Carl—and she told me to give Elena up so my daughter wouldn't possibly one day have to grow up motherless......

Tears spring to my eyes and I turn abruptly toward the ocean. "Why didn't you tell me, Mom?" I whisper into the breeze. My heart hurts. My bones hurt. The ache in my side that I felt when I woke up this morning hasn't gone away. I prop my elbows on the railing and put my forehead in my hands as I cry, my tears so plenteous that the wind can't dry them. I have never wanted to hug my mother so badly. But she's not here. I forgive her for the lies. I forgive everything she has unintentionally caused. She did every bit of it out of love. Oh God, I would have done anything for Elena. And my mom did the same for me when she had no obligation or biological tie to do so.

I cry more loudly, mourning the loss of my mom as I never have. I wish I could tell her I understand now and that I'm sorry for breaking her heart.

After an indeterminate time, my eyes are no longer blurry from tears and I breathe deeply to air out the last of the sorrow. There is more to this story and I need to hear it. Kaylen has been holding her arm around me and she releases me now.

Robert, who has been silent and meditative as I've cried, moves ahead without commenting on my reaction. "To my surprise, you didn't die. All these years I believed it was some kind of miracle... But now we know why. Carl didn't actually do visuo-touch on you. Visuo-touch doesn't require an illness beforehand. Like you, Carl could manifest abilities in healthy people—powerful abilities. So why would he go so far as to give you juvenile diabetes? Or an allergy?"

"Because he couldn't do visuo-touch anymore, and it was the only way to give me an ability—through regular hypno-touch," I supply, picking at a splinter of wood sticking up from the railing, on alert because of what I pick up from Robert: trepidation. I'm not going to like how this ends.

"Yes. I should have made that connection sooner, but I took Leena's word for it that Carl had done visuo." Robert turns his body to face mine, and he looks at me with sincerity. "Wendy, I have lied about many things to protect you, but I did not lie about having no idea how Carl touched people."

"Don't worry about it," I say. "I'm pretty sure Carl lost his ability and that's why he started touching people."

He looks at me curiously. "Oh... So then that was why he needed you..."

"Yep. If you're an evil psychopath, you lose your ability," I say, tempering my anger at Carl that's flaring again.

Without wondering too long about my statement, he continues, "I've kept up with Louise through the years as much as possible. I told you before that I didn't know how to find her because I didn't *want* you to find her. But the truth is I know enough about Louise to be able to locate her if I truly need to."

"Yeah, we suspected as much," I say.

"Yes. My acting never was very good, was it?" he asks with a slight smile, a twinkle in his eye. I don't think I've ever seen his eyes look so lively, but I think it's because he so rarely looked at me directly before. Moby-Dick is getting used to being nearer the surface and he's far more interesting than I thought.

"Louise has never really known the full extent of my ability," Robert says. "That's why she made it so easy for me to find her in San Bernardino. I also don't think she was aware that I've known her alias of Sally Stenworth for some time. It's clear she *wanted* you to find her though, and I am sure she planted that letter to 'help' me find her. The ATM story was a lie, although the goal I ended up focusing on to find her didn't turn out precisely as I thought it would—as you know."

Melancholy falls over him then, but he doesn't bury it in the depths of the sea as I'm used to him doing. He leaves it out for me to see, telling me without telling me that there is something more, and he doesn't want to say it.

I scoot a bit closer to him. I reach out a gloved hand and touch his arm. I've never done that before and it startles him. "Uncle Robert, I've been through hell already. I'm *living* in hell currently. Things can't get much worse. So spill it. All I want is the truth. About everything. So I can start sorting out what I'm going to do."

A cloud of misery moves over him at my words. "They *can* get worse," he says softly, looking back out into the grey. "But you're right. You have proven who you are and what you can handle. I just wish I could spare you hard things."

He turns toward me again, his hands clasped in front of him, one elbow resting on the railing. "Have you been suspicious of Leena's death since you found out about the files?"

I blink at him and take a small step back. "No... Should I be?"

He stands very still, looking down at his feet. "I told you Leena called me when she was diagnosed. She also called a few months later. Aside from giving me instructions about you, she asked me if I'd been keeping up with Louise's past creations. She asked about their health..." Robert looks at me expectantly, but pauses only briefly. "I looked into it and found that a large number of them had died early deaths."

I take another step back, realization swirling through me with dizzying quickness. "Oh no," I breathe. I glance at Kaylen. She's right there with me, the horrified look on her face mirroring my own.

Robert sags visibly. Even his suit looks disheveled all of a sudden. "Hypno-touch kills as surely as visuo-touch. Only slower. And Leena figured it out. Or she already knew it. I'm not sure which."

I put my hand over my mouth. "Oh God... Oh God, no."

Kaylen has her hands wrapped around her braid like it's a lifeline, her eyes wide and her mind moving swiftly.

Kaylen. She is going to die. This sweet girl is going to die. I swear, I cannot picture it. I cannot picture Kaylen's face as anything but full of life, pink cheeks on porcelain skin that seems to glow. No, Kaylen cannot die...

And I'm going to die... Ezra comes to mind, and nausea bubbles in my stomach; my head feels hot and I place the back of my hand over it. Ezra has seen too much death. His mom... Now he will lose both his biological sister as well as his adopted sister. And Gabriel who has become his older brother... Will there be anyone left for him? How will he cope?

And then my thoughts move to the compound and all the people that spent time there: Marcus, Chloe, Corinne, Gina, Jimmy, Will... And they are slated to die torturous early deaths? It's a slaughter. Carl and Louise are serial killers.

"We've got to stop them," I say abruptly, looking up into Robert's harrowed face.

"There is no way to do so. The supernatural nature of their work protects them from criminal charges. I would be laughed out of the police station. Energy touch—something that doesn't even require skin-contact—that causes cancer fifteen years in the future? Not feasible. There are still people out there living with their abilities, oblivious to the future, and I can't take away their peace of mind. What's more, I can't risk them being exploited for what they can do. It's not a kind world for people who are different—gifted."

"You can't warn people ahead of time? There's got to be some way to get to potential subjects before Carl and Louise do. With your ability?"

"I have tried before to warn their new recruits, to tell them what will likely happen," he replies. "But no one is willing to believe that hand waving over the body could possibly be lethal."

We stand looking out over the ocean together for a silent minute. Everyone around me has paid for what Louise and Carl have done and I will not *die* before I put an end to what they have been doing.

"I was thankful when you came back from the compound to hear that you'd resisted Louise's attempts to instruct you in hypno-touch," Robert says finally. "You clearly have better instincts than Carl did. I would have hated for you to endure the guilt of unknowingly harming someone."

I snort. "Don't be so sure about that."

Robert turns his head to look at me with worry. "You've practiced on someone?"

"Gabriel," I reply hollowly. Instead of being my only concern, Gabriel is the first of what is sure to be a long line of tragedies. "On the compound. The one and only time."

"He's in the hospital right now," Kaylen adds sadly.

Worry turns to dismay on Robert's face. He remains speechless for several counts as he sorts through various responses.

"Don't bother," I say. "Nothing you can say is going to make me feel any better or change how things are one bit." I huff bitterly, not at him, but at the situation. "I came because I was hoping you'd have some answers that might help me figure out how to save him… But instead I learn that everyone is going to die. This is turning out to be one hell of a week."

Robert turns back to the ocean, still thinking, regretful and grief-stricken.

Kaylen has been so silent, still overcoming the news of her fate. And she's angry. Furious. Carl is a horrible human being. How could he justify this cost?

I reach out for her hand, lacing my fingers purposely with hers and drawing closer. There is nothing to say right now. There are only the waves of emotion pulsing over the three of us—and me enduring all of them at once. I close my eyes, dizzied by the tumult, but I don't resist. I let them flow and take me where they will.

Sorrow has a way of building to a peak and then dissolving into utter stillness. I am learning to let it flow so I can get to that point. Holding it in always ends up with me doing something stupid. I'm waiting for my head to clear as I stand beside Kaylen, waiting for my tears to dry in the salty air. I want the stillness. I crave it, but I will not leave Kaylen's side. We will endure together. We will arrive together. And then we'll walk away from here and do… something.

"I'll do everything I can to help you," Robert says finally, purposefully. "I don't know how, but we'll figure it out. Please, don't give up hope."

"I hadn't planned on it," I sigh. "But I also have to be realistic. For Ezra's sake." I glance over at him. "Oh, and Robert? I can touch Gabriel now. I know how it works. My lethal skin."

Robert's brows lift in surprise. "That's wonderful! How did you figure it out?"

"I didn't. He did. I just finally stopped being afraid," I say, unable to find any pride or enthusiasm behind the words.

"I'm glad to get some good news in all this..." Robert says, but then his jaw tightens. "But under the circumstances, I can see the tragic irony."

"Get him back only to lose him again," I say dryly. Then, because I am tired of dwelling on the chaos my life has once again descended into, I say, "You'll come with me to the hospital? Gabriel should be out of his MRI and CT soon. He'll probably be calling and wondering where I am. I'd like him to hear all this from you. I'm... too tired to repeat it."

"Of course," says Robert, understanding. "I cleared my schedule for today before I came here. Do you need a ride?"

I nod as the three of us start walking back along the pier, which has become a little more crowded.

My phone rings then and I dig it out of my purse. It's Gabriel surely.

I answer it without looking at the caller ID, "We're on our way back right now. Don't freak out."

"Wendy?" says a more gravelly voice that definitely does not belong to Gabriel. "This is Mike. You're not here."

I forgot Mike was expecting us in LA this morning at the latest. I sigh. And so it begins. I hope I don't get a call from Gabriel's mother, Maris, today, too. I don't have the energy for it right now—maybe not ever.

"Ah... yeah, that's not going to be happening," I reply, hiking my purse back up on my shoulder and walking again.

"Why not?" he demands belligerently.

Gosh, this guy is rude. "Because Gabriel is in the hospital," I snap, devoid of patience.

There are about three seconds of silence as I figure out how to relay the situation without a long drawn-out explanation. "I'm on my way to *you* then," he says abruptly before I can try. And then he hangs up.

I look at the phone, wondering if the call dropped, but I don't think so. *That was weird.* He didn't even ask what Gabriel is in the hospital for.

Dread settles over me. Mike has not liked me from the beginning, and now he's about to learn that I killed his brother.

This week is getting better and better.

8

$\mathcal{G}$abriel calls before we get to the hospital. When I tell him I'm bringing Robert back with me, he bellows a laugh and says, "Of course you are." He doesn't even berate me for going without him, let alone not telling him. I don't ask how his tests went. I'm not ready to hear it yet, but his agreeableness in the face of going behind his back is a universal bad news tell. My mom did the same thing. I could get away with the dumbest things on the nights before she was set to have tests done. She couldn't bear to be angry at me *and* tell me bad news. I was such an awful daughter... And apparently I subconsciously did the same thing to Gabriel.

When we are about twenty-five yards from Gabriel's room, I pick up the sound of his voice, "What does trust have to do with it? Kaylen is beautiful and you are a boy—You *are* a boy, right?"

"Last I checked," Ezra replies snottily. "But that does not mean—"

"Good," Gabriel interrupts. "Then you have all the equipment I'm familiar with, which makes me qualified to give you counsel. So mind your manners with that young woman and don't do anything I'll have to throttle you for. And I don't just mean your atrocious eating habits."

A wide grin spreads over my face and I walk slower, enticing Robert and Kaylen to do the same. I'm curious how Ezra will respond.

"Mind my manners? Are you kidding?" Ezra says. "My brother-in-law might be on his deathbed, and we're trying to avoid crazy people chasing us. Can you explain to me what manners you're worried I won't have in the middle of all that?"

"Certainly," Gabriel replies. "My apologies. I should have been clearer. No undressing. No making out. No sex. No groping. No hands on anyone else's genitalia. No sleeping in the same bed. No being naked—"

"Ahhh!" Ezra interrupts. "I wasn't serious. Geez, Gabe. Cut it out."

I laugh heartily, garnering a look from Kaylen and Robert both who can't hear the conversation like I can.

"Well don't ask the question unless you want the answer," Gabriel replies. "Although on second thought, I'm glad you did ask. I wouldn't want there to be any ambiguity about Wendy's and my expectations concerning your behavior with Kaylen or anyone else."

"Yeah, yeah," Ezra says, annoyed. "I got it. Keep it in the pants. No worries, okay? So shut up about it already."

"Fabulous. I knew I could count on you," Gabriel replies jovially.

With a grin still plastered to my face, Kaylen says, "What on earth are you eavesdropping on that is so funny?"

"Oh just some unique parenting techniques," I mumble as we reach Gabriel's door.

"You're back!" Gabriel says, hopping up as soon as I come into the room. Ezra is slumped in the chair, arms crossed sullenly, but he jumps up as soon as Robert comes in behind me.

I make a beeline for Gabriel's arms, tucking my head under his chin and squeezing him tight. Inhaling him and ignoring his off-smell, I instead close my eyes to the familiar comfort of his shape against me. His breathing sounds a little better. I think they gave him something to clear his lungs last night and it seems to be working.

Oh gosh… I hope he's not about to jump right into his test results. I don't think I can take it.

He kisses me on the forehead. "Have a sit-down, Robert." he says over my shoulder. "I gather from the fact that you're here that you aren't the villainous man we presumed you to be."

"Thank you, Gabe," says Robert as he takes the only available chair. Gabriel and I sit side-by-side on the bed. I hold a hand out to Kaylen and she squeezes on the other side of me.

Ezra, who has been watching us without a word until now, slouches back into the chair and says, "What's up, Uncle Rob? I guess you've got a pretty good story."

Robert grimaces. "No. I'm afraid it's not good at all."

Ezra doesn't speak but the corners of his eyes tighten a tiny bit as he mentally prepares himself. I've seen the look before and my chest throbs. I hate this.

Robert takes a few silent moments to arrange his thoughts and begins as he did with me. Gabriel leans forward with rapt attention. As Robert explains the files in his office, it jars Gabriel as he finally fully accepts that I have been right about his fate. He questions himself then, and at first I don't know what about. But he takes several short moments, smoothing the unevenness of agitation out until it is replaced with relief. Hollow sadness falls over me as I realize he was taking stock of his own vitals, as if to remind himself that he is still alive. I turn my face away from him to hide the grief in my expression. But Kaylen is there and translates it. She inconspicuously reaches for my hand. Afraid of losing it, I distract myself by defining computer programming terms mentally like 'iterator' and 'bootstrapping'. This distraction requires a lot of brainpower because I'm so rusty. I'm going to remember this practice for future emotional avoidance. Gabriel puts an arm around me at some point, and I realize it's because Robert is talking about the sacrifices Leena made to keep me from Carl and why. But I forge ahead with defining 'parsing'.

Not long after that, Gabriel's voice comes to my attention, "So what you're getting at is..." He pauses, struggling through heavy and somewhat sudden dread. He looks from me to Robert. "You're saying hypno-touch is lethal, too? Within fifteen to twenty years?"

Ezra sits up abruptly, his face pale, his lips trembling.

The devastated look on his face is too much. My eyes fill with tears. "I'm so sorry, Ezra," I whisper, wiping my cheeks.

"Yes," Robert replies quietly.

Ezra's head goes down, hiding his face. His lanky arms, which rest on his legs, twitch, but that's all the movement I see. After several moments he stands up in one motion, turning his back to us, feet splayed as his fingers lace together and rest on the top of his head.

I know how Ezra operates. This isn't the time to comfort him. He has to work through it.

"What age?" Gabriel asks, his voice cracking.

"Excuse me?" Robert asks.

"Wendy and Kaylen. Do we know what age they first had hypno-touch?"

Kaylen clears her throat. "Um, I'm not sure. Three, I think?"

"Wendy was not quite four when Leena escaped with her," Robert says. "So before then."

Gabriel heaves a pained sigh. He knew the answer to his question. I don't know why he asked. "They are both out of time..." he says, more to himself it seems. "And Kaylen... She's had hypno-touch more than anyone. How much time does that give her? It can't be the standard fifteen years. And her ability... so powerful, like the people in those files. How is she still alive?"

Nobody has an answer to that.

"This is bullshit," Ezra says finally. His face is red with anger, his fists tight at his sides. "We need to find Carl and get that bastard to start talking. And then we need to put the world out of his misery."

"I know how you feel," I say. "But revenge on Carl won't—"

"Revenge won't what?" Ezra says. "Won't solve anything? That's crap and you know it. How many people has Carl killed so far, huh?" Ezra throws his hands up. "At least a dozen or so that you know of." His eyes fall on Kaylen. "*You* know it's more than that, don't you? How many people did you see come and go at that compound?" He stares at her and it's obvious he expects her to answer.

"At l-least a hundred," Kaylen stutters as she shakes her head, her own eyes now red-rimmed. "But I don't know if there are other hypno-touch compounds out there."

"A *hundred*," Ezra repeats. "How many more is it going to be? So don't call it revenge. It's *prevention.*"

Gabriel is quiet, and he struggles against wanting to disagree with Ezra, but he has been pushed past logic. He opts to be silent while his feelings are so fresh.

"Nobody is going to be hunting down Carl to exact justice right now," I say, tiredly. "We're going to sleep on it in the very least. We're going to give everything a chance to settle. And then we're going to make a decision after the shock has worn off."

Ezra throws himself back in the futon chair, arms crossed, face turned to stare at nothing.

Kaylen's hand is trembling under my own. I lean into her, touching her head with my own. I have no comforting words for her—for anyone. In this room is my family. Even Robert fits in that category with ease, especially when I know that he is all Ezra will have left. In this room are three dead people walking.

Hope is an absurdly scarce luxury right now.

.

9

"*Y*our brother called this morning," I say, throwing both mine and Gabriel's suitcases outside the bathroom and my purse on the nightstand. Gabriel, by a miracle only he could conjure, convinced the attending doctor to discharge him this evening. Though his lungs sound yucky, they don't appear to be accumulating more fluid. While Gabriel was working on that, I went with Kaylen and Ezra back to Robert's house where we picked up extra clothes and necessities. Robert would have had us stay at his house—for protection reasons—but he said a remodel will be starting on his home tomorrow and it won't be livable. Odd timing, but who am I to argue? Instead, he insisted on putting us up in a ritzy hotel. He wants to make our apartment secure before we go back there. Kaylen and Ezra have their own rooms on either side of us, and even Robert has a room here.

"I suppose you explained the situation?" Gabriel replies, sitting on the edge of the bed and pulling his tennis shoes off.

"No." I unzip my suitcase and dig inside it for something comfy to wear to bed. "He hung up on me before I could say anything beyond the fact that you were in the hospital. He said he was on his way here. Didn't even ask if it was urgent. It was weird. He doesn't like me."

A subtle jump of alarm from Gabriel comes and goes. "He would know it was urgent."

"How?" I stand in the doorway to the bathroom, pajamas, test kit, and toothbrush in my grip.

"He knows I wouldn't consent to be in the hospital for anything less," he says, taking off his shirt.

I have the strangest conflict of emotions as I watch. The sight of so much of his skin has me wanting to touch him—lots of him—because I have missed him and I never take our ability to touch for granted. But I also want to run away from him and cry in a closet because I'm afraid of the things he hasn't said yet.

"Why do you have this assumption that he doesn't like you?" he asks.

"Because he has never, not once, been polite to me. During our wedding, he either ignored me or gave me the stank eye. So unless rude is his natural disposition, he doesn't like me."

Gabriel is worried for a moment but says, "You've barely interacted with him. Even if he *does* have some reason for his lack of warmth, it's not going to last."

"Until he finds out I killed his brother with hypno-touch!"

Gabriel exhales with exaggeration. "Mike knows I did what I did on the compound willingly. He wouldn't be petty enough to blame you for anything. Furthermore, *he's* the one that turned me on to it in the first place. Don't worry about Mike; I'll handle him."

"Please do," I say, turning to go into the bathroom. A rock of trepidation drops heavily into me as I shut the door. It's late, but there are other things Gabriel and I should be talking about: his test results. He didn't bring them up at all today. I know how instantaneous MRI and CT findings are. Even though our time together today has been limited, I would have expected him to pull me aside and gotten it out in the open. Avoidance is unexpected. It's bad. Really bad. Gabriel's background dread on the car ride over was enough to confirm it.

Throwing my meter a little too violently back into my bag after testing twice, I pull out a fresh insulin cartridge. My blood-sugar is way too high. Again. This morning I had the same problem. I don't have time for my diabetes to be acting up this way. I stand still for a moment as it occurs to me that maybe this rather drastic change in my blood sugar stability the last few months might be the start of... dying. The macabre thought has me staring at the now-empty cartridge in my hand with solemn contemplation. Death by diabetes. Fantastic. I guess I better start testing even more. Maybe I should get an insulin pump? A doctor might be a good idea. Eventually.

More dire at the moment is Gabriel's situation, so I throw the cartridge away and change out of my jeans and into flannel bottoms and a tank top.

Gabriel is lying down when I come out, knees bent, hands behind his head. He looks over at me and smiles. "It's good to see you finally."

I plop down on the end of the bed, cross-legged. "Sorry I was gone so much today."

"It couldn't be helped—well, it *could* have, but not by you. It was those confounded doctors refusing to let me leave."

"So what did you do all day, cooped up in that room?" Okay, so it's not *totally* direct. But it does leave the conversation open for him to say what needs to be said.

"I was as bored as an illiterate person in a library. Aside from napping once, I ate a passable breakfast, a decent lunch, and spent the rest of time trying to find a channel on the television worth my attention."

"Did you find any?"

"Absolutely not. And I'm pretty sure I de-evolved with everything I *did* watch: contrived sit-coms with no purpose but to praise apathy and degrade affections, so-called reality shows designed to make the worst behaviors inherent in the human condition appear acceptable, and drama in which all they do is take turns sleeping with one another and talking about it. Utter mediocrity."

Under different circumstances I might find his tirade humorous, but now it's awkward. Yet I can't help carrying on the awkwardness. "Are there any TV shows you *do* like?"

"I haven't much occasion to watch the tube, but I must say there hasn't been a show I've watched on a regular basis in quite some time. The Discovery Channel was always a good standby, but even that one has downgraded to this abominable reality trend."

"I bet you were a *Bill Nye* fan as a kid, weren't you?" I ask, smiling a little as I imagine Gabriel as a child.

"I watched every episode. I believe my mother still has them all on VHS."

"*How Stuff Works?*"

"Nope," he says. "I watched it once. They were showing how frozen pizzas are made. They could have shown how something far more useful is put together, but of all the million things on the planet, they chose pizza. And they acted like it was some big mystery." Gabriel rolls his eyes. "Crust, sauce, cheese, toppings, and a conveyor belt... What more is there?"

A wan smile is all I can manage.

Gabriel sits up and reaches for my hand. His is warm, familiarly textured, and I grip it back, looking at our hands together in my lap. He leans closer and tucks a loose lock of hair behind my ear. "You are so beautiful, even when you're sad."

It aches to hear Gabriel speak with so much tenderness right now, but I *feel* it as well, compounding its effect. The affection and concern and submissive honesty... It gently but insistently probes my ridiculously fragile heart until it actually hurts.

I can't help the moisture that fills my eyes, and then both of his hands are reaching for my face as he sits up and guides my head to his shoulder.

"I'm sorry," he whispers into my hair. "I should not have tortured you this long."

I'd answer that it was my fault as much as his, but I'm afraid if I open my mouth tears will become sobs.

Through our silence, steady breathing, and the stillness of our embrace, the weight eases an increment at a time until I'm calm again.

I sit back and look at Gabriel, unsure of what my expression says, if it *should* say anything. I'm ready. I'm done wondering and being stuck in place. I want to know what we're up against.

With one of his hands still in mine, he says, "Do you mind... sharing? I want to be with you."

Knowing what he's asking, I channel us into the colorworld so he can feel my emotions. Eyes wide open, illuminated colors move forward out of relative darkness, like rubbing away the grime of our world to reveal the colorworld beneath it. I don't know why, but the colorworld has a way of fading the perception of permanence. Emotions are... less encompassing—the negative ones anyway.

I brace myself though, because pain is pain. Gabriel responds with resignation, which brings me guilt. I don't want to make this harder for him. I want to be strong. But how can I listen without turning into a blubbering mess?

He exhales frustration, likely picking all of that up from my brainwaves. "I dislike telling you as much as you dislike hearing it," he says.

I jump to my mental distraction of earlier. I was on 'class' I think. It should keep me relatively placid. So I start:

Class...a template in object-oriented programming that defines objects. They contain the same data type and—

"What on earth are you thinking about?" Gabriel asks, interrupting my definition. "You're as blank as a blackboard, but your brain is whirring like a machine. Are you trying to distract yourself?"

I stare at him in surprise. "Uh, why would you be so sure I was distracting myself?"

He raises an eyebrow. "Odd how someone can pick thoughts right out of your brain, isn't it? Especially when that person claims they can't read minds?"

I offer him a half-smile. "Sorry. I thought it might, you know, help me take the news." I swallow the lump in my throat. Obviously I'm going to have to be at rapt attention or he will know I'm purposely ignoring him. "I'm good now."

Gabriel's smile disappears completely as he takes in my misery that's no longer clouded by distractions—I'm obviously *not* good. He starts thinking intently, surely searching for a gentle way to deliver the news. I know that's a fruitless effort. I hate seeing him agonize over causing me hurt so I say, "There's no easy way to say it so just spit it out."

"Yes, yes," Gabriel says quickly, taking a short breath. "The good news—possibly the only good news—is that there are no tumors as yet in my brain. I guess I use it too much. It's probably the healthiest part of me."

His mouth moves into a grimace. "The bad news—and there's a lot of it—is that there are lesions of varying sizes in other areas. Lymph nodes, bone, liver, and one of my adrenal glands. Right off that bat, that indicates a malignant cancer. The largest tumor is in my left lung and they biopsied it during my CT. After much finagling, I got the doctor to tell me he strongly suspects small-cell lung carcinoma. We should have biopsy results to confirm tomorrow or the next day, but I think, based on what we learned from Robert today, that it's as bad as it sounds. The doctor said surgery is most likely not an option at this point because of the multiple metastases, but chemotherapy should yield results. We'll know more about treatment once we confirm the diagnosis." He looks at me expectantly.

It takes me a while to process his words. I blink at Gabriel several times as they become reality. My hand goes slack in his as I lift the colorworld from my view to see his body—his seemingly perfectly healthy body. His tanned skin. Toned chest and arms. His expressive eyes and fine-textured hair. Every bit of him is the picture of wellness. Regardless of my very *low* expectations leading up to this moment since yesterday, I'm at a complete loss for words, for understanding. I can't be sure, but I think I wasn't expecting it to be quite this bad already. It's *everywhere*? How can that be?

Gabriel absorbs my mental state silently and squeezes my hand in both of his as if to be sure that I'm still with him—or to remind me that he's still with me. I look into his searching eyes. His concern for me seeps through the cracks in my mind, looking for a way in. Like always, Gabriel can touch my heart like none other and the experience is no less intimate than being touched physically. He knows how to love better than anyone I know. How is so much disease able to survive in someone so full of such fearless love? I find it hard to believe. I have known this. I have expected really bad news, and now that I'm getting it I don't believe it. What is wrong with my brain?

"Are... are you sure?" I ask, my voice shaking.

"Ahh... as I said, it's not yet confirmed. But it's the most likely diagnosis. If it's not small-cell, it's... some other cancer that has metastasized," answers Gabriel, bewildered by my response. He isn't alone; I'm bewildered by it myself.

"How is this possible?" I whisper to the room. "How does someone so healthy get so sick, so quickly?"

They don't. I know that. It's not something that happens under normal circumstances. It's like the guy in Robert's files who developed hemophilia as a middle-aged man, or the triathlete who got diabetes. Stuff like that doesn't just happen. Gabriel's body being riddled with cancer in a few months' time *does not* just happen. But my life is full of *just happened* type of things. A flyer for an allergy study *just ended up* at my feet. A statue I made as a grief-stricken teenager *just found its way* into my future husband's parent's home. My ex-boyfriend *just happened* to work at the *one* gas station Gabriel, Kaylen, and I decided to stop at.

No, I refuse to look at *anything* from now on as *just happening.*

I was dragged kicking and screaming back to Gabriel over and over. I am exactly where I am supposed to be. I will not ignore what I learned that night right after touching Gabriel. I refuse to believe that the view of my terminally-ill husband is merely what it seems. It's right in front of me, clouded with impending devastation, so how can I possibly see it with any perspective? I don't know what this moment will look like to me in a decade—if I live that long—but I do know it's built upon moments and hours and days and months and years. Touching Gabriel taught me that.

"I'm going to fix this," I say, surprising myself. Fix what? Him? How? The words have found their way out of their own accord, like some part of me that believes them wanted to make itself known. I look at Gabriel, and in the colorworld his essence permeates my senses—the joy of breathtaking determination, the courage and utter insanity he is capable of doling out when in pursuit of his goal. The unparalleled tenacity and earnestness every one of his actions is possessed with was meant for more than this. Within Gabriel's essence is the purpose I have always intrinsically known. Gabriel is not done. I am sure of that.

Ridiculous. He's dying. Like all those other people. I look down at our hands as the war between logic and hope rages within me. It's clear, however, that hope is winning by a landslide. The reasons elude me, but the feeling is strong. Perhaps at any other time logic would easily win and visions of a future without him would overwhelm me, but at this moment I am possessed with something that reaches beyond understanding. I don't know what I'd call it. Faith maybe? I have never felt so self-possessed in my life. My soul burns with conviction, and my body is too weak to fully contain it. For once in my miserable life, I am utterly in control of my body, my mind, and my emotions.

"I'm going to fix you," I tell Gabriel fervently again, thinking this is where I start.

Gabriel's emotions, I realize, are diluted when compared to the light that consumes my soul. I also realize he has released me, though I can't remember when it happened. I only know I am no longer in the colorworld and his hands are no longer in mine. "What are you saying?" he says, disbelieving. "You think you can figure this out? Wendy, I want that as much as you, but we have to face the reality of our situation. I most likely have extensive stage lung cancer. It has already metastasized. Even if it *hadn't* arisen from supernatural circumstances, the prognosis would be horribly bleak. But in my case, bleak is now terminal—end stage. I don't want you to have your hopes so high only to have them disappointed. I know what that does to you. Please, by all means, have hope, search for a cure—especially for yourself and Kaylen, but be realistic. I am at least weeks and at most a few months from death."

I have never thought of Gabriel as anything less than a force to be reckoned with, but at this moment I find in him incredible weakness; he has never felt so frail to me. Without the colorworld to reaffirm the qualities of his essence, I find only a man before me.

"You don't know that," I say. "Why are you so pessimistic?"

"Everyone dies, Wendy," he says firmly. "*Everyone* does. If we would stop clinging to the hope that we are the exception to that rule, we might live brighter, more productive lives. We are to *utilize* the hand we are dealt rather than fighting against it."

I stare into his eyes with fervor. "You are the most important thing to me ever. I will *not* accept defeat. How can I have less hope when it comes to you? And how can I not have faith after everything we have been through?"

"But Wendy!" Gabriel digs his palms into his temples, stonewalled by my reaction. "You don't get a reprieve from suffering simply because you imagine you've met your fair share of it. Life has so few happily ever-afters, and there is no way to guarantee them. You can only control how you handle the journey, whether you are happy or sad. And I want this time with *you*, not with fading hope and worry over how you will handle things when I don't survive. Sometimes you have to listen to the odds, accept them, and spend your time making the most of what you have. To set your expectations so high as I can tell you've set them, and to have them dashed, will crush you. I can't go on knowing that. I just can't."

Gabriel's eyes fill with tears, and when I reach for him he scoots away from me, consumed with confused anger. I have never seen him withdraw like this before. He is always the one pushing me, forcing me to deal with my emotions, helping me through them. As I ponder it, I think I know why he let go of me earlier: he couldn't stand to endure my level of hope. I have completely put aside the possibility of failing. I understand his reasons. I know how I must seem: insane perhaps. To be insane is to be out of your right mind. And maybe that's what I am: out of my mind and going on the intuition of something else. But I wouldn't trade this experience for anything.

How ironic that he would have dealt better if I had just given up in anguish, clinging to him and telling him he couldn't die and lamenting over what I would do without him... I am not going out like that, and neither is he. This is an impossible fight. It will require impossible hope.

"Gabriel…"

He turns away from me, lying on his side. I scoot closer and lie down to wrap an arm around him. Outrage burns through him at my touch and I let go, cut by his rejection but knowing it won't last. I need to let him work through it. He will come back to me. Gabriel fluctuates on extremes. He doesn't do love halfway and he doesn't grieve halfway. He'll grieve his life he thinks he won't be able to give me, and then when he wakes up in the morning—or maybe sooner—he'll realize he's still alive and he can either march his way to his death or he can help me save it—no matter the outcome. He *will* get past this.

"I'll come back later," I whisper near his ear, and then I get out of the bed and grab my key card off the nightstand to go take a walk. I open the door to our room and step outside, closing it noiselessly behind me. I stand in the hall and breathe in my life, sensing all my years at once. I want to remember this moment. I memorize the sensation of it in my chest, my hands, my shoulders, and my stomach. But most of all in my soul. I want to remember it when the moments I will face later try to tell me this night did not happen. I don't know what to call it, but it's a weightless enlightenment. Peace and excitement, and even anticipation for having all this play out. For when it does, I will prove that I can trust what I have *become*.

This happened, I tell myself. *This is real.*

And truly, I have never felt a moment more real in my life.

10

$\mathcal{G}$abriel's arms are around me when I wake up in the morning. I take it as a sign of forgiveness and acceptance on some level. In retrospect, I can't blame him for how he reacted. I don't have a stalwart past when it comes to dealing with despair. I'm new to this whole faith thing.

I'm still riding a bit of the high from last night, but I've submerged back into life somewhat, and down here it's easy to get lost in singular moments and concern over an unknown future. And truly, the future *is* unknown. I only know I have to save Gabriel. He once said he was made for the relationship with me when we couldn't touch. He was right. And I was made for *this.* Saving Gabriel. I was the one who did this to him, and no one knows the colorworld like I do. Including Carl. And if I can save Gabriel, I bet I can save all those other people that Louise and Carl have sentenced to early deaths. Which means Gabriel and I meeting at the compound was another one of those *just happened* scenarios that will ultimately serve a purpose if I'm willing to see it through. Thinking in such a way is still new to me, and I have to muscle past my usual cynicism, but it's easier than I expected.

With Gabriel asleep, it's the perfect opportunity to go into the colorworld with this new outlook. I sit up gingerly, and, careful to keep from touching his skin so as not to wake him, I pull the familiar colors of that place into focus. Maybe it's because I've scarcely woken up, but it takes me longer than usual to adjust to the brilliance.

Turning my attention to Gabriel's swirling purple strands, I watch them move for a long time, searching for insight. The most obvious characteristic is how disjointedly they flow about his body as compared to someone who has never had hypno-touch. It was something I noticed at the compound even before I could decipher the strands themselves. Normal life forces—those that haven't been manipulated by hypno-touch—have a characteristic whirlpool pattern over the chest. Everyone outside of the compound, such as Robert and Ezra, have life forces with this same chest swirl. Hypno-touch disrupts the normal flow of the life force. I think if there is some way I can get his life force back into that pattern, there is a possibility that Gabriel's body can heal itself.

The question, of course, is a big fat *how*? Manipulating strands is how we got into this mess to begin with. I could very likely decrease his life expectancy even more if I start screwing around with things I know nothing about. As urgent as the situation is, I'm going to need some time to think about this. I can't make Gabriel an experiment. Things aren't *that* dire yet.

Withdrawing my hands from his life force to leave the colorworld, my stomach rumbles. Breakfast sounds good. I ease out of the bed and the dull ache in my side announces itself. I have definitely pulled a muscle. After yanking flannel pants on, a sweatshirt over my head, and slippers on my feet, I leave a note for Gabriel.

I ride the elevator down to the lobby, and when the doors open I spot Robert sitting in a chair, using a tablet device, and mumbling to a lanky, balding man in a suit standing beside him whom I've seen before occasionally. Robert looks up and meets my eyes immediately as if he knew, without looking, exactly where I would be.

He nods at the tall man who then leaves without a word. Robert stands up and comes toward me. "Good Morning, Wendy," he says. "I've been waiting for you."

"Is everything okay?" I ask.

"Oh yes," he replies, touching my arm just barely and leading me toward the dining room. "I didn't get a chance to discuss some things with you yesterday, and I think that you had better know everything there is to know going forward."

"Okay," I say hesitantly. *More secrets? I thought we already did this.* "Um, did Kaylen and Ezra already eat?"

"Yes, I got them off to school this morning. And don't worry. I sent protection with them."

Oh yeah, they go to school. What kind of guardian am I that I can't even remember that they should go back to school?

After I tell the maître d I'll opt for the breakfast buffet, Robert leans toward me. "I'd recommend the pancakes. Join me after you get your food." Then he takes a table in the corner of the room.

Even without Robert's suggestion, I would have chosen the pancakes anyway. They're blueberry. In fact, I stop for a moment, stunned that they are also whole wheat. My mom used to make me whole wheat blueberry pancakes because I *love* them. I am so sensitive to flavor, and to me whole wheat have always tasted better than regular pancakes. I glance behind me at Robert who is thumbing through his tablet again. I wonder if I should make

77

anything of my favorite breakfast food being part of the buffet. Deciding to accept it as a good omen on the first day of my journey to save Gabriel, I stack three on my plate and head back to the table.

Robert is in Moby-Dick deliberation mode at the moment, so I dig in, closing my eyes as nostalgia hits me. I realize at that moment that I haven't had blueberry, whole wheat pancakes since before my mom died. She was the only one who ever made them for me. A bite catches in my throat as grief stabs me momentarily.

"Are they okay?" Robert says, inaccurately deciphering my wounded expression.

I take a moment to gather myself. "Oh yes. They're amazing," I reply. "It's just that they made me think of my mom."

Robert contemplates that before saying, "I hope it sweetens the experience rather than embitters it."

I think about it, letting the clearest memory of my mom giving me pancakes like these settle over me in all its many nuances. I think my most pointed memory was when we moved right before I started middle school from the one place I ever considered a home—it was an actual house. There were real neighborhood kids there, not apartment walls and dingy common hallways where people avoided each other's eyes as they passed. When we had to move back into the city, back into an apartment, I was so distraught and combative that my mom said she was going to make whole wheat blueberry pancakes for me every day until I smiled again. And she did. Of course, the problem was that even blueberry pancakes get old after a few days—which ended up being the point. I told her about four days in that I'd had enough of the stupid pancakes; I was never going to smile if I had to eat the same thing every day. To which she replied, "Exactly, baby. Don't be afraid of change."

I haven't encountered that memory in a very long time, how I made faces at her back while she did dishes as she listed off all the things that were different about our new home. I remember Ezra was at the table, too. And he started copying my faces, which made me giggle under my breath. Then he said, "Mom, Wen is smiling. Can we stop having pancakes for breakfast now?"

I smile fondly now and say, "Yes, it's a good memory."

"Good!" exclaims Robert, somewhat relieved. Then he calls the maître d over. "Give our compliments to the chef, and tell him I appreciate his carrying out my request perfectly," Robert says to her as she sets a steaming mug of water in front of him.

"Your request?" I ask as she walks away.

"Yes," he says, opening a tea packet and putting the teabag in his mug. It smells like lemon and ginger. "I asked Ezra this morning if there was something you'd like to eat for breakfast that might put a smile on your face. He immediately said the pancakes. And I made sure the kitchen was careful about the ingredients."

Left speechless, I look at Robert and then down at my plate, eyes brimming now from the overwhelming warmth of being loved, not just by Ezra, but also by Robert who took the time— and probably liberal tipping—to make my morning a little bit better. My heart softens even more toward Robert. How did I ever imagine this man might be a villain?

"Why aren't you married, Uncle Robert?" I ask when I manage to take a bite without choking on tears.

Robert seems accustomed to the question and, without looking up from his cup of tea that he stirs slowly, says quietly, "I was once. A long time ago. She passed away though, and I never remarried."

"I'm so sorry," I say.

"That was a long time ago." He glances up with a friendly smile. "I live a fulfilled life, and while I do miss her, I have no complaints. I stay so busy now that it's possible that no woman would choose to stay with me." He chuckles and tests his tea, his emotions held comfortably in check in a way that I translate as an exercise he's used to and possibly does automatically. He's truly at peace with it. I wonder how he's come to this place. Carl lost the love of his life as well, but he obviously handled it terribly. Considering how similar Carl and I are, I think I ought to make a more in-depth study of my uncle. My respect for him grows as I sit pondering his meticulous thoughts and hoping I can learn how he does it.

"Any decent woman would recognize your dedication and commitment for the good thing it is," I point out. "She'd probably follow you all over the place, no matter how busy you got."

Robert feels flattered and a little uncomfortable with my blatant, unapologetic compliment. He doesn't speak as I put forkfuls of pancake into my mouth, though I pick up a tiny pulse of gratitude from him. For once, Robert seems unconcerned that I'm reading him. In fact, I wouldn't recognize the subtle invitation of it for what it was if I hadn't already spent the entirety of our acquaintance with his obviously more guarded self. That he was able to wall himself off from me so effectively for so long and in so many different situations is impressive. The longer I observe his emotions, the more impressed I become with the purposeful nature of everything he thinks about. He kind of reminds me of Gabriel that way. I can't believe I used to think Robert boring. The man is a master of himself, and when he does allow himself to feel, it is powerfully evocative. The quietude of his emotions demand attention. Moby-Dick is no ordinary whale.

Once I've cleared my plate and don't demonstrate that I'll be getting seconds, Robert says, "Ezra explained the extent of Gabe's illness yesterday. I take it you and Gabe have spoken about it?"

"Finally."

"I'm going to do everything in my power to save him." Robert looks at me pointedly—an expression I don't think I've ever seen on him before. "I want to, so please let me do it."

"What did you have in mind?" I ask, putting an elbow over the back of my chair and tucking a leg under me. I recognize the casual nature of the pose only after I've done it. Suddenly my relationship with Robert has taken an about-face. I have *never* felt this comfortable with Robert before now. I must have subconsciously reacted to his more transparent mind.

"For one thing, I don't want you to have to move elsewhere, but I would like Gabe to have access to the best doctor, one experienced with his illness, whatever that may be."

Robert looks at me critically now, and after several silent moments I come to realize that he has spent a great deal of time prior to this conversation considering his next words. "You realize the likelihood that the cure ultimately lies with you. Am I right?" he says.

"Yes," I say, reaching for my ice water. "The sickness isn't conventional, so I don't see the treatment being conventional. I'm sure a doctor will help keep him alive longer, but I *am* more interested in finding a way to cure him with my abilities."

"I agree," Robert says. "And I may be able to help you with my ability—though I'm still somewhat hesitant to offer."

I tilt my head. "What do you mean? Doesn't this goal *not* involve you? I thought you couldn't focus on the goals of other people."

Robert closes his tablet case and zips it, the act seeming to put away any remaining indecision as well. Once finished, his hands still resting on the case, he looks at me directly. "I have had a rule for a very long time: I do not interfere with life and death. Because I can focus on any goal at any given time and come up with a place, no matter who or what it's for. My ability is not limited by anything but my own personal desires. I will *always* get a vision. But as I told you, I often get a place that doesn't help me because I don't recognize it."

I experience a twinge of discomfort from him and I wonder how many people Robert has told this to—and why he's telling me now. "Discovering what I could do came easily as a child," he continues, "I would get seemingly random pictures in my head, and they increased in prevalence the older I got. I started drawing them because they'd be stuck up there. I made the connection a bit later as to what the visions meant. Anyway, the point is that I was having visions all the time because I had *desires* all the time. Humans have desires rambling around in their heads constantly, both unconsciously and consciously. Desires for themselves. Desires for others. Some big. Some fleeting. Some good. Some bad. My ability is in effect for anything I want at any given moment."

Robert is expecting me to make some connection, and I imagine what he has described. Thinking about all of the major ambitions I've had over the course of my life—and how they would have destroyed me if I'd gotten them—I understand the problem. Seeing recognition cross my face, Robert says, "I had a difficult adolescence. It was addicting to make things happen for myself even when what I saw was not an ethical means to accomplish something. What I *see* in my visions is ultimately dependent on my motives. A quick example. Say I wanted a good grade on a test. Well, if I was not committed to coming by the grade honestly, I'd see a place where an opportunity to steal the test answers might arise rather than my classroom or the library. More often than not, I was faced with temptation. It became the worst kind of burden. For a long time I was consumed with getting what I wanted—it seemed easier than spending the time agonizing over ethics."

It makes me a little ill to imagine it. How on earth did he get free of that kind of power?

"It did take practice to get it to work right for me," he says, "but considering how easily visions came, I had plenty of opportunities. I had visions constantly. It's like having a television going on in your head all the time, except the channel changes every moment along with my thoughts. Overwhelming is an understatement. And while I have tamed it a lot more these days, back then it was nearly unbearable."

Lips parted in shock, I picture it. I never imagined that Robert's ability would function that way. All this time it has seemed tenuous—so limited. But it actually sounds dangerously accurate—and torturous. "How do you manage it?" I ask. *And where are you going with this?*

"Self-imposed rules. You remember what I told you about compounding visions?"

"If you don't recognize the first vision, you can use another vision to find it," I say.

"Yes, and I can compound visions infinitely. Layered goals like that will help me find anything I want, *do* anything I want, and *accomplish* anything I want."

"But you said that's dangerous. You said you stay away from compounding visions."

"Exactly. Miracles always come with a price, and someone always pays it."

"But you obviously *do* use them," I point out. "You used one to find me."

"I did." He sets his mug down and leans forward. His eyes don't meet mine as he crosses his arms on the table in front of him. "It was a series of terrifying, humbling, and heartbreaking situations that led me to understand that the gift I had was meant to be used with temperance. Even in the best circumstances, with best of intentions, I can inadvertently cause death and destruction simply by affecting the natural flow of events in the smallest of ways—the future is a fragile thing. The farther up the vision stack I go to achieve my goal, the flimsier my connection to the place I see, and the more drastically I impact the natural flow of events there—often to someone's detriment. I believe the reason is that I don't *belong* there, and my presence disturbs things too much. Things never go the way I intended because the goal is so far removed from me and the original vision. I can almost always accomplish a goal, but the cost is usually too great. And because I can never know the cost ahead of time, it's best to steer clear."

I'm sure my face says how confused I am as to what this has to do with Gabriel, but Robert is unconcerned, almost distracted. He takes one of his long pauses while I wait impatiently, about a hundred questions bouncing around in my head.

"It took years of practice and meditation to put my ability in check," he says. "In the end I had to come up with rules. The overarching rule is that goals must focus on *helping,* not on acquiring something for myself. It is the only way I have managed to be successful in a way I can live with. When I focus on *gaining* it always ends up *taking* from someone else. So I visualize things like wanting to give someone truly talented the opportunity to shine in their field."

"Uncle Rob," I say, trying out the more casual moniker that Ezra uses, not quite sure it fits our relationship. "That reminds me. One of the first things that made us suspicious of you was learning about your talent scouting. You've put a lot of exceptionally skilled people into big-time positions—people that seemed like they might be supernaturally talented."

Robert turns bashful, and doesn't look at me when he answers, "They were—*are*. They're individuals I've kept up with after they left the compound. I've been able to track down a few of them. With their shortened life-spans in mind, I wanted to give them opportunities to make their mark. I suppose it's somewhat like what your mother tried to do for you: I wanted them to be able to live their dreams. A sort of penance, I suppose, for having had a hand in helping fund Carl and Louise's research."

A long pause ensues as Moby-Dick plunges into a dive to get over the discomfort of having exposed so much of himself out of the water. Robert does *not* like tooting his own horn. I am stunned, once more, by what I'm learning about him and how quickly I am learning it. He has become more complex, existing in three dimensions when before I only saw him in two.

I decide then that I don't want to call him Uncle Rob. I've never liked shortening the names of people I like—which is ironic since I've let so many people over the course of my life shorten *my* name. I *have*, however, often called people nicknames in my head. And Robert deserves more than just an 'Uncle Rob.'

"Goals to help others, while not always immediately beneficial, inevitably turn around and help me in some way," Robert says, continuing his earlier explanation. "But I've come to think of the benefits to me as side-effects. For someone in my position, self-promotion is an easy trap. Whatever I gain, I have to be sure to deposit. For example, if I gain a new contract, I might give everyone on the team a bonus, or donate the majority of the proceeds. Whatever it is I do, it has to stretch me. Managing my ability takes a great deal of discipline. And even after all these years I am still tempted to vary from my rules. Like life and death for example. That is the hardest want to ignore." He looks at me pointedly again.

"Why are you telling me this?" I sigh, crossing my arms.

"Because I want your permission."

My heart pounds. "For what? Whether you can visualize a way to save Gabriel? After everything you've just told me, why would you ask me that? Are you *trying* to tempt me?" My feelings are in flux.

"If I said yes, what would you say?" he asks. I can tell he honestly wants my answer.

A cyclone has blown through me. I can't separate anything definite out of the rubble. "Are you serious?" I ask.

"Yes."

"But why?" I ask. "Why on earth would you ask me if I want you to save Gabriel when you very well know how *badly* I want to save him?"

"Wendy, I'm asking you if you want me to," Robert says. "Stop looking for my motive. I told you all that so that you could have full disclosure. Whatever the cost is, it likely will not be paid by me. So knowing what I've told you, if you were me, and you could see what I see, would you use it to save him?"

I brace my back against the chair, one foot flat on the floor while I outline a diamond pattern in the carpet with my other foot over and over. If Robert weren't so calm, I'd think he was messing with me. I run through possible reasons why he's making the offer, but I realize I'm only stalling. In the back of my mind I'm scrambling for what he offers. I fluctuate between glorious excitement and wary confusion. I can't reconcile the two. When I allow myself to settle on accepting his offer, my stomach knots in anxiety over the possible and unforeseeable consequences. But when I think about rejecting the offer, I feel like an overcautious idiot. Did I not say I'd save Gabriel? How can I turn down something with so much promise?

I don't know how long I sit there struggling while Robert watches my face, expectant. The waiter refills his mug with hot water, and Robert puts his teabag back in, stirring it around and adding honey calmly as if he hasn't just offered me free wishes like some genie.

When Robert's emotions fail to reveal any answers, I really consider his question, moving past all of the confusion and desperation going on inside me. Only last night I made such a strong commitment to saving Gabriel. And now, as if confirming that I made the right choice, I have Robert offering me a likely solution. It's serendipitous, like so much of my life in recent months.

But Robert said there is a guaranteed cost that someone will have to pay, and I can think of plenty of costs I'm not willing to pay. Like someone dying. That was Carl's mistake. He wanted to save my mother, or maybe avenge her memory. I'm not sure. Either way, Carl crossed a line.

I don't want to be *anything* like Carl. I won't trade an unknown payment for Gabriel's life. And neither would Gabriel.

"Thanks, Uncle Rob, that's... really generous of you to offer," I say finally. "Clearly you have worked really hard to maintain your rules. I don't want you to break them for me or Gabriel. If he's going to live, I will make that future without your help."

Moby-Dick crests, splashing me rather suddenly with his distress. He *really* wants to save Gabriel. At first, I think it's that he's disappointed that I won't accept his offer. But then I realize it's something else. It's affection for me and for Gabriel. It's compassion for our situation. I don't think I've realized before how much he has come to think of us as his family. That's what I feel right now: a familial connection. Father-like—not that I have much experience with that. But it's how I imagine it. He's proud of me. A great upwelling of pride spills out of him, dissolving my discomfort over his offer.

"Wonderful," Robert whispers with relief, and he all but collapses against his chair. "Then I believe I truly *can* help you. With your permission, of course."

"What do you mean?" I ask, worried he's really going to start pushing this cure vision thing on me.

"Wendy, I don't merely visualize my own goals. I can visualize anyone's if I align myself with wanting what they want," Robert replies. "I don't ever do it because I have no way of knowing the true intentions behind the goals of others. Their heart, if you will. If I attempt a goal *for* someone else, it is always affected by what motivates them above all else. And how can I know what that ultimately is?"

I lean my elbows on the table and rub my temples. "You are confusing the heck out of me."

"My question was a test. I needed to know your honest answer because it would tell me if I could focus on a goal on your behalf whose vision wouldn't be distorted by misplaced motives. I apologize for putting you through the agony of indecision, but there was no other way to know your real passions underneath your more fleeting ones."

"I don't get it. You said miracles have a cost. I thought that wasn't limited to bad goals."

"Oh yes. There is a cost. Whether or not you take my offer, there will be a cost to saving Gabe's life. But pure motives ensure that those costs are worth it. And by testing you, I forced you to truly ask yourself how far you would go to save Gabe. It caused you to establish your own boundaries and now those boundaries will govern what I am able to see for you. Remember I said that my ability is only limited by desire. With noble ambitions, the cost can remain within acceptable bounds."

"*Can?*" I say, still skeptical. "*Can* and *will* mean two different things. And I thought you didn't deal in life and death."

"Correct on both counts," Robert says. "I maintain acceptable costs by sticking to my rules. As for avoiding questions of life and death, there are other goals that might help you on your way *to* the goal of saving Gabriel. If he ultimately can be saved, we can get there by choosing a goal that doesn't violate the rules. No compounding visions. I think that should be something we mutually agree on. That no matter what we see, we will not try to see past it. Agreed?"

"You're the expert."

"I was thinking something like helping you gain more information about how the body interacts with the life force. Seeking information is almost always a safe bet in my experience. It doesn't involve attempts to affect the futures of others. It's a method I have always been able to count on as long as my motives are pure. And since yours are, I believe it will work for you, too."

"Okay…" I say tentatively. I can't think of anything *wrong* with it. "That sounds alright with me."

"Perfect," Robert says, picking up his newspaper rather abruptly and scooting his chair back. "I should get back to you this evening some time."

"Really? I thought visions come instantly when you focus on a goal."

Robert smiles. "They do. As I said, people have a floating list of wants bombarding them all the time. If I want to make sure I get the *right* vision, I have to focus long enough on the right thing."

"Ah," I reply, standing up with him. I move around the table to take him in a hug, which surprises him since I'm always so careful about my skin. He smells like ginger and wool. "Thanks, Uncle—" I still don't know what to call him. 'Uncle Robert' doesn't sound right because I called him that when I wasn't comfortable with him. I think for a moment as I release him; I've learned so much from this one conversation with Robert. His skill with his ability astounds me, and it hits me how his life force is so bright. The man has incredible power that would allow him to have and do whatever he wants. Yet he has limited himself dramatically simply to live morally and not be ruled by petty wants. The man's willpower is incredible and explains everything about him that I thought was flat and annoying and tedious.

"Thanks for everything, Uncle Moby," I say.

The nickname isn't lost on him, but instead of asking about it, he says, "My pleasure." Then he walks away from me toward the exit.

I once thought that Robert the whale had a lot more going on beneath the water's surface than I knew. I was obviously right. But I also think that what I just found out about Robert was merely a taste of the wisdom he has to offer. I'm definitely going to be paying closer attention to him from now on. He is not an average whale.

Uncle Moby is definitely the right name for him.

11

Coming out of the hotel restaurant, a to-go carton of food in my hand for Gabriel, I stop in my tracks as soon as the lobby comes into view. Gabriel is there, dressed in a pair of sweats and a white t-shirt, his back to me and sitting in the corner. On the other side of the coffee table in front of him sits his brother, Mike, who is dressed in a grey compression shirt—which only someone of his vast musculature can pull off so well—and black basketball shorts. Even from here I can smell stale sweat on him. I think he drove straight here from the gym, and if the slight bloodshot of his eyes is any indication, he drove through the night.

Mike spots me with surprising quickness over Gabriel's shoulder, and his expression is impassive. I halfway wonder if he recognizes me. But then the slight tightening of his eyes tells me he does. Gabriel is in the middle of explaining the tests he's had and what they mean. Even though Mike's dark brown eyes are on me, I feel like he isn't actually *seeing* me. I am too far away to pick up either of them—having stopped next to a potted plant near the hall—so I watch Mike's expression for signs of what he thinks about the news.

Gabriel says something about statistics for his survival, and Mike now looks... queasy, his features slack and his arms wrapped around his middle. Anguish tinted with guilt grips my own stomach.

Gabriel finishes his piece by the time I reach them, and now Mike's emotions hit me like a punch in the gut: devastation and confusion. Instinctively, I step back to get away. Taking a moment to steel myself, I step forward again and sit on the arm of Gabriel's chair. He looks up at me but stays quiet. He puts an arm behind me though and I lean forward to place the food container on the table in front of us.

"Hi, Mike," I say, trying not to sound timid, but I must admit Mike scares me a little.

Mike doesn't look up. He puts an elbow on the arm of his chair as he leans forward, staring at the floor, too consumed with shock to properly acknowledge me—although I'm not sure he *would* acknowledge me even if circumstances were not so dire.

For a couple of utterly silent minutes, I can do nothing but endure Mike's raw emotions that circle with rounds of icy disbelief, hot anger, and spasms of grief. The blueberry pancakes I ate are no longer sitting well. Mike seems to remember I'm here and he looks up, stares directly at me. He makes some assessment, and then he says, "And what are *you* going to do about it?" His tone is somewhat mocking, and definitely irate.

"Mike," Gabriel says in reprimand.

I put a hand on Gabriel's shoulder, my eyes not leaving Mike's. "I'm going to fix it," I say simply, searching for more comforting words. But the truth is I know there *aren't* comforting words in this situation. And I don't know if Mike would care if I made such a gesture.

"How?" Mike demands. I was right; he blames me and it twists the small dagger of guilt I've been walking around with since learning of Gabriel's condition. I obviously bear some responsibility for what has happened, but with Mike being related to Gabriel as well as the son of Maris and Dan—both of whom have never acted with anything but grace—I don't understand how he can be so petty. He hasn't liked me from the very beginning and I have no idea why. I also don't know why that stings so much, which results in my sarcastic side rearing its head as a defense.

"Magic!" I answer, throwing up jazz hands.

That takes both Mike and Gabriel by surprise. And for a moment they both react the same way—with amusement. The similarity in the way they experience humor is so unexpected that I'm taken with surprise. But only for a moment, because Mike quickly opts for annoyance instead, as if deciding that my attempt to make him laugh was offensive—and I suppose I kind of meant it to be. But I'm still intrigued by what I just felt from the two of them. When their mental currents converged, the sum became far greater than the parts. Usually when I feel two people at once, I have to choose which to focus on or they jostle into an undecipherable mass. But I felt Mike and Gabriel together clearly, at the same time, as if they were one person for that moment. I guess Gabriel was right when he told me that he and Mike are close. Odd, since they are so very different in almost every respect. Even now, Mike's emotions are wrought with sharp edges, as if he invites his anger and misery over Gabriel's illness, accentuating it, projecting it until it becomes perfectly clear that he is directing it toward me. He *wants* to blame me, so badly even that the effort is exaggerated enough to be clumsily obvious.

Mike, aware that I must be reading him—probably because I'm staring at him—becomes all the more incensed by my attention. "It's a good thing you *like* being mentally violated," he says, looking back at me as if in challenge, but I know that was directed at Gabriel. "I personally would not be able to stand it." And that part was for me. Then he turns his head only slightly to move his attention to Gabriel, but it's so deliberate and well-complimented by his distaste for me that it has the same effect as if he had turned his back on me entirely.

I hate that my initial reaction is chagrin. I try not to show it though. Instinct has generated a host of possible retorts, but I have to keep reminding myself that Mike has just received devastating news about his brother. I'm no stranger to lashing out, so I have to assume that's exactly what this is. It doesn't explain why every time I encounter him he's even ruder than the last time, but I vow to let it go for Gabriel and not give this guy any more reasons to dislike me. I need to kill him with kindness... or something like that.

"I'm sorry," I say, searching for remorse so it sounds genuine. "I can't help reading you when you're in range, but I guess I don't have to try so hard."

That catches Mike off-guard, which makes me feel somewhat victorious. With my confidence given a boost, I say, "I guess I can focus on Gabriel more since he doesn't mind. He's a lot more pleasant to endure anyway."

Oops. I frown at the floor. I didn't mean for that to come out *quite* that way. Although I don't know *how* I meant for it to come out...

"Mike, *must* you be so belligerent?" Gabriel says tiredly.

"I can be whatever the hell I want," he says. "If she doesn't like what she reads, she should stop reading me."

Gabriel glances up at me and then at Mike. "Well I *can't* read you, so I have no idea *what* you're telling her with your mind. But I *can* hear you, and I don't like what I'm hearing. Feel what you want; Wendy doesn't expect you to control that, and neither do I. But you *do* have control over what comes out of your mouth. I expect you to use it."

Mike, egged on by Gabriel's reprimand rather than abashed, leans back in his chair spreading his legs as if he couldn't be more comfortable with the situation. His lip curls just barely as he crosses his arms. Usually I'd read that as defensiveness, but I'm pretty sure Mike did it to look more intimidating. It's working.

"Sure thing, Gabe," he says. "How can I refuse my dying brother?"

"Your bonhomie is inspiring," Gabriel replies dryly.

"Deja de hablar a mí," Mike says, waving a dismissive hand. And then Mike starts a Spanish monologue. Though I can't understand any of it, it's laced with anger and defensiveness.

Gabriel replies in Spanish, his voice sharp and decisive, like a reprimand. Then he stands up and pulls me to my feet. "If you'll excuse us, Mike, I have some things to attend to."

"I'm not done, Gabe," Mike says angrily, standing as well but keeping his arms crossed. Man, the guy is ripped. "You haven't told me anything except that you probably have lung cancer. Were you even going to mention it the next time I talked to you? Instead I have to hear that you're in the hospital from a stranger, and when I show up here to see what I can do to help you, you brush me off like you dying is none of my business." Mike glares at me, his blame finding its mark.

Stranger?! What a creep. I cross my arms and grit my teeth, fuming. Gabriel slumps a little in exasperation. "Mike, I promise I will explain everything to you, but I really do need to get going."

Mike again delivers his response in Spanish, and this time the words are full of mocking. He's also jealous and worried, which I feel bad for until I hear the words 'Doña Perfecta.' I know what that means. And I know he's talking about me. It's something a guy I briefly dated during my vindictive years used to call me sarcastically when he thought I couldn't hear. But with my hearing at the time, I always heard. It means 'Miss Perfect.' The sarcasm was well-deserved then, but coming from Mike now in a similar way, it's infuriating. I grit my teeth and cross my arms tightly. As I watch Mike's face, I think of all the clever retorts I could give. I've got his number. I know exactly how to handle guys like him.

I frown at the floor. Except when they are my husband's brother…

Throughout their clipped conversation, however, I recognize how distant Gabriel is being. He's keeping Mike at arm's-length, and Mike, unused to such treatment, is responding out of confusion.

Despite Mike's utter dislike for me, I feel bad for him. Mike deserves to know what's going on without having to wait in line. If these two really are as close as Gabriel has let on—though this particular encounter has me doubting it—I don't want to be the force that separates them.

"Oh just go out to lunch later or something," I say to Gabriel when there is a break in their exchange. "You two obviously need to catch up." I glance at Mike, but my offer doesn't seem to do anything but aggravate him, as if he can't stand the idea that I might be able to get Gabriel to spend time with him when he couldn't. Sheesh, this guy is such a baby. I can do nothing right by him.

"What are you going to do?" Gabriel asks, slightly suspicious.

I shrug. "Take a nap maybe. I didn't get to sleep until late last night."

He frowns, repentant about our fight—which we still haven't discussed. I reach for his hand. "Not because of that."

"You're not going to…go *see* anyone without me, are you?" he asks.

"You don't want me to see other people?" I laugh, wanting to put a smile on his face after Mike's unrelenting antagonism. "Don't worry, Gabriel. So far you're the only person of the male persuasion not related to me who can touch me. I'm pretty much stuck with you." I sigh. "Unless fate would have some stranger unwittingly come into contact with my skin and live. Then I simply have no control over what happens next."

A half-smile forms on Gabriel's face. "You would have me believe you're a dilatory woman, but I know better." He spreads his feet, hands on hips as he gives me a once-over. "And your diversion tactics are useless on me."

"Only when I'm not trying," I say, raising an eyebrow.

"I don't doubt that," Gabriel says, looking at me slyly. "And I'm fully amenable any time you want to try out new diversion tactics."

"Okay, seriously," Mike says, backing away out of my range and looking disgusted, "have some consideration. And did I hear you say you could touch him? When did that happen?"

"Not long ago," Gabriel says.

I thought Mike knew, but we've mostly been communicating with him via Dan. And clearly Mike and Gabriel haven't spent much time talking. Confused, Mike says, "I thought you two split up because you wanted to kill yourself. Idiot." Then he looks at me. "Don't feel too bad. Gabe always gets what he wants." He says it reassuringly, but I know it's meant to rile me.

"I won't deny the idiocy," Gabriel replies. "But fortunately Wendy's fortitude in enduring my transgressions in logic saved me from myself."

"Then how—" Mike starts.

"It was her doing," Gabriel say proudly. "Not mine. I'd already given up my convictions about touching her."

Mike's mouth opens a little in skepticism as he translates that. I nearly groan aloud at Gabriel outing me. If blaming me for giving Gabriel cancer weren't enough, Mike is now going to be pissed at me for endangering Gabriel by touching him. But knowing Gabriel, that won't have occurred to him.

Sure enough, Mike looks at me with a taut jaw and hardened eyes. I notice that the angrier he becomes, the darker his brown eyes turn until they are almost black. I'm glad I can't read him. He turns to Gabriel and says, "Wonderful. It's no wonder you're dying. You found someone as foolhardy as you are. Sounds like a winning combination so far."

"Mike," Gabriel says in a low voice that's almost a growl, his hands balled into fists. "You are out of line. I'm going upstairs now to shower. If you intend to go to lunch, I'll meet you down here at noon. And then you can have the opportunity to talk to me alone and tell me what your bloody problem is since Wendy's presence turns you into a raving adolescent."

Mike grins in a self-satisfied way, as unbothered by this jibe as he was by the one earlier. "Really Gabe, that's all I've been asking for. And apparently insulting your wife is the way to get it. Maybe next time we can skip all this if you spare me a phone call and a few minutes of your precious time."

Gabriel shakes his head and puffs in aggravation. He turns around, putting his arm around my waist as he leads me out. "Noon," he calls over his shoulder.

"My gosh. What in Hades is his *problem?*" I say once we reach the elevator and Mike is out of earshot. "I have *never* encountered someone so openly hostile. Even Louise the psycho knows how to speak to people. Please tell me he isn't like that all the time?"

"I admit he was rather short with you," Gabriel says, stepping into the elevator.

"*Rather short?*" I say incredulously, leaning against one of the walls once the doors shut. "Gabriel, the guy is a complete asshole."

Gabriel winces, reaching out to press the button for our floor. "Using such vile language only makes you look immature. It's evidently something you and he have in common."

I stare at him, dumbfounded. He's quibbling over my word choice after... *all that?* I'd think he was purposely goading me, but I can tell he just doesn't like me talking like that—he never has. So I take a calming breath. "If the shoe fits, Gabriel. It's a perfectly good word to describe someone like that."

"He's not usually like that."

"I'm not sure if that makes me feel better or worse."

"Me neither," Gabriel replies, preoccupied. If that wasn't normal behavior for Mike, I have no idea why Gabriel doesn't care more about it. I waver between asking him to explain it and dropping it. We have more pressing things to be concerned about. And I woke up in such a decent mood… Mike has spoiled it.

Remembering that Mike has just learned that his brother is dying, I feel the first stabs of guilt. I really should give him a break. Anger was probably his way of coping. "He's probably just… in shock," I sigh. "And I'm a good target. I know what it's like to want to blame someone."

Gabriel comes forward as the doors open, taking both my hands in his. He kisses me on the forehead. "That's not really it, I don't think. He thinks I made too hasty of a decision in getting married and he's taking it out on you." Gabriel says, annoyed.

"I think you're wrong. A quick engagement is no reason to hate me *that* much. I felt him so I know exactly how much he blames me. I'm okay if that's what he needs to do right now. I do share some responsibility and I can accept that."

"Wendy…" he says, pressing the open button for the door before it can close. We step out. "Having hypno-touch was my decision. Not yours."

"I know that. I didn't say I bear *all* the responsibility. But I could have refused to do it as easily as you could have refused to have it done. Louise is to blame—and so is Carl—but a bad decision is still a bad decision. We both made one."

"Fine. I'll allow that," he says as we walk down the hall. "I think blame is Mike's way of justifying his *other* feelings. You have to understand our relationship. We've always been close, always conferred on everything. We are…… best friends and brothers. But when it came to you, I never asked his opinion. And I told him explicitly that I didn't care about his concerns when he tried to advise me against marrying you. He was so vehement about it and wouldn't leave it alone, and I don't deny that I shut him out entirely. Completely. For a number of months I did not speak to him so I wouldn't have to hear about it—especially while you and I were separated, because I needed conviction rather than doubt, and Mike was sure to infuse doubt. I was trying to send a message to him, but it appears that rather than being offended by *me,* he chose you instead. He began to see my uncharacteristic avoidance as *your* doing. His issue is not you. It's his refusal to accept your place in my life. And it was my erroneous idea that the silent treatment would convince him of it. I never imagined it would scar him the way it has. He's had a lifetime of my tactics so I expected him to read between the lines. But he didn't. I just have to find a way to repair the rift. And yes, he's also in shock, which makes the situation worse. Don't worry. I'll handle it."

"Wow," I say, waving my key card over reader on the door. "So he thought our marriage was a mistake... because I couldn't touch you?"

"I suppose that was part of it," he replies, pensive as he sits in one of the chairs in our room and I shut the door. "He knows every detail of my rather unsuccessful history with women. He did not expect our relationship to be any different. If I were to look at things from his perspective, I can see where his doubt stemmed from, but I admit I still don't understand why he has been so utterly intractable about it. But I'm done conjecturing on his motives. You and I would be better served talking about last night."

"I don't know what more to tell you about last night. I still mean every word of it." I sit down in the chair on the other side of the small table.

"Then *I'll* talk," he replies. "I didn't like that you refused to accept the likely possibility that I may die."

"I know."

He looks at me expectantly. "Wendy, I'm probably going to die."

I remain silent.

"Why are you so sure that's not the case?"

I infuse my expression with assurance. "Hindsight. Sometimes it also gives you foresight."

"And what if you're wrong?"

"I have everything to gain by hoping. And everything to lose by giving in."

He spreads his fingers on the table, frustrated, and then searches my face for a long time before saying, "I'm trying really hard to understand where you're coming from, Love. The only origin for this sudden confidence that *I* can pinpoint is your decision to touch me. I fear your success made you overzealous."

I sit back in my chair and cross my arms. "Gabriel, you have a double standard."

"I do not," he says indignantly.

I snort. "Yes, you do. You based that theory of yours about who can and can't touch me on scant evidence. You were so confident in how you saw it you refused to look at things any other way. *Come on.* You explained your theory to me exactly this way the night we split up. You said, and I quote, 'I had an idea. It was reasonable.' And then you proceeded to make decisions as if it was one hundred percent right."

"You know I regret every bit of those two months," he protests. "What I did to you should never have happened, and you shouldn't base your decisions *now* on my egregious example *then.*"

"What you did to enforce what you believed is a separate issue. Regardless, you never stopped believing in your theory. And it's not like it offered the highest percentage of likelihood and that's why you picked it off a shelf of possibilities. You like to think you base everything you do on logic, but logic is subject to perception. And that's something I finally get. And sure, I get that you *perceive* what I'm doing is reckless. But I have a different view than you do. I see a past that prepared me for this. I see myself in a repeating cycle that my father failed to break out of. I see a problem he started that needs to be fixed. And I see myself as the only one capable of doing it. And I see you…" My voice catches.

I reach across the table for his hand. "Do you remember what it was like when we met? How instantaneous? Gabriel, I fell for you after only one short conversation. It was unrealistic and nobody would believe it—look at your own brother. And then all the crap that *should have* kept us apart? I wasn't kidding when I said we collide. We're like magnets or something. I am *supposed* to be here with you. And it can't be to watch you die."

"I agree the circumstances of our relationship are baffling," he says quietly, squeezing my hand back. "I don't deny that. I simply want *some* kind of indication that you aren't setting yourself up for being shattered when this doesn't go your way. If you follow this path you are set on with expectations so firmly in place, having that faith crushed will alter your ability to believe in yourself ever again. I felt your state of mind last night. Your expectations are *beyond* unreasonable. It literally hurt to endure it."

"Gabriel, if I can't figure this out, I'm dead anyway. Why are you arguing about a future you and I both know I won't have if I can't do this?"

"First of all, that's not set in stone. We don't know for sure if you've simply gotten lucky so far, or if you may be immune to the effects of hypno-touch. Aside from that, I'm concerned that you can't do what needs to be done in the available *time*. Time is something I don't have a lot of. I desperately want you to figure this out—for yourself if need be as well as Kaylen—and I believe you can. But most likely not for me."

I withdraw my hand and look down at the table. "If it will make you feel better to know I have doubts, then yes, I have them. I *am* human. But it doesn't make me happy to entertain them. And it sure doesn't help me. Don't ask me to embrace a part of me I might finally be letting go of—one that has brought me nothing but unhappiness."

Gabriel thinks about that for a while, and then I suddenly remember the pancakes I wanted him to eat. "Crap, I left your pancakes downstairs," I say.

"It's okay. I'm not hungry," he says, waving his fingers dismissively. Then he sighs in resignation. "I can't argue with your reasons without going somewhere I don't want to go again. I want you to be happy and if you say blind confidence in me living makes you happy, I'll support it."

I lean across the table and kiss his cheek. "Thank you. But for starters, supporting it means you have to try your hardest to live. That includes eating. I'll go get your pancakes while you shower."

He wrinkles his nose. "That sounds like a terrible plan. You're going to force feed me *and* I have to shower *alone*?"

"I'll be quick. And I promise the pancakes are worth it. Robert had the kitchen make them for me special." I stand with my hand on the door handle.

"Robert? You saw him this morning?"

"Yes. We had… quite a conversation over breakfast. I'll tell you about it when I get back."

Gabriel's instant excited curiosity makes me laugh as I leave the room. And then I smile at myself for laughing. Maybe I *am* delusional. But I'll take delusional and happy over sane and miserable.

When I reach the lobby, Mike is still there. So are the pancakes; Mike's *eating* them.

I contemplate ignoring him and going to the restaurant to get more, but he's spotted me again so I walk up, arms crossed. "Enjoying Gabriel's breakfast?" I ask. I peek into the tray and see that he's only got a few bites left. I really hope the kitchen can make more.

"Oops. Were you saving these? Here I thought you left them for me," he says, licking syrup from his fork and looking entirely unrepentant. He even leans back in his chair and props a foot up on the coffee table.

"I would have if you'd asked."

"Why? I'm a jerk, remember?" He forks in another bite.

"Because you're Gabriel's brother. That's pretty much the only reason."

"Can I ask you something?"

I lift my eyebrows. "If I said no, wouldn't you ask anyway?"

He looks pensive for a second. "Probably."

I wait.

"Do you really think you can save him?"

"Yes."

"Why?"

I shrug, not willing to get into my deep-seated reasons. "Because I know more than anyone about life forces. I can do things other people can't."

He swallows the last bite. I haven't put him in range, so I don't know what kind of animosity he's harboring behind those dark brown eyes. But he seems less antagonistic at the moment. "Did you have hypno-touch at the compound, too?"

"Right before I went there. I also had it done years ago, as a child."

He looks at me with surprise. "Really? Why?"

I crease my brow, keeping my arms crossed. "My dad was a life force-obsessed nutcase who wanted to make sure I had the same abilities as him. It's a long story…"

Mike looks confused for several beats and then asks, "So… you had hypno-touch done by your dad—the concentrated kind like you did on my brother, but you're still alive? That doesn't make sense."

I shake my head. "No, my dad only did regular hypno-touch on me."

"What?" Mike says, even more confused. "I thought you two had the same ability. You mean you have a *choice* of what kind of hypno-touch your hands do?"

"I don't think so." I sigh, not wanting to get into the nitty-gritty details. "But when my dad did it, he didn't have—I mean we *think* he didn't have his ability. Which means he did regular hypno-touch. Look, there's a lot to it. Ask Gabriel about it when you guys chat." I turn to go.

"So *that's* why you touched him…" Mike says as I walk away. "You realized you'd already killed him. Not much of a risk then, is it?"

My chest cramps and I try hard not to let his words get to me. I turn slowly. "No," I whisper. "I didn't know."

I'm not sure if he believes me, but he laughs. "You sure won the lottery, didn't you? You have a killer touch no matter how you slice it. If your skin didn't kill him, your hypno-touch would. With those odds, why the hell couldn't you leave him alone a year ago?"

I suck in a breath and look down. Against my will, tears find my eyes. "I tried."

He snorts. "I actually believe you on that one. So, how many people at the compound share the same fate as my brother because of you?"

I turn my face away, guilt ripping through me and pushing more tears to the surface. I wipe them with the palm of my hand. "He was the only one," I say hoarsely.

"No shit," Mike says. "Figures. Gabe always thinks he's bulletproof. Exactly why he married you. He's always liked throwing himself at danger."

I look up. "If you actually think that, you don't know him at all."

"Are you really claiming that you know him better than I do? After what? A few months?"

I try to calm down, but Mike pushes every button I have. "No. I said *if* you think that. I don't actually think you believe the words that came out of your mouth. I think you're hiding behind… whatever this is." I gesture at the length of him. "You're hiding from your own guilt. We all know exactly how Gabriel ended up on the compound in the first place."

"Really?" Mike asks sardonically. "You're blaming me because I told him about the compound? The compound didn't kill him!"

"Whether or not I would have been there, he still would have had hypno-touch. Which means he'd still die a horrible death, just a little later. At least now I'm in the picture and have a chance at saving him. You're welcome," I spit, glaring at him.

Mike leans forward, putting both feet back on the floor. His brow knits in agitation for several beats, and then he says slowly, "Are you saying regular hypno-touch is lethal also?"

"Yes…" I say. I guess Gabriel didn't get to that part in his explanation. "It's just slower."

"Must be awfully slow if you're still alive."

I frown. "About fifteen years. By our calculations I should be falling ill any day now."

Mike gapes at me, but snaps his mouth shut as soon as he realizes it. Then his face bears an expression of intense thought again. "Damn," he breathes. "Damn." He hops up abruptly and I flinch. But he doesn't move toward me. Instead he puts his hands on his hips and his face evolves from bewilderment to pure fury. But for once I think it's not directed at me.

Then, without another word to me, he heads for the door.

Crap. What did I just do? My shoulders deflate. I didn't mean to guilt him…

Yes, you did.

The only placation I have is that he would have found out anyway. At least I got the pleasure of seeing him knocked down a notch.

Actually, I didn't get pleasure at all. The guy just learned his brother is terminal, and I told him it's his fault.

If Gabriel brings out the best in me, his brother definitely brings out the worst.

12

"*W*hat just happened?" Gabriel pants, staring up at the ceiling. I lie beside him, my feet tangled in the sheets, hands cast out to my sides, overwhelmed in every sense of the word. I feel as if I've been electrocuted and it has stimulated every one of my nerve endings.

I'm utterly spent.

We're in the colorworld, which makes emotions a dual-experience, but this was *not* like the last time we made love while in the colorworld together.

"You got me," I reply, breathing heavily. "That was... *Wow.*"

As the tingles of ecstasy ease, something inexplicable remains: a connectedness that leaves me aware of Gabriel's body. I lie still, trying to put my finger on it. It's not exactly the way I am aware of myself, but it's almost like his body is an extension of my own, or a shadow in the background. The more I think about it, though, the less I can hold on to the sensation.

"You're fading," Gabriel says, mirroring my thoughts. "It was... as if we shared somatosense."

"Which is what?"

"Tactile sense. Or less accurately, touch: temperature, pressure, the nuanced sensations felt by the nerve endings in your skin. It's mostly gone now, but I think I even felt some of your motor movement as if it were my own. You're picking up the same thing, am I right?"

"It's almost gone. But yeah. That sounds right." More silence passes as we both try to remember the experience, but the magnetism felt between where our skin touches is all that remains. Somewhere in my psyche, however, is an empty place where Gabriel's body once was and it's a bit like an itch I can't reach.

"I don't like this," I say, although I'm not sure what I mean by that.

"I think I've got it—well the discomfiting part of it," Gabriel says. "It's like having a phantom limb, only in this case it's more like a phantom body."

"Phantom limb?" I say, still slightly afraid to move. "Um, is that like when someone has their arm or something amputated and they can still feel it?"

"Precisely," Gabriel replies. "I believe in some sense we were sharing somatosense—feeling what each other felt—and it was like having an extension of our own body. But somehow that connection has left and it's like losing a limb—or several of them."

"Okay," I say, nodding. "There were some moments there where I couldn't separate us, so I can see that. But how did it happen that we shared... somatosense in the first place?"

"The question of the hour..." Gabriel says, shifting so he can turn on his side to face me. Being in the colorworld with him now, I unfocus my eyes so I can see his face. He reaches out carefully and runs a finger down the length of my arm. I can tell that he's doing it for observational purposes—seeing if we can share feeling again. As far as I can tell, it doesn't work. But I'm so oversensitized that his skin moving against my skin is overstimulating and I shiver.

His finger stops and he watches my reaction for a moment before moving his finger again. I flex my bicep to escape the sensation, and again he stops. "If I pay close attention I can almost feel what you do," he says. "But why was it so much stronger earlier?"

"Uh. Ecstasy turns the somatosense-sharing switch on?" I offer.

"Perhaps," he says. "But something must have changed. Last time you and I were intimate, it was an exalted experience due to the emotion-sharing. But it was not like this."

"It's my ability gone wonky again," I say. "Just when we think we've got it figured out, it does something new and we're back to square one."

"So far I have no complaints," Gabriel says, giving me a knowing look. "And the answer to why it has changed must be that you improved your ability." And then he props his chin on his hand and moves into lightning-speed thought while I hold his other hand in between both of mine. A mixture of horror and intrigue comes over me as I look at it and recall what it felt like to have this hand against my skin as the we were lost amid one another's ravishment. I wouldn't call it *sharing* feeling. It was more like... multiplying pleasure.

"I think I've got it!" Gabriel says, interrupting my ponderings. "Move your hand slowly down my arm."

He closes his eyes then and I do as he asks. As my hand moves the length of his arm, a shiver moves through me involuntarily.

"Whoa," I say, stopping my hand on his wrist. "How did you do that?"

He opens his eyes and grins. "It functions precisely like your telepathy. I have to *think* my sensations to you—in this case the sensation of your hand moving down my arm."

"But I didn't feel that exactly. I felt the effect it had on you—the shivering."

"It's a bit difficult to think precise somatosense *toward* someone," he explains. "Probably if I practiced more, I might be able to induce a clearer 'picture' of what I'm feeling, so to speak. Only part of the experience is 'getting through.' I have to practice concentrating on the precise feeling to transmit it accurately."

I nod, getting it. "And intimacy pretty much demands all of your concentration—so that's probably why it came through so clearly without us really trying?"

"Yes. I think you are absolutely right."

"If this is really my ability improving, when did this happen?" I ask.

"The last time we were in the colorworld together was… last night, right?" he says. "During our fight?"

I was in the colorworld earlier today, but I was careful to avoid touching Gabriel then. Although I remember how much brighter things were…

"Something changed between our intimate encounter a few days ago and today," he says. "You improved your ability that much in that short a time?"

I shrug. "I think it's related to the magnetism thing. So maybe it's not all that drastic. Whatever it was that caused it, I'll take it." I roll over to mirror his pose. "Do you realize that we've gone from completely incapable of touching each other to experiencing each other more intimately than probably anyone in the history of humanity?"

He smiles softly. "Indeed. And I have a new idea."

"Of course you do."

"It's clear that we were both passing somatosense to one another—two-way. I think that may mean we can also speak telepathically both ways when you're sharing your abilities."

That sounds reasonable. Without moving because we're in the colorworld now, I concentrate and think toward Gabriel, '*Can you hear me?*'

His grin widens. '*Yes! So touching in the colorworld does make it two-way!*'

A knock sounds at the door right then. I lift my head to look past Gabriel at the clock. "Crap. I think that's your brother. You're late."

"You're right," Gabriel says, though he's reluctant to get up.

I hop up, yanking us out of the colorworld. We must have been sharing some of each other's awareness after all because I feel the break between us like an invisible link has broken. It's a bit disorienting and I sit back on the bed a moment to adjust.

"That is most awful," Gabriel remarks, sitting up carefully. "Wendy we're either going to hate each other really soon for this or fall more madly in love."

I laugh. "Please. More madly in love." Another knock sounds at the door and I yell, "Just a *minute!*"

Then I notice Gabriel hasn't moved. He's watching me, his eyes soft and brimming with adoration. It renders him motionless, but completely happy and satisfied.

"What is it?" I ask nervously, though my whole being warms in response to his feelings. Gabriel's reverence for me so often feels undeserved. I guess sitting here naked has me imagining that he's going to see my inadequacy all of a sudden.

He does not speak, but gazes at me, his eyes moving over me, a measure of disbelief over what he sees. And he seems in no hurry to get up and get dressed. "I love you. So much," he says finally. "Your features are the same as yesterday, yet... you are more gorgeous than I remember. It's as if what I perceive as ideal beauty has changed. And you are now the standard... I don't know how or why, but I desire nothing more than to simply behold you."

Yet *another* knock comes from Mister Rudely Impatient, and I grimace.

"Mike," Gabriel booms, though his eyes do not leave me. "I will be downstairs in ten minutes. *Go away.*" And then more softly, he says, "He is lucky. You've intoxicated me. I do believe I'm too drunken on you to be irritated at him. Perhaps our time together at lunch will be pleasant after all."

"Ah..." I say, unsure how this odd mood of his strikes me. "I think maybe this is post-intimacy endorphins."

He raises his eyebrows. "I can't think you're beautiful without biological triggers?"

I shrug. "You tell me. You're the biology expert."

He waves a hand and sits up. "We know there are things outside of biology that drive us. We've seen them. And *you,* mi encantadora doncella, are strikingly lovely in both this world and in the colorworld." He reaches for his shirt.

After dressing, he leans over and kisses my forehead. It reactivates the draw between us, like an invisible rope connecting us, holding more tightly the closer he is. So many odd and unexplained feelings between us. I can't possibly make sense of them all. Maybe one day I will be used to them enough to analyze their meaning. He brushes my cheek with his hand, stares into my eyes for several seconds, and wordlessly turns to go. As the distance increases between us, the rope loosens. When he closes the door behind him, the connection lingers. And then it fades slowly into nothingness. It is definitely related to the somatosense thing Gabriel talked about. Somehow the colorworld links us in ways I've yet to fully explore. I still don't fully understand what we just experienced.

Whatever it was, I've been given a new tool in the fight to save Gabriel. Not even a day after making the decision.

13

*W*ith my hands raised over Gabriel's body and submerged in his luminous strands, I pull gently at them. I hope to be able to move some of them aside so I can determine what it looks like beneath them. I want to know how they might connect to the body—*if* they connect to the body. I'm careful to move slowly so as to avoid that awful sound that hypno-touch makes. I recall how when Louise did it, the sound was not nearly as grating as when *I* did it. I think that means the worse the sound, the more damage.

My efforts make the music I know well. It sounds harmless, but unfortunately it doesn't allow me to manipulate the strands enough to move them away from Gabriel's body.

"My own life force keeps moving through your strands without me actually *gripping* anything," I tell Gabriel who is eager to know what I'm seeing.

"What does it look like when it makes the terrible sound you talk about?" Gabriel asks.

I groan. Gabriel and I just had a fifteen minute argument about how rough I should get with his strands. He claims a second or two of watching his life force while I tug at his strands won't kill him any faster. I beg to differ. Gabriel would have me experimenting on him without restraint if it were up to him. But the reality is I need to know what's happening. At least a little. So I suck it up.

I close my eyes, focusing on what I *feel* rather than what I see. "There's a slight tug…" I say, cringing as I wave my hands through him, alternating between quick movements and slow ones to note the difference. "Only when the awful sound happens. And it's only when I start jerking my hands around."

I open my eyes now, this time to *watch* what happens with the horrid noise. I lean in closer. "My *hands* don't actually connect with your strands; my own *life force* does the manipulation. It's like it gets tangled up with yours. The quicker my movements, the more tangles."

"Fascinating," Gabriel breathes, launching into his mental analysis.

I try several techniques, holding my hands at different angles and positions to see if I can get my strands to connect with his enough to part his life force without harming it. I wince and grit my teeth, stopping abruptly any time I hear the beginning of the wrenching sound. But no matter what I do, I can't get enough control to see anything beyond his cocoon of silken threads. It's like trying to separate water, the way his strands move to fill in whatever gap I begin to make.

I groan in frustration. How am I supposed to get the strands to move where I want without doing damage? I can't stomach the thought of getting more forceful. There's a good chance that if I do that, I'll make Gabriel worse. I might kill him.

"I wonder what happens if I do it while I'm touching you?" I say, curious.

"Good idea!" Gabriel says. He lifts up his t-shirt to reveal his toned chest.

Placing my palms against his skin, I soak in the connectedness to his body. Ever since our experience of somatosense, I've craved that feeling, although I couldn't say why other than that it's lonely in my own skin. We've experimented a few more times, and it has become clear that sharing bodily sensations definitely takes practice. It doesn't happen without purposeful concentration usually. I won't be able to fully enjoy it now since I need to focus on Gabriel's life force strands.

I note the blending of our souls is just as I remember: seamless. Hopeful that this will work, I keep my hands against his chest as I spread them apart.

My anticipation drowns in disappointment and I shake my head. "My life force doesn't do anything. Even when I move fast. It has even less of an effect than I did when I wasn't touching you."

My life force moves through his, connected to it, part of it. Keeping my hands on him, I close my eyes. Sensing my misery through his connection to me in the colorworld, he pulls me down to his chest.

There is obviously no way to manipulate Gabriel's soul without possibly harming him. As amazing as my ability is, it does not give me nearly enough precision. I bet this is the exact problem Carl ran into. I bet he was hoping this wouldn't be the case for me.

Gabriel, knowing that my experiment validates his skepticism over me curing him, remains quiet, which I'm grateful for. I haven't given up, but I can't stop the helplessness that overtakes me suddenly and forcefully. I drown in it for a while, struggling not to cry. It takes concerted effort to hold the tears at bay and to push the debilitating disappointment away from me enough that I can find the parts of me that haven't dissolved in the murkiness of the future.

Gabriel continues to hold me, observing my emotional trek. Breathing with purposeful control, I force my thoughts to the past: a time that I find more comforting than the present. On the compound Gabriel accurately predicted that the solution to my death-touch would be found in the least likely place. He was right. I should not expect this to be any different. I may not know where to go next as far as a solution, but if I keep my eyes open, a direction will come. I'll figure this out and the solution will wow me so much I'll wonder how I never guessed it.

Gabriel chuckles. "You are a fascinating woman, Love. I wish I could have listened to your internal logic just now. It was exhilarating. Like a roller coaster. Up down up. What brought you to such a positive conclusion?"

"Some good advice someone gave me once."

"Mmm. And who might that be? I need to meet them. They seem to have a positive effect on your mood."

"You," I reply.

Surprised, he squeezes me and sighs. "Wendy, I will do everything in my power to help you succeed. You know that right? I may be concerned about feasibility, but it does not mean I will try any less."

"I know. This is not something I think I ever would have had the courage to go after, but with you... even impossible doesn't feel out of my grasp." And then I tuck myself closer to him, craning my neck up to smile at him. "What I am now is all your fault."

***

"I don't get this!" Kaylen whines, slumping from where she sits on the floor and throwing her pencil on the coffee table.

Ezra leans over to get a look at Kaylen's paper. "You balanced the equation wrong," he says immediately. "That's why you're coming up with the wrong limiting reagent."

Kaylen brushes a lock of hair out of her face and stares at Ezra for a second before mumbling, "Annoying math geniuses" and bending over the problem and picking up her pencil again, eraser at the ready.

"The dynamic duo," I say, having come into the common room of our hotel suite to find Ezra and Kaylen doing homework. "Back at it." I like to see Kaylen and Ezra doing normal kid things again. When I was living with Robert, they did homework together every day. Ezra would help Kaylen with the math things, and Kaylen would help him with everything else.

Ezra points to somewhere on Kaylen's paper with his pencil, having scooted even closer to her. "On this one, the atomic mass of magnesium isn't twelve. That's the atomic *number*."

"I got the right answer though," she says.

"Only because you had a fifty percent chance of being right," Ezra says. "There are only two reactants. It had to be one or the other."

She narrows her eyes. "Thank you, genius. I'm not a complete idiot."

"I'm only trying to help," Ezra says, holding up his hands. "What's wrong? You had this stuff down before."

"I guess I forgot it all while we were on 'vacation'," she says, holding up air quotes. It was sort of a vacation, but mostly we were on the run from Robert at the time.

"But we worked problems every day then," Ezra says. "How would you forget?"

"You did problems every day?" I ask. "While we were hotel-hopping?"

Ezra glances at me before taking his own eraser to Kaylen's paper. "Yes. Someone had to make sure we got an education."

"And by we he means *me*," Kaylen corrects him. "I don't even know why Ezra goes to high school at all. He should be in college."

"Social interaction," Ezra replies. "And I suck at writing."

"Stress," Kaylen says, slumping against the couch. "That's why I can't remember how to balance a stupid equation. All I can think about is... you know."

I sit down and prop my feet on the edge of the coffee table. Kaylen has a right to be frazzled. Aside from not knowing her fate, we still haven't gotten the results of Gabriel's biopsy even though it's been two days since he had it. We need to start thinking about treatments and right now we're in limbo, although I've spent a great deal of time watching life forces. It'd also be nice if we could get out of this hotel—even if it *is* the nicest hotel I've ever stayed in.

At that very moment, however, Gabriel walks through the door, accompanied by Robert.

"Well," Gabriel says, stopping in front of the closed door and putting his hands on his hips. "I got the call finally."

I lean forward and put my feet on the floor. Kaylen and Ezra twist around to look at Gabriel.

"Small-cell lung cancer. Chemo first, radiation later, but no surgery. They want me in for my first infusion tomorrow. A second one on Friday. And then next week it will be Monday, Wednesday, Friday," he says matter-of-factly.

Since I've been expecting as much, the official diagnosis comes as far less jarring than the original news of a tumor in his lung. I lay my head back to ponder my lack of reaction and Gabriel plops down next to me, taking my hand. Robert takes one of the arm chairs, looking pensively at nothing and stroking his goatee. I wish the news relieved some of my stress, but it doesn't. In fact, I think it doesn't change the way I feel *at all*. That's disappointing.

After a few silent moments, Ezra says, "Anyone else agree that was the most anti-climactic terminal cancer news they've ever gotten? I think I actually felt relief right there."

"I guess it helps to accept it ahead of time," Kaylen says.

Well *that* part is a relief. So everyone has been mentally preparing themselves for this.

"Too bad we didn't expect something even worse like pancreatic cancer," Ezra says. "Then we could have thrown a 'Congratulations On Only Having Lung Cancer Party.'"

That makes us all chuckle, and I shake my head at Ezra's comedic timing. I have to admit I'm more interested now in what Robert has to say. He called earlier to tell me he was stopping by to talk to us about progress on getting a vision. With Gabriel's diagnosis no longer on the horizon, it's time to get to work.

I look at Robert now. "You're up, Uncle Moby."

"Oooh," Ezra says, shifting into a cross-legged position on the floor. "This is about the vision thing? Wen told us about that yesterday. You got something?"

"That relates to Wendy learning more about how the life force interacts with the body? I believe so," Robert says, and I can tell he's trying to be clear that his vision is not about Gabriel and his illness. "Time will tell because right now the vision is blurry. So most likely it's further in the future. I'll need to keep trying it out every day to see when it becomes clearer."

Ezra, unable to wait for Robert to finish his characteristic pause, prods, "That's it?"

"All I can tell so far is that it's outside of a building," Robert says, drumming his fingers on the arm of the chair. "I think I'm seeing a lot of trees. They're all evergreens except one. I think it doesn't have many leaves. If this place is somewhere in southern California, my guess is that the time in the vision is probably in the next week or two."

"Is this good or bad?" I look over Gabriel who is looking back at me. I told him in more detail than Ezra about my conversation with Robert over breakfast two days ago. He knows that if we don't recognize this place, we won't get another shot. No compounding visions.

"At this point... I'm only a little concerned," Robert says carefully. "Outdoor visions are always either a godsend or an utter disaster. The edge of a building is in the scene, which is much better than in the middle of the woods somewhere. We have to hope it's a place one of us recognizes when it clears up."

He's a *little* concerned? I think I'm a *lot* concerned.

"Wendy, this is still good news," he says, picking up the skepticism in my silence—and probably my expression.

"And how is that?"

"First, this is a primary vision. And second, it's static. When it's this far in the future, it's unusual to get something that doesn't shift. In my experience that means it's based on a good goal."

"But why does it matter how good the goal is if you have so little chance of recognizing the place in the vision?"

"I understand your concern and it's a good question. Let me see if I can explain." But instead of diving into it he stands up and takes a mug from next to the sink, filling it with hot water from the coffee maker. Then he produces a tea bag from somewhere and puts it in the cup. It smells like ginger. Looking back, I remember Robert always smelled faintly of ginger; I just never acknowledged it because I didn't take a vested interest in him before.

"Every action we take has consequences that reach far beyond ourselves," Robert begins, turning around with the mug grasped in his hands. "Each person on earth has an effect on every other person. We are bound through our past, our present, and our future. The future itself is manufactured by the most microscopic moments. For that reason, there are possibly innumerable paths to a goal. If you think about that fact, you have to wonder how it is that I can *ever* come up with a static vision."

I put my elbow on the arm of the couch. That makes sense. There are obviously a lot of ways to get things done for a regular person having a regular goal *sans* supernatural abilities. But for someone like Robert, who has access to the future, the number of ways to cause something to come about would grow exponentially.

"As I told you before, visions are governed by the motives of the person whose goal it is," Robert says slowly once I've had time to process what he's said. "When motives are selfless, the goal becomes more than merely *your* goal. It becomes... what I call a *collective* goal. It benefits more than one person. The greater the number of people who benefit from a particular goal, the easier it is to accomplish."

"Because you've got more people on your side," Ezra says, nodding.

"Yes," Robert says. "And here's where it gets tricky. The goal must accommodate all their singular wills and their varied possible futures. Therefore it *limits* the means by which the goal can be accomplished. It narrows down the possible visions."

"More data points... more accuracy," Ezra mumbles.

"Exactly," Robert says. "The greater the number of people to benefit, the more precise the vision gets. So when it becomes static despite being so far in the future, that means it has been narrowed down due to a huge number of people—those it ultimately benefits. Are you with me so far?"

"It's like... if a treasure was buried somewhere and you decided to look for it by yourself because you didn't want to share it with anyone," I say, paraphrasing so I can be sure I'm following. "That would be a selfish goal. But if you decided you'd share it, you could get a bunch of people involved. You might actually find it then... That's why people usually work in teams rather than solo."

"Yes!" Gabriel says, squeezing my hand. "Brilliant analogy, Love."

"Okay, *that* actually made sense," Kaylen says, gesturing at me with her pencil.

"Well... yes," Robert says, surprised. "And in fact, you've touched on the overall point I'm trying to make: why it is this method of a collective goal has a higher probability of success. Using your analogy, change the hidden treasure to a *moving* target instead because it's in the future and the future is directly and indirectly affected by every person's actions. If you have many people pursuing the same treasure, all coming from different directions, taking different paths, and the treasure itself is moving in response to *their* movements, predicting where it will end up becomes easier because, quite simply, they are closing in on it, driving it toward one place—even *determining* where that place will be."

"It's chaos theory," Gabriel says, awed.

"Predictability increases as new data points affect possible trajectories," Ezra gushes, eyes bright. "And you can see the event further out because that predictability allows you to!"

Kaylen shakes her head and frowns at them. "Annoying geniuses. Is it really that exciting to speak in a language only a certain IQ population understands?"

"Gabe is right," Robert says, impressed. "It precisely *is* chaos theory."

Kaylen throws her hands down. "You *too*, Uncle Rob?" Then she looks at me. "Please tell me you don't know what chaos theory is."

I shake my head. "No way. But I think I can rephrase what Uncle Moby said: It's hard to find something by yourself and even harder if that thing is moving because all you can do is chase it from one direction. It's easier to find something with a bunch of other people because they can all come from different directions and drive it where they want it."

Robert and Gabriel both chuckle. Ezra nods emphatically, and then Robert says, "Yes. Visions, no matter what they are based on—good goal or not—are ultimately governed by the majority. If the path to something I want conflicts with what the majority wants, (in other words, goes against the desires of too many others), it will be much harder to get a viable vision. Achieving my goal will likely require compounding visions. And as I said, things never go right then. Make sense?"

"Yep," I reply. "The future of one is shaped by many people because... the future of many... can be shaped by one person. Gonna take a while for that palindrome logic to sink in though."

"Palindrome logic?" Gabriel laughs. "Your life lesson cliff notes are superb. You make things almost *too* simple."

"I don't actually simplify. I paraphrase," I correct him.

"I'm just glad you don't know what chaos theory is," Kaylen says. "I thought I was going to have to find a group of average people to be friends with so I don't have to feel stupid all the time."

"So you see how this vision I've gotten for you is shaping up perfectly then," Robert says.

"Yeah," I reply, relieved. Robert's ability continues to wow with its sheer scope of possibility. But then I remember his rules about life and death. I'd like to ask him how that fits in, but I need time to wrap around this latest insight. "So we wait," I say. "And when the vision clears up, you'll show it to me and hopefully one of us recognizes it. Right?"

"You've got it," Robert says.

"Thank you so much for your help. You're pretty amazing, Uncle Moby," I say.

"It's my pleasure," Robert replies, sipping his tea.

Ezra, I notice, is scribbling on a piece of paper—probably equations. I asked him once a long time ago what they meant, and he said he was writing his thoughts out. His mind operates in math; it's the language he understands and speaks best. In fact, when he was little other people would tell my mom that Ezra had a developmental disorder because he didn't do typical kid things like make-believe and role playing. Ezra also didn't like books unless there were pictures involved. Metaphors and abstract ideas eluded him. School turned out to be a nightmare for him—even math lessons because of how Ezra would always skip steps, or scribble something the teachers could never follow. My mom never believed the doctors or the teachers. She was Ezra's translator and his advocate. She knew how to speak Ezra's language better than anyone. I remember how Robert told us our mom was a math prodigy as well, and I can't believe that I never caught on to that as being the reason she got Ezra so well.

Though my mom was always on his side, two things changed Ezra's life: comic books and taking French as a freshman. Comic books were actually my mom's idea, I remember. She brought one home and Ezra latched on to it immediately. Comic books presented theoretical ideas in a format Ezra could follow and then translate internally into his own language. I think it allowed Ezra to relive the imagination of childhood that he missed out on because he was orienting himself in the world differently than other kids. Once he understood and appreciated the importance of imagination and creativity, he had a much easier time relating to people. The process of learning French taught Ezra how language is constructed and how it builds upon itself. It allowed Ezra to understand why it was he couldn't communicate effectively. The vast majority of people only know the basics of mathematical language, and Ezra has always been fluent. He explained to me once what it was like for him to use words, "Try communicating in English only in basic noun and verb sentences all day, no adjectives, and no abstract ideas. No cultural phrases or slang. That's what words are like for me. I can see and understand so much more of the world in numbers and angles and shapes and patterns than I can with words. Words limit me."

Once Ezra got this about himself, he started tutoring in math. Because he realized he had to learn the language of others if he was going to be able to do anything with his gift. And it helped him tremendously both in communication and confidence. Now, you'd never know Ezra was a social outcast or a relative mute when he was around other kids. Now he can teach Kaylen how to balance chemical equations without getting impatient. I am so proud of my brother. That my mom always assured him that there was nothing wrong with the way his mind worked was why he actively sought ways to integrate socially. And *that*, I realize, was why Mom kept him in public school and had him complete one grade at a time like the other kids.

*Ezra needs to know that math problems aren't the solution to everything, namely people. He will have to grow up soon enough...*I put my hand over my mouth as I remember those words my mom said to Mrs. Logan, the school counselor, on the phone once.

"What's wrong?" Gabriel says softly, and I realize I'm crying. Ezra is still scribbling and Kaylen is asking Robert how the remodel is going at his house.

"Just thinking about my mom," I whisper. "It just occurred to me that she knew she was going to die. She knew *I* was going to die. She prepared him—Ezra." I look up at Gabriel. "She made sure Ezra had the skills to be able to cope."

"She does sound like quite a lady," Gabriel says, though he's still confused about where my seemingly random thought came from.

I shake my head in wonder. "It blows me away how much more I feel like I know her now than I did when she was alive."

"Death seems to do that."

"And maturity."

"Yes. That, too."

14

*T*he first day of chemo starts off well. It's not until halfway through that Gabriel starts to wake up periodically, behaving more and more incoherently. He mumbles my name like he's asking for me even though I'm right next to him, holding his hand. Then he starts babbling in Spanish. And then Russian, French, and who knows what else. He looks right at me at times, but there is no recognition. Later, tremors rack his body in fits and starts. He's still having them when the infusion finishes. I ask the nurse about it several times, but she keeps saying it's all normal.

He's taken up to a room where he'll stay until tomorrow's infusion. He rests peacefully there for about half an hour. But then he wakes up suddenly and vomits violently all over the bed, the floor, and me. He falls back and I think he falls asleep instantly. Whimpering a few times as I try to ignore the smell, let alone the feel of being doused in Gabriel's stomach contents, I buzz the nurse and then call Ezra to have new clothes brought to me.

"I thought you gave him anti-nausea meds," I say to the nurse as she cleans him up.

"We did. Sometimes they aren't very effective," she replies, going about her job methodically and expertly.

"More like not effective *at all,*" I say under my breath, standing very still so the wet shirt doesn't touch me any more than it has to. I remove my gloves. One of them is completely soiled.

Gabriel starts moaning as soon as the nurse leaves the room and I rush to his side, but don't touch him. I'm halfway to deciding to lose my shirt and just walk around in my bra. "I'm here," I tell him soothingly, stroking the top of his hand.

He grips my arm suddenly, and his eyes flash open. A look of horror crosses his face as he looks around the room. Then he launches out of the bed, throwing me to the floor to get me out of his way. His IV pole jerks forward behind him, but one of its feet catches on a chair next to the bed, falling over and into me. Caught in my flailing limbs, the pole doesn't move any further. Gabriel doesn't have enough slack in his line to make it to the bathroom—his destination apparently. Instead of stopping, however, he jerks his arm to free it from the IV line, which not only rips the cannula out, but also yanks the top of the pole into my cheek just below my right eye. Putting my hand to my smarting face, I see Gabriel drop to the floor and put his face in the toilet. He retches over and over, oblivious to the blood dripping over his hand and me lying in appalled confusion next to his bed and wrapped in his IV line.

I get myself disentangled just as the nurse shows up again. She stops in the middle of the floor, looking from me, to the IV pole and line on the floor, to Gabriel in the bathroom. "Are you alright?" she says to me.

"Physically? Yes," I reply, peeling my shirt off once and for all. At this point, I could care less who sees me in my bra.

The nurse, who has gone over to coax Gabriel back to the bed, isn't phased by my stripping. I guess you see a lot of crazy things in the oncology wing.

Gabriel doesn't seem to be listening to her. His head is bowed over his knees like he's resting. But I, frankly, don't care if he wants to hang out in the bathroom the rest of the day. I can't help being irritated at him for all but trampling me, ripping out his IV, and leaving me in a puddle of his vomit. Okay, so it's really only on my shirt, but I'm a sorry mess.

I scoot across the floor over to the wall, which I lean against to recover, drawing in deep breaths to calm down.

And then Mike walks in.

"You've gotta be kidding me," I say under my breath, absolutely *drowning* in embarrassment over being shirtless and doused in vomit in front of Gabriel's brother.

He has stopped at the door, having spotted me, but then his eyes dart to the empty bed, the IV pole still toppled on the floor. He walks the rest of the way into the room, seeing the nurse still working on getting Gabriel to his feet. He ignores me and walks into the bathroom to help her. Actually, he single-handedly lifts Gabriel, almost putting him entirely over his shoulder and carrying him to the bed. He gets him arranged while the nurse calls for help.

Mike leaves the room, but returns in moments, a hospital gown in his hand. He holds it out to me wordlessly.

I eye the fabric. "Did you grab that out of the laundry pile?"

A few silent seconds pass between us, and Mike is close enough for me to tell that he's amused. Deciding to *act* amused, he actually laughs. Then he waves the gown back and forth. "Might have. Might not have. I guess you'll have to trust me, won't you? Or you could go out into the hall in your bra and find one you know is clean..."

I lean forward and snatch it out of his hand, careful to keep my skin far from him. "No, I don't. I have an excellent sense of smell. I can tell."

I ball it up and take a sniff while eying him. "Yep. Clean," I say, pulling it over my shoulders and wrapping the ties just right so it actually covers me.

Mike has located the bed pan and now sits on the other side of Gabriel, trying to get his attention with things like, "Hey, Jackass. You just horked all over your lady and ripped your IV out. If you need to throw up, use this." He puts Gabriel's hand on the edge of the bed pan. Gabriel opens his eyes briefly to look but says nothing.

I stand off to the side while two nurses get the pole back in place and the IV tubing changed out. An orderly comes in to clean the floor. Meanwhile I'm feeling out of place, unsure about coming closer. I'm a little traumatized. Gabriel has never been remotely violent with me, and even though I know he's not quite in his right mind, it still cuts me.

"How long has he been like this?" Mike asks.

I shrug, forcing back tears. I do not want to cry in front of Mike. "Since the end of his infusion. Totally out of his head."

"And this is normal?"

"I don't know. The nurse says it is."

Ezra shows up then, an overnight bag in his hand and I rush to take it from him. "Thanks," I say.

"You okay?" Ezra says. He can tell I'm close to losing it. And my cheek must bear evidence of the IV pole incident because he's staring at it.

Determined not to lose composure in front of Mike, I say, "I'm fine. But I've got barf all over me. I need to take a shower." And then I turn for the bathroom.

"You're not supposed to use that," Mike says before I shut the door.

I stop and glare at him. "What are they going to do? Come drag me naked out of the shower? They can kiss it." And then I slam the door behind me.

***

I've pulled myself together by the time I'm done with my shower. I'm ready to do this. I simply didn't expect Gabriel to have such a drastic reaction to the chemo. I've got my game face on now. Mike is still here. Ezra has gone, but he left me a sub sandwich. The room still smells like vomit, and I heard Gabriel throw up in the bed pan at least two more times while I was showering. But I'm too hungry to care about unpleasant smells.

Mike watches me while I sit on the futon, check my blood sugar, and then approximate my insulin. I ignore him while I eat my food, giving myself pep talks. Gabriel will probably not remember what happened. I need to get over it. I also wonder how long Mike is planning on staying. There's something I want to try with Gabriel and I don't want Mike around while I do it.

I'm contemplating what I can say to Mike that might provoke him to leave when I hear a chiming sound. Mike gets his phone out of his pocket and then commences to have a text conversation. After about five minutes of this, Mike's face turns red. He's outside of my emodar, but I could swear he's fuming.

He stands up abruptly, shoving his phone back in his pocket. "I have to be somewhere," he says. "I'll be back tomorrow. Are you going to be able to keep him in bed this time?"

I glare at him. "Get lost, Mike."

He smirks before turning and leaving without another word.

My tension leaves with him, and I look at the clock. Eight PM. I wonder what kind of urgent business Mike has at eight PM on a Thursday? Not going to complain though. I wanted him to leave anyway. I stand up and slide next to Gabriel in bed. Keeping the bed pan within arm's reach, I put my hand on his skin and tap into the colorworld.

I take a moment to test my experiment from yesterday with his strands again, to see if anything different happens while he's asleep.

Nothing. While touching him, I have just as little influence over his life force as before.

Exhausted, I get comfortable, hoping I can get a short nap in before Gabriel wakes.

I can't sleep though. My brain hops from one thing to the next—all the things I wish I was doing right now instead of watching my husband suffer through chemo. Like having a *life*. *Not* in a hotel. A job. Maybe school. Buying a house like Gabriel wanted and having Ezra and Kaylen live with us. I want that normalcy. It sounds like heaven. Peaceful.

New awareness tickles my daydream. After several moments of feeling as if part of me is waking, I realize it must be Gabriel. I open my eyes and wait to see if he is going to reach full alertness.

Nausea begins to distract my efforts though, and I wonder why until Gabriel's emotions become clear to me. And then I know that the nausea is his. As soon as I recognize this, I quickly snatch up the bed pan, holding it at the ready. I watch him though, absorbing this new sensation of discomfort that isn't really mine but that I can feel as if it is. From what I can tell, he's not fully aware yet. Gabriel said in order to pass somatosense, we have to purposely think it *toward* the other person, just like telepathy. I don't think Gabriel is aware enough to have that kind of concentration...

Maybe, because it's discomfort, it projects more easily. Or maybe my ability improved again. I don't know. What I *do* wonder, however, is if I can give him any relief. I close my eyes and do my best to think about... projecting my wellness onto him. I don't know if it works. I don't feel any different.

Gabriel's eyes flutter a few times and finally open, and for once I see all of him there rather than the daze of earlier. Startled, it takes him a moment to get what's going on. "Hello, Love. Doing research again?"

"Gabriel!" I say in a high-pitched voice, tears of relief springing to my eyes. "It's you!"

He glances down at himself and back up to my face. "Were you expecting someone else?"

"You've been out of it all day. It's nice to have you finally know who I am. You scared the crap out of me today."

He cringes. "I can't remember a thing. It looks like my tolerance for those ghastly poisons is low. I feel horrible. This is supposed to be *treatment?*" And then he gives me a close-lipped smile. "But these colors are nice to wake up to—as well as the beautiful woman at my side." He reaches up to brush my hair over my shoulder. And then he frowns. "My stomach feels like it's being tossed around in the washer."

"I can't tell if I'm helping at all," I say. "I'm going to let go of you a second. Tell me if you feel any different." I let go of his skin but not the colorworld. I still experience his discomfort though—which I guess is expected. If I'm in the colorworld, people can speak to me telepathically even if they aren't touching me, just not the other way around. That must mean they can transfer somatosense to me without touching me.

Gabriel, on the other hand, gasps and grips his stomach. It's clear that *he* feels different. Quickly I put my hands on him again and he relaxes.

"Good heavens," he pants. "That is the most effective upset stomach relief I've ever encountered." Then he looks at me and frowns. "But does that means you feel my queasiness, too?"

"I think I'm feeling exactly what you are now," I say. "I think we split our... somatosense between the two of us. My good feeling cancels out some of your yuckiness." I smile widely, thrilled with being able to actually *help* him.

"But... how?" he asks. "I'm not purposely passing any feeling to you."

I consider it a moment, but the answer seems pretty clear to me. I start tentatively, "I don't think you actually have to *try* to pass your pain. Because of the emotion that goes along with it. I can always tell if someone is hurting physically." I look down, disliking that I have relive this. It's been a long time since I thought about it. "It reaches outward, scrambling for relief. Emotionally, pain feels like... a person that can't swim being thrown into the deep end. Desperate. And if it's bad enough, it's the terror of being suffocated but never dying." My eyes are wet as I think about it and I wipe them with a free hand, looking away from him and stifling the memory of my mom that has become so clear all of a sudden. "Pain grabs on to whatever it can find. So yeah. Yours reaches for me even without you trying."

He sighs. "Well I'd like to argue that I can take it like a man, but after that it sounds worse to put you through the emotional torture."

I snort. "Yeah, a stupid man. Anyway, I don't have to try to pass my own feeling to you because pain is powerful enough to pull my somatosense into you all on its own. This new ability is pretty useful. It multiplies pleasure and divides pain. I should have been in the colorworld with you as soon as you started getting your infusion. Then maybe you wouldn't have thrown up all over me and ripped your cannula out."

"I did that?" he says, aghast.

"Yep. I wanted to punch you."

"You should have," he replies in wide-eyed dismay.

I rest my head next to him, so glad to have him back. "I'm over it. And now I can help you instead of just holding your bed pan."

He sighs, still a bit annoyed at me sharing his nausea. "I don't think they had this in mind when they invented the phrase 'in sickness and health.'"

I look up at him and chuckle. "Or a death-touch. Or mind-reading. Or crazy counting. Or hypno-touch-induced cancer."

"What does my counting have to do with testing our vows?"

I shrug. "I have no idea. But I'm not going to discount it as the possible cause of some future strife just because it *seems* straightforward."

"My Wendy," he sighs. "You've become quite the open-minded thinker these days."

"I learned from the best."

He puts his arms around me and squeezes. I expect him to conjecture more on this newfound ability or ask me more questions about his chemo and the hours he doesn't remember, but I notice he lacks his usual vim. His curiosity that knows no bounds doesn't seem to be able to make it up his steep hills of reason. It slides back down as if the way has become too slippery. He gets lower and lower.

"What are you thinking?" I whisper.

I can tell that speaking exhausts him, but then to my mind he says, *'Oh nothing positive.'*

A lump forms in my throat and anxiety intensifies the nausea I share with Gabriel in the colorworld. Gabriel is almost never down. I don't know what to say to this version of Gabriel.

'Tell me anyway,' I encourage softly.

'I hate this,' he replies. *'Putting you through this. I'm angry. At a past I can't change. At being rendered an invalid. I can't believe I vomited on you. And I know there is something else that happened that you won't tell me. I feel your distance. And I'm not sure I want to know what it was. Which makes me a coward.'*

Stunned by his perception, I take a moment to find words. "Distance? How so?"

'I don't know. I can just tell. It's like part of you is missing.'

I bite my lip. I had no idea I was acting different... And I don't want to tell him. He's going to feel awful. Crap, he probably picked all that up just now...

Sure enough, he groans. *'It's as bad as I imagine, isn't it? Is that what that mark on your cheek is? I know it hurts.'*

I put my hand to my cheek without meaning to. I forgot about that. We've been in the colorworld all this time, which means he had to have unfocused his eyes to see my face.

'Tell me,' he insists.

'You didn't mean it. You weren't yourself.'

"What did I do, Wendy?" he demands aloud now, command in every word.

"You just knocked me down in your rush to get to the bathroom," I say, wincing in preparation for his reaction.

He pushes away from me, forcing us both out of the colorworld, and sits up. "I did *what*?"

"Knocked me down," I repeat obediently, frightened by the darkness that settles over him as he takes on the full brunt of symptoms. I don't reach out to him, which leaves me confused. I should not be afraid of Gabriel, yet I can't help my automatic reaction.

He shakes his head, and collapses back into the mattress, gripping his stomach and gasping in agony a few times. "How did you get the bruise under your eye?" he demands, and though I know he is furious, I can no longer tell if it's directed at himself or me. It's just... rage. He's sinking back into delirium.

I leap out of bed and away from him. I buzz the nurse, heart pounding. For the life of me, I cannot calm myself down.

It's Gabriel, I tell myself. Only it's not. This is not Gabriel. This raging person is *not* Gabriel. And instinct is telling me to stay far away.

Backing into the corner, I wrap my arms around myself and cry. "Gabriel," I beg. "It's me. I'm sorry. I can't... help you. I'm sorry..."

But he is lost again, tossing and moaning in bed. He throws up again, this time all over himself, and I cry all the more at seeing him in such indignity. And I hate myself for being too afraid to help.

The nurse comes in. She takes one look at me, one look at Gabriel writhing, and then she calls out orders into the hallway.

By the time a male orderly runs in, Gabriel has already tried to get out of bed, only to fall to the floor. He grabs the leg of the bed table and flings it out of the way. It crashes into the wardrobe. The orderly fights with Gabriel to get him back in bed. A third person appears with a syringe, and she pushes it into Gabriel's IV line.

I'm nearly hyperventilating as tears and sobs fight for an exit. I slide down to the floor, put my head between my knees, and take deliberate breaths to calm down. I thought I'd gotten over this embarrassing habit, but I guess feeling threatened by the love of your life can create mental instability.

Being irritated at myself over this brings control quickly. Before I lift my head, however, I feel a hand on my arm. My *bare* arm.

"Don't touch me!" I yell, throwing my head up to see it's the nurse. "Don't ever touch me!" I yell, terrified of the familiarity of this moment.

She jumps back, jolted by my outburst. But alive. I watch her for a few seconds before relief floods me. She's immune. Collapsing against the corner as the adrenaline ekes out of me, unspent, I gasp, "Sorry. Just... Don't ever touch me. I'm... OCD."

It sounds so lame considering I just screamed at her, but it's all I've got.

"Are you alright?" she asks carefully. "We've got your husband sedated. He should be able to rest tonight. Maybe you should get some rest as well? It's been a rough day for you. Is there someone I can call for you?"

"Is that normal?" I demand. "Psychosis? He was in a rage. I have *never* been afraid of my husband. But that scared the shit out of me." Okay, so I *have* been afraid of Gabriel before today, but not because I thought he would get violent.

She hesitates but says, "I have personally never seen that. But chemo affects everyone differently. I'm going to make a note of it in his chart for the doctor in the morning."

"It better be a big *fat* note," I say.

"Is there someone I can call for you?" she repeats.

I puff out a breath, pushing the last of my own hectic thoughts back down. "No. I have a phone. I'll call someone."

She nods and goes back over to Gabriel, checking his vitals and then helping another nurse expertly change Gabriel's sheets, his gown, and giving him a sponge bath.

On wobbly legs, I find my way over to the futon where I collapse, reach for my phone, staring at it for a moment, deciding who to call. It's ten PM. Gabriel is unconscious, and I almost killed someone.

Holy hell. I almost killed someone. Sitting up, I dig in my bag for my extra pair of gloves and pull them on, instantly calmer. Better but exhausted. If Gabriel is sedated, I should probably just stay here and sleep.

When the nurses are finally done, I turn off the lights and snuggle into the futon, which really isn't very comfortable. But I fall asleep anyway, hoping that I won't have to relive today's events in my dreams.

15

*D*espite my heavy misgivings, the doctor decides to discontinue yesterday's drug but commence Gabriel's treatment the next day with a different drug. He says Gabriel's reaction, while he has never seen it occur so quickly, is not unheard of. He's not taking it as seriously as I'd like. The doctor orders anxiety meds prior to Gabriel's infusion in order to stave off possible 'psychological reactions' as if what I saw yesterday was merely a panic attack. I know panic attacks. That was not one.

Gabriel is still sleeping when they start his infusion—he still hasn't been coherent at all. Everything within me rebels, but what else can I do? Gabriel needs treatment. We need time. Chemo is the only option for that.

And so it begins. But this time symptoms start only thirty minutes into his infusion. First, he starts sweating. When I make the nurse aware of this, I can tell she is surprised. Chemo side-effects generally take a lot longer to kick in. But she doesn't seem inclined to worry. Instead she checks his vitals and notes on his chart that his heart rate is somewhat elevated.

Once the sweating stops, he gets a fever, which the nurse gives him something for. Then his right leg starts twitching. After watching this for an hour, I can't stand it anymore. I put my hand on his skin and channel us into the colorworld.

Gabriel is not fully awake, so what I pick up from him is foggy. He's not in pain at least, so I let go. I don't want to risk anyone touching me again so I put my glove back on.

Not long after this, as I'm listening to his vitals like I do every so often, I sit up and look at the clock. I count his heartbeats. And then I buzz the nurse.

"His pulse is elevated," I tell her. "Like 120."

She takes his pulse. "Has he mentioned any shortness of breath?"

"No. He hasn't woken up."

"He hasn't woken up?" she says, surprised. "At all?"

I shake my head.

"Have you tried to rouse him?"

"No," I say, more anxious at her concern.

She looks at his IV. It's three-quarters of the way done. "See if you can wake him. I'm going to page the doctor. He hasn't been given any sedatives so he shouldn't be out this long. And that heart rate is a bit high."

I stand up immediately and start shaking Gabriel vigorously. "Please. Wake up, Gabriel," I say, my voice catching on terror.

Nothing.

I keep shaking him. Talking to him. Pleading with him.

At last, his eyes flutter open and he looks at me groggily. I smile widely. "Gabriel! Thank goodness. How do you feel?"

When he just furrows his brow at me in confusion, I say, "Nevermind. I can check." And then I channel myself into the colorworld.

No pain. That's good. But he's becoming more agitated by the moment.

"What is it?" I ask, scooting his legs over a tad so I can sit down.

His eyes flash to his legs and then to my face. *'Wendy. My legs! They're numb!'*

My mouth opens and I look at the outline of his legs under the sheets. "You... you can't feel your legs?" He must be wrong. I reach out and pinch one of them, hard.

He doesn't flinch, and being in the colorworld with him, I feel nothing.

'Wendy... one other thing,' he thinks to me, swallowing back panic that flutters in my own stomach.

"What?" I ask, terrified of what he's going to say next.

"Why can't I hear you?" he asks loudly.

***

"Deaf?" Mike says. He puts his hands on his hips, head bowed. I've come to recognize this as his worried stance. He steers clear of my emodar so I have to rely on body language.

I turn back to Gabriel, who is sleeping, and gently squeeze his hand. "Side-effect of the chemo. Likely permanent," I say evenly, although inside I'm furious at Mike. "And the numbness indicates nerve damage. He's scheduled for an MRI on Monday morning."

"How much of that crap did they give him?" Mike asks in an accusatory voice, as if *I* was the one that did the administering. "And Monday is three days away!"

I try to breathe in calm but even the air tastes hot and angry. "An average first dose, Mike. And Monday is the earliest they could schedule him. Plus, he's likely to have more damage between now and then until the drugs get out of his system."

I don't know if I'm too far gone for another breakdown or just really tired, but I'm livid at Mike for paying a visit this late. It's 3 AM. Not that I was sleeping. We're in the ICU now, and there are lots of monitors to watch. Gabriel had to be put on oxygen, and his pulse is still elevated. He hasn't been awake since earlier today when he told me he couldn't hear.

"So they do a different drug then," Mike says.

"They already did that. Besides, he's got to recover some first," I say. I think I hate Mike. I know I should be attempting to translate why it is Gabriel is reacting so poorly to chemo and if there may be an alternative way to safely treat him, but my brain is on auto-pilot survival mode. All I know is hypno-touch is to blame. And it's up to me to fix it. And Mike is nothing but an infuriating distraction.

"You need to sleep," Mike says after several minutes of blessed silence.

I ignore him.

"I'll stay with Gabe," Mike says. "Look, I know you don't like me, but this is my brother. What do you think I'm going to do? *Not* take care of him?"

I glare at him and then turn my back to him again. I'd like to ask him where he's been all day, why he's only just *now* paying a visit. But I don't want to argue with him. I'm glad he wasn't here to see me fall apart anyway.

"You're being idiotic," Mike says. "I thought you were supposed to be figuring this thing out. Research and all that bull you promised? How are you going to do that in your state?"

My shoulders slump a tiny bit. He's right about that. But what if something happens while I'm gone?

I don't know. I can't think beyond my trepidation over Gabriel's reaction to the drugs. And every time I try to think about it, my mind hits a block. I am utterly incapable and stupid for ever having thought I could do this. *If Gabriel can't handle chemo, how will you keep him alive long enough to save him?* The inevitability threatens to send me into an anxiety attack, so I have to force my thoughts elsewhere. Besides, if I stay in this room with Mike for a second longer I'm going to start screaming at him. And he clearly has no plans to leave.

I close my eyes. I don't want to think about any of this right now. I want to be asleep.

Standing abruptly, I say, "Fine. But you call me if *anything* changes. Got it?"

I don't wait for an answer. I brush past him, picking up his hollowed-out worry.

***

Three hours. That's all I got in the sleep department. I don't feel rested even a little. But maybe I *would* if Mike hadn't just called to tell me Gabriel had a seizure.

"Hold it together," I coach myself softly as Robert's driver shuts my door. It's probably a good thing I'm not driving. I'm on the edge of hysteria.

"Hold it together," I say again, but this time my voice gets higher and I bite my lip, hard, focusing on the pain of it so I don't have to experience the constriction caused by unintelligible, terrified imaginings. Like arriving at the hospital and finding Gabriel dead.

"Please no," I whisper, grinding my palms into my eyes. I can't take this. The stress is going to suffocate me.

I reach out then, out of habit, to pick up the driver's emotions. He's a little concerned and curious, which is *way* better than what I'm feeling. Unfortunately, my rampant fear won't be ignored. It's like a twitchy leg, heavy and demanding in the background. I need a bigger crowd, one to get lost in to take the edge off for a while so I don't lose my sanity.

"No go, Wendy," I tell myself, shaking my hands out like it might dispel my frenzied thoughts. This time, I must endure it. I can't run away, and that means memories of my mom rush forward. If I'd spent any time thinking about it before now, I would have remembered how poorly my mom did with chemo. All the times she was hospitalized, it was because of chemo side-effects. Yet she lived for nine months after diagnosis. But that was because of surgery. She had a double-mastectomy right off the bat and that bought her quite a few healthier months. In Gabriel's case, however, surgery can't be done.

I put my head in my hands. I need Gabriel awake so he can figure this out. What do we do if he can't receive chemo?

The bigger question is will he even survive long enough to get a chance to think about it?

When I arrive at the hospital, I leap out of the car and dash for the doors. Once I reach ICU, I slow, and my hand automatically moves to the incessant pain in my side. Mike and my uncle are outside Gabriel's cubicle. I hear lots of movement going on within. Ignoring Mike, I look at Robert expectantly.

"He's in a coma," Robert says. "They think it's due to lack of oxygen. The drugs lowered his red blood cell count too much. They're giving him a transfusion."

Heart catching in my throat and then dissolving until I can't perceive it anymore, I look from my Uncle Moby's kind face to the tiled floor. I consider sitting down right here, but the prospect doesn't sound as inviting as it usually does because my body is so restless. Shifting my line of sight upward to the flimsy curtain in front of Gabriel's door, I can't figure out what to do with myself. Utterly helpless, I'm incoherent. Like I'm drowning in emotion. The pressure weighting my chest ties itself there more firmly.

The bottom edge of the curtain flutters slowly, and with my superb eyesight I watch it closely, purposely focusing on the loose weave of the light blue fabric, stretching and bending. Such drastic microscopic movement is involved in the simple shift of the curtain. How is it, I wonder, that I can see so many details that nobody else can see, watch the collaborative effort of thousands of tiny cotton fibers, yet I couldn't tell that hypno-touch was going to harm people? Why on earth did I imagine changing the appearance of a person's soul wouldn't have devastating effects?

Compassion reaches out to me in my moment of intense guilt and I look up. Robert, I now realize, is close enough to read. And his peaceful steadfastness grows by increments. Gently it works its way past the desolation banging inside my head. Wanting more of what Robert offers, I move forward and tuck my face into his shoulder—he's about half a foot taller than me. He puts his arms loosely around me and knows words aren't necessary. I breathe him in, inhaling past his surface scent of ginger. Beneath that is his intrinsic scent, one of the sweetness of decaying leaves of fall, a scent I know becomes even more poignant in the colorworld.

As his stillness surrounds me, the strain dissolves until anguish becomes clear, and then tears sprout from my eyes. And the sobs are close behind. But it's a blessed relief to cry. It has never felt so good. The last three days I've watched and waited, full of anxiety and trepidation, dreading the inevitable outcome, thinking I would cry then. But I need to now.

Robert hugs me a little more tightly, and I wet his button-down shirt. He relaxes, as if he's been waiting for me to cry.

Releasing him finally, I give him a small, close-lipped smile. "Thanks for letting me use your shirt as a tissue."

He chuckles softly. "Thank you for considering me tissue-worthy." The warmth he emanates is a balm from my head to my toes and I have no desire to be away from that feeling.

"Where'd Mike go?" I ask, noticing his absence.

"I believe he's picking up his mother. I understand she is flying in this morning."

My shoulders fall. Oh no. What am I supposed to say to Maris?

Robert reaches out and squeezes my arm. Reading my expression, he says, "Wendy, I believe Maris is a strong individual. She will be more of a help to you than a burden."

I guess Robert did meet her that one time at my wedding... I also wonder briefly if it's his fortune-telling that has given him that information. And then I berate myself for always jumping to that conclusion rather than assuming Robert is simply perceptive.

A couple of nurses come out from Gabriel's cubicle then. "Mrs. Dumas?" the shorter one says, looking at me questioningly.

"Yeah. That's me," I reply.

"You can sit with him while his transfusion finishes. We've been monitoring his brain activity and he's still been having minor seizures. We just gave him anti-seizure meds, but we're hoping that as his oxygen saturation goes up, they'll stop. We have to wait and see."

"And this is from the chemo?" I ask.

"Most likely," the short, dark-haired woman says. "We'll discontinue treatment until he's healthier."

I cross my arms and walk past her into Gabriel's tiny room. I sit on the small stool and roll it over to his bed. I reach for his hand. His face is half covered in an oxygen mask. I don't turn when I hear Robert's quiet steps.

"We can't do chemo anymore," I say. "These side-effects are happening too quickly, too severely."

"Yes, I got a call about that this morning," Robert says. "From Carl."

I turn to look at him, expectant.

"He suggested looking at his past case files to figure out a course of treatment," Robert continues. "So I brought them with me. Mark has them. He's out in the waiting room when you're ready. That's how I ended up here this morning. I was on my way to deliver them to you and Gabe."

I turn back to Gabriel. I channel myself into the colorworld to look at him. I don't sense his body or emotions at all, so he is definitely asleep. *A coma.* His life force looks the same, but I can't decide if I should be happy about that. "That's a good idea," I reply, my voice devoid of enthusiasm. I am sure the files are going to tell me exactly what I already know: chemo will kill him even faster than cancer.

16

"It's still blurry," Robert says, "but you pulled a lot more detail out of my vision the last time. Maybe you can do it with this one, too."

I drag a chair around Robert's desk to sit next to him. Robert's call could not have come at a better time. Gabriel had his MRI this morning and it delivered the only good news of the weekend: he doesn't have any bleeds. The bad news is far more plenteous. He still isn't awake. He's also had three more transfusions in three days to keep up with the endless destruction of his red blood cells caused by the chemo. The doctor is flabbergasted. His regimen isn't supposed to target red blood cells. They give him drugs to combat the side-effects only to find that the side-effects of *those* drugs cause problems. Right now they're worried about decreased kidney function. But I'm over the 'impossibility'. Hypno-touch cancer doesn't work the same way as typical cancer, therefore it can't be treated the same way. I've had Ezra looking through the files because I'm too frazzled and I'm too inept to make medical recommendations. And Ezra is good at spotting patterns to draw conclusions.

Meanwhile, I've been sitting through hours of Gabriel's inhales, exhales, and heartbeats along with Maris' constantly mouthed prayers. She may think her less than a whisper is silent, but it's pretty much deafening to my sensitive ears after forty-eight hours of it. I need Robert's vision. Because so far I am *failing* at what I promised to do.

I rest my gloved hand on Robert's arm and pull myself into the colorworld, taking a little longer than usual because of the state of my mind.

The vision appears slowly, but even as Robert struggles to bring it into focus for me, I gasp, knowing exactly where it is.

"The compound!" I say. "Just outside the research building." I know the tree that has lost its leaves in the vision, too. I sat on the ground, leaning against it while Gabriel sat across from me. Not only did he count the leaves on that tree to demonstrate his counting ability, he told me funny stories about his parents after I lamented Robert's influence on Ezra and my misgivings about being at the compound.

"It's a good thing I can show you my visions, isn't it?" Robert says, leaning back in his plush leather office chair. "I would never have recognized it."

"Why would the answer be there?" I ask, confused. "I was there for weeks! What am I supposed to do? Go there?" I don't like where this is going. Maybe asking for Robert's help wasn't such a good idea after all.

Robert is far less concerned than me. Clicking a pen, he rolls his chair toward one of his desk drawers and takes out a small but thick journal with white lettering engraved on the cover that I don't catch. He starts writing. "What would you like to do?" he asks without looking up.

My eyes widen. "Do? Storm the compound with a SWAT team and put Carl and Louise in jail."

"I meant, what would you like to do about the vision?"

"I know that," I snap. Then I sigh. "Sorry, Uncle Moby. That wasn't directed toward you. But the only reason I see to go to the compound is for Louise and Carl. I swore to myself only a week ago that I wouldn't seek them out for help and now your vision is telling me I should—"

"The vision isn't telling you to do anything," he interrupts, closing his notebook and replacing it. "Don't make guesses about *meaning*. As for Louise and Carl, I think you're mistakenly discounting them. There is no doubt that the situation you are in right now is exactly what they hoped for."

"Which means I should play along? Go beg them for help?" I say, incredulous. "Why? I don't have anything to hold over their heads that I'm willing to exchange for information. I want to be free of them. I don't want to think about them and wonder and guess at the things they *haven't* told me. I don't want to *need* people like them. I can't best their kind of crazy."

Robert crosses an ankle over his knee as he swivels around to face me. Fingertips meeting fingertips that rest under his chin, he looks at me for a long time, and he's somewhat expectant, waiting for me to speak. But he's also working through something, analyzing it maybe, so I wait. Silence and Robert go together and I have a great deal more patience for it now.

But I have nothing to say. My brain hasn't been working at full capacity since Gabriel had his first fateful chemo infusion. It's like he took half my brain with him into his coma.

"Let's go visit Briona," Robert says at last—and somewhat abruptly. And then he uncrosses his legs and stands up.

"Who?"

Robert doesn't answer, but holds an arm out to me like a Victorian gentleman. It's something I might expect Gabriel to do based on the sort of old-school mannerisms he uses to put on the charm, but on Robert it's more natural and adds to his persona of agelessness. It occurs to me that Robert seems both old and young at the same time. I have no idea what his age actually is.

Without a word, I stand and take his arm lightly. He leads me out to his lobby, telling Lacey he'll be back in time for his two o'clock meeting.

We step into the elevator, Robert still not releasing my arm, and he says conversationally, "Did you know I ended up writing that letter to you back when it was just you and Ezra because of my visions?"

"Really? What was the vision?"

"It wasn't *a* vision. It was many. I very rarely use only one vision for anything."

"You're using only one *now…*"

He doesn't answer, and I wonder to myself if that assumption is wrong. I actually have no idea how exactly Robert came up with that vision of the compound. After several moments of silence, I say, "Are you going to tell me about writing the letter?"

He glances at me with a raised eyebrow, his expression mischievous with a slight curl to his lip. I've never seen that look on him before. He seems… lighthearted. "No," he says.

The elevator dings and opens. Robert holds out his arm again and I tentatively take it. He's being awfully cryptic.

As we walk down the grey carpeted hallway, Robert is so calm that I can't properly read anything else from him. I want to interrogate him about his visions, but I restrain myself. There has to be a point to all this; I need to be patient.

"Here we are," he says as we reach an open door. Robert knocks on the casing. "Briona, do you have a moment?"

"Fah yuh, of course, Missa Rob," a Jamaican accent says. It belongs to a wiry woman sitting at a desk. Her smile is the first thing I notice. Her skin is so dark that her brilliantly white, perfectly aligned teeth stand out like lights. Her hair is short, put into a bunch of little twists that stick out almost an inch all over her head, kind of funky and cute at the same time, especially because she's also wearing a tailored pantsuit. I don't remember her from when I worked here, and I'm sure I would have. Her expressive eyes land on me and her smile gets wider. "An who might dis be?"

"Briona, this is Wendy, my niece." Robert says. Then he looks at me. "Briona transferred here from our D.C. office."

"Hi," I say, glancing around the sparse office that overlooks the street. She obviously hasn't had time to personalize it yet. "Sorry to barge in on you while you're working."

"Reespek, Miss Wendy. Deh is nuh such ting as barging when de door is open," she replies, coming around to shake my hand with both of hers. The glove doesn't phase her either. She's genuinely pleased. "An nuh such ting as barging when Missa Rob is de one knocking."

Robert points me to a chair and Briona returns to her side of the desk. "Wa a gwaan?"

"Briona, I'd like you to tell Wendy about the Obeah woman," Robert says.

Briona's eyebrows arch, and she puts her elbows on her desk and clasps her hands, glancing quickly between me and Robert. "Yuh sure bout dat?"

"Yes," he says.

She nods and turns her attention to my bewildered expression. "My best bredren in college was into dis Obeah ting an he wanted mi to let dis scientist hypnotize me. De ooman said it would help mi sickle-cell disease, zeen?"

"A woman wanted to… do hypno-touch on you?" I ask, my eyes wide, but then my shoulders slump as I recognize what this means for the woman. She must be one of Robert's charity cases.

"Yes. That's wah they called it. But it didn't work on mi disease."

"But something else happened?"

She nods. "The Scientist a put Obeah pon mi."

"Uh… excuse me?"

"A spell," she clarifies. "She put a *spell* on mi. In mi culture, wi call dat Obeah."

"What kind of spell?" I ask, certain she must mean that she has a life force ability.

"Mi see death."

More confused than ever, I look up at Robert, but he has mysteriously disappeared. I turn back to Briona and say, "I'm sorry. I don't follow."

"I see when death is near yuh," she says slowly.

"How?"

She puts her hands flat on her desk and looks down at them as she speaks, "When someone come close to mi, mi knows it."

I stare at her for a few silent moments, wondering several things, not the least of which is whether she senses *my* imminent death. "So you know when someone is going to die?"

She shakes her head. "Nah exactly. I know when someone will come near it. Sometimes dey die. Sometimes dey dohn. Ah up to di future." She looks at me directly. "Are yu like Missa Rob? Yuh naa waan know when death a nearby?"

Why did Robert bring me here? To find out from this woman if I'm going to die as a result of following through on his vision?

I wave a hand. "Isn't everyone near death all the time?"

"Yu a smart lady." She grins. "Some times neara dan oddas. I sense ow close at de time."

"Well I already know I'm near death. I don't really need anyone to tell me."

She looks at me with consternation and opens her mouth to speak but then closes it.

I have no idea what her face means. And she's too far away to read very well. But I swear I don't want to know. I have enough probable deaths to worry about without *also* freaking out about my own and how imminent it might be. "So this woman you met…" I say. "She had long silver hair?"

"Yuh know har?"

"Unfortunately."

"At di time wi met, De Scientist was suh close to har death, she wers all darkness."

"Who is the Scientist?"

"De ooman. Shim ah till alive?"

"As far as I know."

She nods pensively. "When I told har, she lost har mind. Locked harself inna har ouse fah a week. She paid mi fah years afta dat to watch fah har death all di while. She neva went anywhere without consulting mi first. I was har leash and she was usually tied up. I got tired of it, doh. Ah hawd ting tuh be around suh much fear. But when I tried to leave, she locked mi up. It wers Missa Rob who gat mi wey."

"You worked for Louise for *years*?" I say, shocked.

"Louise… I call har De Scientist. She wers always getting har hands inna Obeah."

"Obeah…" I say. "Spells?"

"Ah like wah yuh call voodoo."

I chuckle. "Voodoo. Yeah, that's about right. So you knew Carl then?"

"Who is dat?"

"I mean Kevin... He went by Kevin maybe?"

"Ah yes. Missa Kevin. Poor sad mon. Obeah ooman spelled his mind."

"Spelled his mind?"

"I mean she controlled him wid fear."

"How so?"

"Missa Kevin was always afeard. Looking ovah his shoulda like di debil himself was behine. But he wers right. Dat ooman wers de debil's demon. Dem deh two... carry on like bredren but neida trusts de udda. It wers him who planned to kill De Scientist when I met har. I warned har, but I wish now dat mi hadn't."

"Kevin planned to kill Louise?" I say, stunned.

"Back den, yes. Dey neva did trust each udda. I tink yu would call it er necessary alliance."

"An alliance from who?"

"Mi uh suh sure. Dey didn't tell mi much. But I tink deh yeyes wers too red."

"Their eyes were too red?" I ask, confused.

"Jealous of each udda," she clarifies. "Dey were both bandulu. And when yuh are dat bad, yuh duh nah know ow to trust anudda. Yu always tink demma outa to get yuh. Paranoid, zeen?"

"Oh..."

"Dat was why I wanted to leave. It was neva... comfortable. Being between dem. And neva knowing wah was going on wit de science."

"Seriously," I mumble in agreement, pondering this new information about Carl and Louise. After a while, I say, "Is there anything else I should know about Louise? And Kevin?"

"Ah depends pon wha yuh waan fi know."

I shrug, propping my elbow on the arm of my chair. "What they were after maybe?" I guess I kind of know, but it sounds like Louise and Carl may have had different ideas if they didn't trust each other.

"De Scientist and Missa Kevin spent all de while searchin. De wers looking for sinting. Ah had sinting to do wit Missa Kevin's dawta. When De Scientist waan fi spell him wit fear, she would remind him what would happen ef dey didn't find har—his dawta. Missa Kevin always wers guilty. Mi dohn know why exactly, but mi think wers sinting er long time ago, an ah gat de feeling his dawta was inna daanja. An he needed fi save har. But mi dohn think De Scientist waan har fah dat. She waan sinting

137

else. Missa Kevin's dawta wers jus a ransom she used against him."

Briona's words stir something unexpected within me. I didn't know I cared whether Carl thought of me as his daughter or not. I never got the impression that he *did* see me that way. At all. He has always been laser focused on his agenda, thinking that I *belonged* to him by virtue of relation. Just how strong *is* Carl's guilt? Most of all, how much of the Carl I've met is a product of Louise's manipulations—which I know well—and how deep have those manipulations gone? Was this why Robert wanted me to talk to Briona? To find out more about what makes those two tick?

"Thanks, Briona," I say quietly, fingering the cuff of my sweater.

Briona is on the edge of my emodar, so it surprises me when she gasps. "Jah!" Then she slides her chair back. Her eyes scan the length of me, seeing something she didn't before. "Yuh!" she breathes. "Yuh a di dawta!"

I hold up my hands in surrender. "Yeah. That's me. I take it there's a resemblance?" I wrinkle my nose at that.

She gets a hold of herself finally and rolls back forward. "Ah sorry. Yu took mi by surprise." She glares at the empty doorway. "Dat Missa Rob! Ramping his Obeah cards!" She shakes her head, though I don't think she's truly upset, just shocked. "I should ave known when he brought yuh inna here and asked mi tuh tell yuh tings him neva waan know."

"Don't worry. He didn't tell me who *you* were either."

She smiles. "Him ah a good mon. Always know mod an he says."

"I'm figuring that out." I stand up. "Thanks for your time, Briona. I hope... Well I hope I'll see you again soon." *So I can save your life.*

"Any time, Wendy," she says. Before I can turn to go, she adds, "Yuh are Missa Rob's niece? By blood?"

I nod.

"So Missa Rob is... Missa Kevin's bredda..." she says, taking it in. "Dat Missa Rob and his crazy Obeah..."

"Bye, Briona," I say as I leave. I see Robert down the hall next to the elevator, on the phone. He spots me immediately and wraps up his conversation as I approach him.

Shaking my head and clucking my tongue when I get closer, I say, "You are quite a trickster, Missa Rob."

He suppresses a grin, but it shines through the rest of his face anyway. "I take it you had an enlightening conversation?"

"You would know."

"No, actually. I don't know." He pushes the elevator's up button.

"You don't know that Briona worked for Louise and Carl? You expect me to believe that? She said *you* rescued her."

"Oh I know she worked with Louise. But when we met, I didn't ask any more questions than necessary."

When we step back into the elevator, I put my hands on my hips. "Okay. What is all this about? You were telling me about your vision, and then when I told you I didn't want to do it, you suddenly wanted me to meet Briona. On the way down here you tell me about the letter you wrote to me months ago and you refuse to explain anything about it. I hope you don't expect me to think that question was random. That's not you... And then you disappear while Briona's talking to me. And now you're acting like you have no idea what she said to me."

Robert presses the emergency stop button and turns to look at me. He clasps his hands behind him uncomfortably, and I sense he is about to tell me something he hasn't told many people before. "Wendy, do you trust me?"

"Of course I do."

"Do you trust me enough to not have to know everything?"

"What is that supposed to mean? Are you saying you are keeping even more things from me to *protect* me? Uncle Moby, that's—"

"Did you *listen* to me?" he interrupts somewhat pleadingly. "Did you *really* listen when I told you what my ability enables me to do?"

"Yes," I assure him.

"Did you get a chance to tell Gabe?"

"Of course."

"What conclusions did he draw?"

"Uhh," I say, lifting my shoulders. "I don't know. We didn't have an in-depth conversation about it. He was kind of preoccupied though... getting the diagnosis and... other things." I actually told Gabriel the same day we discovered somatosensory sharing in the colorworld. We were occupied pretty much the entire rest of the day, and when I told Gabriel about the conversation, I think I left out important details and the proper excitement because I was still so much in awe over what I was able to do with my ability.

"That was my fault then," Robert sighs. "Gabe is such a thorough thinker that I didn't entertain the idea that he might not come to the right conclusions." Robert looks up at me. "It wasn't my intention to confuse you. Allow me to clarify."

"Please do," I say, folding my arms but then subsequently letting them fall so I don't look on guard against Robert, especially since he is about to tell me something he's uncomfortable with.

"You understand the basics of filming, right? How moving pictures are made? Many still image frames displayed to the viewer within a short span of time?"

I nod, thinking of cartoon flip books.

"My visions come as still frames, but as I told you before, they fluctuate depending on what's on my mind. The more my thoughts roam, the more visions I get. You've dealt with complicated decisions in your life. You know how much time you spend analyzing possible courses of action. With each option you imagine what the outcome will be. In fact, you weigh outcomes, deciding what set of consequences you can live with. You might spend days stressing over a problem because you understand that analyzing every angle is important if you're going to come up with the best course of action, right?"

I think my face blanches as what he's saying clicks, but it's so... unbelievable. "You're saying... it's theoretically possible for you to piece visions together so as to be able to see the future in... more dimensions? More like a movie instead of one frame? That can't be easy... It would take a lot of skill, right?" Of course it would. But Robert has obviously had *years* of experience.

"I am extremely selective about what I expose myself to," Robert says, ignoring my conclusion, but I can tell that I'm on target. "I rarely watch the news, listen to the radio, and I almost never form close relationships. In fact, this familial relationship I've started with you, Ezra, Kaylen, and Gabe is very much outside my comfort zone. To have contacted you as I did back in May was... life changing for me. Prior to that time, staying away from you and Ezra and Leena was about more than simply abiding by Leena's decision. I have avoided anything that might cause me to form personal attachments. It is easier to know I'm being objective about my decisions when I can treat everyone as equal priorities. No favorites. Otherwise, the temptation I face at all times is more than I want to endure."

With my lips parted in surprise, I think I am starting to get what Robert is saying. "I did think of what you might be able to do, but I think I didn't take it far enough. I also never considered what you might do to avoid *wanting* to get visions. You're saying personal relationships tempt you to break your rules?"

"Strict rules I can follow. But there are far more gray areas that cause me to ask questions I have no answers to. The fact remains that I have the capacity to shape the future. I can shape the lives of others—change their course entirely. But as much of the future as I can see, I still cannot see it all. And what I *can* see, there are things I want desperately to change. But I told you before, every present, past, and future of every person is connected. I change one, I change all, and I don't know enough to have that kind of say in what direction the future will take. The future is… not something you should ever wish to know. It is a burden, Wendy. The worst kind of burden and one you can never imagine until you have actually felt it."

"Are you saying my future is bad?" My body tenses with dread over the possibilities. I'm already in the middle of bad. I can't handle something worse right now.

Robert frowns, frustrated. "You're missing the point, yet your question demonstrates what I mean. The future is neither good nor bad. It is simply… circumstance. And it's natural to want to craft our circumstances in a way that we think will bring us happiness. But circumstance has no control over happiness. Happiness does not lie in the future, Wendy. It is right here. Right now. *Fear* of the future is what ruins happiness, and I do not want yours ruined."

After several pondering moments, and still slightly confused, I say, "Then how do you ever decide when to act on a vision? Why did you decide to help me at all?"

He looks at me with eyes whose depths speak of years of weary effort. The wisdom I usually see there is overshadowed by exhaustion that tugs compassion from me so hard that my eyes begin to water. "Because I am only a man," he whispers. "Never forget that. I am only a man. And I have done my best with what I know. And I will continue to do my best. But now you all have given me a family and it will become even harder. That's why I left Briona's office. I brought you there because I wanted you to understand how much more powerful you are than Louise. Louise did not turn left or right without Briona to predict the probability of her death. I believe that is why she failed for so long at finding you. She spent too much time avoiding death. Louise would have been forever content to govern her every action that way. That is weakness. It is the weakness we are all subject to. So when Briona began to tell me her story, I cut her off as soon as I learned what she could do. I never learned Carl was alive from her because I didn't listen to her or wonder long enough to figure it out. On purpose. Someone like Briona presents too much temptation for me. She's a wonderful woman. But her ability and mine are a terrible combination. I avoid a lot of things for this reason. Quite frankly, Wendy, I have enough to think about. I *must* control my wants so they do not control *me*. So when I say there are things I will never tell you, and when I tell you there are things I don't want to know, trust that it is for good reason."

Once again, my perception of Robert shifts drastically. I take a step back, intimidated. The hand bar of the elevator hits my back and my hands find it. Where once Robert came across as a mousy sort of man, now he is more like a force I've only just come to understand exists. When you're a kid, gravity isn't something you acknowledge. And then one day you find out that gravity is what literally holds everything together and you wonder why such a question never occurred to you. Remembering his mention of the letter he wrote to me months ago, I think I get what he was saying: he contacted me for reasons yet unknown to me and he has had an active hand in my life since. I try not to wonder how much of my life is a result of Robert meddling with my future. I suppose a normal person would be completely *not* okay with this. Imagining that one person has that kind of power over your life is an extremely uncomfortable thought. But I am not normal. And I think Robert was counting on that when he told me. I know where his thoughts lie, where his heart lies. I know what his struggle is like. He has shared it with me in the only way he can—through his emotions. It is pain of a different kind. It is a *constant* struggle. How can I *not* trust someone whose agonized confession tells me how much care he puts into his every thought and action?

Despite the fact that Robert just said he keeps things from me, I trust him more than ever. He could probably tell me to have Gabriel wash in holy water to cure his cancer and I'd believe him. I also don't know whether to apologize for being a part of Robert's life now or to be glad that the man has someone. *Everyone* needs someone to love them, don't they? Even powerful forces of nature like Robert? Life, which I had finally started to understand, has suddenly become a mystery again as a result of, once more, recognizing my limited vision. Will I ever stop being surprised by what I see when I zoom out like this?

Robert sent me into Briona's office to talk to her about Louise's obsession with death. But I learned about Carl's weaknesses instead. Robert probably didn't plan on that, but I think that he's used to his visions taking him places he didn't expect. I would have thought that Robert could ignore visions that result from passing desires, but really, how can you? You can't *unsee* things. You act on everything you learn. I can't truly imagine what being in Robert's head must be like—in fact, it's kind of giving me a headache to try—but I get how hard it must be now, and how, even if he wanted to, Robert can't just *ignore* what he can do.

Tears spring forth more surely this time, the overflow of love and admiration I have for him. "I'm sorry, Uncle Moby."

"For what?" he says gently, stepping forward and putting a hand on my shoulder. Then he tilts his head. "Why do you call me that? I've been trying not to wonder, but even I can't help curiosity sometimes."

"I'm sorry for what you have to go through on a daily basis," I say. "And I call you Uncle Moby because you reminded me of the book *Moby-Dick* when I first met you." I smile at the memory of that day in his kitchen right after I'd had hypno-touch and gained lethal skin. "I always suspected there was more going on beneath the surface. And the more I know you, that becomes more right than I ever expected." I take two steps and throw my arms around a very surprised Robert, not worried in the least by my skin possibly touching his. There is no way this man is susceptible to my comparatively dim life force. I tighten my embrace, fiercely trying to infuse it with the loyalty I now feel toward him. I don't want him to be alone anymore. I am *not* sorry for being in his life. I used to think *I* was better off alone, too. But that's not true. When I come away, Robert's expression is full of relief, not over being alive—he must trust my judgment—but over my understanding and acceptance.

"I trust you," I say. "And I don't need to know everything. If you do weird things I'll know why and I'll let it go. I love you, Uncle Moby. And I'm glad you have a family now."

His gratitude and warming affection has made the elevator more cozy. I've never had a real father or male role model before, but I doubt they are quite like this. Robert is the most amazing human being I have ever met, and he's *my* uncle. And Gabriel… another incredible person. I really hit the jackpot on phenomenal family members. It hits me with a new wave of responsibility. I have to figure this out. I need to save Briona and everyone else so I can *deserve* all this.

"Having a family is definitely full of the ups and downs I expected," Robert says as he starts the elevator again. "To watch someone suffer up-close is very different from simply hearing about it. Those moments..." He exhales. "Moments are my enemy." He glances at me, spreads his feet and clasps his hands behind his back. "I want you to know this is why I've not visited Gabe much. And should you fall ill, it's likely that I'll be keeping myself very busy. It won't be for a lack of wanting to support you, but a need to occupy my ever-wandering mind and its incessant visions. To say now that I'll allow things to progress without my involvement is easy. To actually do it when the situation arises is quite another."

I sigh heavily. I wish Robert didn't have such a burden. "I will never allow you to violate your rules for my sake—or Gabriel's."

"Thank you," he says quietly as the door dings open.

I reach to take his arm as we step out, and we head back to his office. The need to be near him and soak in his wisdom is something that has taken me rather suddenly since our reunion. The quickness of my unconditional acceptance of him surprises even me, but I suspect the brilliance of his soul is something that my own can sense—even without seeing it in the colorworld. Everyone is attracted to light, I think, whether they realize it or not.

"Mr. Fletcher and his associates have arrived, Mr. Haricott," Lacey says as we reach her desk. "I showed them the conference room."

"Very good, Lacey. Let them know I'll be about ten more minutes."

Once we reach Robert's office, he removes his suit jacket and puts it over the back of his chair. He's a lean man, and I think he must run regularly, though I've never seen him do so. Not that I'm in on the mundane details of his life. I wish he didn't have to maintain such a distance from us. I'd like to know him better.

Robert pulls out the same book from earlier. He writes something in it quickly before returning it to its drawer. Seeing that I'm not sitting, he holds out a hand to my chair from earlier. "Let's talk about that vision."

Obeying, I say, "I guess I can't just ignore it. And Briona did give me some interesting information about Carl. I thought I wanted to avoid him but... maybe this is about saving Carl as much as saving Gabriel."

Robert closes his eyes and holds up a hand. Like a retreating wave tugging at your ankles while you wade in the tide, he culls stray thoughts with smooth and practiced effort. It's a pleasant feeling. He opens his eyes when he's done. "Rule number one of using visions is 'Assume nothing.' And furthermore, I'd still rather not know what Briona told you about Carl. My need to save him is still temptingly strong—He *is* my brother, after all. In my experience, for someone as far gone as Carl, the only way to escape that much darkness is to allow things to unfold for him as they will. Carl has to save himself."

"Okay," I say, stifling my need to analyze. I pull up a knee, lacing my fingers around it. "In the vision the leaves have almost all fallen. When does that usually happen in Big Bear?"

"I'll have someone double check for me, but I think trees started to drop their leaves last week. I'd say the end of the week. I won't be able to give you an exact date, but the vision is still blurry, which means it's still a fair amount of time out. It will continue to clear up as it gets closer."

"And storming the place to demand answers is out?" I ask, giving him a slightly joking, slightly serious look.

"No assumptions, Wendy," he says sternly. "Besides, if it were that easy, we could apprehend them today and do just that without going through a vision."

I slump. "Right." I bite my lip and think. "Louise never gives away information... So maybe... I'll overhear something if I stake out the place?"

"Now you're getting somewhere, but—" He hesitates over his next words, going back and forth over whether to finish his statement. He looks at me apologetically. "I know," he sighs, realizing I've been 'hearing' his indecision. "This next part is not something either of us will like."

I fold my arms and sit back in my chair. "You sent me to Briona to convince me to go, and now I'm convinced. I'd think you'd want to give me the best chance of making the trip there useful."

His face bunches up. "Wendy. You're assuming again. Assumptions about my motives. Assumptions about my hesitation. Stop that. I'm simply not used to getting visions for others, so I'm questioning how much to tell you about acting on them."

"You mean you didn't consider all that before you told me what the vision was?" I give him a cheeky grin. "Not much of an omniscient uncle after all, are you?"

Robert's mouth curves upward slowly. Then a bellowing laugh escapes him rather suddenly. My grin widens.

"Pardon my... ah... oversight," Robert says, steepling his fingers under his chin and looking every bit the part of an indulgent sage. On purpose.

I giggle at Robert's pun—*and* his expression.

Amusement becomes deep thought for several moments as he rests his arms on his chair and leans back, looking up at nothing. Robert's casualness today has not been lost on me. It feels so good to finally *know* him and to see that he finally feels at liberty to be himself around me.

"Here's what I can tell you," he says. "This is the original vision—not a compounded one. Original visions usually require my direct involvement in some way—or in this case *your* involvement. It usually means that in order to accomplish the goal, you have to be in the spot at the time, not merely overhearing something. It means your presence is necessary in some way to making things come about in the way you want."

I wrinkle my nose. "Fabulous. Kind of has me hoping Gabriel will stay asleep. Because he would *not* be a fan of that plan."

"People often think knowing the future would make life easier. But all it does is complicate decisions and add more responsibility." Robert sighs.

I know his frustration well. People—Louise and Carl specifically—think the colorworld ought to deliver the answers to all questions. And sure, maybe it does some of that. But mostly it *raises* more questions. The camaraderie I share with Robert at the moment over this has me exultant inside, imagining that in some way I may be living up to Robert's example and his trust in me. Exultant feels *so* good after so many days of emotional drudgery.

"Well we don't know exactly what it's about, do we?" I say. "And you did say *usually*, right? Not all the time? So I say we stake it out and see what happens. You know I'm willing to do whatever it takes. And if turning myself over to Louise temporarily is what it takes, I'm going to do it."

"I know," says Robert, sitting up, elbows on the arms of his chair. "But I insist on giving you protection to accompany you. Other than that, I leave it up to you as to how exactly to handle it. You have pretty good instincts. Trust them and not your emotions." He stands. "Now if you'll excuse me, I need to get to my meeting." He smiles at me. "It was good to talk to you, Wendy."

I hop and hug him again, instantly energized by it. "Sorry," I say when he stiffens a little, jolted again. "I'm a hugger by nature, and I'm actually positive I'm not going to kill you. Once you're in my hugging circle, you don't get to leave." I stand back and grin at him.

"It's a pleasure to be counted in your circle," he replies, and then I let him lead me out on his arm again. Just like that, Uncle Moby is a permanent piece of me.

17

$\mathcal{J}$ thought I'd appreciate silence in the ICU, but it's more ominous than peaceful. I think I'd prefer to have Maris back with her incessant praying. When she arrived several days ago, Mike had already explained everything to her, which meant I didn't have to, though I did worry about what spin he put on the story. Upon encountering me, Maris gripped my arms in her hands, stared up at me with those huge doe eyes she has, and said, "Mija, God will see him through this." After that, she was on her phone nearly the whole day with all her church friends who in turn rallied some kind of prayer group back in Bakersfield. Each one wanted to say a prayer with Maris over the phone. The chaplain has been by at least half a dozen times, and then the rest of the family over the phone... That was a spectacle. Sobs and intermittent prayers. Lots of "God willing" this and that. I left the room off and on all weekend, trying to be graceful, but the whole ridiculous show was getting to me. Gabriel is not a religious man and I *know* if he was awake he'd be telling Maris to take her prayers out in the waiting room at the very least.

But today she is gone for a little while. I didn't ask where she was going, but I'd like to think she recognized my agitation and decided to give me some space and some time alone with Gabriel. I even wore my pink tights—Gabriel's favorite—and my jean shorts in celebration of our alone-time. Chances are it will just be me at this date though, and that's depressing.

With Maris gone, I have nothing to capture my attention but monitors and vital signs and the absence of Gabriel's voice. I miss it so much. I lean forward in my chair and lay my head on Gabriel's bed, touching his hand with my own lightly. Like I have every time I've touched him since he came into the ICU, I go into the colorworld with him, assessing where his mind and body are at.

Still nothing.

My throat catches and I take his lifeless hand more firmly and tuck it under my chin—there is no longer any magnetism between our skin and this bothers me more than anything.

"Please wake up," I plead fruitlessly—and more out of habit than purpose. Four days of this and I am losing hope an increment at a time. Even with the prospect of Robert's vision, Gabriel may die before I ever complete it. I'm terrified of trying to do this without him and I hadn't recognized how much I depend on him until now.

Lifting my head, I watch his life force move around his body, looking exactly the same as I remember. It is only here in the colorworld that I get any assurance that Gabriel is still with me. He is just as present here as he has always been—his smell is strong and full of his essence.

"Come back to me," I say, leaving the contact of his skin so I can caress his life force and hear the music that our life force strands make as they glide past each other. I close my eyes as I do so, thinking there is no sound on earth more sweet than this. After a while I open my eyes and for probably the hundredth time observe the disarray of Gabriel's strands. They swirl and wind as if they are in a choppy current. Because I have nothing else to do, I begin to sweep his strands toward his chest methodically—partly for the sound but also in the vain hope that if I do it long enough his strands will move in the direction they are supposed to. I continue for quite some time, putting myself into a trance almost, lost in marveling over the fact that even though I can sweep the strands the same way, the sound changes entirely each time.

In my mind's eye I see the menagerie of the sky over my head in the colorworld that day I first saw it as Gabriel lay beneath my hands even then. I continue to push his strands toward his chest, capable of almost re-conjuring the wonder of that day, allowing his scent to wash over me entirely, filling me through my nose. Goosebumps dot my arms then, the thrill of connection quiet but no less sure.

All of a sudden, someone's skin brushes my arm—which is bare—but before I can react, a haze settles over me and I can barely lift my head off of the bed. Instinctively pushing it away as not my own, I look up to see Gabriel's hand resting on my arm. His eyes are fluttering as he struggles for strength to open them. That small movement crashes relief over me and tears rush forth such that I can't see him clearly anymore. Gripping his hand now in one of my own, I vigorously wipe my eyes with my other. But the tears keep coming and I cry like a baby, unable to get any words out for a while.

I think he tries to talk, but it comes out garbled. And he has an oxygen mask on so that complicates communication as well. We're in the colorworld, so I say mentally, '*Speak to me with your mind, Gabriel.*'

He closes his eyes.

I shake his shoulder. "No! Stay awake!"

But he doesn't respond. I shake him again, scared to lose him to sleep again. Still he doesn't open his eyes. Fortunately, his emotions say he's not completely unconscious.

'*Gabriel,*' I coax him. '*Please let me know you're listening. Remember you don't have to speak. Think the words to me just like this.*'

I wait for an unbearable amount of time. But in reality it's probably only a few seconds before I hear mentally, '*I hear you...*' The 'words' are communicated with a bit of confusion, but I'll gladly take them.

'*Yes! Gabriel, do you know where you are? And what's happening?*'

He struggles to wake, but he's so tired. His frustration grows, but all it does is tire him.

'*Gabriel, don't struggle so much. Don't try to move. Just focus on my voice. You're trying to do too much at once.*'

But he doesn't listen. Whatever I've said has sent him into instant panic. Adrenaline courses through him, shooting his mind with sudden alertness. His eyes flash open. "Wendy!" he shouts in a muffled voice through his face mask. And then his vital monitors start protesting loudly. The nurse will be here soon.

I put a hand on the exposed part of his cheek. "Shh. Yes, it's me. You don't have to talk. Use your thoughts. Think your words to me."

Another wave of panic. "I can't hear? I can't hear!" he yells. His chest heaves and sweat beads on his face. His heart races at a cringing pace.

Crap. I forgot about that again. I put hands on either side of his face and force his eyes on me. '*Calm down. Calm DOWN,*' I order him. '*Talk to me. This way. Stop fighting so much. You're putting too much strain on your heart and I don't want to lose you again.*' Although to his credit, alarm over the situation really woke him up.

'*Wendy. Why can't I hear anything? Why is it so hard to move? What is on my face?*'

"Mrs. Dumas!" a voice says as footsteps rush in behind me.

I hold up a hand before they can say anything else. "Let me calm him," I say. "He just woke up and he's afraid."

The nurse looks at the monitor worriedly, but his heart rate is already slowing. She comes over and checks something, but I pay no attention, instead explaining briefly to Gabriel telepathically what has happened to him in the last few days. Fear tries to break through his composure, his pulse bouncing up and then coming back down again. His trepidation surprises me. Being rendered disabled in any fashion is undeniably terrifying to him. I do believe I have discovered Gabriel's weakness. No wonder he hates hospitals.

He lays in silence for a couple of minutes when I'm done. He's doing a mental check, reorienting himself. I lay down beside him, holding his hand firmly. *'Relax,'* I tell him. *'I haven't heard you speak to me in days. I've missed you. Talk to me.'*

"I'll let the doctor know," the nurse says. "And I'm going to need to do some stimulation and tests to determine the extent of his paralysis."

"He still can't feel his legs very well," I say. "But he moved his hand earlier. And he still can't hear."

I don't think she takes me seriously, saying nothing as she exits the room.

Gabriel seems to have accepted my explanation of what's happening, although his mood sinks. Regretful inevitability settles over him.

'Spit it out,' I demand.

That one phrase I so often use lightens his melancholy. *'Can't keep a thing from you. A man has no privacy with you around.'*

'You knew what you were in for when you married me,' I reply, unable to restrain my exuberance over the fact that he is communicating with me with what seems to be his full faculties.

'So true. I'm bothered because I swore I wasn't going to do this to you—become useless.'

'Believe it or not, Gabriel, you couldn't help this,' I reply.

'I've always been a firm believer that the mind can overcome the body by sheer force of will. I failed at the very first sign of trouble. You, however, are entirely in control of yourself.'

I chuckle even though he can't hear. *'You act like you've been watching me the past four days. How would you know how in control I've been?'*

'It's in your emotions. If you'd been languishing, I'd know. You are as vivacious as the last time I remember.'

I squeeze myself close to him. *'I shut down when my mom was diagnosed. I am determined not to do that again.'*

'Wendy... am I dying?'

My stomach hollows.

'I'm sorry,' he thinks to me, picking up my reaction. *'I just... feel like I'm dying. And if I'm dying I want to know so that... I don't know. So I can be prepared.'*

I take a deep breath. *'You're dying. You've been dying. You have lung cancer, remember? But you just woke up from a coma that the doctors told me you had only a twenty percent chance of coming out of. And now that I can talk to you, I might have a chance of making this right. I need your help.'*

That was a lot harder to say than I thought it would be. I don't like putting so much pressure on Gabriel, but I have felt incapable of doing anything while Gabriel has been asleep. I need him. I'm lost without his confidence around.

This is exactly what Gabriel needs to hear. His intellect fires up, filling the mental space he shares with me. *'Tell me everything you've learned so far,'* he thinks.

So I give him every detail I can recall of the last few days, starting with his terrifying chemo symptoms—minus the knocking me over incident. He remembers none of it. I tell him of Mike's annoyingly mysterious in and out visits, Maris and her incessant praying—which elicits and audible grumble from him—as well as our conclusions about the lethal nature of chemo.

'It sounds like you're on the right track,' Gabriel replies. *'Ezra's a good man for the job. I'll need to have a chat with him. And I'll need a visit to the library.'*

'You are not *going to the library, Gabriel. You're in the ICU.'*

He doesn't like that. *'Then I expect you to bring the library to me. I can't be of use if I can't research.'*

'Believe it or not, that's actually possible!' I think to him jokingly. *'We call them computers. And these days computers can fit in one hand! And you can bring them anywhere!'*

'If I could move you would regret that snarky reply.'

I poke his side—which actually gets him to flinch.

'If my mother comes back, tell her I'm still in a coma,' he adds.

'No way! I am not putting up with that dog and pony show of hers another day!'

'But if you tell her I woke up, she'll think it's because of her prayers and I'll have to hear about it from now until next year!' he whines.

'You're saying you want me to lie *to her?'* I prod. *'I thought lying was beneath you... Oh wait, so you don't mind other people lying on your behalf?'*

'Fiiiine,' he replies and even the drawl comes through mentally. *'Thank heavens I woke up. I almost missed the pink tights.'*

I look down, having forgotten about them. I smile. *'I wore them for you. I planned to have a hospital room date with or without your eyes open.'*

'I try not to miss dates with beautiful women in pink tights.'

'I've missed you,' I think, squeezing his hand.

'What else can you tell me?'

I relay my day yesterday with Robert as accurately as I can. Though he shares his disapproval through his emotions when I get to the part about the vision, he is definitely enthralled overall. About Briona. About Robert's ability. His intellect moves like a bullet train and I involuntarily grip his hand harder to endure it.

'That is... possibly... the most incredible thing I have ever heard...' he thinks in wonder when I'm done.

'I was floored,' I reply.

'Then to think Robert has managed to maintain his moral character through all that is just... astounding! The man has earned his light rightfully.'

'Absolutely,' I agree heartily.

Gabriel wiggles his fingers, an attempt, I think, to squeeze my hand. *'Truly you and Robert are cut from similar cloth since you resisted the temptation to breach his rules. He offered you a wish. And you didn't take it.'*

'You would have done the same thing.'

'I'd like to think so... but you never know until you're faced with the possibility, do you?'

'True. But Robert... he hasn't just resisted it once. He's resisted over and over every day for years. Robert basically has to resist being a god among men every day of his life.'

Gabriel grunts. *'Discipline is what makes a god. Obeying those rules he has made for himself is the only way he's been able to be successful in the first place. If he hadn't, I have no doubt Robert would have self-destructed in some fashion years ago. Cheating isn't sustainable.'*

'Yes, yes,' I reply, waving a hand. *'I remember now. God doesn't go against the laws of reality.'* I smile as I remember Gabriel's lecture in the museum a few weeks ago about how reality would implode if God started poofing things into being. I had no idea I'd encounter the same novel concept twice within a two week period... The first time I heard it, it was just a theory. But Robert is a walking example of it.

'Try convincing my mother *of that,'* Gabriel snorts mentally. *'I declare, I shall never understand how religious people would rather believe God operates by magic powers possessed only by*

deity than by the beautiful simplicity of science. It's absurdly ironic that mankind claims God to be the most powerful being in the universe yet limits him or her by claiming he or she cannot operate within the very laws created by that supreme being! What kind of flawed system of reality is it that everything we see and experience cannot be comprehensibly explained? And what kind of benevolent god throws his beloved creations into an incomprehensible terrarium as he sends down magic beams to serve only a select few who deny the laws and beauty of his creation in favor of repetitious supplications for so-called 'divine interventions'? Foul play! Hogwash!'

'Okay, Plato. Calm down,' I tell him. '*Sheesh. Put you in a coma for four days and you come out a raving atheist.*'

'*That was decidedly not an atheist argument. That was an anti-religion argument. And Plato was not an atheist. He just had the good sense not to bring religion into a logical argument.*'

'*Well whatever it was, you lost me. I'd rather hear what you think of Robert's vision.*'

'*Sorry. My mother's religious devotions put me in a bad mood. And so does Robert's vision.*'

'*Yeah. But I'm doing it. I just need to figure out* how *to do it.*'

'*I can honestly say there is nothing about any possible plan that I like. Especially because it looks like you'll be carrying this out in a couple days and I can't even lift my head currently.*'

'*I was thinking about staking it out, seeing if I can overhear something.*'

'*Okay. Now that sounds better. You should have suggested that from the beginning.*'

'*I was willing to see if you had a better idea first,*' I point out.

'*No, it looks like you've had everything under control while I've been... indisposed. You are well on your way to accomplishing what you set out to do. I love you so much, Wendy. You're more amazing every day.*'

'*Let's not get ahead of ourselves,*' I say. '*We still don't know what the vision is about. Who knows if it will help me learn something about my ability that will actually help things? Just because things are looking good doesn't mean they will turn out the way they look.*'

'*Oh I* know *they won't turn out the way they look. I still can't say that my life will be saved in all this, but I can say you are most definitely going to accomplish something.*'

18

"*D*r. Altman, you are a very unpleasant man," Gabriel says, without a hint of animosity. But he has said the very thing we've both been thinking.

It's Wednesday; Gabriel woke up only yesterday and since then has changed over to a nasal cannula for his oxygen and found his voice. He has made incredible improvement just in the 24 hours since he woke up, able to move his arms and hands with concerted effort and wiggle his toes. If he concentrates really hard, he can bend his knee. He can even hear some. Not enough to understand people though. It turns out, however, that Gabriel can read lips. It's something that he picked up incidentally as part of his process for learning languages. There are apparently a great many things I still do not know about my husband.

Dr. Altman, the prestigious doctor Robert found, flew into town today and came by to consult with us about Gabriel's case. I think it's kind of useless. Gabriel will not be continuing chemo. But the appointment was scheduled last week and we might as well go through the motions since he's here already. But he has the worst attitude of any doctor I have ever encountered. I have no idea why he came when he so obviously doesn't want anything to do with us, let alone Gabriel's case. I hope Robert didn't shell out too much for him to come here.

Dr. Altman looks up from his tablet and I expect to see indignation there. Instead, he's completely apathetic. "I almost never give personal consults," Dr. Altman says, glancing back to his tablet, his glasses perched on the end of his beak-like nose. "So I haven't had much patient contact in many years. When Mr. Haricott contracted me to come here, he assured me you wouldn't mind my brusque methods, that you were only looking for treatment advice. Is that not the case?"

Gabriel and I look at each other, somewhat surprised, and he is the first to answer, "That is correct. We don't require whitewashing. But there is a difference between brusque and antagonistic. Since you arrived you have done nothing but complain about how you should never have been called in on such a case, how as soon as I reacted poorly to chemo, the appointment with you should have been cancelled. And despite the fact that I am actually improving and the chemo damage is being reversed, you continue to assert that there is no hope for me since I cannot tolerate treatment. Apologies if it offends you sir, but as a scientist my case is unusual and ought to interest you a great deal more. That you are not even a little curious as to why I reacted the way I did pins you, in my book, as someone disillusioned by your own field and too complacent to expend your brain any more than absolutely necessary."

"Dang!" I mouth to Gabriel, floored that he put it to Dr. High and Mighty like that.

Dr. Altman lowers his tablet, seeing us for the first time I think. His ears turn red, and I can feel the heat of his anger at Gabriel's words. I expect him to walk out or say something about us disrespecting him, but he doesn't. He just stands there all mad-like.

Finally, when his temper abates somewhat, he says tightly, "I assure you that cases like yours are not unfamiliar to me. I group them into a category I label anomalous due to their untreatable nature. I have had my eyes on almost every case of small-cell carcinoma in the last thirty years. I know their behavior inside and out. And I have looked for patterns in anomalous cases like your own and I assure you there are none, other than their untreatable nature. They are no respecter of age, region, or genetic predisposition. And they die far too quickly to gather any categorical data that might help future cases. And there are too few of them. I am sorry to say you are one unlucky man, Mr. Dumas. And that is just how it is. If we can ever manage to cure lung cancer in the more typical scenario on a consistent basis, that may be the day that cases like yours could have hope. Today is not that day."

Whoa. This dude sure knows how to take any hope a person has and grind it into the floor with his foot right in front of them.

I'm about to let my tongue loose, (since all of us are apparently being so *open* today), but Gabriel's sudden interest stops me. "How many other anomalous cases like mine?" he demands with wide eyes.

That was *not* what Dr. Altman expected, and for the first time it piques his curiosity rather than his irritation. "Forty-six in the last forty years."

Gabriel's mouth opens for a second as he thinks. Then he looks up. "Have most of them been more recent?"

"No. There are pockets, but they occur fairly consistently."

"And all of them—even the ones, say, thirty years ago—have behaved the same way?" Gabriel asks. "Untreatable due to treatment side-effects? Did they happen prior to forty years ago?"

"Yes to the first question, although every case varies in the body's reactions, but that's because we aren't clones of each other. And yes to the second question. Though my data is not as detailed for that time period so I couldn't give you numbers or what the earliest recorded case is. Treatments have evolved so much since the nineteen-forties that it's not helpful to use treatment data that is so old. But I have no doubt anomalous cases have been in effect since the birth of cancer—so, always." He removes his glasses. "I have to ask, Mr. Dumas, why do you want to know?"

"Is there any way to get my hands on those cases?" Gabriel asks. "I don't need names or personal information. Just the data."

Dr. Altman chuckles. "Why? Because you imagine you'll develop an effective treatment plan for such cases when I haven't?"

"Shall we wager it?" Gabriel says, a challenging curve to his lip.

My mouth drops open. I can't believe it. Gabriel is challenging the most prestigious small-cell lung carcinoma doctor in the nation to his own game.

Dr. Altman is highly amused, and not at all concerned. "Certainly. Stakes?"

"First, the terms," Gabriel says. "What is the life expectancy for anomalous cases?"

"Hard to say," Dr. Altman says, spreading his feet and rubbing his neck. He looks like he's enjoying himself for the first time since he walked in here. "Typical oncologists don't recognize cases like yours for what they are and continue with different treatments until they kill the patient. But since you are ahead of the game in that respect, you are guaranteed to live longer than those patients. So I suppose if we base it on how long you'll live if you go untreated…" He looks at us. "Which is what I recommend, by the way. It will give you the best quality of life for the longest time. Given your metastases, I give you two months, tops. But we're not talking about life expectancy. We're talking about effective treatment. You'll need to shrink your lung tumor by thirty percent to garner my attention. Because at the rate you're going, that's what will kill you first."

"Okay, so you agree to give me all of your data on past cases, and if I can shrink my lung tumor by thirty percent or more, you will concede defeat."

Dr. Altman looks like he swallowed something sour at the sound of the word 'defeat,' but he says, "Agreed."

"If I win, you will return the fee that Robert Haricott paid you for this consult," Gabriel says.

Dr. Altman chuckles. "If you win, I will do that *and* become your personal, exclusive on-call oncologist either until your remission or death."

Gabriel smirks. "You'll regret that level of cockiness, Dr. Altman. You had better start clearing your calendar."

I realize my mouth is still open and I shut it. I cannot believe what I'm hearing!

"There is one problem to this plan," Dr Altman says, one hand on his hip, but it's clear from his emotions that he knows exactly what the solution is. "If *I* win, you will probably be dead. How shall I collect?"

"Depends on what you *want* to collect," Gabriel says.

"Your cadaver," Dr. Altman says without hesitation.

"What!?" I say. "You've got to be kidding."

Dr. Altman doesn't spare me a glance. He just looks challengingly at Gabriel.

"Very good, Dr. Altman," Gabriel says, nodding pensively. "I take it no past individuals who fell under the anomalous category were willing to donate their bodies to science?"

"As I said, it's a small group," Dr. Altman says. "Clearly there is something different about your physiology. It would take an in-depth autopsy and extensive study to even begin to understand why it is you react so differently."

"Oh that is so gross," I say, crossing my arms. "And freaking morbid. What is wrong with you people?"

"Agreed," Gabriel says. "I like the way you think. Either way, science wins. You have redeemed yourself, Dr. Altman." He holds out a shaky hand and Dr. Altman steps forward to take it firmly.

"I'll have my office send the paperwork over by the end of the day—as well as the data. The clock is ticking, Mr. Dumas. I must say, this has been the most enjoyable consult I have ever had."

"Likewise," Gabriel replies. "You are the most sensible doctor I have ever encountered. I look forward to having you in my employ." He grins.

I roll my eyes. They are a couple of mad scientists.

"One more thing," Dr. Altman says before he turns to go. "That lesion on your leg is likely not related to the pulmonary cancer. The morphology isn't right. I'll let your oncologist know to have it biopsied ASAP." He smiles as if he has just given us a head start in this bet.

I am so confused by what just happened.

"Thank you," Gabriel replies.

After Dr. Altman leaves, Gabriel rubs his hands together and says, "What a useful consult. I must remember to thank Robert next time I see him." He smiles to himself as if remembering the interaction all over again and gleaning the same enjoyment.

"What a couple of freaks," I say. "Should I go procure some black market body parts for your underground lab? You've got a bet to win and I'd like to keep your body to myself, thank you."

"Oh Wendy, that's disgusting," he says, aghast. "If I die, you are *not* keeping my body."

I burst out laughing and keep going until tears come to my eyes, infecting Gabriel as well. When we're done with our mirthful outpouring, I say, "But for real, I don't want your *dead* body either. I want it alive and well."

Gabriel, I notice, has an uncomfortable look on his face after all the laughter. He looks pained. I waste no time in touching him and going into the colorworld to see what it's about. I can tell immediately that Gabriel's chest throbs as he takes careful, shallow breaths to keep it under control.

"How long has this been going on?" I demand.

"Since this morning," he replies.

I shake my head. "Gabriel, you have to stay on top of these things or you are never going to win that bet."

"Relax, Love. I plan to do so forthwith. I didn't want to miss the appointment with Altman though. And good thing I didn't."

"You are something else, Gabriel Dumas," I sigh. "But on another note... Forty year-old cases like yours? They can't all be hypno-touch-related, can they? Louise has only been doing it for what? Twenty years at most?"

"We have to accept the fact once and for all that we have no idea if anything Louise has ever said was the truth," Gabriel replies pensively. "We have no idea how long hypno-touch has actually been around."

"That would be crazy if it was that old," I point out. "But good job on you. If they actually are hypno-touch cases, that should seriously help."

"I'm counting on it," Gabriel replies.

19

"*T*his bloody cancer is really ticking me off!" Gabriel yells, throwing his plastic spoon across the room. It hits the wall and clatters to the floor.

"Gabriel, I'll be fine," I insist, sitting at the end of his bed carefully. My side is *throbbing* today. I know I should get it checked out, but today is the day I leave for Big Bear. A steady fatigue has begun to blanket me that I'm trying really hard to ignore.

His face is stricken. "You don't know that."

My shoulders slump. "What else is there to do?"

"Wendy," he says softly, entreating. "I cannot bear the thought of you being in peril right now. It's too much. It's not that I don't believe you capable, but the possibility that you could end up in trouble while I'm too incapacitated to help you..." Another flash of bitterness moves through him. "I hate this," he says harshly, aggravated with his own weakness, though he ought to be thrilled. In only two days' time he has found his legs again. They're shaky, but the improvement is astounding. He is still having kidney issues and he had to have a thoracentesis to drain his lungs of fluid two days ago, but he can hear again, almost as well as before. His doctor is perplexed that he has recovered from the chemo damage so quickly. I don't know what to make of it, what it means about his condition overall. I dare not hope that it means he is going to somehow miraculously go into remission from cancer, but it's in the back of my mind as I prepare to leave for Big Bear and the compound. One thing is sure, however: this isn't your average cancer case.

I scoot forward and pull his head to my shoulder. "This is just how it is. And maybe... well maybe the reason Robert's vision was set for right now was because you aren't supposed to be there."

"Terrific," he grumbles into my neck. "You're saying I would have ruined it."

I sigh heavily. "That's not what I meant."

He lifts his head. "I know... I... I want to be where *you* are, not here. And I know you're going to accomplish something incredible and you're going to do it entirely without my help. I... I worry that one day you will no longer need me. It feels like this is the beginning of that... you going off and doing something dangerous without me."

He's serious. How could he think that?

"Don't be ridiculous," I say, almost offended. "I will *always* need you."

"That's what you say until you don't need me anymore."

"Please tell me you understand how irrational that is," I say, not knowing how I can convince him of that.

He sighs. "In my heart, I suppose so. In my brain, no. It's perfectly logical to assume that you could reach a place in which I add nothing to your existence."

"So you don't trust me..." I say.

"Of course I trust you."

"Did I not marry you?"

"Yes, and I know what you're getting at. But I don't want you to stay with me out of obligation. I want you to *want* me."

I have never wanted to roll my eyes at him so badly. In fact, I think my eye twitches as I resist the urge. "Gabriel," I say in a controlled tone, "I am *committed* to you. It was *you* who taught me what that really means back when I couldn't touch you. You are backpedaling on all of that and claiming I only love you based on circumstance. That is just—" I pause to control my irritation. "really hurtful," I finish lamely, but it's probably better than the screaming and yelling I want to do. If he wasn't in a hospital and I wasn't about to risk my life, I probably would have. Thank goodness for cancer to save me from myself.

He pauses to consider it so I strike while the iron is hot. "If you can't trust my vows, you might as well never trust *anyone*. You might as well dump me right here. To say I might choose to not honor that commitment is an insult. Commitment aside, what you have done for me, to make me into a person I finally love, is something I will never be able to repay you for. I want you. In every way. Always."

The last part hits home for him where the commitment part didn't. My guard relaxes at the realization and I chuckle at the irony his emotions betray.

Gabriel looks at me questioningly.

"Oh just realizing you are more human than you let on," I reply. "Apparently all you needed was, 'I will love you forever and ever. The end.' You are as much in need of emotional reassurance as the next person." I lean forward and kiss him on the cheek.

He wrinkles his nose in a bit of confusion still. And I can almost hear him thinking something like, 'Well of course I do. Why is that so funny?' but he says nothing. Instead he leans into me and lays his head on my shoulder again, and I can tell that all he's asking is for me to make time for him, to share a moment together in relative peace until our lives, once again, are upended. Thank goodness for emodar. I never would have figured that out without a huge fight—maybe not even then. How do other people do this marriage thing without it?

I reach up and brush my fingers through his hair—which is miraculously intact despite the chemo. He flinches, but to my surprise, lets me. Gabriel, I've discovered, is kind of a princess about his hair, so losing it would definitely be a big deal to him. Unlike most guys, he uses shampoo *and* conditioner as well as a leave-in treatment twice a week. He doesn't use a lot of styling product, but he blow dries it, which I find hilarious. I always thought his hair fell attractively without effort, but evidently that's not true. And even though he doesn't have it gelled in place, he claims the oil on my hands will affect the way it falls—so he usually won't tolerate me touching it. I can only touch the shorter sides and the back unless I want him complaining and immediately running to a mirror to check his hair placement.

Yesterday Mike visited and I immediately saw myself out of the room. I haven't spoken more than three words to Mike since Gabriel woke up. He has been as nasty as ever with his emotions, but his mouth he keeps shut. I might have left the room yesterday, but I just went to the closest waiting room and eavesdropped—not usually my style, but I felt like I needed to 'see' how Mike behaved when I wasn't around.

What I found was very much a brotherly reunion, full of nitpicking and arguing. It sounded like Mike brought in some rehab equipment and was making Gabriel do pull-ups from bed. At one point Mike told Gabriel he needed a haircut, and the two went on and on arguing about whether shorter was better than longer (Mike's is quite short, but I suspect after their conversation that he may be as picky as Gabriel about his hair). And then Mike started arguing with Gabriel about his soul patch. "Dude," he said, "if you're going to do facial hair, do it all the way. That patch on your chin makes you look like Billy Ray Cyrus' Mexican brother."

I giggled when I heard that. Gabriel loves that small section of facial hair. He calls it his 'Patch of Distinguishment.' I've become a fan of it myself.

Mike's attitude toward me bothers me more and more. I guess I expected he'd warm up to me sooner rather than later. And the longer this goes on, the more I dislike him—probably because I can't figure out what he hates about me so much, and it makes me self-conscious. I hate being self-conscious...

"What are you thinking about?" Gabriel asks.

"Why your brother hates me."

He sits back and shakes his head exhaustedly. "I couldn't say. We talked about it, but he kept insisting that he didn't care what I said. He doesn't trust you, especially since I became so reclusive after I married you. And when he learned about Carl that solidified his distrust. If Carl was your father that must mean you're a bad egg as well." Gabriel growls. "He is so fixated on your presence in my life so suddenly. He won't let it go and I can't do a thing to persuade him otherwise."

"Well I guess I'll just have to kill him with kindness," I say.

"He'll be gone for several days supposedly. He had to get back to work. So it looks like we'll *both* get a break from him."

"Hopefully I'll be back soon so I can enjoy it, but I do have to go now. Robert is probably waiting." I make a move to stand.

He grabs my wrist to stop me. "If you don't want me heading into the woods after you and compromising my condition, you had better return to me."

"I will."

"I'm serious, Wendy. I will tear the entirety of the San Bernardino National Forest apart in search of you if I have to."

I roll my eyes. "I think you're getting a little dramatic."

His eyes narrow and he frowns. "You doubt me? Don't imagine I have limits when it comes to your life. I am a dying man, so I have naught to lose."

"I'll come back, Gabriel." I reach for his hands and squeeze them.

"Wendy. I'm not kidding."

I put a hand on his cheek. "I wouldn't dream of assuming you are."

He smiles devilishly and smacks my butt suddenly before settling back into his pillows. "Okay I feel better now that I've done my cave man duty and made threats about protecting my woman. Go be amazing. Which shouldn't be hard in those pants."

He's talking about the fleece-lined spandex pants that I bought specifically for this trip. They offer warmth and flexibility, and incidentally a good view of my butt. I chuckle as I leave, but it occurs to me that Gabriel hasn't demanded to know my strategy or plans concerning the vision. That he has put this entirely at my discretion means more to me than I would have guessed. He trusts me. He believes in me. And with that, I straighten my shoulders, and despite feeling especially fatigued today, I am ready to do this.

***

"Has it been used since I was there?" I ask, looking through the window at the passing trees that wall either side of the winding road we travel. We're on our way to the head of the main access road to the compound. Robert says the compound itself is about five miles from there. The plane trip zapped my remaining energy so that I'm tired just *thinking* about the upcoming hike through the woods—that's how we plan to approach the place in Robert's vision.

"My surveillance tells me there's been light traffic," Robert says, "but not like before. Now that Louise knows I watch it, she's been keeping a low-profile."

"And the vision?" I ask, my anxiety growing with each mile. I'm moving *toward* my worst enemies and *away* from Gabriel, the person that needs me most. This sucks so bad. "The timeline still looks good?"

"It's crystal clear," he replies, reaching over and patting my gloved hand. "It looks like more of a mid-morning time given the lighting, so maybe tomorrow or the day after? Either way, we haven't missed it."

I relax slightly, relieved that this trip may be much shorter than I expected. My urgency to see a doctor has grown even more since this morning. Thank goodness I'll have four body guards around to make sure I don't pass out alone in the middle of the woods. This is such a dumb idea...

I have to do it though. I trust Robert. I trust his vision. And a week of *no* progress toward a cure in the colorworld demands new information to give me a direction. This is life and death. For Gabriel, for me, for Kaylen, and for all the people out there that have no idea how close death is for them.

I close my eyes. *I can do this.* I summon every bit of my strength, thinking back to that night when things were so clear, when fear and uncertainty had no place in me, when strength didn't come from my body but from somewhere else.

"You can do this," Robert says, breaking through my thoughts and unwittingly reading my mind.

I turn to look at him. "Is that your omniscience speaking?"

165

He chuckles. "Why does everything have to be about fortune-telling with you? Why can't it be that I'm proud of your accomplishments in life thus-far and believe you capable of handling this?"

I roll my eyes. "You and I both know that everything you say is influenced by what you know. And you know a lot of things. Whether you like it or not."

He frowns. "As I have told you, I may know a lot more than most, but 'a lot' is still frighteningly little compared to how much *can* be known. But that's beside the point. I don't need the future to tell me the kind of will and wits you possess."

Will and wits will do me no good if my body doesn't cooperate, but I'm not going to say anything about that. "Thanks, Uncle Moby," I say as the car comes to a stop on the side of the road. A truck pulls behind us. Mark, Farlen, Sam, and Connie, my bodyguards, emerge one-by-one. Connie is the only one I haven't met before. I know the other three from the time we captured Louise in Riverside.

I lean across the seat and hug Robert. "Make sure someone is with Gabriel all the time so he doesn't check himself out of the hospital. He's already talking about it. Plus, I could hear the beginnings of fluid in his lungs before I left and I'm afraid he's going to put it off until the last possible moment again."

"Don't worry," he says. "Ezra will go over to the hospital right after school today. Those two sure have been putting their heads in the books. And Maris is around of course."

"True," I say. I saw Maris briefly yesterday, but she and Gabriel got into an argument about treatment or something and I had packing to do so I didn't stick around. I don't want to get anywhere near an argument between Gabriel and his mom. There is tension between them, brought out, I think, by Gabriel's illness and the fact that Mike had to be the one to tell Maris about Gabriel's cancer. I think she's even affronted that I didn't make Gabriel call her. I just don't have time for family drama like that. I have way bigger things to stress about.

"Wendy, one thing before you go," Robert says and I stop with my hand on the door handle. He holds out a necklace chain with a one-inch Star of David pendant. Memory of it catches my breath.

"That's... how did you get that?" I ask.

"Ezra," Robert replies, stretching it out to me even more. I flinch but reach out carefully. Robert drops it into my palm, the chain slinking into a pile, partially covering the star.

"But my mom was buried with this necklace," I say. "How did Ezra get it?"

"Ezra admits he took it from off of her before she was buried," Robert replies. "He's been wearing it."

"I've never seen him—oh, his dog chain necklace?" I remember when I first saw that chain on his neck I made him show me what it was. He pulled a dog tag from under his shirt. I told him it was silly to wear it *under* his shirt all the time to which he replied dog tags were for ID, not fashion. And I replied, "Yeah, in a state of *war*, idiot. Not in high school." He rolled his eyes at me and snatched his tag away. This must have been under his shirt as well.

"Look on the back," Robert says.

"The inscription?" I say, picking up the pendant. "My mom said the necklace had belonged to her grandmother. It's her initials. She said my great-grandmother's middle name was Wendy—" I stop. That can't be true. Leena, my adopted mother, wore this necklace every day. I couldn't have been named after her grandmother because I *wasn't* her biological daughter. My father, Carl, and biological mother, Regina, named me Wendy.

I rub my thumb over the back once like I used to do when I would sit on my mom's lap and play with the necklace, staring at the initials:

R.W.W.

Regina Walden? My biological mother? *Her* middle name was Wendy?

I look at Robert and a soft smile appears on his face. "This was *Gina's* necklace?" I say just above a whisper.

"Ezra realized it not too long ago, but he was afraid you'd be mad at him for taking it. He was thinking you could wear it. Should you encounter Carl it might... well, it should certainly unnerve him. Hopefully in a productive way."

I stare at the star with new eyes. My biological mom was Jewish? And Leena, my adoptive mother wore it every day because... why? To remember the woman whose child she was raising? I wonder if I will ever know the whole story surrounding the woman who raised me.

"Tell Ezra thanks," I say, looking at the pendant once more before clipping the chain around my neck and putting it under my shirt.

We step out of the car, and over the top Robert says, "Remember rule number one: no assumptions."

"What on earth could I be assuming?" I say. "I have no idea why I'm here."

He gives me a knowing smile. "I've been in your shoes enough times—acting on a vision with no clue about where it will lead. We can't help but attempt to fill in the blanks. Let it go. Focus on one step at a time and pretend you're on a camping trip. But keep your ears open and act on instinct instead of what you think you know."

"Got it," I reply, tightening the straps on my backpack as I look at the wall of trees in front of me.

"We'll be hiking a perimeter to avoid being seen," Mark, the shorter, middle-aged man who is in charge of the others, says as he approaches us. "But it's actually a shorter distance on foot than the road would be. Just over four miles. Do you need me to carry your pack, Wendy?"

Normally I'd refuse, but I think it better to conserve my already-depleted energy. "That would be great," I say, hoping my readiness to hand over my things doesn't strike anyone's suspicions.

"We'll be waiting for your check-in then," Robert says. "Safe travels."

Waving goodbye to him, I toss my braided hair over my shoulder and follow Mark, Farlen, and Connie. Sam takes up my rear as we navigate into the woods. I hear the two vehicles turn around and head back the way we came. We're on our own.

The hike starts off difficult, climbing dramatically uphill, and I'm glad I didn't try to tough it out and carry my pack. Mark and Farlen scout far ahead, cutting through heavier brush with machetes and turning back to make a different route when a way is impassable. I'm glad it's taking them so long to scout the way because I don't think I can move more quickly. A chill is in the air as well, and despite being gloved and wearing a jacket and hat, the cold sinks deeper into me.

Sam starts off walking about ten or fifteen feet behind me. I've spoken to him a few times before, back when Ezra and I lived with Robert. One time Sam came by the house to talk to Robert about something, and while waiting for him to show up, Ezra started ribbing Sam about his t-shirt. It had the silhouette of a beard with the words "Fear the Beard" above it. And truly Sam has a thick but manicured beard. He and Ezra started arguing about whether a beard was manly. I was perusing a magazine, listening to them, cracking up when Ezra pointed out that superheroes didn't have beards, proving that from a marketing standpoint, beards did not make men appear more virile. To my surprise, Sam started rattling off superheroes that had beards. He ended with Green Arrow, and Ezra held up his hands and said, "Okay, you win. Nobody messes with Green Arrow."

I laugh to myself just thinking of it. Since then I've always thought of Sam as "the bearded bodyguard."

After a while, Sam closes the distance between us because I keep tripping over the smallest obstacles and moving like I have two left feet. He helps me up several embankments and finally settles on walking just behind my right shoulder. He's baffled and pitying rather than worried, which is embarrassing because I must look like a clumsy idiot to him. But I'd rather him think that than wonder if I need to see a doctor. I keep reminding myself that Robert wouldn't have gotten the vision if I weren't physically capable of being there. The future has to have taken into consideration my deteriorating condition, right? That's what I'm going on.

As I crouch low to duck under a partially fallen tree, a sharp pain stabs high on my side. I have to restrain myself from crying out, instead falling to one knee and grunting and gripping my rib cage with one hand.

Worried for the first time, Sam takes my elbow then. "Do you need a rest?"

Hiding my face from him because a few tears of pain have eked out, I grit my teeth and crawl the rest of the way under the tree. Standing up and quickly wiping my eyes once I reach the other side, I lean back against the horizontal trunk. Sam hands me a water bottle already uncapped as he scans my form for signs of injury. And then he yells ahead to the others. Connie stops and comes back to where we are. Mark and Farlen continue on ahead to clear the way.

Connie is an Asian woman with an athletic build. I'd put her in her late thirties or early forties. From what I can tell, she's not as comfortable as the others, making me think she's new and unused to working with this group. I notice her eyes are resting on my hand that's holding the water bottle; it's shaking. I thrust the bottle back at Sam and busy my hands by brushing the dirt and leaves from my knees. Sam is oblivious, digging through his pack for something, but Connie watches me. She says nothing though. I'd like to think she's keeping her mouth shut to do me a favor, but camaraderie is not something I pick up from her. Instead, she comes across as strictly professional.

"Here, drink this instead," she says, holding out a small bottle of what looks like some kind of sports drink. She nods at me just barely as if trying to pass some silent message.

I shake my head. "I'm staying away from sugar. My diabetes has been acting up lately."

I'm hoping she'll take this is the reason for my sorry-looking state, but she takes a step closer, hand still outstretched. "It's sugar-free," she says, breaking the seal and looking at me intently. "Take it. You need to stay hydrated."

Not willing to start an argument, I obey. The drink is grape-flavored with a slightly metallic aftertaste. I want to ask her what's in it, but that's only going to raise Sam's suspicions. I wonder if Robert put her up to keeping me in one piece. Maybe he already knows I'm in a sad state—or will be.

After a minute or two, we start off again. Connie moves quickly to catch up to Mark and Farlen, and Sam stays near my elbow. After only another five minutes, I start to feel a little more energy. I look at the half-full bottle in my hand that really is labeled as an electrolyte beverage, but I don't believe it. I glance ahead to Connie's back. What did she dose me with? I wonder if she has more?

In better spirits, and thrilled that the terrain has finally evened out, I say conversationally, "So, Sam, how do you get into doing shady odd jobs for a guy like Robert?"

I can't see his face, but his emotions state that he's hesitant about answering.

"Uh, if it's too personal, you don't have to share," I say. "I was breaking up the silence."

"You are as perceptive as Robert said you were," says Sam.

"Yeah, it's a gift," I say dryly.

"I was trying to decide if Robert would want me to tell you. He's so modest and doesn't like people knowing all his good deeds, so I keep my mouth shut about it usually."

"My Uncle Robert is a constant surprise," I say sincerely. "I'm so lucky to have him in my life."

"He's the best man I've ever known," Sam agrees. "Helped me rehabilitate from addiction and then he employed me to… do whatever he needs. I owe him much more than hiking through the woods as a bodyguard for his niece."

"Oh, Uncle Moby," I say to myself, amazed again at how differently Carl and Robert turned out. Robert is as good as Carl is bad. What went so wrong for Carl? Was it really my biological mother's death that broke him?

As we continue to hike in silence for a while, I occupy myself with Sam's mental processes, which become clearer as I get used to their current. He has a busy mind, full of observations and then questions that he's always in the process of guessing at. I wouldn't call him analytical, but he becomes fixated on one thing to the point of irritation only to be dragged off by some new idea that catches his attention. I think he's an outgoing guy used to engaging in animated conversation whenever he's not carrying out orders. After a while, I notice what I think is one particular question that comes up over and over, but he keeps talking himself out of asking it. Eventually he calms and I think he may be directing his attention on the scenery as a new self-diversion tactic.

Sometimes when I tune in to others for a long time, their emotions become harder to let go of. I guess I become invested in whatever it is that's motivating them at the time. So it is with Sam and his unsatisfied round of questions. I want a resolution even though I have no idea what he wants to know. "After all that wondering... you're going to keep your mouth shut anyway?" I complain. "Geez, I've been on pins and needles up here, dying to hear you blurt something out."

Jolted into a mental standstill, Sam says, "You picked up all that? Wow. I mean Robert warned us but... wow."

"Emotions say a lot more about your thoughts than you'd think."

"No kidding." And then he goes back to his exasperating internal conversation.

As we continue to walk, the underbrush becomes thinner and easier to navigate. I also notice that the ache in my side has dulled. Did Connie give me pain meds?

"Robert keeps such heavy-duty surveillance on you and your family. Just has me curious as to why you're such a coveted asset is all," Sam says, breaking the silence. It takes me a moment to realize he's referring to what was on his mind earlier.

Baffled that he has no idea what I can do other than read emotions, I reply, "Do you even know why we're out here in the woods, Sam?"

"Generally. Louise and Carl are after you because you have something they want. I know you all have gifts that are kind of out there, but for whatever reason *you* are the valuable one to those two jokers. My job is to keep you safe at all costs and do what Mark tells me, but a guy can't help wondering even though it's none of his business, you know?"

I chuckle and glance back at him. "Fishing, Sam?"

He smiles, his grin toothy and slightly crooked. He runs his thumbs back and forth under the shoulder straps of his pack, ruminating with a sly look on his bearded face. "Robert didn't tell me many details about the situation, but he also never said I couldn't ask. And I'm a nosy person. In fact, I'm proud of myself for having kept a lid on it for this long. You don't have to answer, of course. But I like to run my mouth anyway. Can't help it."

"I know someone like that," I say, smiling to myself.

"Who?"

"Gabriel."

Sam snorts. "No way. Gabe likes details. I like headlines."

"Headlines?"

"Yeah. I always want to know what people are up to just for the hell of it. But Gabe wants to know *why*. Never thought anyone was more nosy than me until I met *that* guy. I am way too shallow for all that. Give me the headline and spare me the touchy-feely details."

"Why?"

"Ah, it's just in my nature to get caught up in people's drama too easily. It's a bad habit of mine. Shoot, if I read minds like you I'd be *screwed*."

"You'd figure it out," I say.

"No I wouldn't. Living vicariously through the people around me until I start copying their bad habits is how I started doing drugs in the first place. No thanks. I'll stick with shady odd jobs and keeping my nose in my own business."

"Sounds like you're exactly *not* shallow then," I point out. "Otherwise you'd care less about what other people have going on."

He contemplates that as we crunch over the fallen leaves. I look up to see that we're in an area concentrated with broadleaf trees. Very few leaves still cling to the branches and I think Robert is right and we're right on top of his vision, time-wise.

"I don't know," Sam says finally. "I'm just spouting the stuff my addiction counselor tells me. He says I have to distance myself from people so I don't start copying their coping methods. I'm a copy-cat. Always have been."

"Well if copying people is your weakness, Robert is probably the best person you could copy."

"That's what I'm saying. I stick to him like glue. Best part is Robert's a headline guy, too."

"Headline guy..." I muse. Yeah, I guess I can see that. But it's not out of being shallow. At all.

"Round the clock detail... Two on duty at all times..." Sam muses. "Surveillance technology detection straight out of his own tech collection. I never figured Robert for a paranoid guy, but I started to wonder until we pulled some pretty fancy bugs and trackers out of your apartment and your cars. I've never seen stuff that sophisticated except for Robert's tech... You must be pretty skilled if the people after you are willing to spend that kind of cash... Or maybe you know something and they want to tie up loose ends..."

"You *are* nosy." I turn to grin at him and then say, "There were bugs in my apartment? Round the clock surveillance? Really?"

Sam's forehead wrinkles at my surprise, assessing. "Looks like you've been in the dark... I guess that means you don't know what you're worth to those yahoos either. I thought Robert liked to test out all his gizmos, but Louise and Carl must be some kind of loaded to put up the capital for having you followed everywhere. We stay pretty busy running interference."

I stop and turn, my mouth agape. "I'm being followed all the time?"

Sam nods. "Getting you out of Monterey today without them realizing where you'd gone was tricky."

"Those two are insane!" I turn to start walking again, bewildered. "You think they're just watching or are they looking for an opportunity?"

"Hard to say. They try to stay incognito, but we see signs of them every now and then. My guess is they're just watching. But we don't let our guard down."

"That's crazy," I mumble. Louise and Carl's efforts are so sporadic. Sometimes it's like they're running some rag-tag gang off the street and other times they've got a legion of black SUVs tracking me through Cannery Row with com-links and tranquilizer guns. Ever since Gabriel went to the hospital I had assumed they'd backed off, waiting for me to have a breakthrough. They have to know that if I figure this out, there is no way in hell I'm ever telling them anything about what I learn, so maybe surveillance is the only way they hope to get information.

Considering the time and resources the two have invested in discovering the secrets of life forces, I should never have expected anything less from them. I'm going to have to play this really smart.

20

$\mathcal{B}$y the time we find a spot situated close enough to the research building to set up camp, weakness has settled into my whole body again and I am completely out of it mentally. For the last half mile or so, summoning the concentration required to propel myself forward was all I could manage. I all but collapse against a tree while the others move about, scouting the area. Finally able to let go of willpower, I notice that even though I'm no longer trudging through the woods, I'm still breathing heavily and my heart is pounding. I focus on calming myself down but still don't feel like I'm getting quite enough air.

"Are you okay?" Sam asks, his voice close. "You're as white as a ghost."

My eyes flash open to find him crouched in front of me, the yellow of the setting sun beaming through the trees behind him. "I'm fine. I'm just listening," I lie, but then I realize I actually *do* need to listen. "How close is the research building?"

"Mark says a little less than a half-mile. Super-senses... That's right. Like when you were in that tree the time we went after Louise?" Sam asks.

I manage a small smile. "You remember. It's one of my super valuable skills. Have you figured out what I can do yet?"

"Nah. But I'm now guessing this is why we didn't bring any long-range surveillance equipment. *You'll* be the one doing the listening?"

I nod, closing my eyes to see what there is to hear from here. After a few minutes, I open my eyes and say, "I hear *nothing* from the research building—it must be empty. But there are definite signs of life at the lodge. Not much talking, but I can't understand what's being said anyway. How far is it from where we are?"

Sam looks to Mark who says, "Almost a mile."

"So if we were going to put ourselves equidistant between the lodge and the research building, it'd be what? Another half mile?" I don't know why I'm asking. I don't even think I can stand up. Another half mile tonight would kill me.

"Yep," Mark says. "Do you want to move closer?"

I don't want to miss something, but another hike, no matter how short, is *not* happening. Well, clearly the vision is not going to come to fruition tonight. Maybe some sleep will rejuvenate me enough that we can move early tomorrow morning. I shake my head. "This is good for tonight. Maybe in the morning."

Mark nods and starts pulling food out of his pack. I check my glucose, which is fine for once, so obviously this weakness problem is not a result of my diabetes. Mark brings me a satellite phone and some jerky and cheese to eat. I call Gabriel's cell to let him know we're settled in for the evening but get Maris instead.

"Oh Mija, finally!" she says, an edge of hysteria in her voice, and my already overwrought heart launches into overdrive again at the sound. "He's having fluid drained again. My terco mijo! He's going to kill himself at this rate! He said he wanted to hear from you first before going in, but we had no way of getting a hold of you. It took Robert convincing him. I have no idea what the man said. But I promised Gabriel I would keep the phone on me the whole time, and Robert assured him you were fine."

I put my hand over my chest, trying to calm down. "It's just the thoracentesis then?" I ask evenly, although my heart still flutters anxiously.

"No, Mija. Dehydration also. And this afternoon he received the results from the biopsy on his bone lesion. Osteosarcoma. My boy has *two* different types of cancer!" And then she starts crying and mumbling in Spanish.

I close my eyes. *Two* cancers? Two cancers that can't be treated...

"Why didn't he call me?" she continues, sobbing. "Why didn't my boy call me?"

I can't do this with her right now, and I'm on a satellite phone with a limited battery supply. This isn't the time for a heart-to-heart with my mother-in-law. So I say the thing I think will help her most. "Maris, he didn't call you because he didn't want you to worry, and you also know he doesn't like to be prayed over. Maybe if you could stop throwing it in his face so much, he might not be... such a jerk about it. If you want him to call on you, do the things he says he *needs*. He hates using the computer to research, so I had been going back and forth to the library for him. You can do that. And he hates being coddled. So don't help him with something unless he asks. Now I've got to go so I don't run the battery down. It will be okay."

Connie walks by right then and discreetly hands me another bottle of miracle-juice. I look up at her questioningly, but she doesn't stop, just goes over to sit on her mat and begins unwrapping a protein bar.

Maris is breathing more evenly as I crack open the bottle. I really need to calm down or anxiety is going to make whatever is wrong with me worse.

"Okay, Mija," Maris says with stoic determination. "I'll try it your way. I won't even mention a chest tube to him after his procedure—even though he needs one. You'll work on that with him, won't you?"

"Sure," I say, slumping. Convincing Gabriel to have a tube inserted in his chest on a more permanent basis sounds like loads of fun. "I swear I'll be back as soon as humanly possible. When he comes out of his procedure, tell him everything is absolutely fine. I'll call him tomorrow. Tell him I insist he get some sleep. Maris, drug him if you have to."

"Easier said than done, Mija," Maris huffs. "That boy reads the label of everything they give him, every disclosure, and argues about every procedure. He's been organizing those files from Dr. Altman and now seems to think he's a doctor calling the shots."

"Alright, Maris. Tell Gabriel I love him and I'm fine. I'll be back soon."

After we hang up, I'm antsy but exhausted as I tuck myself into a heavy down sleeping bag. I want some progress so bad. Why am I here, camping in the darkness, trying to hear conversations from a place I lived at for weeks but never learned a thing from except that Louise was evil and should be avoided at all costs?

I try to settle down, but my limbs twitch, making it hard to relax. Sam is still awake, settled against a tree nearby. I assume he must have first watch.

Frustrated by my inability to put my tired body into much-needed slumber, I give up and daydream about what miraculous discovery I'm going to make that will save Gabriel's life. I think about life forces and what they look like, that swirling purple cocoon of strands that surrounds a body—what more can they tell me?

A minute passes and nothing comes to me. I revert back to asking the same questions, like, *what am I here to learn?*

Looking at Sam I remember how Robert hasn't told any of his people what I can do. I know discretion is necessary, but I need a fresh sounding board.

I sit up and pull my mat and sleeping bag closer to Sam who is combing his beard. I laugh as I watch him. I saw him run a comb through it earlier today, too, when we stopped briefly for a break on our hike.

He ignores me and keeps moving the comb in careful, even strokes. He's wearing a beanie on his head and I don't think I've seen him give this kind of attention to the hair on his head. In fact, I think he has a buzz cut.

"Is combing your beard a way to stay awake during stake outs?" I ask when it doesn't seem like he's going to stop anytime soon.

He wordlessly lifts up his coat to reveal his undershirt. It's a black t-shirt with a Nordic-looking man over the chest with a majestic orange beard, a hard hat, and two wrenches crossed behind him like cross-bones. Below the man it says, "Big Iron Bad Ass." The guy on the shirt looks pretty mean.

"Combing your beard is supposed to be a bodyguard intimidation tactic then?" I ask.

He stops combing finally, tucking the comb into his pocket. "Beards serve many purposes," he says in a sage voice. "And they require proper attention."

Grinning, I say, "Is that so? Well I need some advice. So do beards make you wise?"

Sam's blue eyes laugh at me. "If only. I'd talk to Robert if I were you."

I wave a dismissive hand. "I have. I need someone who knows next to nothing about supernatural abilities."

"Okay…" Sam replies hesitantly, though internally he's excited.

"I can see the life forces of things."

Sam looks at me in disbelief. "What are life forces?"

"I'm pretty sure they're souls."

Sam has his mouth hanging open. "You see… *souls*? What do they look like?"

"Human souls are purple."

"*Human* souls? You see *other* souls?"

"Oh yeah," I say, propping myself up on my elbow. "It's a completely different world. I call it the colorworld because it looks like this world only everything there is a different color than it is here. And everything glows like it has an inner light."

Eyes wide, Sam is speechless as he tries to grasp what I'm saying. Then he's suspicious, thinking I'm messing with him.

I make an annoyed face. "I'm not kidding, Sam. Come on. I really need your input here."

Disbelief becomes unease. He even looks right and then left like there's a threat nearby. "Why are you telling me this?" he says in a low voice.

"I already told you why. A second opinion."

"Second opinion?" he says, incredulous. "About what? *Souls?*" He holds his hands up. "This is *way* over my head. You need to ask someone who has some kind of... experience in this area. That person is *not* me."

I snort. "Someone with *experience?* Like who?"

Sam shakes his head. "I dunno. A priest?"

I sit up, drawing my sleeping bag up with me so I can keep warm. "A priest. Really? Why?" I can honestly say that such a thing has never occurred to me.

"That's their business, isn't it? Saving souls?" Sam says, highly uncomfortable.

I laughingly imagine going to a confessional and asking a priest's opinion about how to fix Gabriel's soul. *Oh that's a piece of cake, my child. Thirty-eight Hail Marys ought to do it.* I can't help chuckling aloud, which gets an odd look from Sam.

I lie back down though, as parallels begin to materialize. From my understanding—which is limited to what I've seen on TV and movies, of course—confession is supposed to be a method of obtaining forgiveness for sins. I think the idea is that when you do something wrong, it does something to your soul. Something that prevents you from having an afterlife? And to fix it you have to obtain divine forgiveness. Is allowing someone to muss your soul up through hypno-touch a sin then? I kind of wish I'd been to church a time or two. I'm not exactly sure what a sin is other than the obvious things like killing and stealing.

I guess our theory about what causes a life force to brighten or darken sort of aligns with that, right? Who knows? Maybe a priest would have some insight. Gabriel would probably laugh at me though since he has such a poor opinion of religion. But hey, I'm kind of desperate, and if a priest might be able to inspire me with a new direction, I'll take it.

"Have you ever seen anyone die there?" Sam's says, breaking through my ponderings. I've been too busy with my own thoughts to notice his cloud of amazement until now.

I glance over at him, and he says, "You know, in the *colorworld?* Where does a soul *go* when somebody dies?"

It's my turn to be amazed. "I... uh... don't know."

"Have you ever seen any ghosts?" Sam asks, getting more excited.

I stare back at him. "I... don't think so. And I've never seen anyone die there, so I don't know what it looks like—what happens to them or where they go." I lay back with my hands behind my head, staring up at the sky full of stars. *"Holy crap,"* I whisper to myself. *"Why have you never thought of that, Wendy?"*

Sam is disappointed and I turn my head to look at him again. "That's an incredibly good question. I think I've never thought about it before because everything there is so... alive. Death isn't really something you think about there." Even as I say it, I'm not sure I can articulate why that is. Have I just *assumed* my whole life that souls are eternal, that they don't simply wink out of existence when the body dies? Unarticulated fear grips me. If I've never seen disembodied life forces, does that mean that there *are* none? But then...

"Oh my gosh!" I nearly shout, sitting up abruptly and startling Sam. My head feels like it might explode with excitement. "Sam! You're a genius!"

Memories flood my head. "Louise..." I murmur. *"That's* why she wanted me to kill someone while in the colorworld. She wanted me to see what happened to a life force when someone dies!" Eyes ablaze, I look to Sam who stares back in confused worry. "That's it!" I say, looking around for my bag that has the satellite phone. I need to run this by Gabriel. There has to be a way to watch someone die. A hospice maybe? I bet Robert can help!

As my hand finds the phone, I remember that Gabriel is likely still in his procedure, or at least in recovery. Plus, he needs rest and there is definitely not anything I can do tonight. I'll have to wait until morning. In fact, with this new information, there is no reason to stay here for the vision. I don't think I have the patience to wait for it anyway. I *know* this is the right direction. I clap my hands in excited delight, grinning at Sam. "This is perfect, Sam. You have *no* idea how this is going to help me! Thank you!"

Sam is not entirely convinced, but he says, "You're welcome."

I lie back down once more, begging sleep to claim me. I want to hurry and wake up so I can get a move on. Possibilities roam through my head so quickly that I worry I'm going to be up all night in anticipation of morning. But despite the exultant will of my mind, my fatigued body wins and pulls me into a deep sleep.

21

$\mathcal{J}$ wake up to shouts and scuffles. There's no moon to pierce the blackness, but my eyes pick up everything perfectly. Sam has Connie by the neck and is rolling on the ground with her, trying to restrain her. Connie catches his nose with her elbow and blood drips. Mark and Farlen are looking on in confusion, unsure of what to do. Mark finally clicks a flashlight and shines it on the two.

"She was crouched over Wendy!" shouts Sam, getting the struggling Connie on the ground, face-down. She's pretty strong for someone so slight. "I saw her! I don't know what she was doing!"

"Liar," Connie growls under Sam's grip. "It was my watch. *You* were the one leaning over her."

"*She's* the one lying," I say, having moved close enough to sense the both of them.

Everyone looks at me. "Her emotions are pretty clear," I explain.

"What were you doing?" Sam demands, giving Connie a little shake. She remains quiet.

Mark takes Connie's arms. "Alright, alright. I've got her. Here." He hands Sam a handkerchief for his nose.

Just then, I notice other sounds: footsteps in the brush. "Somebody's coming!" I hiss.

Sam leaps toward me, guarding my body with his while Mark holds on to Connie and turns off his flashlight.

Sam, Farlen, and Mark pull out their guns, surging adrenaline into me. Someone is going to get hurt.

With their backs to me, they point their guns into the surrounding darkness. Mark is crouched, gripping Connie's small wrists in his one free hand, her back under his knee. Connie keeps quiet, and the only thing to be heard other than the usual rustling of leaves in the gentle autumn breeze is our breathing. The movement out there has stopped, so I can't be sure how many there are. All I know is that I heard more than one.

I close my eyes, concentrating as hard as I can on listening. Moving past the sounds of breathing and heartbeats in my immediate circle, I strive to hear the vital sounds of those who lie in wait for us. But I'm not that good, I guess. It's hard enough to pick up such miniscule sounds let alone decipher exactly what direction they're coming from.

An idea hits me. Sam's back is against me, and I reach out a gloved hand to use him to tap into the colorworld. Life forces are like beacons there so I bet I can spot them.

Sure enough, there they are. The luminous blue trees are dim compared to the brilliance of a human soul. Trying to hide themselves is as fruitless as trying to hide a halogen light.

"There are six total," I whisper. "Surrounding us at about fifty yards away in every direction."

Mark finishes tying up Connie's hands with something, but keeps her face down in the dirt with his foot on her back. "What are they doing?" he whispers.

"They've stopped moving," I reply. With bated breath, I watch the souls paused in the distance. All around me, Mark, Farlen, and Sam mentally churn through various strategies. Standing in the middle of the clearing, we are exposed, and the need for flight is strong. If I couldn't tell that fleeing would lead us right into the hands of the enemy, I'd be hard-pressed to resist.

To my disappointment, and as if cued silently at once, the souls in the distance begin advancing again. I hear their faint and measured footsteps as well.

"They're moving toward us slowly," I whisper.

How are we going to get out of this? It might turn into a gunfight, with all of us dead on the ground. If only my bodyguards could see what I'm seeing, then they could fire in the right direction.

"Can you lead us through a gap in their lines, Wendy?" Mark whispers.

"Undetected?" I reply. "Dragging Connie? She could shout and give us away. I don't think that's a good idea."

"We need to get out of this clearing," Farlen says gruffly. "We're sitting ducks like this."

"Let me get Wendy over to that heavy underbrush," Sam says, pointing to a collection of boulders and bushes. "Mark, you and Farlen can take Connie through the trees and maybe they'll assume Wendy is with you and it will draw them off."

"Not with them coming in on all sides," Farlen argues. "Too risky."

"I have an idea," I say timidly because I'm still not sure about it. Eyes moving between the approaching life forces and Sam's soul in front of me, I weigh our chances of getting out of this by any other way.

"Let's hear it, Wendy," Mark urges when I don't immediately reply.

"I can give Sam my sight and then he can see where to shoot," I say, breathless with fright over what I'm offering to do.

Confusion all around, and then Sam says, "How—"

"When I touch people, they see what I can see," I interrupt, looking between Sam's life force and my own. Not as bright as mine, but neither are Kaylen's or Ezra's, and they can both touch me. "Your soul is brilliant. It can take mine." I say it more to assure myself than him. He probably doesn't know what I'm talking about. I don't think they know about the death-touch.

I realize then that I'm already in the process of removing my gloves.

"We need to move," Mark says, clearly no longer taking me seriously.

"Hold your position," I say sternly. "I've got this."

With my gloves finally off, I take a breath of courage. "Sam. It will be disorienting at first. Don't be afraid. Brace yourself," I whisper and place my bare hand on his exposed neck. My hand literally jumps to his skin with a magnetism that startles me, but I keep my hand in place.

Sam jumps back into me and gasps. He hisses a few choice words that Gabriel would call impolite in the presence of a lady, including the phrase 'piss my beard' which I'd find hilarious under any other circumstance.

Finally he calms down and whispers, "Incredible!"

"No time for that," I say impatiently, too afraid of what might happen next for relief over Sam being alive still. "Look over there." I point with my free hand. "The trees are blue and glowing just like I told you everything is. But people are much brighter. Purple. You see them?"

"Yes!" he whispers excitedly.

Far more confident now, I turn to glance at Farlen, assessing quickly that his life force is bright as well. I catch sight of Connie under Mark, confused for a moment that her soul appears to be just as bright as the others. No time to wonder about it, though. "Farlen, you too," I whisper. "Come here. I can help you see."

Farlen backs up closer to me, confused but trusting. He's probably going to be even more stunned than Sam; he wasn't around when I told Sam about my ability.

"I can see the souls of people and things, and when I touch you I can let you see them, too," I explain softly. "It's going to be really bright, but you'll adjust." Then I reach up to place my other hand on his neck. Farlen flinches; his pulse leaping, and, frightened, he tries to pull away from me, but I grip his neck and shoulder to stop him. "It's fine," I assure him.

After too many long moments of waiting for him to recover the shock, I say, "Get it together, Farlen! We're out of time. Look for the purple masses in the trees. Those are people."

"What...?" Farlen says, trying to make sense of all the lights and moving colors that are so much more brilliant in the dark.

"Purple," Sam growls at Farlen. "See the trees? They're blue. See the purple balls? We need to take aim and shoot together. Do you see them?"

"Uh... yeah..." Farlen says, still unsure. "I think so."

"You *think* so?" Sam says. "Do you see them or not?"

"Yeah, yeah," Farlen says, finally dismissing his incredulity and replacing it with the professionalism he usually has.

"Then let's get low and shoot. Now."

At once, all of us drop to a crouch. I flinch at the sound of the gunfire from either side of me. Opening my eyes finally, and surveying the trees around us, I see only three life forces beyond our position rather than six. And it looks like they are retreating. If the other three are dead, I can't say what happened to their life forces; they are nowhere to be found.

"There are three left, Mark," Sam says. "North and west. Looks like they're on the run."

"They know where we are, and they might be retreating to regroup," Mark says. "Sam, you take Wendy east. Farlen and I will get Connie and find some cover behind the trees and draw them off."

Nobody argues, so I let go of Farlen. Sam takes me by the hand and guides me to the edge of the clearing. I don't have much opportunity to look behind me to spot the location of the people coming because I'm trying not to trip. Sam leads me through the trees quickly, still able to see perfectly in the colorworld lights. I hear gunshots again, but they are randomly interspersed, like Mark and Farlen are trying to scare our pursuers off since there's no way they can see to aim in the dark.

We stumble along until we reach a somewhat overgrown trail. Sam stops at the head of the trail and we look around. As far away as we are from our original location, it's impossible to see any life forces through the thick trees.

As my adrenaline wears off, fatigue finds my limbs. "Let me listen. I should be able to tell where they are," I say, needing a break.

"Okay," Sam says.

Sam should be able to hear, too, being connected to me through the colorworld, but he won't have as much practice as I do with distance, so I don't count on his assistance. I stretch out my senses to find voices, but I hear movement instead. Lots. They are being none too careful about moving stealthily now, and I bite my lip in worry over Mark and Farlen. But as I listen more closely, my spirits lift.

"I think they really are retreating," I whisper as the sounds of crunching underbrush move further away. We keep still for five minutes as the steps retreat further into the woods, away from the compound and away from us.

"I think you're right," Sam says, taking note of the sounds as well now that he's paying attention.

"Are you able to contact Mark and Farlen?" I ask.

"Yeah," Sam says, holding his wrist to his mouth. "Mark?" he says into it. "I think we've got them on the run. Are you clear?"

"Clear here," I hear Mark's voice say from the radio in Sam's ear. "We sent Connie off to confuse them further about our location. I think it worked."

"Orders?" Sam says.

"Confirm their whereabouts if you can."

"I think we should move to the research building," I say. "They're moving away from it. And I don't hear any sounds coming from there. I think it's clear for now. But we should stay away from the lodge."

"We're headed to the target," Sam says. "We can call for a pickup there."

"We'll head your way."

"This trail should lead to the research building main path," I say.

"Alright, I think I'm good to see on my own if you want to let go of me," Sam says. "It's hard to move quickly if we're side-by-side and I'm holding on to you."

"Fine, but you need to follow me. Even out of the colorworld my eyesight is a lot better than yours."

I take the lead and travel down the narrow and somewhat overgrown path that I'm sure Kaylen used to frequent with her horse when she lived here. We have to travel uphill for a bit and I beg my legs to get me a little farther; I am so tired now that adrenaline has worn off. I'm focused on my feet to keep from tripping or falling. I know I should be listening, and I do every now and then, but I have trouble focusing because of how fuzzy my head is. Furthermore, my back and side are throbbing in full force, demanding attention. I'm surprised Sam didn't say anything about the pain when he was connected to me—although I barely felt it when I was touching him. We finally break out onto the main path and I can see the research building only about fifty yards away. The lights lining the path are on, and I have to take great care not to collapse against the nearest boulder. But I do rest against it, bringing my head into my hands so I don't have to hold it upright. I'm glad we're going to call for a pickup right now instead of the morning. I need to get to a doctor. ASAP.

Sam crouches near me, putting his hand on my back. "Wendy?" he whispers. "Are you hurt?"

Gasping for breath, eyes closed, I have no idea how to answer that. Instead I take note of the sounds of Farlen and Mark moving in our direction, praying they'll move a little faster so we can get the heck out of here; something other than my health doesn't feel right. It clicks at about the same time I hear footsteps right nearby much sooner than expected: I remember the lights on the path are motion activated... and they were on before we got here.

"Sam!" I gasp, leaping up, but it's too late. Someone is in the shadows just outside the beam of the lights, and he's got a gun trained on Sam and me.

I open my mouth to warn Sam, but he has already whirled around, his gun drawn. The sound of gunfire echoes through my skull again: once, twice. Stunned, I'm not sure who fired until I see Sam's body drop in front of me.

"Sam!" I scream, falling to my knees. A crimson pool spreads over his chest that rises and falls quickly as he gasps for breath. His eyes flit from side to side like he can't see.

"Sam! Sam!" I yell, trying to figure out what to do with my hands. I settle for placing them over his wounds, two holes in his chest about six inches apart. "Stay with me, Sam," I plead, knowing it's fruitless, but begging for it with every particle of my will anyway.

It's at that moment, desperate to find some way to save Sam by my own will, that I remember the colorworld. And with his blood soaking through my gloves, I fight for focus, straining to find the right awareness so I can go there. If I can go there I can find some way to keep his life force attached to his body.

Sam's bright purple soul finally blazes to life in my sight. I'm in the colorworld. Beneath me is a mass of swirling purple flame where Sam's body should be. At least it seems like purple flames at first, but it's not. It's his life force strands, and they're undulating in a way that I've never seen a life force do before. Like waves, they ripple from his chest outward, making his life force appear bloated. I blink, thinking maybe my hazy brain is betraying me. And then in a flash of light, they disappear. I look this way and that, searching for where they went. All I see is Sam's body now. His skin is faintly luminous green. No purple cocoon. Just an inanimate body illuminated like everything else here. It's completely silent.

Realization clicks into place.

Sam is dead. His life force left his body.

At least I think so. I am so attuned to souls in the colorworld—the way the essence of a person permeates my senses there. Now that Sam's purple strands are no more in my sight, I expect the space to be empty of his presence. But it isn't. I can't put my finger on the whys, but it's like being in a dark room and sensing someone is there without seeing them. Sam's life force is here... but why can't I see it? I wave my hand in front of me, searching for it. The air feels... slightly viscous? I close my eyes, trying to get a better handle on the sensation. I'm sure he's here.

Or am I? I lean forward and sniff. I can *smell* him—like early morning dew resting on the leaves of gum trees. Every other sense tells me his life force strands are still near me.

I look down again to see his empty-looking body, my hand over his chest where his jacket has fallen open to reveal his Big Iron Bad Ass shirt. Blood has seeped between my gloved fingers and has almost covered the image of the Nordic man with the orange beard. I have no perception of Sam's body. It's dead to me. And dead to him. It's a striking contrast to what I can perceive of him around me. I could swear he's alive, but this body is no longer him.

All of a sudden, my head clouds more surely. I'm going to faint. I fight to stay awake, but it's no use. I have one last thought before the blackness finds me:

Blood is red in the colorworld, too.

22

"*O*h look. It's you," I say tepidly to the face suspended over me.

Carl's face scrunches up as he examines the length of me. He does not reply.

I reach up to rub my eyes, wondering how long I've been out, and find that my hands are bound together. "You are the most irritating person on the planet," I grumble, noticing the dark reddish brown flakes on my bare hands. It takes me a moment to figure out what it is: *Blood.* Oh gosh, Sam… My chest spasms and my eyes sting with tears as images of him choking on his last breaths fill my head.

Glancing around the room, I recognize it as one of the classrooms in the research building. Mid-morning light streams in through the window and onto the cot on which I'm lying. I look down, seeing blood smudged on my jeans and sweatshirt also.

"You killed Sam," I say, looking sharply at Carl who seems to be waiting for me to talk. "Why?"

Carl sits on a nearby folding chair and crosses a leg, hands clasped over his knee. He wears a pair of casual dress slacks, a polo, and a light fleece jacket. His ease infuriates me.

"Matt shot him in self-defense," he says as if it should be obvious. "You were trespassing. What did you expect?"

Reeling from disbelief, I rewind the events of last night—at least I'm pretty sure it was last night. "We weren't threatening you. We were only watching, and you're the one that had Connie spying on us. *You're* the one that unleashed an army on us in the middle of the night."

I think that catches Carl off guard for the slightest moment, but he returns to stoic detachment. "Why were you watching?"

"Beats the hell out of me," I mumble, awkwardly trying to rub my side that throbs more sharply than ever. But touching it makes it hurt more. Sighing, I relax back into the cot, awaiting whatever it is Carl plans to do with me and wondering what the state of my blood sugar is. I feel pretty jittery. My thoughts move to Gabriel, however, and impatience finds me once more when Carl says nothing. I turn my head to look at him, noticing he has quite a bit of scruff on his usually clean-shaven face. "Why am I here? I thought I was already doing what you wanted me to do— finding a cure to the life force problem you created." I grit my teeth and reel in my temper over Carl getting his way. "You made sure of that when you had me work on Gabriel. So what is it you want now?"

His pale blue eyes move over to me and he smiles in a weary kind of way. It reminds me of Robert's smile. I don't like seeing Robert's gentle vulnerability on Carl's horrible face, and my lip curls in distaste.

"Tell me where you're at on it," he says. "I'm sure we can figure this out."

"No," I say, appalled that he would even ask.

Carl's brow creases and he shakes his head at me like I'm misbehaving. "Walk with me, Wendy." He stands up.

Undecided as to whether I'm going to do *anything* he asks, I lie still for a moment, gathering my thoughts. This whole thing was a mistake. I haven't learned a thing and Sam is dead. Mark and Farlen are... Oh I hope they're alright.

I can lie here and hope my stubbornness wins me freedom, or I can acquiesce to Carl's request, follow him around, and hope he spills some vital piece of information...

Holy crap! I jerk my head to the window again. *Mid-morning.* It's around the time in Robert's vision. I don't know if it's today or three days from now, but chances are I am about to be *in* the vision. That is, if Carl plans to take me outside.

The tree. It's right outside this building.

My heart leaps into overdrive.

Calm down, Wendy, I tell myself, closing my eyes. What is it Robert says? Assume nothing. Pretend you know nothing. Just... act natural. What's natural? Refusing to go with him? Shoot. I'm overthinking this. I need to forget I remembered the vision and just do what I had already planned to.

What did I plan, though? I didn't. That's the problem... I reach up and put my bound hands on my forehead, which is sweating.

When anxiety won't let me lie here any longer, I carefully sit up, cringing and stifling my need to cry out as pain stabs under my ribcage. I have to sit ramrod straight to keep from squeezing whatever muscle or organ is protesting.

A quick glance at Carl reveals him watching me, taking in my careful movements. Lifting myself from the cot completely, I spread my feet to keep from swaying too much. "Can I go to the bathroom?" I ask. "I need to check my glucose."

"We checked only a half-hour ago. It's fine," he says, holding the door open.

Through the door is another man, almost black hair, young, lanky. I recognize him as the person who killed Sam last night. Matt. He's properly outfitted in gloves and long sleeves. I don't spare him another glance, not letting my thoughts settle on Sam as I follow Carl carefully down the hall, Matt taking up the rear. I need to use my head to figure out how to get the information I need. The problem is I don't know what information Carl *has*. I do know, however, that my time to get it is limited. I'm at the compound. Robert is sure to know I'm in trouble when his men don't check in, which means he'll send a legion to get me. That begs the question as to why Carl hasn't hidden me somewhere else. Unless he's depending on his army from last night to hold off Robert. Oh gosh, this could turn into a blood bath.

Carl leads me down the stairs, Matt near my elbow, cautious, probably expecting me to make a leap at Carl with my bare hands. I have no such ideas though. I'm exactly where I need to be. I think. I hope. I notice one of Carl's hands is balled into a fist, and I'm not sure what to make of that.

"Let's go outside," Carl says, holding the exterior door open. Taking several calming breaths, I follow.

"It's such a nice day," Carl says, looking up at the clear blue sky. "Your mother always preferred to have conversations outside. She said it cleared the mind." He pauses, and he smiles a little to himself before glancing back at me. "Plus, you look pale."

I snort. "That's called dying," I say nonchalantly, certain it's true and wondering how it will hit Carl.

He stops and whips around completely, looking at me with wide eyes. "Are you...? What do you have?"

I shrug. I don't know, but I wouldn't tell him even if I did know.

Carl looks around somewhat frantically like he's got a doctor on call stashed behind a tree or something. Pulling his shoulders back, he indicates a horizontal log next to the path. "Have a seat then," he says, resignation settling into his voice, his face suddenly more aged. He clearly believes me. He probably even expected my announcement. He waves a hand at Matt who backs up to the building, out of earshot. I sit, hands bound in front of me, staring down at the gravel path, waiting to be inspired about what to say. Nothing comes. Instead my irritation over my situation grows.

"What can I do for you?" he asks finally as if I've simply dropped into his office for advice on a Tuesday afternoon.

I glare at him. *"Do* for me? You've done enough, thanks. I'll take it from here." Being snotty is natural for me, right?

Carl clasps his hands behind his back. "Why do you have so much anger? You can't think rationally when you're angry, you know."

I grunt. He's right. I hate that he's right. I need to stop being defensive. I'm never going to get anything out of this ridiculous venture if I don't start thinking offensively. Gabriel is always good at staying calm. What would he say? *Carl, old chap, let's all have a sit down and talk this out. I surmise that we all want an end to this chess match.* I hold back a smile, imagining it.

"Carl," I say deliberately. "It is very hard to be rational around you when you kill people all the time. I'm here to—to talk." *Really? That's all you got?* "Although after last night," I add, "I can't believe I bothered to come anywhere near you."

Carl wears a look of indecision. He's too far outside of my emodar for me to tell what he's thinking. He's looking at something in his hand though, the same hand that was in a fist. I can't see what it is though. I look past him to the research building, noticing the gum tree standing next to it, exactly as Robert described. A couple leaves drift to the ground. The colors are exactly like the colors I saw in the vision, confirming that I'm exactly where I am supposed to be. It's not how I imagined it happening, but here I am. Robert's ability never ceases to tangle my brain.

"Wendy?" Carl asks. "Do you have *any* idea what's going on here?"

I look at him, taken off guard. Does he know I'm here because of one of Robert's visions? How could Carl know? A spy?

Forget the vision or you might ruin it. "You tell me, Carl. I'm tied up." I hold up my hands. "My husband is dying. I am, too. Kaylen will be soon. I'm here because I thought…" I have no idea what I thought. But I do believe Carl still knows guilt, and I think some part of him must feel for what he's done to me, so I ought to milk it if I can. "I figured since I'm going to die soon if I can't solve this, you might want to tell me everything you know. Maybe then we might have a chance of undoing everything you've screwed up."

Carl looks beyond me. "There is only one way to get the information you need."

I look at him expectantly, excitedly, but he doesn't continue. "Carl, please…"

His eyes lower slowly to mine, his brow crinkling softly, maybe compassionately. "What are you willing to sacrifice?" he asks quietly.

Probably not the same things Carl is. "Like what? Someone's life? No. And why would I? I'd end up like you. Unable to help anyone."

His expression turns quizzical and slightly troubled. "What would you know about that?"

The vulnerability there reminds me of my conversation with Briona, the Jamaican woman from Robert's office who can sense death. She hinted at Carl's weaknesses.

"I know you have no abilities. I even know why." Or at least a strong suspicion. "You're afraid you're going to die and your whole life will have been a waste."

His face brightens with interest rather than offense as he comes to sit on the other end of the log. Beneath his overt curiosity lies the discomfort of anxiety. "Why?" he asks.

I find it hard to believe that he hasn't figured it out by now, but then I guess you'd have to *believe* in morality in order to entertain that having it might be important for things like supernatural gifts.

"Because you let Louise twist you," I reply. "Life force abilities are powered by your soul's light and when you do things like murder people, you lose that light. No light, no power."

Carl opens his mouth to protest, but shuts it, thinking hard about that, searching for alternative explanations. He turns slightly away from me, looking down at whatever is in his hand again, and I pick up a pang of guilt.

"Why have you let her rule you so long?" I say gently, knowing the answer to the question, but wanting Carl to ask himself. If I can turn him against Louise once and for all, this will be a trip well spent. "Is it because when you lost your ability, you needed her in order to have any hope of fixing things? That's not true, you know. I've felt her. Whatever Louise's motives are for what she's been doing all these years, it's not because she wants to make the world a better place. I know you've questioned the things she does. You knew what she was doing was wrong, but you let her convince you it was for the greater good."

Carl looks down at the ground, lost in thought, listening but distracted.

I brace my hands on my legs, trying my hardest to sit up straight so my side doesn't hurt. But I'm so tired. Weakness begs me to lie down, or at least slump over. Ignoring it as best I can, I say, "Let her go. Walk away. Don't let her ruin what's left of you. You can fix this. We have a chance. I swear I'm going to work until my last breath if that's what it takes." I look at his face, feeling a bit surreal. Sometimes it's easy to forget he's my *father*. Other times his features are so familiar that it hits me all over again who he is and how screwed up that is. He's calculating, so I'm not sure what that means. He seems determined about something, though whatever it is doesn't feel like the moral turnaround I've been shooting for. Actually, the more he considers it, the more I don't like it. It's dark.

"My suggestion is to look at people in the energy world as they die," Carl says confidently. "That's what I did, only I saw so little of it that it was impossible to really tell what was going on. The life forces disappeared too quickly. But you can see more. You should be able to see what they're doing."

That can't be right. I watched Sam die only last night. I saw nothing. His soul disappeared from view before it ever left his body.

Carl looks at his watch, both anticipating and dreading something.

Crap. This is not good. He's expecting someone? Louise? If she comes I am *screwed*. I can't undo her brainwashing on Carl if she's around.

"Have you killed anyone since Don?" Carl asks almost conversationally.

"No," I say, disgruntled. "Unlike you, I don't make a habit of killing people." There goes my father-daughter pow-wow.

After several moments of silence, realizing I need to get Carl talking if I can, I say, "When did you first lose it? Or was it gradual?"

Elbows on knees, hands clasped under his chin, Carl glances at me. "My ability? It was gradual at first. And then gone suddenly."

"What were you doing at the time?"

Immediately uncomfortable, he changes the subject. "So you're unwell. What do you have, Wendy?"

I cross my arms and look away. "I don't know. But something's wrong with me."

"And you thought a stakeout would be a better idea than a doctor?" He chuckles, though it's tinged with an ancient pain. He contemplates saying something more, and it's a long time before he finally says tentatively, "Your mother was like that. We'd been expecting it—her illness—but she wouldn't do anything preventative. She said there was no time. We needed to worry about a cure with my ability, not with medications..." His voice cracks, and, embarrassed, he looks away.

I expect him to continue when he's got it together, but he changes his mind, looking at his watch again. He fights for determination, battling against a familiar doubt. He pulls his fist out of his pocket and looks at it again, and that rejuvenates his commitment. To what though?

"I'll give you what you need if you'll make me a promise," Carl says unexpectedly.

"What's that?" I ask, pulse sprinting forward.

"Next time someone touches you, you watch what happens to them in the energy world."

"You want me to... watch someone die there?" I ask, both repulsed and confused.

"Not just *anyone*," Carl says slowly. "Someone who is susceptible to the ill-effects."

Within moments it hits me and my jaw drops. "Oh. My. Gosh." I leap to my feet and away from him. "*That's* how you lost it, isn't it?" I hiss. "Your ability? You watched what happened when you killed people in the colorworld, didn't you? On *purpose*?" Sickened, I shake my head vigorously. "No way. No. I told you, I don't kill people. Dammit, Carl. I told you that's how you lost it. I wasn't kidding. What happened to you? Why can't you see that's so, *so* wrong?"

He rolls his eyes at me, looking so much like Ezra that it momentarily confuses me. This situation hardly calls for derision.

"Wendy," he chides, "calm down."

"Calm down?!" I shrill. "Tell me it's not true. Then I'll calm down!"

"So full of fiery indignation. I see Sara rubbed off on you."

"Don't you bring my mother into this!" I snarl. "It was because of her I didn't end up a scumbag like you."

Carl shifts in his seat to face me and says deliberately, "Sara was not your mother."

I stamp my foot, indignant that Carl still thinks Sara, AKA Leena, was not my mother. She might not have given birth to me, but she was my mother. "You have no right to even speak her name. You go around murdering people, doing hypno-touch on me as a *baby* even though you knew it would eventually be lethal. You did the same thing to Kaylen and then you all but forced me to do it to Gabriel. And you think you have *any* right to tell me the woman that dedicated her life to loving me and taking care of me wasn't my mother? You don't know what a mother *is*. And you have no *clue* what a father is." Heaving furious breaths I kick at the gravel. Why am I here?

"Do you promise?" he asks as if I haven't spoken.

I glare at him. "You want me to promise I'll watch someone die in the colorworld from my lethal skin? No. I don't plan on utilizing that particular skill ever again. Even on you."

"Why are you so obstinate?" he says. "Why did you even come here if you don't want something from me? I'm telling you I'm going to help you and you throw it back in my face out of what? Principle? You are acting exactly your age, Wendy. I honestly expected better from you."

I don't like Carl having the upper hand here and calling the shots. I might be tied up but surely I can say or do something to turn the tide a little...

That's when I remember the necklace. I restrain the need to reach for it. If I am going to let Carl see it, it needs to happen naturally. If he sees me pull it out, he's going to know I'm using it to manipulate him. So I bite my tongue, literally.

Exhaustion overpowering me, I plop down on the far end of the bench, and cry out briefly from the pain under my ribcage.

"Fine," I say once I recover, summoning as much graciousness I can muster. "If, by some accident, I touch someone who is susceptible to my death-touch, I will watch what happens in the colorworld. But I'm telling you, if that's what it's going to take to solve this, it's not happening. It's a literal hell when someone is dying from my skin so I'm very careful."

"I'm sure you are," Carl says quietly. He slaps one of his knees. "Now, we don't have much time and there are some things I want you to know. If you could contain your temper that would be helpful." He looks at me reproachfully.

I stare back at him for at least fifteen seconds. He fluctuates easily between timidity and command, but with sarcasm weaving throughout as if it's always present, lurking, and looking for any outlet. Could I be any more like him?

I smile disingenuously, struggling between disgust and puzzlement. "Sure, Dad. Just promise you won't say anything dumb, and I think I can control myself."

Carl lowers his chin and looks at me through his eyelashes, brows knit. Though I never had a father growing up, there is no mistaking the 'father-like' reprimand in it, and I involuntarily feel compunction, as if my being intrinsically recognizes him as my father and responds accordingly.

I look away and try to cross my arms, forgetting my bound hands. To my horror I almost huff like a teenager, contributing further to my unrest. This man is *not* my father. This man is a sperm donor. Nothing more.

I have the urge to reach for the necklace again. I think leaning over might make it fall out of my shirt, but my side hurts so badly I'm not sure I can manage that...

Not realizing my awkwardness, Carl says, "Yes, I gave you diabetes. And food allergies. I went to medical school in an effort to solve my skin limitations, so I had the background to figure it out. I did it because I needed ample opportunity to give you the ability to see the energy world as I once could. The *world* needed you to. You might see it as selfish, but it was not for me. Gina was already dead by then."

I open my mouth to protest but he holds up a hand. "Yes, I know you don't agree. I don't really care what you think. I did what had to be done, and one day you'll learn to do the same."

He turns to face me then, his eyes fierce. "Whether you like it or not, you are part of something bigger than you imagine. It will require more of you than you want to give. And trust me, you will want to give up. But you'll have no choice but to continue."

He stares at me for several moments. There is no denying his absolute conviction. Carl never came across to me as a powerful personality, but this moment changes that opinion. I still think he's evil, but this is a very different side of Carl. The side that explains how he has been so dedicated for so long.

I look away and sigh. Yet *another* way I am like him. When we make up our minds we are formidable. And when we confront grief, we tend to dedicate ourselves to the wrong thing. And we see it as sacrifice and therefore justified.

"Sara took away your chances of survival and all because she was afraid of what she didn't understand. I know why she did it. But you can't make decisions based on fear. Remember that."

"Oh sure. Great advice. And you've accomplished so much by following it," I say.

Carl tilts his head. "Maybe not in the way I intended, but I did accomplish giving you the ability I hoped to. I've done my part. Now it's time for you to do yours."

"You are so irritating," I snap. "Don't act like what you've done was destiny or something. You know what I think? This ultimate purpose you keep harping on is your way of rationalizing all the terrible things you've done over the years. Delusions of grandeur. That's what you have."

Carl turns in his seat to face me, looks down at his watch and then back to my face. "Let me make one more point and then I will let it go. I know you know about Robert's uncanny ability to predict the future. He was born with it. And me? I was born with what I could do as well. How is that, Wendy? Humanity is changing. You might want to start asking yourself why."

Focusing on the tree from Robert's vision over Carl's shoulder, I recall it was that tree where Gabriel first demonstrated his astounding counting ability. He counted the leaves within seconds simply by looking. His ability to count is *natural*. I know only three people with natural abilities. And I wouldn't even know about Gabriel if I'd never gone to the compound. I precisely remember Kaylen saying natural abilities were extremely rare. Three people can hardly be considered the whole of *humanity*. Carl is so full of it.

"A few people does not indicate some kind of genetic shift," I point out. "Besides, if people were mutating with supernatural powers in droves, why would you be doing hypno-touch to *give* them superpowers? You're delusional. Why can't you see it? Can you *please* let this dream go?"

"I am as much between a rock and a hard place as you are," Carl says quietly.

"Bull. We *always* have a choice. It only seems like we don't when the alternative looks too hard."

"Oh the naiveté of the young," Carl says wistfully.

I cross my arms. "Oh the pigheadedness of the old."

He chuckles almost imperceptibly. Straightening up, he says, "I told you I'd make my point and then I'd drop it. And just in time. She's finally here."

23

*W*hipping my head around to look down the path, I see a head of long, white-grey hair coming over the hill followed by the rest of Louise's lithe figure wrapped in some kind of peasant dress. My stomach drops. I really was starting to think Carl might let me go. But Louise will start calling the shots and there is no way she's going to let me out of her sight.

It's now or never if I'm going to try the necklace. With my back to Carl, I reach up to search for the pendant. But I can't find it. Reaching a little higher for the chain on my neck, I don't find that either. *Crap.* It must have fallen off when we were crashing through the woods. What do I do? That was my last defense... I swallow a few tears of desperation as I see Louise's ominous figure move closer and closer.

She spots me and her only reaction is to raise her eyebrows. I shiver involuntarily in the chilly November air as she continues toward us. She stops in front of me. "Oh my, Carl. You do know how to deliver surprises. Hello, Wendy, dear. What brings you here?"

I look down at my bound hands, wondering why she would act like I'm making a social visit. I'm not going to speak to Louise if I don't have to.

Louise looks at Carl expectantly.

I guess Carl's face relays whatever his reply is to her unspoken question because Louise looks at me again, shakes her head, and sighs. "*Still* after all this time you are stuck on your own problems. I do not understand how you can subsist that way. It's awfully narrow and suffocating. I'd think that being married to someone like Gabe would have opened your horizons a bit."

She turns back at Carl. "Have you learned anything?"

"Only that she is unwell. And so is Gabe," he replies.

Louise shakes her head pityingly. "One thing left to do then, isn't there?" she says quietly, looking at nothing, but with a pensive set to her lips. Her emotions are too far away to sense.

"You know I can't," Carl says.

Louise nods. "It was always meant to be me. I will not falter this time. And when I succeed, I can right everything that should have been righted years ago."

Eyes wide, I look uneasily at Carl, but he's not looking at me. "I'm sorry," he says quietly to her. "It is clearly my fault we've been unsuccessful all these years. But are you sure?"

Carl's words are completely disingenuous. He *wants* her to do whatever it is she's talking about. *Carl is manipulating Louise?*

"Yes," Louise says. "At this point there is no choice."

"No choice about what?" I blurt.

"To share your sight," Louise answers calmly.

Terrified, I look at Carl, but his head is bowed. I turn my attention back to Louise. *She wants to touch me?* "You can't be serious." And while I can't ever gauge when Louise is serious, I do know that she's crazy. She has just enough crazy to touch me.

I know without a doubt that she will die. Just thinking about it sets my hands trembling. I'd be sweating if the air weren't so chill. I may hate her, but I do not want to experience, let alone cause, her death.

"You'll die if you touch me," I say desperately.

Carl looks at me. "How do you know?"

"Because she's bad," I say. "Her life force won't survive mine."

Carl is pleased and I know now that he asked that question knowing the answer. And he apparently wanted me to tell Louise. *What is going on with him?*

She scoffs. "It's just as I thought. See Carl? She knows I have the strength of will to survive so she makes up lies to scare me."

He waves a hand. "Wendy does hate you. I have no doubt she'd say anything to keep her ability from you. You have no argument from me on that."

"No," I whisper. "It's not a lie."

"Wendy, dear," Louise says, "I know you touch your brother, Gabe, Kaylen, and who knows who else. I worked with you; you forget I know what motivates you. You learned to control it by accident. That is the only way you would've had the bravery to touch people so close to you—because you'd already figured out control."

"No," I insist, shaking my head. "I *cannot* control it. If your life force is not bright enough, you *die* when you touch me. And *you,* Louise, have *always* underestimated what I am capable of."

"Oh ho, ho," Louise says, "is that so? And you think mine is not bright enough?"

"I'm positive," I say.

"Louise, you know I can't prevent you from doing anything, but what if she's right?" asks Carl, though I realize he is triumphant. And I'm not sure why. He is clearly after something from Louise.

"Wait," I beg her. "I'll look and see. I''ll tell you exactly how dim your life force is."

Carl has a jacket on, so I scoot over to grab his arm. He flinches but doesn't move away, I waste no time in channeling myself into the colorworld. I adjust to the brightness and look at Louise's life force before me. I have seen her life force many times in the past when I was at the compound. But I've not seen it since my sight improved, allowing me to see the iridescent steam and the difference in brightness of life forces. But now, with my new capability, her life force is clearly different from what I'm used to seeing. It's perfectly swirled, like a healthy life force, and it even shines, but it's the *way* it shines. Like an inanimate object. Reflective rather than self-sustaining.

I look at Carl. His has the same effect, but I could swear it's not as bad as Louise's. The swirl over his chest is fighting to illuminate itself. Some part of it is still... alive. I look back at Louise's and the sight makes me nauseous. It's a dead thing.

"Louise, you can't," I beg, tears starting to come to my eyes. Her life force is such a tragedy. I know it must have once been a thing of beauty, but it was oppressed, suffocated until it became lifeless. "Your life force can't even hold its own light," I tell her, looking away. But I swear I can still feel it, like a vacuum. I think it's sucking on me. Glancing at it once more, I think it's actually sucking on *everything*. Pulling at the light around it in order to sustain itself. At first I wonder how it is I didn't see this about her when I first saw her in the colorworld at the compound. But as I watch the way her life force reflects light rather than producing it, I begin to wonder if she *seemed* bright then because she was always inches away from Gabriel as she instructed me, and Gabriel's light was feeding hers, making it appear brighter than it was. As I glance at Carl, I wonder how much of the light in him is his own since he is so close to *me*.

As I think about Carl and his eagerness in this moment, realization awakens in me: he *wants* Louise to touch me *because* he knows she will die. That's what he meant when he said he would give me what I needed! He plans to use me to kill Louise and he wants me to watch it in the colorworld!

"Louise!" I cry, releasing Carl, but it's too late. She has leapt forward, and before I can move or even think of what to do, her bare hand is on mine. I have not left the colorworld, sitting close to Carl as I am, so I see every detail of what happens next.

Her life force begins brightening like a lightbulb, and at the same time energy hemorrhages from right where her hand grips mine. And then I hear wailing. It comes from those usually so quiet voices I hear in the colorworld. It reminds me of what it sounds like to manipulate a life force: grating and unbearable. But I can't escape it. I'm frozen where I am, stuck, I think, because *she* is. I *perceive* her just as I do Gabriel when he is in the colorworld with me.

Her life force continues to brighten until it's nothing more than a silhouette. Her body and organs are merely outlines. As I perceive her I realize it's not her body I feel, but her life force itself. In fact, I feel it spread out within her body. I think I'm *seeing* it, too, the part of her life force strands *inside* of her body. I have never actually seen the end of a life force strand before. It is *not* one long strand. There are many strands, at least millions.

Her impending torment gathers at the same time, and I shove at it. *Hard.* I yank my own emotions forward to block hers. I don't question how I manage this so easily, because I'm caught in the moment, and what I see right now with Louise's body holds me spellbound.

Strands are inserted at Louise's chest and also in the top of her head, embedded into her brain. It's with both my sight and my perception of her body that I make out her vascular system stretching out from her heart in rivers of arteries and veins and into the tiny capillaries. Each capillary has a life force strand running through it all the way to its end, each strand thinner than spider silk and illuminating the flesh around it, and I think this is why her body appears transparent. The intricacy is astounding.

And then there is the life force as it resides *outside* of the body. The bulk of her strands have gathered together until they are wound into a thick rope. One end of the rope is divided, part of it going into her head while the other is inserted in her chest. The free end of the rope reaches upward, looking almost like a tight purple flame suspended over her. The rope tugs and twists, and from what I can tell it's trying to pull her strands from where they are embedded into her head and chest.

The rope gives a determined tug and the strand ends in her body retract back toward her heart, retreating from her chest.

With a final jerk the strands in her head come out as well. As soon as they detach, her whole life force disappears. Just as

Sam's did. Then Louise's pale yellow body drops to the ground; her grip on my hand loosening as her heart stops.

But I can still hear the moaning strands that are now invisible to me. They must be moving away because the sound retreats until the other voices here overtake the horrendous cries. I blink into the emptiness, my chest like lead and my body weakened and shivering.

I manage to scoot away from Carl and out of the colorworld. My teeth start chattering and a cold sweat has broken out on my forehead. Bile rises in my throat and I turn in time to retch onto the grass, coughing and sputtering as I grip my stomach and try to hold it together.

Tears fall with the vomit and I realize I am sobbing, too.

"What happened?" asks a voice from behind me. It's not Carl. I think it's Matt who must have witnessed Louise's collapse.

I grit my teeth once the vomiting stops and sink to the ground, swaying on all fours. My side screams in protest, but I'm so drained that I can't have the energy to even cry out. Furthermore, the residue of Louise's terror that I held at bay so easily, now insults my mouth and my thoughts with a putrid aftertaste.

I work to picture Gabriel's face. I struggle to remember what he smells like and what it's like to be held by him, needing some small portion of pleasant familiarity so I can stay aware. That calms my sobs, and while I'm still shaking, I can finally think beyond the thing I just witnessed. It's happened exactly like Gabriel said. I shared my light with Louise and she lit up like a lightbulb, only her life force couldn't seem to take it and it separated itself from her body.

I look up then, rubbing away the tears that have blurred my eyes. I see Carl crouched next to Louise's body, his face harrowed as he looks down at her. He is sad. He pretty much tricked her into killing herself, but I guess it's still a loss to him. As I watch him for a moment, his face slackens. Though I can't feel him anymore, I could swear he looks relieved. Lifting my eyes beyond him, I see the nearly leafless broadleaf next to the research building. And then it dawns on me: the vision was about seeing Louise die. Because now I understand how the life force is connected to the body.

I don't know if what I've seen will help me, and I'm so drained both physically and mentally that I can't find my reaction.

"You killed her!" Matt says, having come closer.

"Wendy didn't kill her," Carl says, his voice quavering. "She killed herself." He looks at me with empty eyes. "Did you keep your promise?"

He's holding Louise's lifeless hand. Her eyes are still open and staring. "Yes," I whisper, remembering the sound of her life force strands screaming in protest. Bringing my head up, I say, "Carl, please. Can you let me go now? I really don't think I'm well. I need a hospital." I can't believe I haven't passed out already.

To my surprise, Carl leaps to his feet. "Matt, remove Wendy's restraints and escort her into town. I'm sure Robert is on his way if he isn't there already."

"Okay, Mr. Fowler," Matt says, looking worriedly from Louise to me.

As I walk away with Matt behind me, Carl says. "And get the other two as well. Send them with her." He pauses and then adds, "It's in your hands now, Wendy."

I don't respond; I'm too hazed but for the urgency to find civilization, a doctor, and Gabriel. Before we disappear over the top of the hill, though, I can't help glancing over my shoulder. Carl stands where we left him, looking down at something in his right hand. But I see a slink of silver chain hanging between his fingers. My hand goes up to my neck, and that's when I realize I didn't lose the necklace. Carl saw it and took it. Somehow that necklace did its part, and I didn't even have to try…

My head spins and I nearly run into a tree, catching myself on its trunk and pushing myself back in the right direction. I want to go faster, to run even, but my legs are dead weights as I shuffle them forward. I nearly trip over a few pebbles that catch my toes.

You can do this. One foot in front of the other. Just make it into town.

"Are you alright?" Matt asks from behind me. "You're moving like you're drunk."

I nod and shuffle forward, thinking nothing but how to propel my feet. *Move, Wendy.* I am sure that if I can't get out of here quickly, something terrible is going to happen.

Something terrible *did* happen. But I don't have any room in my head for replay. I only have room for determination. I need to get out of here.

24

*A*lthough I feel tired enough, I don't sleep on the drive into town. My muscles twitch so much it's impossible. Mark and Farlen are with me again, thankfully. They were captured, but I don't have energy to ask for the story.

I'm thinking of Sam as my head bounces uncomfortably against the car window; I can't hold it up. I became comfortable around him even in the short time we spent together, which is kind of rare for me to experience so quickly, but I think I've changed; I'm more inclined to give people a chance instead of dismissing them. I mourn the friendship that would have been. He couldn't have been older than mid-thirties, but Sam gave his life for mine and for my mission.

A fruitless mission it was. What I learned from watching Louise die leaves me more lost than ever. The complexity of the relationship between body and life force is not something even a lifetime would allow me to duplicate. And even if I could figure it out, how do I move the strands around, let alone do it safely? The more I think of it, the more daunting the problem becomes. I am in *way* over my head.

I am a dead woman walking. My time is limited. It isn't fair that I lived and Sam died. It shouldn't have been that way. Sam's life was not worth this. Sinking further into the possibility of inevitable failure, I have no reason to want to cling to the sliver of awareness I have left. My vision blurs and I have no idea how much time passes until the car stopping jars me. I try to open my eyes but I don't think I can. Someone pulls me from the car and I cry out as my side spasms. I take four labored steps away from the car and half-collapse, half-sit on the ground. At least the pain has woken me up a little.

"What's wrong?" Mark asks, crouching down beside me. "You don't look so good, Wendy."

Sucking in several breaths, I panic at the sensation that I can't get enough air. I lay down entirely to conserve energy, gravel digging into my face, but I don't care. "Hospital," I gasp.

"Did they drug you with something?" Mark asks.

I try to shake my head. "No. I'm sick."

"Can't you see she's in bad shape?" I hear Mark say angrily over my head. "We're at least a mile from town."

A few silent seconds pass and then I hear Matt, "One phone call. Here."

Mark's arm reaches over me.

"Gabriel," I say, barely above a whisper.

"Wendy, we'll contact him, I promise," Mark says, heavy brows drawn together as he dials. "But 911 is more important right now."

Summoning the energy, I lift my hand, knocking the phone from his. I look for him but I can't see clearly. "My skin," I slur. "Nah safe. Gimme Gabriel. He knows who can'tush me."

"But he's in Monterey," Mark says somewhat desperately. "In the hospital."

If Robert is, in fact, on his way here, Gabriel will have broken out of the hospital to come along. "Rob knows ahmmin trouble. Gabriel will 'ave come. Trus' me." I hope they understood what I said.

I want to explain more, but my mouth isn't working. My thoughts are falling apart and it's a fight to stay conscious.

"Okay," Mark concedes, and I hear him dial. But I don't catch the conversation. It becomes murmuring in the background. Everything becomes an echo in the background.

***

An odd pressure in my ears wakes me up and I blink my eyes as a low, soffited ceiling comes into focus. A dim light emanates along the edge. The ceiling looks familiar. Turning my head, I see a small window. I'm on a plane. Robert's plane. It's about sunset and I wonder what day it is. I barely remember the last time I was awake. I vaguely recall being in a hospital and having Gabriel next to me. I remember going into the colorworld but I don't know how long I was there or when I left. I think I remember asking Gabriel what was wrong with me and he said my spleen.

"Gabriel?" I croak, turning to my other side. But he's not there.

Instead a woman in scrubs appears. She's a bit burly with caramel-colored skin, a bun, large lips, and a wide smile that reaches her eyes. "Hello, Mrs. Dumas. I'm Jeanelle. Your uncle hired me to take care of you. You're on your way back to Monterey right now. We just reached cruising altitude. Did the pressure change wake you up?"

"Where's Gabriel?" I ask.

"Mr. Dumas is sleeping."

"Sleeping?" I ask uneasily as I recall the last time that Gabriel wasn't around for me was when he was in a coma. I glance back at the window. It can't even be past eight o'clock because it's not yet dark.

"Yes. He was getting too worked up. It's not good for him in his state."

"He's okay?" I ask, my stomach uneasy.

She nods, but I can tell she's not telling me everything.

"What is it?" I demand, making a move to sit up.

She puts a hand on my arm. I notice she's gloved. "It's nothing to be concerned about. He wasn't really in a state to travel when we left Monterey this morning. It took it out of him. His lungs are stressed and he's fighting an infection. I needed to give him some antibiotics for that so I've got an infusion going to be sure he's well-hydrated."

Trying to force myself to relax, I settle back down in my narrow cot. "So what's wrong with me?" I ask.

"We're not quite sure yet," she replies. "Mr. Haricott insisted on having you stabilized for travel as soon as possible. They'll have more tests done when we arrive back in Monterey."

"Gabriel said it was my spleen. What's wrong with it?"

"It was enlarged."

"What does that usually indicate?" I ask, annoyed with her evasion.

She frowns. "It could mean a lot of things. Too many to speculate."

I roll my eyes. "Assume it's the worst-case scenario. Cancer or some other auto-immune thing. Which would it be?"

Again, surprise internally, but she brings her lips into a stubborn line. I'm about to insist that she get me an Internet-enabled device so I can look it up myself, but at that moment my uncle appears next to her, his face careworn and tired. He smiles thinly.

"Uncle Moby!" I say, his presence easing my tension. I reach out and, slightly surprised but unafraid, he takes my hand and sits down. I squeeze his fingers with my own bare ones, surprised at the slight rush of energy that emanates from him where he touches me. It diffuses into the rest of my body, warming me. I smile at him. "If I can't see Gabriel, you are absolutely the next best thing."

He takes a disjointed breath and I can tell he's keeping strict control. "If only it were better circumstances."

I shrug, noticing the IV inserted in my hand. "You and I both knew it was inevitable. What can you tell me? This stubborn nurse or doctor or whoever she is won't even give me an informed guess about why I passed out and my spleen was enlarged."

Robert glances at Jeanelle. "Go ahead. Wendy is aware that it's not a definitive diagnosis."

Warily, Jeanelle turns her attention back to me, her mouth set in a grudging line. "The initial blood count indicates infection. But you have no fever, and your enlarged spleen and lymph nodes plus the rash on your arms, points to some type of leukemia. You'll have a bone marrow biopsy done once we reach Monterey. That will tell us exactly."

Rash on my arms? I lift one and see red bumps on the underside. I lay my head back and look at the ceiling of the cabin. "Just like my biological mom," I sigh.

"Yes," Robert says. "Gabe already took a look at her file on the flight to Big Bear. She presented with exactly the same symptoms as you. She had T-cell prolyphocytic. It's probably the most aggressive type of leukemia. I've already let the hospital know ahead of time to include it as a likely possibility. It often takes some time to diagnose because it's so rare. Gabe actually insisted on having your blood drawn for diagnostics before you received a transfusion so the results wouldn't be skewed by the donor blood. He was quite prepared—which is why I insisted on taking him along."

"He always is. And I had no idea I had a transfusion. What did that test say?"

"We won't get the results for a day or so."

"Of course not," I say tiredly. "They always take forever. But I think we can assume it's as bad as it could be."

"It will indeed make the waiting easier," Robert agrees.

My thoughts turn to Ezra… This will devastate him. What am I going to say to him?

And Sam. Carl is responsible for Sam's death, too.

And inadvertently so am I…

I glance at Jeanelle. "I need a private word with my uncle."

She leaves without argument.

Robert leans toward me, resting his arms on the side of my cot, and with that motion, his stress of holding in so much cracks a little. It takes him a moment to compose himself, but I catch the red around his eyes and it stabs right into my heart. "I hope you aren't going to tell me what you found," he says. "I'm at the threshold of what I can handle right now, so it's not a good idea."

Watching and feeling Robert, I'm struck with how unguarded he is at this moment. In the silence between us, a sense of security comes over me, a draw to stay near Robert. I guess people would call it a bond, but I hadn't realized how tangible it could feel. With it, I am suffused with joy—odd, one would think, in a heavy moment like this. But connecting with my Uncle Moby fills a lack of something I didn't know I was missing, and I want to enjoy it. Unable to contain myself, I reach up and put my arms around his neck, pulling myself up and him closer. Tears overflow and it takes me a second to get my voice working.

I lie back on the cot, feeling kind of like a child, lying in bed and getting tucked in, but it's not awkward with my uncle. "Uncle Moby, I want to be like you when I grow up."

He squeezes my hand, his own trembling slightly as he holds it together. He manages though, and he smiles at me, his eyes full of warmth that reaches a depth I have not seen or felt before.

"So," I say, "you had your jet fueled up and ready to go before you ever knew we were in trouble. I don't even want to know how you got the hospital in Big Bear to let Gabriel pass out orders, let alone even be with me in the ER. I don't remember a whole lot, but I do remember that. Makes me think you knew exactly what would happen…"

He chuckles. "That was simply preparedness, Wendy. Visions have taken me by surprise so often in the past that I don't underestimate the possibilities."

"I guess you're right," I say thoughtfully. "After all, if you'd known what was going to happen you wouldn't have sent Connie with us." My mouth draws down. "Sam…" I look at my uncle. "I'm so sorry," I whisper, a lump forming in my throat again, this time from sadness. "He shouldn't have died. It was a complete waste."

Robert's intellect plods more heavily. "Yes, that is a tragedy. But let's not ever call someone's death a waste. That's never the case."

"Plenty of people die needlessly," I point out. "Sam died needlessly. How is that not a waste?"

Robert adjusts his seat, staying silent for a minute. I know he's preparing what to say and I wait, eager for Robert's wisdom to sort out my guilt over my part in Sam's death. I keep thinking about the price Robert said would be paid for the miracle. I should never have accepted his help to get a vision. He warned me, but I never thought *this* would be the price. He said it was a good goal, didn't he? Then why do I feel further away from my goal of solving this life force problem?

"Everyone dies," Robert says finally. "It is the final mortal destination for all of us. Every moment we are alive, we are inevitably approaching our death. Intrinsically, it has no value by itself anyway."

"Gee. That's supposed to make me feel better?"

"It's supposed to offer an alternative perspective on death."

I wait, expecting more, but he's waiting on me instead. "But... I didn't gain anything!" I protest. "I'm more lost than ever! If Sam was going to die, at least his death could have benefited a few people!"

"Let's say you *did* gain beneficial information. Would his death have been *worth* it then?"

I open my mouth to say... I'm not sure what. If I say yes, that means I'm assigning my own value on Sam's life. If I say no, that means I place more value on Sam's life than the people that would benefit.

"We humans like to put price tags on everything," Robert says, seeing my confusion. "It's in our nature to label, categorize, valuate. It's how we find assurance, stability, understanding—as tenuous as it is. The problem is that such a currency can't possibly be consistent or hold up to life's surprises. And it's not consistent because we never have all the facts, all the variables involved. Neither do you, Wendy. And *you,* someone who knew Sam and appreciated his life, only have one job when it comes to his death."

"What's that?" I ask.

"Make it add value to *yours.*"

"But I'm... dying," I say, slumping helplessly. "And I have no leads on how to save *anyone.*"

"You've heard of the idea that something is worth only as much as someone is willing pay for it?"

"Yeah..."

"Sam's worth is not determined by circumstances outside of your control. Sam's life is worth as much as you're willing to pay for it."

I furrow my brow, perplexed.

"I need to have a word with the pilot now," Robert says, standing. He puts a hand on my shoulder. "I'm glad to have you back, Wendy."

Before I can protest and demand further explanation, he disappears through the cabin door.

I repeat Robert's words over and over in my head. Sometimes I think I get what he's saying. *I have to make Sam's death mean something. And the only way I know to do that is to learn from it.* Still, full understanding of Robert's words evades me. The only conclusion I can draw is that I should never have asked Robert for help via a vision. I've learned my lesson about using the future to get things done. I won't do it again. From now on, I'll embrace ignorance and muscle my way through with brute determination and good old-fashioned research.

Once again my brain twists in knots. People always say ignorance is a bad thing. But it's clearly not always. Even Robert chooses ignorance sometimes. So does that mean there is such a thing as *the right amount* of ignorance?

I shake my head, exasperated. All I know is I won't be using a vision again. I'm not cut out for dealing with this supernatural stuff. Life sure is easier when knowing the future isn't even an option.

How on earth does Robert do it?

Is it really just his rules?

After about five minutes of pondering it, all of a sudden I hear, "Confound it, woman! I told you I won't be drugged into a coma! I went to sleep, didn't I? It's your own fault I didn't stay that way, coming in here and poking me for the tenth time!"

I hear a cabin door slide open and footsteps behind me. Angling my head to see, I spot Gabriel catch sight of me before he turns back to Jeanelle. "You wake me up to take my blood pressure but not to tell me my wife is awake?!"

In a few more steps, he throws himself at the side of my cot, dragging an IV pole behind him. "Wendy!" he exclaims. "You woke up!"

"Mr. Dumas, I *told* you she'd wake up and you didn't need to worry," Jeanelle says from behind him, her hands on her hips.

He ignores her, looking at me eagerly. "How are you feeling, Love?" he says softly.

"I've been better." I reach up to touch his cheek.

He catches my hand and holds it there.

Jeanelle huffs and leaves the cabin.

While Gabriel's eyes spell out relief, he is burdened under a great deal of suppressed emotion. Likely, while I've been sleeping, he's been coming to terms with the fact that I'm ill. And if he's been looking at my mom's file... Well that sounds like awful bedtime reading material.

"I love you," I say, not knowing what else I *can* say.

He frowns, placing my hand back on the blanket gently. "You don't have to say it like it's your dying confession."

"I didn't! I meant it."

"Oh I know you mean it," he says stubbornly. "Dying people are all about telling the living exactly how they feel."

"You're saying I told you that to bring deathbed closure? I think you've been reading my mom's file too much. That bad, huh?"

He cringes. "Admittedly, that may have something to do with it."

"Well whether I'm living or dying, I love you," I say. I squeeze his hand. "How are *you* holding up? I leave you alone for a day and you almost drown in your own lung fluid."

"I beg to differ," he says obstinately. "Whatever my mother told you, she was exaggerating."

I roll my eyes. "Whatever. I'm just glad to see you acting like yourself."

"Now that you are awake, I am doing much better. Earlier I upset Jeanelle so much I almost made her quit her job on her first day. I think she hates me."

"I'm pretty sure everyone in the medical profession hates you. You should stop jabbing hornet nests with sticks."

He smiles widely. "Oh I've missed you."

"I saw you only yesterday."

"I know. I can't miss you after one day?"

"You only missed me because I was unconscious and I'm dying."

His brows knit. "Don't say that."

"You did earlier."

"I was merely pointing out that *you* believed you were dying. Telling me that you loved me proved that you believed it."

"Gabriel..." I say, exasperated.

His expression deflates. "Sorry. But in my defense, I'm banking on your assertion that you can save me. And if you can save me, you can save yourself. Which means that though you are ill, you will not die. Therefore you are not dying. What did you discover?"

My mouth turns down as I think about Louise's life force and what it looked like leaving her body.

"I learned that hypno-touch does the equivalent of unraveling a Persian Rug."

"It sounds like you learned a lot then. Why do you look so down?"

I grip his hand. "Because I know nothing about carpet weaving. And what's worse is I have no idea what the original pattern was. I think you may be right. It's something I simply don't have the time to figure out."

He looks down at our hands and then back at me worriedly and tentatively. "Well... perhaps you'd like to hear about some progress on my end then. There's a chance I may have figured out how to give us more time."

25

Eyes wide, I stare at Gabriel, open-mouthed. "It's... perfect," I say. "How...? Oh forget it. I know how. You're smart. You consider everything. Things that no one else would *ever* consider."

We're taxiing down the runway, having just landed in Monterey, and Gabriel has just laid out the most unlikely solution for how to deal with aggressive hypno-touch disease that doesn't respond well to conventional aggressive treatments.

"Wendy, it's merely a theory," he points out. "One I haven't worked out all the particulars to."

"But you will," I say excited for the first time in days. Time is the thing I've worried most about since discovering Gabriel's poor reaction to chemo. And I really think Gabriel has bought more of it.

"Wendy," Gabriel says in a warning tone. "Don't depend on it until we know for sure it will work."

Jeanelle walks in. "I'm not done with this discussion," he mumbles to me, moving out of her way.

I ignore him, offering Jeanelle my arm to check my blood pressure, mocking his expression with pouty faces over her shoulder. After a little while he finally cracks a smile, satisfying me that he's not so opposed to his own idea that he's going to make much effort resisting. It also makes *me* feel better, making him smile. I've had enough melancholy.

But it's also my desperate attempt to distract myself from the dread of the upcoming reunion with Kaylen and Ezra. I'm going to reunite with them in a hospital. The happiest place on earth.

When we finally reach the ER, I find that arrangements for my admission have already been made. I also learn that they've been preparing a room. A double room. Gabriel and I get to share it. Miracle of miracles. Robert must be behind this.

While waiting for someone to take me up to my room, and after they take Gabriel away for a chest X-ray, Kaylen and Ezra show up with Robert. Ezra behaves exactly like I expected: stone-faced, rigid. He barely looks at me. Kaylen looks over at him at least four times, expecting, I think, for him to say something. I think she was prepared to 'wait her turn' to speak to me. Giving up on him, she moves in, leans over, and hugs me. "I'm so glad you're okay," she says.

"Sort of," I reply, giving her a wry smile, knowing Kaylen will appreciate the openness.

Stepping back, she mirrors my smile and shrugs. "I guess I should have said I'm so glad you're alive."

At that, Ezra spins on a heel and walks out of the room, tearing off a piece of my heart in the process. Tears spring to my eyes.

"Oh Wendy," Kaylen says, *her* eyes now watering. She sits on the edge of my bed.

Robert gives me a look and I nod. He turns to follow Ezra.

"I hate this," I whisper, looking at the empty place where Ezra stood only moments ago. And then I can't help it. I sob, and the weight of the last few days presses down on me at once.

Kaylen wastes no time climbing into the bed next to me and squeezing my hand, tucking her head next to mine. She says nothing, but I can feel what she's communicating. To be so obviously cared about somehow hurts, but it's a good hurt. Besides, I'd like to do this—cry so I can move on.

Kaylen seems to get this, though I can hear her quiet weeping next to me. To my relief, I don't sob for too long. And when I'm done, I'm instantly tired, but also more peaceful with the weight of Kaylen's cheek on my shoulder. I'm comforted, as usual, by having her near. Her presence is light, like always. Even when she's sad, she's not a burden.

A nurse shows up and informs me she's going to take my blood. I wasn't expecting that, but when I see that she's gloved already, I concede. Gabriel told me that in Big Bear I woke up briefly to take us into the colorworld so he could look at the life forces of the people working on me, and evidently I can stay in the colorworld even while half-conscious. I don't remember any of it, and he says it's because I was severely anemic at the time. He also learned that Latex is effective in preventing the transfer of energy. So this nurse should be good to go as long as she keeps her gloves on. I heard that Robert told the staff here that I am not to be touched without gloves. I'm amused to find out that they are using the same excuse I have in the past: that I have severe obsessive compulsive disorder, and whenever someone touches me I'm compelled to spend fifteen minutes washing my hands thoroughly afterward.

The nurse takes so much blood, however, that I look at her purposely and say, "You *do* know some of that isn't mine, right?"

213

She looks at me questioningly and with some irritation. Apparently she's not used to her pincushions talking back. "I had a transfusion earlier today," I explain.

"It's procedural," she responds blandly, though I think I surprised her a little and she actually *didn't* know that. She removes the needle expertly after taking about seven vials without speaking.

No wonder Gabriel hates hospitals.

"Why don't you just tattoo my arm with a number? Then you won't even have to look me in the face to identify me," I say smartly.

"They'll take you up to your room shortly," she says, ignoring my aggravation and leaving the room.

As her mental presence leaves my emodar, I taste the residue of it. In retrospect, I think what I picked up just now wasn't bored detachment, but purposeful. If I didn't know any better I'd think she knew I could read her and was trying not to *let* me.

Maybe my previous oxygen deprivation is still affecting me. I am definitely exhausted, and I don't much care what the nurse thought.

"Wow," Kaylen says, as surprised as me. "She's got a warm and fuzzy disposition."

Robert shows up then looking weary. "Ezra will be alright. Said he needs time to think through it."

"He's in the cafeteria doing math problems. Right?" I say.

Robert raises his eyebrows at first, but then heaviness fills his heart. "Oh dear. Realizing the reason you knew that so perfectly may be the saddest thing I've ever heard."

I give him a half-hearted smile. "It may be sad, but his consistency gives me a little assurance. Ezra made it through the last time this way. If he started acting out of character, then I might worry more. He'll come around by tomorrow."

"You look like you could use some serious sleep," Robert points out.

"I fully expect to pass out once they get me to my room."

"Should I stick around and wait until he's ready to go home?" Robert asks.

I shrug. "You can ask him. But most likely he'll want to stay. He'll figure out where my room is when he's ready. I'm sure I'll wake up in the morning to him staring at me and ready to talk."

"Very well," Robert says. "Kaylen?"

Kaylen looks at me.

"Go home and get some sleep," I tell her. "I promise I won't make any announcements until you get back. I seriously want to be unconscious right now."

"Okay," she says, giving my hand one more squeeze and standing up.

She and Robert say goodbye just as the orderly comes in to wheel me up.

When I reach the room, I want to stay awake until Gabriel gets here, but my eyes are begging me to close them. I oblige. Gabriel will understand. But before I fall asleep completely, I feel familiar pressure on my forehead: Gabriel's lips. I smile blearily to acknowledge him without opening my eyes, and I hear him whisper, "I love you, Wendy."

The moment becomes perfect. I may be sick, but I'm home whenever Gabriel is near.

***

Ezra doesn't look like he slept in a hospital. He's in different clothes. That, and the fact that he showed up at the same time as Robert and Kaylen, tells me he actually *did* leave with them last night. I wonder how they managed that?

Scraping the last bit of yogurt from the container on my breakfast tray, I say, "Hey guys. Boy did you miss all the action. The doctor just came. He said absolutely nothing. Before that was the new nurse. Gabriel is becoming an expert at winning them over. At least I get some entertainment around here—and extra apple juice from Nurse LeAnn who took a shine to Gabriel."

"Yes, and you should have seen Wendy trying the same tactic on the doctor," Gabriel says with a smirk, pushing his own tray out of the way. "It was a riot."

I give him the evil eye. If he was close enough, I'd smack him. "You know what, Mr. Dumas? You're lucky all the nurses have been female so far."

Kaylen plops on the end of my bed with a smile. "Don't worry about it, Wendy. I could swear Gabe has some kind of supernatural ability when it comes to schmoozing to people. It's not really fair."

Ezra takes a nearby chair and crosses his arms. He snorts. "Yeah, but it only has a temporary effect. He obviously doesn't know how to control his powers yet, because if he keeps talking too long, people realize what a weirdo he is."

Gabriel opens his mouth to deliver a comeback, but then his face screws up like he just tasted something sour. "Heavens, I cannot find fault in that argument. It's true."

Kaylen giggles and then bounces on the bed. "Enough of that. I'm dying to find out what you learned at the compound."

"Me too," Ezra says. "I need a mental distraction from the fact that you are deathly ill with something that doesn't have a diagnosis yet but it doesn't matter anyway because there's no way to cure it."

I'm not sure what to do with that. Making light of bad news is not something I've seen Ezra do before…

"I need to get to work," Robert says, jingling his keys in his pocket. "I just wanted to bring these two by. But phone me if you need anything. And I hope you're both planning on staying with me when you're finally discharged. You should not be alone. And I've already hired help."

"What about your remodel?" I ask.

"It's done," Robert says.

"That sure was fast," I say.

"What?" Ezra complains. "You're not even a little curious about what Wen learned?"

"It's fine, Ezra," I say. "I already spoke to Uncle Moby on the plane about it." That's not really a lie. I *did* speak to him about it. I just didn't tell him all about it. He didn't want to know. And now isn't the time to expound on the reasons with Ezra.

I reach out. "Hug before you go," I tell my uncle.

He smiles and comes toward me. Taking him in a one-armed embrace, I whisper, "Thanks, Uncle Moby." I'm saying thank you for a lot of things. The offer. The talks. The advice. The *room* that I'm staying in with Gabriel which I am sure was his doing. I'm also sure Robert knows I'm saying thank you for all these things.

He pats my hand before walking out.

I turn my head to see Gabriel watching me from his bed in pensive silence. "You're different with him," he says thoughtfully. "It's like watching two old friends that speak volumes without needing words. It occurs to me I haven't had much opportunity to see you together before now."

"You got that from watching us for three seconds?" I ask.

"I'm an expert at body language. It's part of my foreign language-learning process. It gives verbal words context. Not really something I can explain."

"And I definitely don't want you to try right now," Ezra says impatiently. "So?" He looks at me. "What happened?"

Pushing my tray table away, I begin, trying to recall all the details. I even include my conversation with Sam.

Ezra interrupts after I tell about Sam's death. "Crap, are you serious? Sam was the guy that used to drive me around back when you were at the compound. I used to make fun of his beard obsession. He's *dead?*"

"Yes," I say, sad again over the brief but meaningful connection I made with Sam. It upsets me all over again and I wish I hadn't gone to the compound in the first place. Pressing on, I talk about Carl and what I learned about him. Kaylen wants to force herself not to care, but I can tell she is hanging on everything I tell them Carl said and did. You can't sever yourself entirely from the person who had the greatest hand in raising you.

I finally finish the story, surprised that Gabriel hasn't asked a single question all this time. Instead, he has maintained his 'thinking face.'

Leaning back in his chair finally, arms crossed, his expression making him look very grown up, Ezra says, "And what do you think about all that?"

I suck in a few deep breaths to stall because I haven't figured out how to answer that to myself let alone him.

He stares at me for several seconds, and when I don't answer, he says, "It's not a trick question, Wen. Just... tell me how you feel about it. Because you obviously don't like it. Why do you think I was so upset last night? If you had good news, you would have been running off at the mouth about it when I first saw you."

I guess that's true... Laying back on my partially-upright bed, I cross my arms. "I've been pretty upset about not learning anything that would help me. Sam died and that makes me sad and angry. I wish I hadn't gone..."

"Wait, you don't think you learned anything helpful?" Gabriel interrupts, bewildered.

I shake my head. "How is learning that the life force is woven through every capillary in the circulatory system helpful? How does that get me any closer to figuring out how to fix what's wrong with someone who has had hypno-touch?"

"You sure relinquished all your positivity in one fell swoop," Gabriel points out.

My shoulders slump. "Yeah... I suck."

"Uhhh, Wendy," Kaylen says. "You learned how someone's *soul* attaches to their body. Plus, Louise is dead. That's *huge*. You saved countless future lives."

I don't like Kaylen's gleeful satisfaction when she talks about Louise's death, but I'm not sure how to address it. I can't really argue with the benefits, but I'd rather not dance on her grave—especially not when I know that what Louise became had to have been a process. She wasn't born evil. She gradually lost her light. It was sad and heartbreaking to see her that way. I don't know that I'm an especially compassionate person, but the colorworld tells a different story than what we see on the surface in this world.

"I know. I know," I sigh, deciding to ignore the Kaylen-hates-Louise's-mortal-soul thing. "That's what I've been telling myself, but it's not working... I think it's Sam's death. I... Things are suddenly *real*. There are real stakes and someone *died* to help me. I think... it was seeing how complex a life force really is that has me worrying that I don't have the skill to be able to do this. All of a sudden it's too big for me. I'm messing with people's *souls*. What if I screw something up? Sam asked me if I'd ever seen anyone die and if I knew where their soul went afterward. Do you know I had never even *considered* that? How is it I completely took for granted what the colorworld actually is? Aren't souls supposed to be immortal? Intended for an afterlife and all that? What the hell am I doing thinking I can 'fix' them? As much as I don't like it, maybe I was just supposed to keep this from going any further. With Louise dead maybe Carl will finally back off and no one else will have to suffer. Maybe it was just supposed to end with us. Maybe that's what I was doing on the compound. Robert said the vision would work to benefit a lot of people. He didn't say whether it was prevention or helping people *now*... Oh my gosh, someone please stop me. I'm babbling."

Gabriel brings his legs over the side of his bed. "Too many questions surrounding a problem often make that problem appear impossible. And missing the obvious can often steal our confidence. But these are both part of the natural progression of scientific inquiry."

Ezra gives Gabriel an annoyed look. "Seriously dude. This isn't a research lab." Then he looks at me. "The real problem is you're trying to take too much on by yourself."

"What?" I say defensively. "I am not."

"Wen," Ezra says, scooting to the edge of his chair, annoyed but also relieved. "The only reason you feel like this is because you've been assuming that figuring things out is all on you."

"Ezra, didn't I delegate the whole 'we need an effective cancer treatment' problem to you and Gabriel?" I point out, aggravated. "Pretty sure that is the exact opposite of taking everything on myself."

"Will you shut up?" Ezra says. "Yeah sure. You passed one thing to me and Gabe. Good job on control freak sobriety in one part of your life. But you took the most important part—the cure part—and put it all on yourself. Remember when it was just me and you? I wasn't allowed to help you with anything. You wouldn't even let me cook dinner when you had a school assignment that you needed to do."

I wrinkle my nose. "But you can't cook, Ezra."

He rolls his eyes. "Yes. I know. But I *can* make a sandwich. Geez, woman. That's not the point. What I'm saying is that even when people *want* to help, you don't let them. Here you are, all stressed out because you think you're going to have to knit souls back together without an instruction manual, and you're caught up in all these dumb moral questions. But you're not even asking the people who *need* the knitting what they think."

"Ezra is correct," asserts Gabriel. Then he looks at me curiously. "Did you actually imagine you'd be discovering a solution all by yourself?"

I frown. "Yes, I did. Because everyone else thought it was hopeless."

"Oh that's not fair," Gabriel says. "I never said it was hopeless. I merely asserted that it was unlikely you'd have time to discover a solution in time to save me."

"Neither did I," Kaylen says. "I never said you couldn't do it."

Ezra shakes his head. "It doesn't matter what we would have said. You still would have assumed it was up to you to fix it."

Throwing my hands on the blanket, I say, "Fine. I stink at including people in decisions. It's clearly not my strength. Now that we've established that, I'm waiting to hear how what I saw Louise's life force do is going to change everything."

Satisfied, and settling into thinking mode, Gabriel says, "We know that the life force is made up of lots of strands, correct? And we know that some strands go in the head. Some go in the chest. Where do the *other ends* of the strands go?"

"Maybe they're loose," Kaylen suggests. "Like hair."

"I've never seen the loose end of a strand, have you, Wendy?" Gabriel asks.

"No. But I think there are millions of them, and I've never been able to separate them. So the ends could be buried underneath the bulk."

"Unless strand ends *tend* to stay buried, I'd say it's statistically unlikely that in all the time we've spent looking at life forces, neither of us would have ever seen a loose strand end," Gabriel says.

"Okay. So they come out of the head and chest and the other ends are attached somewhere else? How? Where?" I say, knowing I'm asking the same question Gabriel just did. But it's *the* question of the day.

After several moments of methodically twisting her hair over her shoulder, Kaylen slowly settles on some idea and says, "You said the end of the strands inserted at the head and chest came out last, right?"

I nod. "They were twisting and struggling to come out of her at the end."

"So we think strand *ends* are the problem then?" Ezra says. "And not that the swirl is getting pushed out of place?"

I shrug. "I have no idea. But it seems more likely that the swirl is getting messed up *because* strands are getting pulled out from somewhere."

"Assuming that they aren't free-floating, the end of the strands outside the body probably came away first, right?" Kaylen says, wringing her hair slowly and staring at nothing. " They detach more easily, right? Compared to the chest and head?"

"Ahhh," Gabriel says. "You're positing that hypno-touch may be pulling the external ends away rather than the head and chest ends *out*, since they appeared to come away first in the case of Louise?"

"Yeah," she says. "Plus, the external end placement is probably what makes the chest swirl do its thing, and if those ends are detached, things don't swirl right. Maybe displacing the external ends is what's causing the wonky swirls. I mean… that should be a lot easier to fix than trying to actually thread a strand into the right vein inside someone's body, right?"

"By external ends, we mean the ends that are *not* supposed to be in the head and chest, right?" Ezra asks. "Just wanna make sure we're all on the same page…"

"Yes," I say.

More silence as we wonder how to make the loose ends go back where they belong. I hope Kaylen is right. I can't fathom putting a strand back in the right place *inside* the body. But something in me—the memory of the sound of hypno-touch I think—has me doubting this. It is the sound of strings being rubbed against each other discordantly. The life force doesn't care how strands get jostled *outside* the body. People, in the course of natural interaction, move each other's strands around, creating a musical sound even. But in hypno-touch, we always start somewhere around the chest—one of the places where strands are inserted into the body.

"This is assuming, of course, that the external ends are the problem," I point out, a wall forming in my head by an egregious lack of information. This is no better than guessing. We can't operate on a mere guess where a person's *soul* is concerned. I wish I'd watched Louise's life force more closely as soon as she touched me. "We have no way of knowing. I have no idea how they are supposed to be attached. That part happened too quickly."

"I think I have an idea," Ezra says, leaning back in the chair.

"Well?" Kaylen says when he doesn't immediately explain. But he looks like he's still working it out.

Ezra looks at me. "Chest and head, right? We know the chest has a swirl. Does the head have one, too?"

"Intriguing," Gabriel says, turning to me with excitement. "I've never paid attention. Have you?"

I shake my head, immediately reaching for Kaylen's hand and closing my eyes to look in the colorworld.

I hear Gabriel's footsteps coming to where we are. "Yes!" he says, having already touched my arm while standing over my head. "The head indeed has a swirl!"

Stretching to sit up higher so I can get a look at Kaylen's head, I see that he's right. Kaylen has a beautiful head swirl.

I gesture to Ezra, who comes over and crouches by the bed so I can see his head—he *is* the only life force healthy person in the room and therefore makes a good control subject.

His head looks like Kaylen's.

"So the head swirl appears to be undamaged..." Gabriel says, standing beside the bed and able to see all three of us at once.

Ezra stands then, touching my bare arm, caught up in wanting to get a look himself. He looks at the top of Kaylen's head as well as mine, but then says, "Gabe, lean down so I can see yours."

After only a couple seconds, Ezra says, "Shoot."

"What?" I say, looking up into his brilliant purple mass and unfocusing my eyes so I can see his face.

Ezra looks at all three of our heads again before letting go of me and sitting down in his chair, elbows propped on his knees and his hands under his chin. "Gabe's head swirl is a perfect golden spiral. And it—" He looks up then. "I need a mirror. Two actually. Do they work in the colorworld?"

I nod. "I tried it at the compound before to see if I could see anything weird about my own life force."

"Wendy and Kaylen *don't* have golden spirals?" Gabriel asks, looking at my head once more. "How can you tell?"

Ezra shrugs. "I can just tell."

"Is this like that isomectrodon thing from the museum in San Francisco? You can tell the *proportions* are off?" I say.

Ezra guffaws. "You mean icositetrachoron? Yeah, it's like that."

I grin. "Okay. So Gabriel has this golden spiral thing. Which is what then?"

"And you want to see what kind of spiral *you* have?" Gabriel interrupts, speaking to Ezra. "That's what you want the mirrors for?"

"Exactly," Ezra says. "A golden spiral's arcs grow by a factor of the golden ratio. About 1.61803. Basically where a over b is the same as the sum of a and b over a."

"Uh. Okay. Besides the equation, is there something special about the ratio?" I ask. Gabriel, apparently, already knows the significance. He is on the phone with someone—sounds like one of my uncle's guys running security—trying to get a small mirror brought up.

"Oh yeah," Ezra replies excitedly. "The golden ratio is found all over the place in nature. So is the golden spiral. Mathematicians are obsessed with it because it's everywhere. All kinds of geometric shapes and symbols use it."

"Mark's going to fetch us one," Gabriel says, eyes shining. "Good heavens, Ezra. That's quite something to spot. To me, Wendy and Kaylen's head swirls look just right."

"They almost are," Ezra says. "But yours is perfect. And it has more arcs."

"It's bigger," I say.

"Yeah," Ezra says.

Kaylen throws her hands up. "Okay geniuses. What does all this mean?"

"It means not only are chest swirls off, but so are head swirls," Gabriel says.

"Except for yours," Ezra says. "Which is weird..."

Kaylen starts twisting her hair again. "Well..." she says. "I've seen lots of energy sessions and I've never seen them actually work on the top of the head. So maybe it doesn't get out of whack as much because it doesn't get messed with as much."

"That's ace, Kaylee!" Gabriel says, using his pet name for Kaylen.

"I agree," I say. "I was thinking of that before Ezra brought up the golden spiral thing."

"But obviously they *do* get out of whack a little," Ezra says. "Otherwise you'd have a perfect head swirl like Gabe, right?"

"I only worked on Gabriel once. Maybe it takes more than one session to get the head swirl out of place."

Farlen shows up then, a small hand mirror tucked under his arm and looking confused. "Mirror?" he says, handing it over to Gabriel with a smirk. "Is this really the time to be fluffing your hair?"

"Thanks, Farlen," I say. "And yes, Gabriel is *always* worried about his hair."

Farlen smiles at me, his thin eyebrows arched in amusement and expectation. "Anything else?"

"No thank you, Farlen," Gabriel says. "And this isn't for a vain purpose. It's a scientific instrument today."

I roll my eyes as Farlen grins and leaves the room. We shuffle into the bathroom, pulling IV poles and keeping our lines from tangling us up, as I bring us into the colorworld again using Kaylen's hand. Ezra grabs on to me with one hand and angles his head in front of the mirror. Gabriel holds the extra mirror over Ezra's head. It takes some adjustment, but once the mirrors are in the right place for Ezra to see the reflection of his head swirl, he nods. "Yep. Perfect golden spiral. But still not as many arcs as Gabe's." Then he steps away from the bathroom mirror, looking at his chest. "Yep," he says. "My chest has a golden spiral, too. I can't believe I didn't catch that before."

"Probably because we're the only ones you've spent much time looking at in the colorworld and our swirls are all wonky," I say.

We move back into the room and I sit on my bed.

"Again, why is Gabe's head swirl perfect while Wendy's and mine are messed up?" Kaylen asks.

"Natural ability?" I offer. Gabriel takes Ezra's mirror and crosses the room to set it down on the table. "You know…" I say, watching Gabriel. "As far as life forces go, now that I'm looking, yours is actually a bit… bulkier than others. Stop right there for a second. Kaylen, can you go stand next to him?"

Kaylen hops up and Ezra and I look between Gabriel and Kaylen, comparing their life forces.

"Oh yeah," Ezra says, nodding. "Gabe is definitely fatter."

I give him a look. "Oh stop it. It's not fatter. It's bigger."

"That's kind of the definition of fat," Ezra argues.

"Do you think it's an age thing?" Gabriel says. "I am the oldest, and if you think about it, children always have life forces that 'fit them' as if their life force grows along with their body."

"Maybe when people talk about egos, they are literally talking about souls…" Ezra says. "Would *totally* explain why Gabe's is inflated."

I elbow Ezra and answer Gabriel, "No. It's like you have a bigger life force in proportion to your body. We need to get a look at Robert… Although I could swear Robert's is normal-sized."

"Let's just accept that Gabe is a freak of nature and not use him for comparison purposes ever," Ezra says. "Besides, why Gabe's life force is the way it is isn't actually relevant to the problem. What we need to know is how to get swirls back to golden spirals."

Nobody has an answer for that and silence prevails for a full minute.

"It will come to one of us," I say, trying to sound encouraging. "As soon as Gabriel and I can get out of here, we'll take a look at a lot more people, see if the golden spiral idea is consistent all the time. Maybe we'll see something helpful."

26

"This is not helping me," I say, frowning at Gabriel.

He pushes the bed table holding my empty breakfast tray to the side and puts his hands on his hips. "Wendy, he's my brother and he wants to support us. You're lucky I managed to convince my parents that we needed their help getting our things moved over to Robert's. That's the only reason they're giving us space today. I'll call them later to give them the diagnosis."

"*Us* space?" I shrill. "They were here all day with *me* yesterday. You left me for hours!" Gabriel was discharged yesterday, and he wasted no time in leaving me alone with his mother.

"I had to go to the library," he says as if that satisfies everything. "Research. *Someone* has to work on keeping us alive."

I huff at his low jab. "Your mom said fourteen prayers over me. I counted. She'd sit over there doing her knitting thing, and all of a sudden she'd drop her needles, close her eyes and say some prayer aloud in Spanish before crossing herself. She tried reading the Bible to me a few times. Then she even brought the chaplain in to talk to me!"

Gabriel smirks without looking at me, sitting down on the futon and picking up the journal of oncology he's been reading— or rather, memorizing. "And did he save your immortal soul?" he says mockingly from behind the pages. And then he laughs. "Actually, you should have told him that was *your* job—fixing your life force and all…"

I glare at him even though he can't see me. "He asked me if I knew Jesus. I told him I was pretty sure Jesus died thousands of years ago, so no, I haven't met him, let alone know him."

Gabriel throws the journal down on his knees and looks at me wide-eyed. "Did you really? What did my mother do?"

"*No, Mija,*" I say in my best Maris impression. "*What Father Lizette means is, have you accepted him as your Savior?*"

Gabriel's jaw drops. "And?"

I snigger at his expression, sit back, and sip the juice I've been holding.

"Wendy, what did you say?" he demands breathlessly.

I shrug. "I can't remember." Then I look at him. "If you'd been here, you could have heard it in person."

"Wendy! Please tell me you didn't insult her religion. She takes that malarkey as serious as genocide!"

"Calm down," I tell him. I take a sip, watching him over my straw, keeping my expression as cool as possible. "I know she takes it seriously. That's why I told her that as soon as I get out of the hospital, you and I will gladly go with her to mass." I shrug. "She was overjoyed. Even kissed me on both cheeks." Then I look at him. "Don't worry. I'd already checked out her life force."

He stands up abruptly. "You did *not* promise that!"

"I did," I say, weaving my fingers around the cup in my lap as if it's a mug of coffee.

He stares at me, stock-still for about ten seconds. He's on the edge of my emodar, coming to a conclusion about my motives. Then he collapses in his chair. "You are an awful, manipulative woman."

"And you are an awful, pansy man. Avoiding your own mother at the *library*. Like you can't memorize what you want in fifteen minutes and come back here and read it from your head. I saw how you waited to come back until your dad got here last night. Don't you dare leave it to me to run religious interference. Unless you *want* me to start going to church all the time. Because I will. Just to keep her happy. And now your *brother*? Why now? What are you trying to do? I'm about to give my own brother and adopted sister my diagnosis. I do not need your jerk of a brother standing in the background and giving me an 'I wish you would die already' look."

"He does not wish you would die," Gabriel says, rolling his eyes. "Stop being dramatic."

"Don't trivialize this! You know he doesn't like me and I *know* you have an ulterior motive just like you did with your mom. I just haven't figured it out yet."

Gabriel crosses an ankle over a knee and leans forward. He sighs. "I'm sorry. I should have at least prepared you for what my mother would try to do when she came. I didn't think I could be here while she did it. I'm not good at biting my tongue where religion is concerned. I still don't know how to tell her to back off without completely offending her. You have a bit more tact than me so I hoped you'd do it for both of us. But I swear to you, Wendy. I do *not* have an ulterior motive when it comes to my brother. I'd be perfectly happy to let him keep his distance from you, especially now that we have so much to do. But he asked about you, wanting to know your diagnosis. I didn't think it right to tell him before we told Kaylen and Ezra—even if they do already expect it—so I told him to come by this morning. Mike... well he said he was sorry for being, in his words, 'a dipwad' to you. I think he wants to make peace before... well you know what I mean. I don't know what's going to happen to either of us. And I don't want to chance going while at odds with my brother."

I roll my eyes. "Oh fine. Play the 'I'm dying' card. You know I can't argue with that."

Gabriel hops up, comes over, and kisses me on the forehead. "Wonderful," he says, unplugging his phone and stuffing it in his pocket. "I'll be back in a flash. I told him I could pick him up from the airport this morning and bring him over. Ezra and Kaylen should be here soon. You'll be alright until then?"

"What if I say no?"

He smiles. "Then I'll call my mother and have her come over and keep you company until I get back."

"You do that, and I'll commit us both to church for a month. We *do* need to make peace with our maker before we cross to the other side." I raise my eyebrows tauntingly.

"You'll be fine," he blurts before disappearing around the doorway.

I have to admit, despite him leaving me with his mom yesterday, I'm glad to see him being so upbeat and casual again. It took him a while to find his groove after I was admitted. He was adjusting to me being sick. And this morning we got my diagnosis: T-cell Prolymphocytic Leukemia. Exactly what we expected. Exactly what Gina died from, and it's nasty even under normal circumstances. And my diabetes is out of control to top it off—I am having an insulin pump installed sometime this week. I called Robert this morning to tell him and to have him send Kaylen and Ezra over so I could give the news to them in person.

I'm ready to get out of the hospital, but that won't happen until after I've started treatment. Gabriel and Ezra have a plan for that, which they'll be fine-tuning this week now that they have my official diagnosis to work with, and I'm hoping it will buy us the time we need. But I'm trying desperately to keep my perspective flexible in all this. Gabriel left Gina's file with me yesterday and it gave me an unsettling déjà vu. Aside from the symptoms of my diabetes deteriorating, I have followed her symptoms exactly. Her death destroyed Carl because he was so sure he could save her. He didn't do hypno-touch on me believing he was killing me. He imagined that using me would ensure everyone's cure. But he ignored morality 'for the time being' in favor of a perceived future, in favor of 'making things right,' thinking he knew what right was.

Like Carl, I feel responsible. I have been fixated on saving Gabriel. I have been fixated on a future that I intended to make. But Louise's strange death took my confidence down several notches. And Sam's death knocked the wind out of my sails, but in a productive way. It has me going about this more cautiously. I want to be sure I don't make decisions based on an outcome I believe will happen. Robert showed me how being stuck on the future can ruin our actions *now*.

I have repeated so many of Carl's mistakes. I do not want to repeat any more. And part of that is being open to the possibility that figuring out life forces may not lead to the outcome I imagine. I may not save anyone in time. But I still believe I will do something. And that is the only assurance I want to hang on to. I want to let everything else go—like the need to spare my brother and Kaylen more heartbreak, or that by my actions I can make life more fair to them.

In the past couple days I have measured my life and realized how 'unfair' it is. I did a lot of stupid things. But I also had a lot of stupid things happen to me by no action of my own. Yet I don't *feel* unlucky. I *feel* fortunate because I have so many incredible people to call my family. And I have gained such an astounding amount of wisdom in the last few months. The paradox of so much peace while being so sick still boggles my mind. But I guess that's what facing your death does to you.

***

"What are your plans for treatment?" Mike says, his burly arms crossed over his white T-shirt. These are the first words he has spoken since his initial greeting, which sounded contrived. He's kept a comfortable distance since he arrived, so I've been unable to pick up his emotions. Kaylen and Ezra didn't do much more than sigh when I gave them the official diagnosis. They've been expecting it. We all have.

I look over at Gabriel before answering, "There's actually some good news on that. Gabriel and Ezra have been working out a treatment plan based on a theory about why hypno-touch-affected bodies can't handle conventional treatment."

Mike looks at Gabriel and then at me with disbelief written clearly on his face. "You're kidding, right? Since when are you an oncologist, Gabe?"

"Since they methodically went through the visuo-touch files that belonged to my father, Mike," I say, trying not to snap at him,

228

but I do catch my voice on his name a little too much. "Neither of us has cancer that's going to behave typically. And Dr. Altman gave us every case resembling Gabriel's. It was very helpful. And it supports Ezra and Gabriel's theory."

"That doesn't make oncologist involvement useless," Mike says, and I can hear him trying to keep his voice calm. "They understand the mechanisms of cancer inside and out. You just need to work with one you can trust and share your information with."

"They never said they aren't using a doctor," Ezra says. "Can you listen to the theory first?"

Mike huffs. "Any theory of Gabe's is going to be so crazy no doctor will go along with it. I know how to read between the lines. They might as well be saying they aren't using a doctor. And everyone is going to go along with Gabe because he's going to talk over everyone's head."

"Mike, stop putting words in my mouth," Gabriel objects. "And as Wendy told you, I haven't been working solo. Ezra's ability to spot even the most obscure patterns in data has been indispensable. The data supports the theory."

Mike throws his hands up. "This gets better and better. A teenager and my cracked brother working on cancer cures."

"It's not a cure," Gabriel says sternly. "It's merely an effort to prolong life."

Mike grits his teeth but manages to keep his mouth shut. So much for his regret over being a dipwad. I swear, it's like my mere presence sets him off.

"How does it work?" Kaylen asks.

"First, let me explain what I believe hypno-touch is doing biologically," Gabriel begins. "Looking at the visuo-touch case files, it's clear that the resulting illnesses involve DNA in some way. So it's clear that hypno-touch is having an effect on DNA. Cancer was, by far and large, the most common type of illness. I'll focus on cancer since that's what both of us are dealing with. We know that people can be predisposed to cancer. Whether or not that predisposition actually goes into effect is the result of environmental triggers. My theory is that hypno-touch causes individuals to be more susceptible to environmental triggers. The more damaged a life force is, the more susceptible the body is. The more susceptible, the quicker malady develops."

Ezra holds up a hand. "This also explains why it allows people to have superpowers. Expression of genes that are not usually activated."

"This isn't X-men, Ezra," Gabriel says disdainfully. "Nobody has sprouted wings or shot lasers from their eyes. We're talking about *feasible* genetic mutation."

Kaylen giggles and I could swear Mike cracks a smile. I could kiss Ezra for making this very awkward family meeting not so awkward by being his snarky self.

Ezra rolls his eyes. "Doesn't matter. The point is our genes have the ability to allow us to do more than we currently can. Hypno-touch is just effed-up epigenetics."

Gabriel lets out an exaggerated sigh and I can tell these two have spent a lot of prior time arguing over this.

"Epigenetics?" Kaylen says, and I can hear frustration easing into her voice as she struggles to follow.

"It sounds fancy," Gabriel assures her, "but it's basically the notion that genes can be turned on and off based on environmental factors."

"Like having your soul screwed with," Ezra says, grinning.

"Yes," Gabriel says patiently, "like having your life force strands stirred the wrong way."

"Waiting for the genius treatment theory part," Mike says.

Gabriel's eyes grow bright. "As I said, I believe hypno-touch is sensitizing DNA to environmental triggers. Think of your DNA as a room full of switches. Normally your body buffers your DNA from these triggers—I believe it's the life force that aids this, essentially locking the room with all the switches and regulating what enters. But when damage is done to the life force, it fails at this job. What happens then is the equivalent of unlocking the door and letting a bunch of children into the room. Both good and bad genes are getting flipped, such as those controlling Wendy's stem cells, causing them to react to and readily bind with a carcinogen, damaging the DNA in such a way that the stem cells go haywire."

Kaylen's brow furrows. "Okay. So why do treatments not work?"

"Oh they work," Gabriel says. "Too well, actually. The results of my latest CT show my cancer shrank ten percent just from the two days of chemo. I've also read through every single file. And in almost every case, the cancer was being eradicated, but the chemo was also causing a great deal of problems. Chemotherapy drugs are cytotoxins—cell killers. And in a hypno-touch compromised body, they kill cancer cells, but they also kill other cells, important ones that are part of essential organs. The people in the files never died of their original cancer. It was always some complication with treatment. Treatment had to be slowed or stopped so that whatever part of the body that had been damaged could recover. But it was almost always too late. Average time from diagnosis to death was about two months. It's a shame no one ever got all the patients together under one roof. They might have realized what was happening and tried what I am proposing."

"Which is what?" Mike says impatiently, taking a step forward.

"*Trace* doses. Doctors would never even consider giving such low doses because millions of cancer cases have spelled out what a body can handle and what is required to kill cancer cells. But hypno-touch injured bodies are different and really shouldn't be lumped with other cases. They are extra sensitive. They react to and kill pathogens incredibly quickly—hence why I managed to get over my recent infection quickly in the face of my immune-compromised state, which is actually a great benefit since infections are a complication a lot of cancer patients die from. I think we only saw one case in the files where someone died of infection. Most of them died of some type of organ failure."

"Let's assume this works," Mike says—and I think he's finally considering Gabriel's theory might not be crazy. "What makes you believe it can't offer a cure?"

Gabriel grows solemn. "Logically, it could temporarily. But there are a few reasons I don't think it will ultimately. First of all, Wendy's brand of leukemia even in 'normal' scenarios has an incredibly low survival rate. And secondly, what our bodies have become because of hypno-touch can't survive in this world. We are bombarded with environmental triggers constantly. And in our state of hyper-sensitivity to that environment, we are far more susceptible to those triggers. Even if by some miracle we survive this particular bout, either relapse or an entirely new cancer will beset us. I believe the fact that I have two cancers at once is evidence of this. My goal for this treatment idea is simply to slow the progression down. I believe a healthy life force is the only way to cure."

"That is really interesting," Kaylen says, her eyes unfocused.

"It's genius," I say, smiling at Gabriel.

Sitting down next to me and taking my hand, he sighs. "I don't like that you have to be a guinea pig though."

I reach over and squeeze his arm. "Gabriel, you are suggesting they pump me with *less* drugs, not more. If there is going to be experimentation involved, I can't think of a more ideal trial."

Mike sinks back against the wall and says, "So does this mean you're *not* going to accept my offer? I told you they'll take her into a clinical trial. It won't be chemo."

"Wait. How on earth would *you* get me into a trial?" I ask, glancing at Gabriel. I'd expect such a feat from my uncle who has innumerable connections and money, but Mike is a personal trainer for goodness sake.

"I know people," Mike says. "My clientele includes a lot of doctors. Especially research doctors."

"Thank you for your concern, Mike, but no," Gabriel replies, casting a quick look at me. "What we're going to be doing is already experimental enough. Furthermore, Wendy won't be having chemotherapy treatments under this plan either. The most current and effective drug for T-cell Prolymphocytic Leukemia is a type of immunotherapy."

"I hear you," Mike says. "But give them your data. They can accommodate her with the most cutting-edge medical treatments available. Medical confidentiality will protect you."

"Mike, even if we trusted the information to someone else, they wouldn't believe us if we tried to explain hypno-touch," I say. "Nobody understands life forces like we do. This isn't *normal* disease. And medical trials are intended to provide new treatments for *normal* people. And frankly, I don't trust anyone with information and access to me, especially when I know that hypno-touch affects the body as much as it does the life force. I've already got Carl out there gunning for my abilities. I don't intend to extend opportunity to anyone else. This stops here."

Mike's face is stony. "That's the dumbest gamble you've made," he says, ignoring me and looking at Gabriel. "And you've made a *lot* of dumb gambles with your life. And now you're going to do that with your *wife* too? Gabe. Come on. You're being ridiculous. You don't know what you're doing. Who is going to write your prescriptions?"

"I am on board with this, Mike," I seethe. "Gabriel doesn't make decisions about my life. I do."

"Robert has already hired a doctor that will attend to our needs," Gabriel says calmly. "Wendy is right. This stays in-house. It's not about gambling her life or mine. It's about protecting future lives."

Mike's hands turn into fists and he releases a rapid litany of Spanish, which Gabriel answers in kind. Back and forth they go,

Gabriel growing angrier by the moment until he walks over to Mike, takes him by the elbow, and leads him out of the room, uttering rapid and insistent Spanish.

I watch in disbelief as they leave. Once they're gone, I see that Kaylen and Ezra are watching as well. "It's like someone took all the nice out of Mike and gave it all to Gabriel," I say quietly. "I swear that guy has anger issues."

"Maybe he takes steroids," Ezra says. "He's pretty buff. I hear that stuff can make you a little nuts in the head."

"Maybe," I say, thinking that might be a really good explanation. I'll have to ask Gabriel later.

"It's so counterintuitive," Kaylen says, her brow furrowed, her hands wringing her hair over her shoulder methodically—she's done that so much lately. "But at the same time, it makes total sense."

"What? The steroids?" I ask, confused.

"No," she says, looking up. "Gabe's treatment idea."

I smile widely. "Yeah, I know. Simpler solutions are usually the right ones, though."

27

*T*he week after my diagnosis is mostly spent outlining a specific treatment plan. Gabriel and Ezra are the think-tanks and I'm impressed with the sheer amount of data they've gone through: dosage levels based on age, weight, and relative health; chemo combinations; radiation effectiveness; and every other drug used in the course of treatment for our particular cancers. There are a thousand variables, a thousand possible courses, and the two of them have to narrow it down to one. And then they have to plan for what to do should that course need alteration—which is pretty much guaranteed. The stress level has been a bit high around here.

Robert secures a consult with the foremost authority on leukemia who, like Dr. Altman, has a list of patient files cataloging untreatable cases that he has no qualms about handing over. It becomes clear, however, that thirty years of cases with my kind of leukemia are not as helpful as they were with Gabriel's type of cancer. T-Cell Prolymphocytic Leukemia, or T-PLL for short, is rare and has had a terminal prognosis for even normal people until about ten years ago. But Gabriel and Ezra manage to isolate about four cases in that time period that they think might be hypno-touch related—they even figure out which one was my biological mother's.

Kaylen takes it upon herself to put their treatment plans into two notebooks: one for Gabriel and one for me. She organizes the list of drugs with their new specifications for us, as well as fold out charts to plot my blood workups and Gabriel's CT findings. She also designs a detailed calendar where symptoms and vitals will be recorded hourly as we progress through treatment. Kaylen is seriously good at organization and the finished product is a masterpiece that any oncologist would be jealous of.

Mike, after being absent since my diagnosis, shows up on Friday afternoon after I have my central IV installed. He brings a man along wearing loafers, a casual button-down shirt, and carrying a leather bag. The man shakes my gloved hand smartly, and introduces himself as Byron Spellman. I can immediately tell he's a very intelligent person. His intellect is always moving, observing, drawing conclusions, and reacting accordingly. He's a computer—if computers had emotional currents. He informs me that my case has been brought to his attention and he'd like to offer some assistance with making my diabetes more manageable.

He's a researcher whose company develops cutting-edge glucose testing. The current product they've developed is a contact lens that has a built-in microchip to monitor glucose constantly and transmit readings wirelessly. He'd like to take me on as one of the beta testers for the new prototype.

"That's nuts!" Ezra exclaims, coming over and squatting down eye-level with the table and squinting at the tiny contact lenses suspended in clear fluid. Miniscule copper wires run around the edge of them and into a microchip about twice the size of a piece of glitter. Given my eyesight I can see the microscopic design, and I am thoroughly impressed with the intricacy.

I gape at them before saying, "Seriously?" I actually got an insulin pump a few days ago to monitor my blood sugar more closely, but this is... maybe the most impressive technology I've ever seen if it actually works.

"I understand you'll be using your PICC line for your insulin as well as your other medications," Spellman says, "and this device will allow your glucose monitoring to be constant, precise, and immediate. In fact, you shouldn't experience the need for even minor corrections while using it."

I raise my eyebrows at the man, then glance at Mike whose trunk-sized arms are crossed like a bouncer, a daring expression on his face. Ugh. Jerk.

I turn to Gabriel who watches me expectantly from where he sits, still holding whatever piece of data he was agonizing over when his brother showed up.

"You knew about this?" I ask Gabriel, translating his reaction as indication that he has been entirely in on this.

Gabriel nods. "Since Mike offered his help, I told him you could use a better method of blood sugar management—especially now. Mike sent me the specs for the product, and I told him it would be up to you to decide whether you wanted to use it. You can use the pump monitoring as a failsafe if you want, to be sure the tech is doing its job. But as I understand, the lenses each have sensors in order to duplicate readings and avoid error."

"That's correct," Spellman says. "A failsafe is built in. If either of the lenses stops working, your monitor will let you know immediately."

I'd like to ask how on *earth* Mike seems to know all the right people for every medical issue imaginable, but I'll wait until later, *after* Mike leaves.

"Uhhh," I say, glancing at Spellman. "You *do* know I have terminal Leukemia, right? That's not going to skew your trial run, is it? Don't you want to try this out on... I don't know, relatively *healthy* people first?"

"Your central line makes you an ideal candidate," Spellman explains, unphased by my blunt declaration that I'm terminal. "This technology is intended for a delivery system that's going to allow for immediate and automatic corrections. Right now, central IVs are the best route for that. But the risk of infection they present is too much to justify in typical diabetes patients. Most of the individuals we target for the beta study have extremely labile diabetes. Many of them are waiting on more extreme measures like pancreas transplants. These are the people that need this technology the most. Why shouldn't they have it first? And Leukemia shouldn't affect the function of the device or your need for constant glucose monitoring."

I'm still skeptical, but Gabriel has evidently already checked this guy and his technology out, so why not? I doubt it will make me die any faster. I shrug. "Okay. So what do we do? Don't I need to be fitted for the lenses?"

"Not necessary," Spellman says. "Our lenses are crafted from a special gel that will mold and harden slightly when it comes in contact with your tears. The technology is so sophisticated it needs to be an absolutely perfect fit."

So Spellman uncaps the lenses right there in my hospital room, and one by one he expertly instructs me how to put them in my eye. I have to hold my face upward and close my eyes for fifteen seconds after each one to aid the molding process.

"I understand you have one of our pumps and it's already connected to your central line?" Spellman asks.

"Uhh, I do?" I ask, lifting the edge of my shirt to show him the line connected to my pump. The pump itself is the best one money can buy, specifically designed for intravenous insulin delivery. Gabriel argued my doctor for it vehemently even though they usually don't use such things unless you're staying in the hospital the whole time. It even has a wireless wrist control. The pieces are falling into place, and it appears that Mike and Gabriel have been conferring about my diabetes for a while now.

Spellman takes my wrist monitor, messes with it expertly for a few minutes, and then hands it to me with a smile. "All set."

I take it from him and fasten it to my wrist. The little screen gives me a read out of my blood sugar level, which is slightly elevated.

Spellman explains how the system works and warns me against subcutaneous injection while my pump is hooked to my central line—basically all the things I was told earlier after I had the thing installed. He answers Gabriel's questions about what kind of data they'll need in exchange. Apparently the wrist device records everything and will upload it automatically. I'm a little uncomfortable with that, but the technology, if it does its job the way Spellman claims, will make a huge difference in my health.

"You're like a real-life cyborg," Ezra says laughingly, leaning close to me and looking into my eyes to see the microchips.

"They look pretty," Kaylen says, squeezing next to Ezra to look. "Like eye jewelry."

"More like eyeball implants," Ezra says. "And she's all wired up, stays in contact with the mothership constantly, and has tubes everywhere. She's a total cyborg."

I wrinkle my nose at him and then turn to Gabriel and Mike who are having a loud conversation about my treatment. Mike is once again trying to convince Gabriel to use his contacts. He is possibly as relentless as Gabriel, but with a huge mean streak.

Spellman has left, and I look at my watch monitor, noting that my blood sugar is already going down. Wow, that's fast. I've been outfitted with top-notch technology, and Gabriel and Ezra have just about narrowed down mine and Gabriel's treatment plans that will start on Monday. Everyone is working so hard to give me as much time as possible to figure out a cure, but I am no further ahead with that.

I confirmed this week that Gabriel's life force is still the only one so far that looks so... large. He is definitely an anomaly and I have no idea why. Robert and all his men have perfect head swirls and perfect chest swirls, just like Ezra.

Mike escalates into Spanish and I am not interested in hearing the two of them argue again. Ezra is looking at a page of numbers and writing out equations, so I link arms with Kaylen and tell her we're going for a walk.

Mike catches sight of me leaving and says, "Don't lose any of that. You're wearing a half a million dollars in technology."

I roll my eyes at him. "Thanks for the reminder. I'll try not to forget any of my *life sustaining equipment* in the bathroom."

"I'm talking about the lenses," Mike says, shaking his head at me. "They *will* come out in the shower or when you're washing your face if you aren't careful."

I snap my heels together and salute him. "Yes sir."

Mike turns back to Gabriel and continues their heated debate. I pull Kaylen along with me, deciding where we'll go first.

Other than hypno-touch victims—and Louise's death of course—the only time I've seen a life force do anything different was when Sam was dying. I'll have to talk to Robert about arranging to... be around when someone dies so I can watch more closely, but I *am* in a hospital. I might as well look at some other 'normal' sick people to see if there are any differences. The chemo clinic is on the first floor, so I decide that's a good starting point.

When I reach the elevator, I press the button and Kaylen groans, "Once you guys start treatment, that is going to be ten times worse." She thumbs over her shoulder toward the room where Ezra, Gabriel, and Mike are. "Gabe is going to quibble over every single one of your side-effects. He's going to totally stress himself out."

I realize she's right. I have been too preoccupied with the life force problem to consider how my treatment might actually go. It seemed so simple... but how will we know what side-effects are 'acceptable' for our extra-sensitive bodies?

I shrug though, knowing there is no way to do what we're doing without some trial and error. Ezra has been saying as much. Plus, I'm more interested in what Kaylen and I are about to see.

I channel us into the colorworld as the elevator doors open. We round the end of the hall and emerge into the chemotherapy clinic lobby. A number of people are scattered around, reading magazines or talking, oblivious to the purple luminous masses that surround them. It is the largest number of people I have encountered in a long time in the colorworld, and I'm busy looking and comparing. Kaylen stands next to me, looking around silently, though I can tell she wants to ask me about what she sees—she hasn't been in the colorworld with me nearly as much as Gabriel has.

As we examine the souls around us, it becomes clear that a life force reacts to its body's illness. And I would say a good number of the people here are very unhealthy—no surprise for a cancer clinic of course, but I'm thrilled to find that it's obvious in the colorworld. Among the sick are loose swirls, lopsided whirlpools, and sagging arcs. It's astonishing and quite varying. One man has what appears to be a perfect chest swirl, but I can tell something is very off about his head. It appears swollen, and if I could see the top of his head I'm sure the swirl would look very wrong.

One lady, who is thin and frail and sitting in a wheelchair looks very much like someone who has had hypno-touch done.

The only difference is that her life force in general looks excessively bloated—not like Gabriel's, but slack. She must be very close to death based simply on the way her soul clings to her body. There's a desperation to it that can only be sensed; I can't really articulate why she comes across that way. I gasp at the sight of her though, and Kaylen and I exchange a moment of pity and sadness for the woman. You can't look at her and not feel a foreboding. Intermingled are people with perfect life forces, drawing the contrast more surely, and it can only be assumed that they are accompanying others here for treatment or appointments.

'*I can't believe I have never looked at sick people before now,*' I think to Kaylen, using my recently-discovered skill of being able to speak to people telepathically in the colorworld.

'*So people's swirls can get messed up by hypno-touch, which makes them sick... but they can also get messed up... because people get sick? What happens in a normal scenario first? The disease or the messed up swirl?*' she replies.

'*I think disease,*' I reply. '*But who knows? Either way, it's clear that in order to be healthy, you have to have healthy swirls. Head* and *chest.*'

'*Should we... go up to the long-term care floor?*' Kaylen asks tentatively.

'*Might as well,*' I reply, catching my eyes on the woman in the wheelchair again, her hands folded in her lap, her head bowed. I'm sure I'm staring but I can't keep my eyes off her disheveled life force. A tear escapes my eye for this deathly ill woman I don't know. Kaylen pushes the button for the elevator again and we wait nervously.

The hallway we emerge into from the elevator is silent, and we walk slowly, pausing at the first barely-open door. Through the crack we see a man whose age can't be determined due to his feeble state. He's sitting up and spooning soup into his mouth slowly and carefully. His wife, maybe, sits in a chair beside the bed, her back to us, steadying the bowl as the man dips his spoon in.

The man's life force looks like the woman we saw below in the lobby, only even more distended. If there weren't literally billions of strands that make up a life force, I'd expect to be able to see beneath them to his body. But I can't, even though his strands seem to be relinquishing their hold on his body somehow.

"He must be so close to death," I whisper solemnly.

We continue on, our steps careful in order to maintain the quiet. Each room with an open door is much the same. Some are worse off than others, made clear only by how swollen their life forces are and how un-swirl-like their chests are. No wonder Carl couldn't see much in natural death and was willing to kill Louise using me in order for me to watch how it happened. It's an entirely different death.

Almost at the end of the hall we tiptoe toward a room with the door wide open. A woman lies in the bed. There are two people with her, life forces intact, who are in their own silent state of meditation, presumably waiting for the death of the woman in the bed. I can only guess this is the case because the woman's body is so still that she must to be in a coma. But even more telling is what I see her strands doing. Aside from the bulgy nature of her life force that I've come to expect now, her stands are moving around her body, undulating in gentle waves, almost like they are massaging the body beneath—preparing it maybe for their departure?

'*That's exactly what Sam's life force looked like just before he died,*' I relay to Kaylen.

'*What's it doing?*' she asks.

'*I don't know...*' I reply, pondering what we've seen and what we're seeing. '*But I... I'm starting to think that strands are coming out of the chest or head when someone is sick or when they've had hypno-touch. I know we were hoping that wasn't the case because it'd be impossible to thread them through the circulatory system the right way, but it's the most obvious conclusion, don't you think?*'

'*Yeah... if they got pulled out of the body, all that slack would make them look bloated. And maybe the sicker people get, the more the strands come out...?*'

'*When Gabriel was in a coma though, his life force never looked... loose like this.*' I point out. '*I'd still call his life force compact even though it looks fuller than most. So maybe in natural disease, the strands come out because they don't like a sick body. And maybe in hypno-touch they get* pulled *out but* want *to go back in, so they stick close to the body.*'

'*That makes a lot of sense,*' Kaylen replies as we begin walking slowly again. '*And it goes along with hypno-touch theory. Louise always liked to point out how people close to death would have experiences that proved they possessed supernatural abilities. They seem to like... know things and see things other people don't. Hypno-touch is supposed to be tapping into potential that we aren't capable of experiencing usually. But if people are having the same thing happen to their strands while*

240

they're dying, it's because the strands are pulling out of their bodies... giving them those deathbed abilities, right?'

'*Kaylen! That's genius! I bet you're absolutely right,'* I think excitedly as it all starts to come together. '*I bet even in mild illnesses like allergies and diabetes the strands have started to loosen. That's why Louise could manifest abilities in people like that. She even said the sicker people were, the more powerful their abilities. I bet that's because the sicker someone was, the more strands they already had coming out, making it easier to pull them out even more. And the more strands you get out, the stronger the ability!'*

'*And that's why we'd continue to do hypno-touch in order to strengthen someone's ability!'* Kaylen says. '*Because the only way to strengthen the ability is to pull out more strands!'*

We stop in the middle of the hall and look at one another. "Imagine what would happen to someone who was already really ill and had hypno-touch done on top of it…" I whisper.

"They'd die way more quickly," Kaylen replies. "Louise had to have known it all along."

"But she was hoping to find a way around it," I say. "With Carl and then me."

We walk back toward the elevator and Kaylen says worriedly, "If we assume we're right, and strands are getting pulled out of the chest and head, and if we figure out some way to isolate those strands, how do we know where they go, chest or head? And how do we get them to insert into the right place inside the body?"

Anxiety builds in my stomach—That's happened a lot lately since being confronted with the impossibility of this task over and over. I wish she hadn't asked that. I needed this little bit of progress so bad. But like all progress in the past few weeks, it doesn't move me any closer to my goal—it just asks more questions.

While the elevator climbs up to our floor, I close my eyes. As I've done many times the past few weeks, I imagine leaning against the door outside my hotel room when I decided I would save Gabriel, the sensation that my chest would burst as it pulsed out a rhythm of confidence and hope. I was unstoppable then. This moment should be no different, but it is. Hardship would be so much easier to overcome if we could just hang on to moments like that and remember them with the same power. It's not fair that they should fade when they felt so impenetrable at the time. This sucks.

"A piece at a time," I say finally as Kaylen and I step back out of the elevator. "I've only ever managed to do anything by pushing ahead even though it seemed pointless. We'll figure it out a piece at a time. A day at a time. A moment at a time."

Moments are my enemy, Robert told me. I totally get that now. Moments that seem like they'll go on forever. Moments that were so happy they now taunt us with what we no longer have. Moments of indecision that our future hinges on. Moments of weakness that happen too often. Moments that tick away the remaining seconds of our short life. Moments of suffering.

I think moments are *everyone's* enemy. And I am about to have a whole lot more of them.

Part II

28

$\mathcal{F}$alling to my knees next to Gabriel's hunched form, I rest my arm across his back. I wouldn't call it an embrace—I know from experience that sometimes even the slightest touch can be irritating—but I still want him to know I'm here and that he's not writhing alone in the dark on the bathroom floor. He's been throwing up all night, which isn't unusual for a Monday. Anti-nausea meds give Gabriel migraines so strong that he becomes delirious, so he doesn't take them. It's a Catch-22 because his mouth and throat are so covered in sores that he can't swallow, and throwing up makes the sores so much worse. To keep them from getting infected he has to take additional antibiotics, and adding new drugs is always tricky. The dosages have to be specially calculated, sometimes guessed at. They cause side-effects of their own, and for both of us, balancing side-effects and drug effectiveness is a constant battle no matter what the drug is. Gabriel has been losing so much weight from not eating that he had to have a feeding tube put in. But that just gives his stomach something to throw up.

We have been in a constant push and pull between drugs and our diseases. We spend all of our time on keeping ourselves alive—tweaking, recording, vitals, tests, tweaking again. And of course, actually *receiving* the drugs and then enduring the subsequent side-effects. There's the nausea of course, which is Gabriel's biggest nemesis, but my least favorite one is when the warming starts in my veins that starts during my infusions and always fades into an itchy sensation beneath my skin for hours afterward. I can usually be found in the shower, the water turned really hot to hide the itch so I don't scratch my skin off. This is mixed with a host of other symptoms, and each time we record them—the constipation, odd arrhythmias, shortness of breath, chest pains, twitching, shaking, and incoherency—we have to decide if side-effects are too dangerous and then change drugs or dosages. But when you feel like you're dying, it's hard to be objective.

Several times I have asked Ezra in a fog of loose consciousness, "Am I dying? I think I'm dying. We need to write this down."

"What does it feel like?" Ezra will ask me, trying to be calm but always terrified, pencil at the ready.

"Like I'm falling apart," I'll answer, and then I might start giggling or crying. It's anyone's guess when my head gets like that. When I start scratching though, Ezra knows to get Kaylen or Jeanelle, our doctor on call, to get me in the shower or I'll scratch my skin raw and not realize it with my mind splintered like it is during and after my infusions.

I welcome delirium, but Gabriel hates it. He will take any side-effect over losing his mind any day of the week. It means he ends up like this though, hunched over the toilet and down to ninety pounds. He has two types of cancer, so he gets a larger selection of drugs, but it's killing him. The cancer itself is shrinking, but I sincerely worry that Gabriel will die of malnutrition or a heart attack or renal failure before he ever gets close to remission. I think the only reason he is still alive is because of something else we discovered about our bodies: they recover much more quickly than other people's such as when Gabriel came out of his coma. Most people have on and off days to their treatments in order to give their bodies time to recover. We started off that way as well, but ended up finding that our side-effects are much shorter-lived than would be expected and blood workups show that we're holding our own. So we receive infusions every single day. Gabriel even gets two infusions on Mondays and Fridays. It means we pretty much don't get breaks, but we had hoped that it would get us closer to remission.

Maybe it does, but it also means Gabriel's cancer builds up a resistance so quickly that he has to change drugs every single week. He cycles through cycles, not sticking with the same one too long. Treatments for my Leukemia are extremely limited though. We managed to bring my inflated cell counts down significantly in the first two weeks of my treatment, but since then we've only kept them stable. And it's been six weeks of that. I've lost my hair because I added chemotherapy to my drug roster a couple weeks ago, but for the most part, I think I'm healthier than Gabriel.

Gabriel lays his head on my lap unexpectedly—he usually doesn't welcome me coddling him during his moments of greatest indignity—but his emotional wheels begin to fall off in that moment. His shoulders shake and he gulps at the air amid tears, clutching his stomach and curling into a ball as tightly as possible.

"Oh Gabriel," I say softly, strength leaving me as his mind folds and his will fights to keep it standing. I move my hands to stroke his hair. As I do so, a chunk of it falls out in my fingers. It's dark in the bathroom, but my eyes can see clearly the tuft of nearly-black hair—hair that Gabriel loves. I paste my lips together and breathe shallowly in order to keep the tears away. It may seem a silly thing to be upset over, but I've been looking to his hair for weeks now. It has been a miracle that it hasn't fallen out given how many different drugs he has had, so I've begun to think of it as my personal sign of hope. A message to me to keep going.

And now that small bit of encouragement is gone. Gabriel is losing his hair.

As he shudders in my lap, I don't know what to say or do. Guilt overcomes me for reasons I can't really articulate. And then agony fills every orifice of feeling and I cry out. I can't hold the tears back anymore as I hold his head in my arms and stroke his face. I channel us into the colorworld—something I never do when we're enduring side-effects of chemo—which is most of the time. For one thing, Gabriel hasn't let me, and for another we'd be hard-pressed to offer each other relief when we both feel so terrible.

I close my eyes and hiss at the sensation of my stomach being clenched and then forcing its way upward into my throat. The nausea comes from there rather than in my stomach. I grip his hands and grit my teeth, waiting for it to fade as it balances between us.

Once it levels, I sigh with relief. Even Gabriel has relaxed. But still I cry, partially from relief, but also from desperation. This is too much for him. And I'm done watching it. If what I just felt was how he has been enduring nearly every day for the eight weeks since we started treatment together, it's too much to ask.

I've not had a lot of time for introspection during that time. And until now I've never been able to feel both emotionally and physically where Gabriel is at when in the depths of his suffering. Whenever we've shared time in the colorworld, it's been when we've both felt relatively well for the brief window of time between infusions. I'd like to say I've made progress in uncovering the secrets of life forces, but I haven't. And I've avoided talking about it—another reason I haven't pushed spending time with Gabriel in the colorworld. If he spends enough time with me there, he'll know how discouraged I've become, how I fight back hopelessness every day. And I can't *think*. Not in these circumstances. All I think about is the infusion I'll get the next day and looking back on another day of failure. I can't even enjoy the few hours I get each day of feeling well because the anxiety over tomorrow is debilitating. And Gabriel... how he has managed to stay on top of treatment changes and plans is beyond me, especially when he feels like this so much of the time. I basically forced him into this, promising to find a cure, yet I've never gotten any closer. It's not right, what I've put him through.

'*Gabriel,*' I speak to his mind. '*I'm so sorry I put you in this place. I didn't even ask you.*'

'*Ask me what?*' he asks, gripping my hand in return.

'*If this was what you wanted. To suffer like this in order to give me the chance to figure out how to save us. It's not worth it. If I had known... This is nothing like I imagined you'd be going through.*'

He turns his head in my lap to look up at me. He closes his eyes and inhales deliberately. I know he's taking in my scent in the colorworld. I do the same with him all the time. He opens his eyes and reaches up to stroke the length of my nose with an index finger. '*Don't be ridiculous, Wendy. Of course I want this. I'd do anything for you.*'

'*I don't want you to do this for me. I want you to do this for you.*'

He looks at me in confusion for a moment. '*Everything I do, I do for you. I'm not about to change that because of a little health hiccup.*'

My eyes widen. I reach up and gently brush my fingers through his hair. I hold up the small tuft that falls out in my hand for him to see. '*Health hiccup? Is that what you call this? How far are you going to go to keep yourself alive as my life force experiment?*'

His eyes rest on the hair, but rather than upset, a twinge of resignation is all I pick up from him over it. And then he stares into my eyes. '*I believe in you. What more do I need to know?*'

'*You have to draw a line. You are the one that has to endure it. It's not fair for me to expect you to stick around in pain just so I can satisfy my convictions.*'

'*Suffering is irrelevant when you believe in a cause. And I believe in yours,*' he replies.

We regard each other for several moments. I read his stalwart commitment, and I know it's no use arguing. Gabriel is doing the only thing he knows how to do: taking his decision to help me as far as it can be taken, to dedicate every moment of his suffering, and to donate every cell of his being to helping me succeed.

But I am failing.

I hold his face to my chest. I cannot bear the thought of losing him. I cannot bear the thought of the *world* losing him.

Who can go through what he has been through in the last eight weeks, have no end in sight, and have even more conviction than when he started? Gabriel was always doubtful about my ability to save him, and he certainly has no more evidence in my favor. When did he change?

And that's when I figure it out: the man has given me his will. No wonder he has been able to accomplish staying on top of treatments and charts, all while suffering so egregiously. He's focused in a way only Gabriel can be. He has put his whole self into giving me what I asked for all those months ago. And Gabriel doesn't do anything halfway. He can't believe in me and help me while also harboring doubt in what I say I can do.

I think my heart is breaking. I'm not sure if it's a good break or a bad break, but it hurts. Like maybe my heart's DNA is rewriting itself, integrating Gabriel into every available nook and cranny. All I know is I love him, only it's too much to comprehend at once. I couldn't say where it comes from, but apparently, somewhere in me is a bottomless well of it. My body cannot contain the love I have for him. It leaks out of my eyes in the form of tears, and I hold him close, wetting his face.

"I'm going save you," I promise him, thinking that *not* saving him would be a slap in the face after all he has done for me. If Gabriel can focus and keep us alive, I can pick every piece of the colorworld apart and find possibility once more.

"Mija!" a voice whispers all of a sudden. It's Gabriel's mom of course. But I wasn't expecting her in my bathroom at midnight. She's been staying at Robert's house with us, just down the hall.

"He's fine," I say, knowing how we must look, tangled on the bathroom floor like this.

Gabriel grumbles when she tries to fuss over him. With only half of the nausea of before to endure, he stands up. But I don't let go of his hand. I follow him to his bed and lay down beside him, refusing to let him do this alone anymore. It's clear he needs some relief, and I'll give it as long as I'm able, and he really can't stop me. It's clear he *won't* stop me if I say it's what I want.

Maris asks us if we need anything, to which both of us decline. But she seems set on staying in the room anyway—we're used to it. She sits down on her rocking chair, the one Robert had brought in some time ago. He does that all the time—provides everything we need without us even asking. I'm not sure how he always knows when we need something since he's rarely around, but I guess other people must be telling him.

247

In fact, we learned when we moved in with him the week of my very first treatment that the supposed remodel he was having done was for us. He had several large air purification units installed throughout the house. Gabriel's and my room has one unit by itself and I imagine that we can't possibly be in a more sanitary environment. Our shower is a large walk-in space with several places for sitting. The most astounding thing we found was the elevator that was *definitely* not here before. Our room is equipped with everything you'd find in a regular hospital room, so we haven't had the need to return to the hospital except for Gabriel's CT scans, which happen every single week. A lab is also attached where equipment for blood analysis resides. Jeanelle is our personal doctor on call all of the time. She acts as nurse as well, coming to check and record our vitals every couple of hours when we're not getting infusions, and every fifteen minutes when we are. We have a personal cleaning lady. She sanitizes our room and bathroom at least twice a day. We have a chef as well. She prepares a special diet—for me anyway since Gabriel hardly ever eats—that's supposed to significantly decrease the possibility of infections occurring from food.

Our every need is taken care of, except for one: Robert himself. I miss him so much. He checks on us a few times a week, but it's always brief, and never during an infusion. I understand since he did warn me this would happen before I ever knew I was sick, but some days I wish he would sit with me and divine some wisdom that will point me in the right direction.

I stare up at the dark ceiling, unable to go back to sleep because the nausea is not something I'm used to feeling. Maris is praying. It's in Spanish, but I've come to recognize what her different cadences generally mean. This one is definitely a prayer.

"Mamá," Gabriel croaks. "Must you?"

"Sí, Mijo," she replies gently, her chair making a dull creak as she rocks in the darkness.

"Why?" he asks. "You have prayed a thousand times over me in the last ten weeks alone, and to what end? I am still here. Still stricken with illness. Still making the same effort to live that I would if you weren't praying at all. The same laws of biology and anatomy apply whether or not you pray. So why do it?"

Her chair continues to creak rhythmically for about twenty seconds more. And then she says, "Why do you complain so much? What is it to you that I pray? Does my voice offend you? If you cannot accept God's existence, then it should be to you as a child playing make-believe—harmless. I cannot live in your world, Mijo. I was not blessed with your intellect or your faith in merely the workings of creation. But I was blessed with a love for prayer, something to keep my mouth and my mind busy while my heart weeps. When I fail to understand, prayer brings me peace. When I am desperate to *do,* prayer gives me an outlet. What else would you like me to do?"

"Pray, Maris," I say before Gabriel can answer. "I know what you feel when you do. And while I don't know if it reaches God, I do know it reaches the space around you. Our emotions affect everything around us. Although I couldn't tell you exactly how, I know your prayers do *something.* And I don't think we can afford to turn any help down, no matter what confusing shape it comes in."

Gabriel makes a sound of acknowledgment for Maris' benefit, but to me he thinks, *'So true, Love. Thank you for reminding me. Chemo turns me into an awful human being and I speak without thinking. My poor mother. I have no idea why I give her such a hard time about her religion. It* does *offend me. But I couldn't tell you why anymore.'*

'Because you don't understand it. And she does it so well. It's like she can see something we can't. She speaks to God genuinely and honestly. I feel it from her whenever she prays. So either she's completely crazy for imagining God so well, or we are completely blind. It's as if we see the world with entirely different eyes. Either way it's disturbing, isn't it?'

'Good heavens, you're right!' Gabriel thinks in astonishment. With that, he's off in a whirlwind of thought.

I watch Maris' life force in the darkness-enhanced room in the colorworld. She's got that energy vapor coming off of her. Her embodied prayers? Whatever it is, I ought to try and understand it more. I need to go into the colorworld as often as my eyes are open. It's easy to say that, but I know it will be much harder to do, especially come infusion-time tomorrow morning.

But with Maris' desperate prayers in my ears, her genuine desire to help, I remember my brother and my sister. They would do anything they could to help as well. And both of them are counting on me to solve this. It's clear I need them in order get the colorworld time that I need. How much peace and satisfaction do I have in this moment that I can bring relief to Gabriel? I am a selfish, prideful person for having kept that from Kaylen and Ezra as well. Why do I always think I have to do everything myself?

29

"*A*re you joking? All this time you've been able to and you haven't mentioned it even once?" Ezra asks, crossing his arms.

I bite my lip, playing off my discomfort by using the controls on my bed to incline myself into more of a sitting position. "Well... it didn't occur to me."

"It didn't *occur* to you in two months?!" Ezra says, his face stricken. If he cries I am going to lose it also. "I have watched you and Gabe suffer for *two months!*"

"I know," I say, my tears really threatening to come now.

Ezra puts his hands on his hips, huffs, and then crosses his arms again. "I am so pissed at you right now... I'd like to just let you suffer. Do you have *any* idea how many times I've wished there was some way to do that but had to accept that there wasn't? That's messed up, Wen. Like, *really* messed up. You know what it's like on my side! You know! How could you do this to me?"

I lower my eyes in shame as Jeanelle walks in with my meds and begins working on my IV lines. "Because I'm a selfish jerk. I'm *sorry,* Ezra! What do you want me to say?"

Kaylen is already in bed next to me. She hopped in as soon as I said, "share side-effects" earlier. Ezra, obviously, was immediately offended that all this time he could have been sharing my discomfort and I didn't tell him.

"Jeanelle, could you move my bed right next to Gabriel's, please?" I tell the brawny woman as she connects my central line to the IV line.

"No," Gabriel says, not opening his eyes. His infusion started an hour ago.

"Jeanelle, please move my bed next to Gabriel's," I say to her again when she looks undecided—not knowing, of course, why I'm asking or why Gabriel is disagreeing.

"Don't be stubborn," I tell him. "I need your head in this, too. I can't do this by myself."

Gabriel turns his head and opens his eyes to look at me for a long moment, deciding, I think, whether I'm serious or if I'm trying to guilt him into letting me help him feel better. I stare back, undaunted.

"If you're manipulating me, I'll know it straightaway," he says, closing his eyes again.

"The truth is I need your help. I also want to help you. I can't help that both of those things are accomplished by touching you," I point out.

He grumbles something in Spanish.

"Here we go," Jeanelle says, turning a valve on the line.

"Nothing like a little Beelzebub to start the day!" I say.

Gabriel looks at me and chuckles. "Beelzebub? You are hilarious. It's called Alemtuzumab."

I stick my tongue out at him. "Sounds like Beelzebub. Which makes more sense anyway. Look what it does to me." I look at Jeanelle. "The bed, Jeanelle?"

She looks at Gabriel nervously—she's intimidated by him. I have told him before that he bullies her too much. He treats her like an orderly rather than the doctor she is. It's not limited to her though. When he goes in for his CT consult, he argues with the doctor as if he himself has a medical degree. Though I suppose at this point you could argue that he does considering all the research he's done for our conditions. The only doctor that earns any of his regard is Dr. Altman. Gabriel calls him up almost daily to update him on his numbers. For one thing, Gabriel has already exceeded Dr. Altman's two month prognosis by a week. And he's sitting right at a twenty-five percent decrease in tumor size, only five percent away from winning the bet with Dr. Altman, who has come to see him four times to take notes.

Ezra plops down on the other side of me then, motivated by the fact that Gabriel is so opposed.

Gabriel grumbles and waves a hand at Jeanelle.

She pushes Gabriel's bed and IV toward me and I say, "Thanks, Jeanelle!" Once she leaves the room I reach across Kaylen to put my hand on Gabriel's arm and say, "Gabriel, she's not your personal assistant. Be *nicer*."

"Me?" Gabriel complains. "*You* are the one that has her moving beds around."

"The point is I ask nicely. You, on the other hand, wave a hand at her with your eyes closed as if sending her for a latte."

He makes a surly face. "My eyes are closed because all of the yammering in here upsets my stomach."

With Gabriel, Kaylen, and Ezra touching me now, I channel us into the colorworld. A whirlwind of confusion happens as discomfort fluctuates and distributes itself among us.

"Gosh, that's freaking weird," Ezra says. "So this is what we all feel at once, blended and divided up among us?"

"Yeah," I reply. "Pain distributes itself automatically. Less intense feeling has to be directed telepathically. It's like when we speak telepathically. You have to direct the feeling if it's not very strong."

"Well I'm assuming that leg pain is Gabe's," Ezra says. "If that's a fourth of your leg pain, dude, you need to do something about it or they're going to amputate it."

I cringe. Gabriel and I have argued about his Osteosarcoma so many times. I think he needs to have surgery to remove it because it seems entirely resistant to chemo. But I could swear Gabriel is secretly terrified they're going to cut the whole leg off while he's in surgery and that's why he won't agree. Sometimes the man can be so irrational.

Resolving not to make an issue of it at the moment, I start looking at life force strands, comparing them, watching them swirl and move. Whenever I have been in the colorworld the last couple months, I keep coming back to the same problem: is there a way to move life force strands that is more precise than hypno-touch hand movements? They *do* move seemingly on their own though, or maybe to some unseen wind. Is there a way to harness whatever it is to move the strands where I want?

Gabriel groans in what I am sure is relief but he says nothing. I bask in the moment though, sensing a lightness move through me. I ascend higher and higher as the heaviness in ourselves and the room slowly dissipates. None of us speak, caught up in our connection in the colorworld. I feel a pang of guilt, realizing I've been holding back relief from Kaylen and Ezra and even myself all this time. They have been hurting, too, just in a different way.

Why did I do this to them? Why?

"I'm sorry," I say softly.

"You all are meddlesome fainéants," grumbles Gabriel. "A body can't even endure in silence in this establishment without every Tom, Dick, and Harry wanting to share in the macabre fun. You see what you started, Wendy? And all because you *had* to make yourself miserable by touching me last night, talking about how you need my help. Nonsense! Now you've got two under-aged miscreants in on your glaikery. And missing school! Good heavens! It's just a little delassation. Possibly it might get worse now with all this hovering."

Ezra laughs, "You know he's feeling better when you can't understand a word he says. Maybe we should let him suffer so that he'll start talking English again."

Kaylen giggles and I start laughing, too. Finally, I say, "That was top form, Gabriel. Even I barely followed that tirade. There were at least three words I've never heard in my life."

Gabriel wrinkles his nose. "How's this for English: You. Guys. Are. Annoying."

"Wow!" says Ezra. "I don't think I've ever heard you use any of those words before even though I know they're English. Wen! He's bilingual! But I don't know what that other language is that he speaks."

"Inmaduros hijos! Usted no sabe Inglés adecuado si te mordió!" exclaims Gabriel, and while the words are mocking, he can't hide his lightheartedness from us, not here.

I burst out laughing. Gabriel is clearly happy to finally be a source of fun and not misery. I know his mouth hurts when he talks, so that dampens his inclination to speak. I can feel the dull pain of it now, spread among the four of us. I really don't know why I didn't do this sooner. I guess because people want to escape suffering, but we don't want anyone else burdened in the meantime. Even though when a burden is shared, it's practically weightless. I'm given a gift to be able to share suffering in a way no one else can and I don't use it. I am an idiot.

"Yeah, that makes as much sense as what you said first," Ezra mocks. "Was that the Spanish translation? What language is it you were using before?"

"Who's the nut in X-men with the blue hair?" Gabriel asks, stroking his chin. "The smart one? Beast? Yes, that's right. Maybe he can tell you what language it is... Ooooh wait. He's not real. Don't fret Ezra, we all had to learn Santa Claus and the Easter Bunny weren't real either. The disappointment will pass, I assure you," he taunts.

"Good one," says Ezra appreciatively.

"In Ezra's defense, some of it actually *is* real," Kaylen says. Then she lifts up the colorworld-glowing rocking chair sitting across the room with just her will.

"That's right, man. Kaylen's like the embodiment of Jean Gray," says Ezra. "And Wen's like Rogue, but cooler cuz she sees this crazy stuff and can actually *give* people powers instead of stealing them. And you... you're like some kinda cross between Rain-Man and Prodigy."

I hear what Ezra is saying, but I don't process it. Instead, my brain is forming a new idea as I watch Kaylen hoist the chair with her will.

"Kaylen!" I almost shout, sitting up abruptly.

Everyone startles and looks at me and then at Kaylen.

Tempering my voice, I say, "Can you manipulate life forces telekinetically?"

30

"Like move them around, you mean?" Kaylen asks, sitting up to face me, considering it.

"Yes!" I exclaim, unable to contain my excitement.

"I'm not sure," she replies. "I can't move people because of the water content, but maybe their life force is different... I can try."

Gabriel and Ezra both know where I'm going with this, and after a few seconds of thought Gabriel says, "How exactly are you going to have her manipulate them?"

That's a good question, but the better question is whether she actually *can* move them.

"Can you just, like separate them a little?" I ask evenly to suppress my enthusiasm. "Just to see if you can?"

Kaylen looks at my life force and then Gabriel's. She bites her lip.

"Try mine, Kaylen," Gabriel says.

I give him a look because I know he's offering himself as the pincushion, but I don't think it will help to argue. *Someone's* got to be the experimental subject.

Kaylen takes a breath. "Okay, I'll try to move the strands apart for starters. They're so small though... Hmmm, maybe create an air pocket? Yeah, that sounds safe."

We all watch Gabriel's life force to see where the manipulation will appear. I wonder if it's too small to see, or if I'm looking in the wrong place when Kaylen says, "That didn't even cause a blip. I wonder why?"

My heart sinks.

"I would presume, Kaylee, that life force strands are as unaffected by air pockets as they are by clothing," Gabriel says. "They are intangible and invisible outside of the colorworld. I think you're going to have to manipulate a specific strand or strands."

"Aaaaand the brain is back! Excellent intuiting, Gabriel," I say, anticipation soaring once more.

"Thank you, Love, but not nearly as bewitching as your intellect when engaged," he replies with a smile. It is *such* a relief to see it on his face after so many weeks of pinched eyes and gritted teeth.

"Okay, you two, you can get a room later and talk about your intellects all you want. Can we stay on topic here?" says Ezra.

"Where should I try it?" asks Kaylen.

I almost look to Gabriel, but decide against getting his opinion. He would likely do something a lot more risky than I would. "Maybe his arm," I reply. "If strands might be coming out of the chest and head after all, then we should probably stay as far away from those areas as possible."

She nods but looks like she's starting to sweat. I'm nervous, too.

Heads bent over Gabriel's left arm, we watch as a few strands twitch as she tries to pluck one, only to release it in fright. She swallows and then tries again, this time getting a hold of one, which stops my breathing as it loops up and away from Gabriel's body. I have never seen that happen with the life force strands before. They always stay close to the body and to each other—or to the life force of another. They never invite being manipulated so individually like that, but the plucked strand flows and swirls in on itself in the air and then settles back in toward the mass of strands.

"I suspect that's not you making it curl up like that, is it, Kaylee?" asks Gabriel.

"No," whispers Kaylen. "I'm so terrified. What if I lift one and it doesn't go back? I can hardly get a hold of one because it slithers out of my grasp. I'm afraid to hold it more firmly."

"Don't be. Try again," breathes Gabriel.

Kaylen sighs but concentrates again. This time the strand lifts up and even farther away from Gabriel's body, floating and twisting. It's about a foot away from his body now and, to the terror of everyone in the room, it stays where it is for several frightening seconds, and then it slowly draws itself back into the flow. Hearts beat wildly with relief.

"It finds its way back, see?" says Gabriel consolingly.

"No. Stop," I say.

"I agree," Kaylen says with relief. "That's way too scary."

"Wait, but what if you push a mass of strands aside? Then you aren't manipulating just one—you're keeping them together as a group," says Ezra, desperate for something to be accomplished.

Kaylen looks at me for permission, and I think for a moment. What is there to lose but time? It sounds relatively harmless. "Go ahead," I say warily.

She concentrates on the life force again. So slowly that it's nearly imperceptible, a small collection of strands, perhaps a finger's-width thickness, raises itself up and away. But like the single strand, it floats in the air, clinging to itself but hovering above Gabriel's body.

"Are you holding it?" I ask fearfully.

"No," Kaylen whispers, even more terrified.

"Crap," I say, as the bundle of strands continues to hover. It looks like a huge run in a giant piece of cloth. I keep listening to Gabriel's heart and glancing at his face for signs of ill-effects. As we watch the strands, I will the snag back into place, but it stays put. It swirls and twirls in the air and I gasp because I'm sure I see the end of a strand, then two, then three. I can't tell if I can see any more than that because the motion makes it difficult to count.

"You've got to put it back," I insist, leaning close to the strands as if I can blow them back into place.

"How?" asks Kaylen frantically. "Do I push the whole thing back down? Do I do it strand by strand?"

"Uh... Let's go for pushing it back altogether first," I say.

Kaylen wastes no time. The strands lower back to the rest of the life force and are lost amid the other strands. I sigh in relief, although I'm still unsure. I didn't like seeing all those strand ends. Where were they from?

Gabriel sighs. "Ten ends," he says. "I saw ten distinct ends. And you think they belong inside the body?"

"That's what I keep leaning toward," I reply. "But we still don't know how everything attaches—some are clearly supposed to go in the head and chest, but the opposite ends should attached where...? Or maybe free-floating...?"

After a minute of silence, Ezra says, "One way to find out." We look at him.

"I'm the only healthy life force here, right? So Kaylen does the same thing to my life force that she did to Gabe. If we don't see any strand ends, I think it'll be clear that the loose strands are the problem, right? That they are *supposed* to be attached. And if we *do* see some, we'll know loose ends are normal and the problem is something else."

"No way," I say. "We are *not* messing with your healthy life force."

There is a clear divide immediately. Kaylen and I are against the idea. And Gabriel and Ezra are for it.

"Forget it," I say, wanting to demonstrate my unwillingness by letting go of Gabriel *and* Ezra. But then Gabriel will have to suffer alone. So I hang on and tell them by my emotions that I absolutely will not go along with this. Kaylen, meanwhile, shifts even closer to me on my bed to emphasize her stance on the matter as well.

Ezra sits back and glares at me. "That is such bull."

"What's bull is *you* being willing to throw your life away for an *experiment.*"

"Stop exaggerating," Ezra snaps, his face turning red. "We're talking about—"

"Not happening, Ezra," I interject, holding up a hand.

Ezra jerks his arm away from me, livid. Then he hops up and leaves the room without a word.

My throat catches tears. We all feel his absence as Gabriel's nausea affects each of us a little more, the pain in our mouths— Gabriel's pain—grows a few increments, thus validating my assumption that it spreads among all the people touching me. I also feel the lack of Ezra in a different way. Strong somatosense sharing seems to forge a stronger connection in the colorworld. Being cut off suddenly is always difficult to adjust to. Plus, for some reason, Ezra's outrage cuts me deeper than I would expect. I obviously hurt him, and I felt that hurt as if it was *me* I lashed out at. Knowing so intimately how I caused pain to my brother stabs me with self-loathing. I handled that badly.

"Stop mothering me, Wen," Gabriel says in a higher tone. "Why do you always want to do everything yourself?"

I glance at Gabriel, trying not to laugh at his Ezra impression. He is seriously good at that, getting the intonation and speed exactly right. Blame it on his language skills I guess.

The last time he impersonated someone, it was Quinn, my ex-boyfriend and father of my deceased child. The role-playing was beneficial then, so I decide to play along.

"This is *not* about doing everything myself," I reply. "It's about risking *your* life. And I won't do it."

"Whether or not I risk my life is *not* your decision. You're my sister. I want to help. What if you die and this would have made the difference? You want me to live in guilt when you're gone?"

"Oh that's low," I say, glaring at Gabriel who is doing a pretty good job of mimicking Ezra's annoyed expression.

"This is getting really weird," Kaylen points out—she's between Gabriel and me.

"But it's true," Gabriel says to me, crossing his arms.

"Ezra, I can't let you do it. It's not right!" I whine. "If I don't figure this out, and I've messed up your life force, too, I won't live with myself."

Gabriel pulls one corner of his lip in. It's something Ezra does when he thinks someone has said something dumb and he's trying to figure out a polite way to point it out. Then he turns solemn—an expression that's more like Gabriel than Ezra. "You won't have to endure guilt long if you don't figure it out, will you?" he says quietly. "I, on the other hand, will have the rest of my life. I'm not an idiot, Wen. I've thought it through. Give me some credit. I'd rather risk my life knowing I tried than live knowing I could have but didn't. You *owe* me this. Especially after what you kept from me the last two months."

I wince. That hurt. And I know that is *exactly* what Ezra would have said if he hadn't gotten so offended and left.

I look at Kaylen. "What do you think?"

"That Ezra, er—Gabe is right," she says, looking confused for a second. "Well no matter who said it, they're right." She sighs, looking at the door where Ezra disappeared. "You *are* treating him a little bit like a kid when... I mean... you had him working on those cancer files, figuring out dosages and stuff. You have *no* idea what kind of pressure that's been on him. He won't say because he doesn't want you to tell him to stop working on it. But when you asked him to do that it was like... major. That you trusted him with your lives like that..." She looks at Gabe. "He gives you a hard time, but he seriously looks up to you and he knows how smart you are. That someone as smart as you valued his input so much gave him a serious confidence boost." She looks at me now. "But now you're backpedaling to treating him like a kid again. You know?"

I look at the empty doorway, wondering why I never guessed everything Kaylen just said. After seeing how much Gabriel agonizes over our treatment, I have no idea why I wouldn't assume the same pressure was on Ezra as well.

"If I had a normal life force I'd do the experiment on myself," Kaylen says. "For the same reasons. I'm just afraid of screwing up, that's all. But obviously if I can move life forces the way you need, I better stop being afraid of them."

I close my eyes. "Okay. Go get Ezra."

Kaylen climbs out from between us and heads for the door. With Gabriel and I now the only ones sharing his symptoms, it's a lot harder to manage. Gabriel, however, is used to much worse, so this is nothing to him. "That young man is stalwart. I never guessed either. His focus has been without fault." He looks at me. "He knows the risks. He can handle this. Don't worry."

"I know. I just... mother him." I smile at Gabriel. "Nice job, once again."

He chuckles under his breath, and then wrinkles his nose, saying, "Like the burning when you swallow liquor. But through your whole body. That is an odd and uncomfortable sensation..."

It takes me a second to realize he's talking about what I'm feeling from the chemo. I didn't even notice. Probably for the same reason nausea isn't bothering Gabriel at the moment.

"This is nothing," I say. "In another half hour it will feel like ants crawling under your skin."

Ezra shows up, looking sullen, Kaylen behind him. I hold out a hand. "Sorry. I can't help... you know, always wanting to look out for you. It's built-in."

"Wen..." Ezra says, looking down and searching for the right words. He also seems really uncomfortable, and I think I know why.

Gabriel will be okay for a minute so I let go of him and sit up all the way to take Ezra's hand, pulling him down to sit on the end of my bed.

'*It's just me and you,*' I tell him mentally.

Ezra is startled for a moment, but relaxes as he remembers what's going on. I have only spoken to him once before this way, to experiment with how many people could speak to one another at a time. It turns out that anyone connected to me in the colorworld can speak to anyone else individually, but it takes a lot of practice to focus on the person specifically rather than the whole group. Most of the time a mental message directed to one person ends up being heard by everyone, because the 'speaker' can't distinguish one person from the others well enough.

'*I get what you're saying now about the colorworld telling you about people,*' Ezra thinks. '*Before it was always a jumble... Too much to take in. But I guess I'm getting better at it because... this is going to sound so weird...*'

'*I know,*' I reply, squeezing his hand. '*In the colorworld a person's smell gets into you. It tells you without words what a person is made of, the things that make them unique. If you're paying attention to it, years of bonding can fill ten minutes there. It's really intimate. So probably kind of weird, yeah. But only if you let it be.*'

He exhales in relief. '*Yeah. That's what I mean. I never paid attention to the smells before now. And I realized how much of yourself you've given to me over the years. I realized all the things I want to learn from you and it made me want to save you so bad...'* He takes several halting breaths. *'And I remembered how much I love you all at once. And then when you told me I couldn't help save you, it really hurt. More because I was in the colorworld I guess. That's what Kaylen says anyway.'*

I know *exactly* what Ezra is saying. If I had spent any time remembering what experiencing someone else in the colorworld is like, I would have recognized his vulnerability in that moment and I would have been a lot more sensitive. But with Gabriel's *and* Kaylen's emotions also in the mix, I would have had to make the effort to pick out Ezra specifically.

'I'm sorry,' I say. *'I really am. I take even the colorworld for granted, I guess. I'm so used to it that I forget what it's like for other people.'*

"Alright, well I'm done with awkward," Ezra says aloud now. "Let's do this." He scoots closer to me and I reach for Gabriel as Kaylen puts a hand on me.

"You are officially discharged from school until further notice," I tell them both as the physical discomforts of the moment fade into obscurity. "Because you guys are serious chemo-buffers."

Kaylen gets right to work, staring at the life force covering Ezra's arm. Just as she did with Gabriel, she ever so carefully gathers a bundle of strands until they are self-suspended over Ezra's arm. I hold my breath the whole time, staring until my eyes sting, to spot any strand ends.

"Not a one," Gabriel says after unbearable amount of time staring at the run in Ezra's life force. "I see no strand ends whatsoever."

"Put it down now!" I squeak at Kaylen, gripping Ezra's hand.

She obeys immediately, pushing the strands back into place. We all exhale.

Jeanelle appears then to take our vitals and Gabriel says, "Nevermind that for a moment. Could you please bring me the hand mirror from the bathroom?"

I swear Jeanelle's eye twitches at being relegated to Gabriel's errand-girl. But I don't chastise him this time. Ezra needs to look at his life force and tell us if it's still healthy.

Jeanelle obeys though, returning from the bathroom with the twelve-inch mirror in-hand.

"Thank you," Gabriel says to her as she begins to take his vitals.

Ezra holds the mirror out from himself while in the colorworld still. Within three seconds he nods. "Perfect golden spiral." He even tilts his head just so to take another look at the top of his head, as best as he can manage.

I throw my head back on the upright bed. "Thank goodness."

"Okay, so that means that loose strand ends *are* the problem?" Kaylen says. "And for now we're sticking to the idea that they're getting pulled out of the head and chest during hypno-touch?"

"Getting pulled out *completely* is what appears to be happening," Gabriel says. "Remember the wind and pull technique, Wendy? I remember you hated that one the worst— probably because it was most effective at yanking strands out since for you it would be a literal winding since you can grip them so much more easily."

Kaylen nods. "More strands out equals more ability, but it also means disease happens sooner."

"Exactly," Gabriel replies, pensive. After several silent moments among us, he continues, "Kaylen could insert some of those loose strand ends we saw into my chest and see what happens."

I turn to look at him, my eyes wide with horror, and if I didn't have emodar I would wonder if he was joking. He isn't though. "Absolutely not."

"Why?" he asks.

"You really need me to list the reasons?" I say, my voice rising.

He stares at me resolutely, waiting.

Shrugging off everyone's hands to disconnect from the colorworld, I hold up my hand and count off on my fingers. "One: we don't know whether the strand ends go into the head, chest, or somewhere else entirely. Two: you're talking about having Kaylen *dig through* your life force to find loose ends, something which could very well do more damage. You saw what the strands did when they separated from the life force. Three: your life force is your *soul,* Gabriel. It is made up of *pieces.* Which means it can be *broken, separated, mutilated.* Look, I don't care what you think about God, an afterlife, or whatever, but I am *not* taking the chance that I might do permanent damage to your soul. If there is an afterlife to be had, you're going to *have* it if I get any say in it.

And when you go there—wherever it is and whenever it happens—your soul will be put together."

I'm breathing heavily when I finish. I've considered the idea of an afterlife before, but I couldn't have told you whether I believed in one or not. But with the real possibility of damaging Gabriel's soul beyond repair on the table, however, my very being revolts against such actions. Endangering a part of Gabriel that encompasses his very being sounds heinous.

Gabriel has opened his mouth to protest but, seeing my face, rethinks it—thank goodness. He ponders again for several beats and then crosses his arms, lies back in his bed, and says, "Well then we'll need to find some way to spread them all out, unwind them—while they're still attached to the body, of course."

"Gee. Why didn't I think of that?" says Ezra with annoyance.

"Ezra," I warn, grateful I don't have to start an argument with Gabriel. "Sometimes just saying things that seem obvious in your head out loud can lead to an idea. It helps the creative process."

"I know," he sighs. "I'm just frustrated that we aren't getting anywhere."

"What?!" I say, irritated that both he and Gabriel are so ready to jump the gun all the time. "We know Kaylen can manipulate strands one by one and we also have a really good theory that some strands have come out of the body. We'll figure it out. Rome wasn't built in a day. Geez."

I don't know that I'm trying to be reassuring—which seems to be what Ezra needs—but I do know I'm afraid of being bullied into doing something I'm not ready to do.

"Apologies," Gabriel says. "You are correct. I'm so thrilled that we've discovered such a major leap in solving the problem. Success always drives one to seek for more of it immediately."

I relax in relief.

"Yeah, you're right," Ezra says. "I'm just impatient to see you well. What we've discovered today is major."

Kaylen shivers with excitement then. "We're going to do it," she says. "We're actually going to do it!"

Her thrill moves through our whole group since we're connected in the colorworld, but it doesn't stop. It reverberates like ripples on the water's surface, but instead of fading, the ripples grow in size as we each grasp on to her joy and take it as our own. It bounces back and forth among us, growing in magnitude as if we are mirrors. Caught up in it, we remain silent and still, basking in this moment of hope that more fully consumes us with every passing moment until we feel utterly unstoppable. It reminds me of the moment outside of the hotel room I shared with Gabriel, after I had decided I was going to find a cure. This time, however, it's not myself I have such confidence in. It's *us*. How many times over the past month have I wished I could more poignantly remember what that night outside my hotel room door felt like? And we just created it simply by sharing a small moment of happiness that started with Kaylen.

"What an incredible phenomenon," Gabriel remarks after a while, all of us high and on a cloud that none of us wants to leave. "The colorworld's secrets never cease. It adds new dimensions not only to life force abilities, but to regular, everyday abilities, too."

"And I think it has given me an idea," Ezra says, sitting cross-legged on the end of my bed, touching the skin of my ankle. "So you said some strands are in the head and some are in the chest. You're sure that one end isn't in the chest and the other in the head?"

"Positive," I reply.

Ezra nods to himself, and then says, "Jeanelle? Could I please see the top of your head?"

Jeanelle, who is sitting in the rocking chair and recording our latest vitals, looks up but hesitates for only a moment. She is used to us talking about things that don't make any sense to her. We make her wear gloves around us twenty-four seven and have instructed her to never touch my skin. She also is well aware of how unconventional our treatment is, yet can see how drastically we react to even the smallest drug doses. She is paid enough to not question.

She leans her head down tentatively, glancing up through her eyelashes to see if that's what Ezra is asking for.

"Perfect," Ezra replies. "Hold right there." He closes his eyes for about two seconds, and then looks carefully at Jeanelle's life force swirls, which are now both in view at the same time. The motion of Ezra's intellect is mesmerizing. I don't think I've ever felt him think so hard—and maybe the colorworld has altered his ability as well—but it's like watching someone draw lines between points in a connect-the-dots picture—a picture I can't see because I can only feel it forming. Whatever it is, I *wish* I could see it.

After about twenty seconds he says, "I need some other people. Farlen and Mark maybe? Is Uncle Rob here?"

His intensity commands immediate action. We then call in Mark to find every person in or around the house for Ezra to look at: the cleaning lady, Farlen, two of their guys stationed outside, Maris. And then he insists he needs Robert. It's clear that Ezra is on to something, though I have no idea what yet. He keeps asking for more subjects, plowing ahead mentally like a machine, and I think we're all afraid of getting in the way. Ezra now has a piece of paper in-hand, and he's writing unintelligible equations when Robert finally shows up, looking rushed as usual. He's like this whenever he's around us now. I want to talk to him, ask him how he's doing, but I'm afraid of interrupting whatever steel bars he has erected within his mind to avoid knowing or acting on the future. What torture it must be...

"Can you bend your head down slightly, Uncle Rob?" Ezra asks. "And stand right there while I check something?"

Robert, as is his character, doesn't ask questions. He simply bows his head, asks if that will be all when Ezra says he is done looking, and exits the room, taking a piece of me with him. I want to reassure him, tell him how we aren't suffering when we're connected, and that he doesn't have to stress so much now...

"I've got it," Ezra says suddenly.

"What?" the rest of us say nearly simultaneously. Patience has been hard for the last hour of Ezra's swirl inspections.

"First of all," Ezra says, looking up from his notepad, "I have no idea what you three are supposed to have because your life forces are all messed up. But everyone else has more arcs in their chest swirl than in their head swirl. Except for me and Uncle Rob. We have more arcs in our head swirls than our chest swirls."

"So by more arcs you mean the chest swirl is bigger than the head swirl in everyone but you and Uncle Rob?" Kaylen says.

Ezra nods, writing something else down.

"Really?" I say. "Why would that be?"

"What else?" Gabriel says, staring intently at Ezra.

"There's something else?" I look between them.

Ezra looks reluctant.

"Ezra, trust your instincts," Gabriel says.

Ezra exhales. "There's something about the relation of the chest swirl size to the head swirl size. It's consistent from one person to the next. Unless we're talking about me and Uncle Rob. The relation is the same, just reversed since our head swirls are bigger than our chest swirls."

Kaylen's mouth is open. "You can *see* that?"

"Ezra has a sixth sense about patterns," Gabriel says. "I've become familiar with his skill in the past months."

Ezra shakes his head and begins to write on a scrap piece of paper. "Spotting a pattern or an inconsistency in a single geometric phenomenon is one thing. But visual measurements to the point of being able to calculate precise correlations is another. It didn't occur to me that I might be able to do it—let alone *trust* that I could do it—until you said the colorworld can add facets to even natural abilities."

"So you can give us the exact ratio then," Gabriel says, "between chest swirl size and head swirl size?"

"No way," I say, looking from Gabriel to Ezra. "Can you really do that?"

Ezra looks unsure, but Gabriel says, "Just try."

"I have no idea if it will be correct," Ezra says. "I have no data to back it up."

"Sometimes you don't have backup," Gabriel says. "I count hundreds of thousands of things in seconds and I can't properly explain how I do it. I just have the capacity to keep track of what I see. You have something similar. Trust that what you see is accurate."

Ezra bends over his paper again and writes as he talks, "Patterns are the result of repetitions, and while most people can only spot simplistic patterns, I can spot complex patterns—those that are the result of compound repetitions. Essentially patterns on top of patterns. I come up with equations by breaking down patterns visually. Now nature, while it's orderly and predictable, is also flawed down to the very basic layers. This makes it impossible for me take precise measurements visually because math and inconsistency don't go together. In fact, when I come up with an equation for what I see, it's always approximate and contains a margin of error." Ezra looks up now. "But this is the first time I have seen something with my own eyes, not computer generated, that is precise. Healthy life force swirls are precise. Perfect. In fact, the significance of seeing that in the hospital months ago didn't even occur to me because I'd never dealt with it."

"Fascinating," Gabriel says, leaning forward. "What about the rest of the life force? Is there a pattern to the way it moves?"

Ezra shakes his head. "Outside of the golden spiral arcs, the strands don't appear to move to any rhyme or reason. It's as if they are influenced by some outside force we can't see. But *inside* the swirl, that's where the magic happens. Everything is exact.

Except for you three of course. You look like someone took a blender to your chest." Ezra writes a couple more lines of math-speak on his paper and then looks up. "The relation between the chest swirl size and the head swirl size is the golden ratio."

Kaylen throws her hands up. "Fine. Got it. Lots of golden thingies. How does this help?"

"It helps because now we know precisely what a life force is supposed to look like," Gabriel replies. "Now we have to figure out how to get our life forces looking that way."

Ezra twirls the pen between his fingers. "You want my guess? You said some of the strands are in the chest and some are in the head. I think the *number* of strands in the chest and the *number* in the head are correlated by the golden ratio. So for Uncle Rob and me, the number of head strands to the number of chest strands is proportional by the golden ratio. For Jeanelle and everyone else I've seen, that ratio is flipped, chest over head. Considering how prevalent the ratio is in a healthy life force, and how precise everything is, I'd place my bet on that. And if we make that assumption, I'd say we're looking at strands pulled out of the chest or the head, and that's what's making the swirls wrong."

"Brilliant!" Gabriel says, eyes wide. "We simply need a way for me to see all the strands so I can count them and Kaylen can get the right number in the right place..." His mind takes off at lightning speed.

"Wow," I breathe, laying back on my bed. "That sure was a giant leap in one day."

"Funny how we always have those when you finally stop trying to do things by yourself," Ezra says.

31

"*N*o," I say firmly as I tug a sweatshirt over my head and then sit on the corner of the bed, exhausted from standing for just a couple minutes. Gabriel is well-dressed for once, wearing a linen button-down and dressy slacks. Maybe he's expecting good news at his CT appointment today. I don't want to ask though. At this moment I just want him to leave because I'm not interested in the conversation I know is about to ensue.

Gabriel throws his pen across the room and swivels his chair to face me. "Then when?"

"Maybe never," I snap. "I will not put your soul at risk. I'm done talking about this, Gabriel."

"I'm not," he says, his jaw tightening.

Kaylen walks in right then wearing a pair of heart-printed pajama pants, a glass of juice in her hand. She holds it out for me "Are you going with Gabe today?" she asks. "Farlen wants to know."

I take the juice from her and shake my head. "Thanks, Kaylen."

She sees my face, then Gabe's, and lifts her eyebrows in recognition before turning on her heel to walk out. She knows what's going on. She and Ezra both avoid us like the plague whenever Gabriel brings up turning his life force into an experiment—which has happened at least once a week in the three and a half weeks since we discovered Kaylen's ability to manipulate strands telekinetically.

"You should get going," I say, swinging my legs up onto the bed and laying down.

I can feel Gabriel's eyes on me, but I don't look his way, instead pretending that I'm reading something on my phone.

"Wendy," he says. I can hear the censure in his voice and it makes me absolutely livid.

I throw the phone down on the bed beside me and glare at him. "Gabriel."

"We need to do something. We already know how the life force is supposed to look. You are letting fear rule you again."

Oh that does it! I have endured his pleas week after week, keeping my cool, patiently explaining to him again and again that I am *not* using him for an experiment. But I have *had* it. Attempting to align this situation with events in the past is low, lower than I would expect for Gabriel. "Enough!" I yell. "You are a *bully,* Gabriel Dumas. You resort to guilt trips because you have nothing else to argue with at this point. But I am not going to put up with it anymore! I want to fix this. I do! But not this way!" I heave in a few breaths, and since I am finally not fighting back my words I say, "I will let you *die* before I disfigure your life force any more than it already is! Mark my words. This is *not* negotiable."

He tilts his head, taking in my clenched fists and flared nostrils. Something in him deflates, though I see no indication on the surface. "Noted," he says, swiveling in his chair and putting his back to me. He writes something down. "Death it is."

Furious, I want to hurl sharp objects at his head, to scream obscene things. But the sight of him... the bald head, the frail frame, protruding shoulder blades, the rattle in his every breath, the subtle shake in his pen strokes that only my eyes can see... it yanks my emotions the other direction. He also carries a small bag that collects the fluid from his lungs via a plastic tube. He's ill. Deathly ill. I can't reconcile my anger and my guilt at that moment as they threaten to pull me apart. So I stand up and stride into the bathroom, slamming the door as hard as I can behind me.

Collapsing onto the bench by the shower, I put my head in my hands to get a hold of myself. My throat is thick, but I really don't feel like crying. For one thing, it's exhausting in my state. For another, they won't be cathartic tears. When I'm done sobbing, the same problems will still be here.

"I don't know what to do next," I whisper into the cavernous space of our bathroom. It echoes back to me—a sound only my ears can hear. I catch sight of my face in the mirror: sunken eyes; pale, sallow skin. Beneath my layered clothes are bruises. Lots of them. I have a nasal cannula for oxygen usually, but I was planning to go with Gabriel to his CT scan and wanted to smell the outdoors. Not now though. I don't think I can stand to be near him at the moment.

We've grown apart the last few weeks because of his increasing badgering to turn himself into a proverbial life force pin cushion. The four of us, Gabriel, Ezra, Kaylen, and I, share discomforts in the colorworld every day, but I never go there with just Gabriel. Instead I let him bleed into everyone else so I can't distinguish him. If he isn't looking over charts and numbers and reading oncology journals, he dozes during those times because that's when he finally feels well enough to rest. I spend the entire time watching the colorworld though, hoping for inspiration. But

I've seen it so much now that I know I'm overlooking something, only I don't know how to change my vision. A few times Kaylen has manipulated Gabriel's strands, testing whether she can isolate strand ends from the rest of his life force. She can do it, but it's a tedious process to isolate even one strand and Kaylen is always shaking by the end of it. Sure, she can grab a loose strand and shove it somewhere, but what if it's the wrong place?

The bathroom offers no inspiration and this bench is killing my bony posterior. I need to lay down. I heard Gabriel leave a couple minutes ago, so I guess I can come out now.

Collapsing on the bed and staring at the ceiling, I relish the moment alone—something I rarely get these days. People always seem to be around, either in the colorworld with me, or poking me, or sitting with me. I hardly ever get my own emotions to myself. Right now I feel... stressed. Like I can't fully exhale. I know it's primarily from spending weeks guarding against Gabriel's next emotional manipulation tactic. In fact, the more I think about it, the more upset I become. Why can't he let it go? It wasn't like this before we discovered that Kaylen's telekinesis works in the colorworld. It's like he doesn't trust me to figure this out anymore. To him, experimenting with his life force is the only way to learn how to fix mine and Kaylen's. And because he thinks that, he's trying to force it on me, and as a result I don't have the mental space to devote to solving the problem. I'm expending my energy on keeping him at arm's-length.

Just like last time...

Disappointment weighs me down at that realization. Old habits die hard, I guess. For both of us. It's clear I'm going to have to talk to him about it, but I don't know if he'll listen. He's so obsessed with keeping us alive another day. Always updating his charts... recording data.

I don't ever pay attention to them—the charts—even though there is a giant one on the wall recording my daily blood counts. I don't like to live my life according to what my blood workup says about how imminent my death is. I disagreed with Gabriel on putting the chart up, but in the end I decided it wasn't worth fighting him on.

I turn my head to look at it now though, curious about it for once.

My heart jumps, but not in a good way. I push myself up abruptly, thinking I'm not seeing it right.

Nope. It's right. And that's when I remember Gabriel had Jeanelle take another blood sample from me this morning because he said the sample last night must have been corrupted. But apparently it *wasn't*. The line graph, which plots my counts from one day to the next with several lines, shows a dramatic increase in my white blood cell count since yesterday. It's been climbing steadily, but the last reading jumped more dramatically than it has at any other time.

"Shit," I breathe, seeing Gabriel's attitude this morning in a new light. Pulsing with adrenaline, for the first time I'm frightened of dying.

What the hell, Wendy? I've been terminally ill for months and I only *now* think about dying like it could really happen?

Tears flood my eyes then, and I'm ashamed of them, feeling weak and stupid. I've got Gabriel and Kaylen counting on me to save them and I'm broken up over *my* dying? I fall back on the bed and curl into a ball, choking on my own breaths. I am a selfish, selfish person.

I hear footsteps over my own crying but I don't turn to look. Whoever it is stops at the door. I quiet my sobs, not wanting to talk to whoever it is about why I'm losing it. It's probably Maris. I think her hearing is almost as good as mine because she shows up whenever I'm doing something out of the ordinary.

"I don't want company right now, Maris," I say loudly without turning.

"Apparently you and Gabe both woke up on the wrong side of the bed today," a rough voice says.

I sit up and snap my head around in one motion to find Mike leaning against the door jamb, his giant arms crossed and his face clear of emotion. I haven't seen him in at least a month. I know Gabriel has spoken to him, but I have had no interest in trying to gain Mike's favor with everything that's been going on.

He looks over my head at something, his eyes scanning. "Well, well. That explains it then. Having a death-bed pity party?"

"Go to hell, Mike," I say, my eyes narrowing to slits.

"My life force isn't mangled, so I doubt that's going to happen any time soon."

"Gabriel's not here," I say. "Get. Out."

He actually chuckles. "Oh c'mon, Wen—can I call you Wen? You're just pissed at Gabe. Don't take it out on me."

I smile sweetly. "Actually Mike, I *am* pissed at you. It's my constant state where you're concerned, see?"

He tsk-tsks and shakes his head. "I'm barely here. What a waste of time staying pissed at me constantly."

I lay back on the bed. Maybe I can call Mark to have Mike muscled out of here. He doesn't seem to have any intention of leaving.

"If there's one thing I get, it's the frustration of being mad at my brother," Mike says. "He can't even argue right. He makes you waste your energy on being mad at him to wear you down. And then he springs whatever his point of contention is at the exact time when your guard is down so you'll give in. Manipulative bastard."

I look at him. He's exactly right. "Well he must think I'm an idiot if he thinks he can force his solution on me. He thinks I can't fix this now. And Gabriel hates being wrong, so he's going to 'help' me figure this out by sacrificing himself. So then at least he can die and give himself a better chance of being right at the same time." I snort bitterly and look back at the ceiling. "Jerk."

Mike laughs. "So that's what it is? And you're surprised by this?"

"No," I say, still not looking at him.

A few moments of awkward silence pass and then Mike says, "What about your uncle?"

"What about him?"

"My brother says you revere him and clearly you're in a bad place. Seems like you'd go to someone you think that highly of when you're facing probable death and my brother is being an asshole."

It bothers me that Mike knows how much I look up to Robert. I don't like that Mike knows anything about me.

"It's complicated," I say.

"My mom says you avoid him."

Just how much do Maris and Gabriel tell Mike about me? Those two need to leave me out of their conversations.

"I don't avoid him. He avoids *me*."

Mike guffaws. "Let me guess. Your stunning personality."

"Mike," I say, irritated. "I told you it's complicated. What's it to you anyway? Why are you here?"

"Because Gabe brushed me off and I have nothing better to do than irritate you."

"I'm going to call my bodyguard and have him kick you out."

"Yeah right."

I turn to look at him. "You doubt me?"

"Yes, actually," Mike says. "I doubt everything about you."

I heave in several breaths, utterly shocked by Mike's audacity. I don't even know how to respond. We regard each other for several seconds, and when I fail to come up with an explanation for Mike's belligerence, I say, "What have I *ever* done to you?"

"You're killing my brother."

His words punch me in the gut and I stop breathing.

"But mostly I'm pushing your buttons because I can't figure out what everyone loves about you so much," Mike continues. "My mother. My dad. My brother. Robert. I just talked to him you know. Checking to see what the news was because Gabe wouldn't talk to me and you are probably the *last* person I want to see. I asked Robert what you were up to on your end. He said he didn't know. I was like, 'why?' And Robert said you hadn't spoken to him and he, quote, 'respected your choice.' Look, I know Robert has resources, and it's now clear you aren't using those resources. The fact that you are trying to figure this thing out with life forces all on your own is absolutely asinine. You're what? Eighteen? You tell me you don't get help from Robert because it's 'complicated' which is really your way of saying you don't want to be any more of a mooch than you already are. And that means you're letting my brother die because of some misguided principle, and that, frankly, pisses me the hell off."

Mike is obviously completely wrong, but I don't care about that right now. What I care about is what my uncle supposedly said to him. "Robert told you he respected *my* choice?" I ask, sitting up.

Mike is thrown off momentarily, probably having expected me to blow up at him, but he recovers and says, "Yeah. In fact, I even asked him why you weren't using him and he said, 'Wendy will come to me when she's ready.' That's a bunch of bull. From what I can tell, you're out of time. What are you waiting for? Permission? Well I give you permission to die already so Gabe won't feel obligated to turn himself over to your nonexistent life force experiments and get some real help."

I stand up and yank my hat on my bald head—it's colder downstairs. Mike flinches as I walk toward him. But I don't care about him. I just want to get through the door. Just before I pass him though, I say, "Make sure you're gone by the time I get back." And then I brush past him, on my way to Robert's office.

32

"*G*ood morning, Wendy. Is everything alright?" Robert asks, looking up from his computer monitor, his salt and pepper goatee a little longer than he usually wears it.

I stand in the doorway and stare at him. When Mike said he talked to Robert, my suspicions were immediately aroused. Robert almost never works from his home office *during* a business day. And then when Mike told me Robert said I would talk to him when I was 'ready' I knew Robert was waiting on me to do something. I want to ask him if he knew ahead of time that I'd be coming to see him, but I bite my tongue. He probably wouldn't answer that question.

"No. I'm dying more than usual," I reply clippingly. I immediately regret it when I see a slight grimace distort Robert's mouth. Stupid Mike. I can't stand him. Somehow I become exactly what he treats me like, which is trash.

I saunter over the empty chair on the other side of Robert's desk and collapse into it. His concern and worry hits me at that moment and I suddenly want to cry—this time out of sadness rather than anger. To hold the tears back I start babbling about my argument with Gabriel, our passive-aggressive distance from each other, and my sudden increase in white blood cell count. "And I'm still no closer to figuring this stupid cure out," I say, biting my lip. "But I can't mess with Gabriel's soul. I didn't listen to my instincts in the colorworld before, and look what happened? How can he ask me to do this? And then make me feel *bad* about refusing? Even if I get him to stop hounding me about it, he won't let it go, not really. It will just morph into something else even more crazy."

I only now realize how true that is. I think that's why I'm still irate at him: I see no way out of this stalemate between us.

Robert is leaning back in his chair, twirling a pen between his thumb and index finger. He doesn't reply, just waits.

Well, if I'm going to whine about my life, I'm going to do it right, so I keep talking. "And you. Hiding all the time. I've missed you and nobody knows how to give me good advice. Maris just reads the Bible to me. Or prays. I don't know what to do. I'm completely stuck. And now I'm out of time."

"What kind of advice are you looking for?" Robert asks, still twirling that pen between his fingers.

I open my mouth in confusion for several beats. "You know… Uncle Moby wisdom. The kind that makes me think in a different direction. The kind that gets me out of my rut."

An amused smile curves his mouth. "What am I? A wisdom vending machine?"

I wrinkle my nose and purse my lips. "Pretty much."

He crosses a leg over a knee and sits back in his chair more comfortably. "I don't deal in life forces, Wendy. What advice could I possibly give you about it?"

I think for a moment and then say, "I don't know. But you don't think I should do what Gabriel wants, do you?"

"It sounds risky. But again, life forces are not my area."

I throw my hands up. "They're not mine either! That's the point!"

"What is it you're asking of me, Wendy?" he replies, this time his eyes boring into mine with that rare but powerful force he possesses.

"You tell me! Mike said you were waiting on me to come see you. So here I am!"

"I *was* waiting for you to come see me, yes. But it's clear you aren't *ready* to see me. So why are you here?"

I put my hands on either side of my face in frustration. "You aren't making sense, Uncle Moby."

"I know. It's because you're here too soon. How about you come back when you're ready?"

My jaw drops. I think he's absolutely serious. And I don't know what to do but obey. So I stand up and back through the door, wondering if he's going to stop me.

He doesn't. And when I get back to my room Mike is gone but Maris is there in her rocking chair, working on the purple afghan she's been making. She glances at my bewildered face questioningly, but when I don't answer and flop on the bed she goes back to her knitting.

***

Gabriel stops abruptly as soon as he enters the room, having spotted me sitting on the bed closest to the doorway, waiting for him. I heard him come in downstairs, and I positioned myself like this to give the impression that I mean business. And I do. I've been building up for hours now, ready to handle any argument he dishes out.

"What is it?" he asks, not sparing any formalities. He's eager, and I try not to get upset at his obvious assumption that I've come around to his way of thinking.

I uncross my ankles and cross them the other way, gathering my wits, reaching for the words I've been planning to say to him. "Gabriel, I need you to trust me."

His brow lifts and he puts his hands on his hips. "I do."

"No, you don't. If you did, you wouldn't assume I've been acting out of fear. It's very hurtful. And it's been holding up my progress."

"Wendy, so far you have not demonstrated that you have an alternative direction. And furthermore, you told me you *needed* me in order to figure this out. So I'm helping you in the only way I can. Why won't you let me?"

I bow my head. "When I say I need you, it does not mean I need you to sacrifice yourself. It means I need you to support me, to believe in me."

"Will you allow me to be frank?" he asks.

"Gabriel, when have you ever *not* been frank?"

"Plenty. I *do* have tact."

I wave a hand, not willing to argue semantics with him. "Please, be frank."

"You have consistently demonstrated that you do not act unless pushed. I'm not asking you to go my direction. I'm asking you to go *some* direction. I'm simply exerting pressure because I know that's what motivates you. If there is some other way to get you to act, I'd love to hear it."

For the second time today, my jaw drops, this time because of Gabriel's harsh honesty—which he did warn me about, but I guess I never expect it to come out quite the way it does... calculated... purposeful. I don't know whether to be disturbed or impressed.

"Is there something else you would like to discuss?" he asks, coming to sit by me as if the last month of distance didn't happen.

"You're kidding, right?" I say, flabbergasted. "Do you realize how stressed out I've been about our relationship? I've spent all this time angry at you and trying to keep my cool instead of focusing on fixing the life force problem. It's been the exact *opposite* of helpful."

He wrinkles his nose. "Wendy, you really ought to learn to let things go."

I turn entirely to face him, bringing a knee up. "And you ought to learn to not try to control me through emotional manipulation! Geez, Gabriel. It's like our separation all over again! Can't you just like... talk to me or something?"

"I did. Repeatedly. You kept saying no. And it's not like I can *make* you do anything. So really, it's not like the separation at all."

"Emotional blackmail? It absolutely *is* like our separation!" I throw my hands up.

"It wasn't intended to be emotional. And it was not blackmail. I asked a question, and each time you answered it in the same way. Why are you so upset?"

I throw my hands up. "Because sometimes you act like a freaking robot! It's as impossible as communicating with a rock!"

Gabriel reaches for my hand, but I scoot away. He hesitates, but finally says, "Wendy, the only person who has been upset in this scenario has been you. Sure, I have picked up on your distance the past month, but I assumed it was frustration over no progress. And I've been involved in other things, choosing to dedicate my time to keeping us alive so *you* can have more time." He chuffs to himself then. "Forgive me, but I think it's rather funny that you've projected your grievances on me rather than the problem. In fact, if you truly examine it, I think you'll realize that it's not *me* and my willingness to be a test subject that you're upset about, but something else entirely."

I grind my teeth and glare at him. "Like what?" I say, struggling to keep my voice even. He is so patronizing. And full of himself.

"You're worried about doing permanent damage to my life force, that much is clear. But I think you've been reacting the way you have because you're afraid. You *do* understand that if and when you figure this out, it's going to require *someone* being a guinea pig, right? And you're going to have to move life force strands? And it's probably going to require being comfortable with some unknown variables? It's going to require you *change* the state of my life force as well as Kaylen's and your own. Even though we know what it's *supposed* to look like, that's a terrifying thought, isn't it?"

I open my mouth. Close it. Open it again. I look down at the floor, cross my arms. Lay back on the bed.

"I hate you," I say, not looking at Gabriel.

"Well that's not very nice."

I glance down at him. "Love-hate. It's a thing. It means you drive me absolutely bonkers. And then you… make perfect sense. Why does it take you making me hate you to come to a turning point in my thinking? You couldn't tell me all of this back when I first told you no?"

"I'm not a mind-reader, Love. You, on the other hand, are. Why didn't you pick up that I haven't been upset with you—that I might be motivated by something *other* than sacrificing myself?"

"Because I purposely didn't pick out your emotions. But you *were* upset with me today."

"That's true," he concedes. He sighs heavily. "I'm a little sensitive to the idea of you moving closer to death. Your numbers—"

"I know," I say. "I looked after you left." I turn my head toward him. "How was your appointment?"

He shrugs, and then deflates inside. "I don't want to think about it."

"That bad?" I ask, bracing for bad news.

"Ah, actually, technically it's not what other people would consider bad. And on any other day I might consider it good, but in the face of your decline, I am hard-pressed to call it good."

"Oh just spit it out, Gabriel," I say, propping my head up with my elbow. "I have no idea what you're saying."

"My tumor has shrunk thirty-four percent."

A smile comes over my face. "Really? Dr. Altman is going to eat his words! Wait. How is this even *remotely* a bad thing?" I watch Gabriel's downcast expression for about three seconds and I get it. "Wait... Seriously, Gabriel? You're upset that I'm dying faster than you?"

"You're younger," he says. "And we need you. You have the sight. I certainly can't fix life forces without you. And you've overcome so much! You've had such difficulty in life. It's not fair!" He cringes. "I know nothing in life is intended to be fair. But I can't help it. You deserve more time. I have eight years on you. Eight more years of life. I want so much to give those to you. I counted I would at least be content if I could die before you. But at this rate, not even that will happen." His eyes have turned misty and his jaw trembles. "I am furious at Carl. You should not be bearing the price of his mistakes."

I sit up and reach for him, tucking my head under his chin. "Gabriel," I say quietly. "No matter what happens, whether I figure this out and save the day, or whether I die, I would not change it. I wouldn't change what Carl did to me. Because it brought me to you. Sure, I've done stupid things, suffered a lot, but..." I sit up and look at his face, holding his hands in mine, finding words that I don't think I've ever spoken to myself let alone someone else. "I would take every bit of the hardship of my life for who I am now. And I became this way because of *you*. For you I would live a life walking through fire. Love-hate. I have never felt so many different things for one person. I've never felt so much, *period.* You…" Warmth glows in my chest and tears come to my eyes. I look down, finding my voice. Looking back into his eyes, I say, "You brought me to life. If everyone could live and change so much in only twenty years, no one would care how long their life was—"

Realization strikes me like a lightning bolt. Gabriel is completely overcome with my words, and though I meant every single one, I understand something that I didn't before.

"Sam," I whisper, looking over Gabriel's shoulder at nothing.

Gabriel, obviously confused, but seeing my expression, says, "Sam? What about him?"

"I need to go see Uncle Moby."

33

$\mathcal{R}$obert looks amused when I come into his office again, this time with Gabriel trailing me. But his expression is subtle—and knowing. Like he said, he's been waiting for me to ask him for something. And I know exactly what it is.

"Sam's death totally threw me off," I say, stopping in the middle of the spacious room. "You said there was a price for the last vision, but I assumed the price would somehow be... less since you said the goal was good. When I realized that the price was Sam's life, I swore I'd never cheat with a vision again. I hated that my actions caused his death. He deserved a longer life. Recovered addict. Sticking by you because he knew you were worth emulating. Trying to do something with his life. To be better. He *was* better. It wasn't fair that just when he figured things out, his time was cut short.

"Gabriel just said the same thing to me—about *my* life. You know what I said? I wouldn't take it back. I want to live, but I don't know for sure if I will. Sam wanted to live when he went on that mission with me, but he didn't know for sure if he would. He made the choice because he trusted what you said about the importance of what I was doing. I don't have the right to take that away from him."

Weakened from standing, I take a few more steps to sit in a chair. Gabriel follows close behind, curious about where I'm going. Robert is on the edge of my emodar, but I can tell *he* knows where I'm going. "Just like Gabriel doesn't get a say in whether Carl's actions all those years ago were unfair to me. This sounds like... so messed up, but I don't think there's anything that has happened in my life that I have been *more* grateful for than what Carl did to me. Even though I didn't want to admit it, I expected a solution that day at the compound with Sam. Sam's death for a solution *would* have seemed like an acceptable cost, because you're right: we weigh the cost of everything, including people's lives. We do it without thinking, even though it's wrong. And it's wrong because we don't have all the facts. We don't know the future and the impact we have on it—most of us anyway." I smirk at him before continuing. "Compounding visions cause so much trouble because they cause you to skip steps. Steps that would have helped you navigate the 'final' vision better. Just like me showing up in your office earlier today. You said I wasn't ready to see you yet. I had to have that fight with Gabriel first. I had to understand I was wrong about Sam, about visions. Skipping that step might have meant I went into this with my head in the wrong place."

Robert is smiling outright now, unable to help himself, I think. Gabriel, whom I can sense from behind me, is awed but questioning still.

"You told me on the plane after he died that the only thing I owed Sam was to make his life add value to *mine*." I say. "You said his life was worth as much as I was willing to pay. The only way I know how is to put everything I have into this, take another risk, and see this through to the 'final vision.' You said the first one was a good vision and I trust that, so let's take the next step. I want another vision. This time I want to find a way to safely unravel life force strands so I can see them better."

Even though I just said the words, my intellect is still having trouble holding on to them all at once. The logic is a bit circular, which I always encounter when I talk to Robert, even though he hasn't said a word. I swear just being around him opens up my mind and makes the words come. And I know they're true.

"Good heavens, Wendy," Gabriel says, putting a hand on my shoulder. "Your ability to grasp the impact of Robert's ability is astounding. Sam's death... what a beautiful explanation."

Robert is nodding slowly, placing steepled fingers under his chin and still smiling. "Those who have known death more than most always have a finer grasp of its place in life. Death forces us to reconcile it. Mortality quails in the face of it above all else such that we avoid even thinking about it. Therefore being forced to see it up close is usually the only way we can gain an accurate perspective on life."

"So, the vision?" I ask. "Does that sound like an okay goal?"

"It sounds exactly right," Robert says.

"Do you already know what the vision is?"

Robert shakes his head. "As I've told you before, visions are affected by so many different variables. I couldn't have gotten a safe vision for you earlier if you'd asked me. Your motives were too unstable."

"How long do you need?"

"It should only take a few minutes," he says, folding his arms on the desk. "But before I do, I hope you might describe in more detail what a life force looks like. I told you I hold goals in mind with a combination of words and images. I have purposely blinded myself from information in this case until now so I wouldn't see something too soon that I couldn't handle navigating. But in order to get a good vision of what you need, I need a frame of reference."

"Frame of reference? How about I *show* you?" I say, realizing that I have never actually shown Robert the colorworld.

His chair creaks as he sits back in it, grimacing a little. "I don't know about that... Seeing what you see... it may be dangerous for me."

It's odd to see Robert move so easily between confident and all-knowing to tentative and afraid. Robert is clearly only comfortable with using his ability in specific ways. I think I can understand how seeing the colorworld would get his mind going in directions that wouldn't be welcome though.

"I think if you aren't comfortable seeing the colorworld, then you aren't comfortable getting the information she's asking for from the vision anyway," Gabriel points out. "Because unraveling a life force the way we need it is no small request. You have already opened that door leading into dangerous possibilities simply by offering. Wendy fears doing this without enough information. So let's do it smartly, shall we? I'd rather you use an *actual* life force for reference so that we can be sure to get accurate information. All or none, Mr. Haricott. Completely through the door, or shut it tightly."

"A smart assessment," Robert says, nodding thoughtfully. "I'll buy it."

"Excellent," Gabriel says, moving a chair next to me for Robert to sit in.

When everyone is situated, and I've explained to Robert all of the weird sensations that accompany the colorworld, I pull off a glove and rest my hand lightly on the top of his. And then I channel us both in.

As I wait for Robert to acclimate, I look around his office and almost immediately recognize that I can see more detail in the colorworld than ever before. With my usual vision, all inanimate objects have a kind of fluctuating illusion of color about them. Their hue changes as I adjust my angle of sight. But now I can tell that it's the structure of the objects that make them appear that way. Their surfaces are multi-faceted. I can see into them as if they are partially transparent and composed of a crystalline structure, though I can't make it out very well.

I can also now see the energy vapor, even in the well-lit room. It rolls off of Gabriel's life force, which is even more stunning than usual. I can make out more than just tiny silken strands. His strands are multi-faceted as well, crystalline and reflective. Their brilliance comes from a mirror effect present in the structure of the strands, refracting his inner light both within and between strands. And there are the tiniest hints of other colors now. Kind of like looking through a prism. Little rainbows glint and shift, disappearing and reappearing as Gabriel's strands shift and move.

"You were being literal about the strands," Robert says finally, breaking me out of my wonder. "They're absolutely lovely."

"Uh, yeah," I say. "But this is a lot more detailed than I'm used to."

"It is?"

"Yeah..." I breathe. I was just in the colorworld yesterday. Have I somehow improved my ability since then? I look down at my hand as if I can tell the difference in my light, but that's when I see Robert's life force bonded with mine. And I get it.

"I think you're improving my ability, Uncle Moby," I say.

"How is that?" he asks, still looking around incredulously at the sights.

"Your light," I reply. "Hang on. I can check." I let go of Robert's hand but keep close to his life force so I can stay channeled into the colorworld. As I do so, the colorworld dims a bit and the vapor disappears and the details fog. I can't believe that the colorworld now looks blurry compared to what I just saw with Robert.

I put my hand back on his arm and the intricacy moves back into focus. "Yep," I say. "I equalize the light between people. That's why some people die—their life force is too dim to handle my light. Since you're brighter than me, you're sharing your light with me, which intensifies my ability. Things are more detailed here and I can see the energy vapor that I can usually only see in the dark."

"Is that helpful?" he asks.

"It's not harmful," I reply. "We're both still alive!"

"Alright, well this is marvelous. Do you have any idea how many strands there are?" Robert asks, looking at Gabriel's life force now.

"No idea. But enough that they correspond to capillaries in the body and points in the brain," I reply.

"Tens of billions," Gabriel says.

I have no doubt Gabriel didn't throw that number out randomly. His estimate is based on definite observation. But it makes both Robert and I balk a little. To think Gabriel wanted me to insert misplaced strands willy-nilly...

"I'll focus now," Robert says then. "And I think it may be more helpful if you let go of me now. The sensations are quite distracting."

I release him, the haze of the visible world moving into focus, as if it's being superimposed on the colorworld—a place both simpler and more complex at the same time.

Gabriel is now sitting on the carpet, and both of us wait. It takes only a few minutes before Robert opens his eyes and sits back in his chair, hands folded in his lap and looking flabbergasted.

"Well what did you see?" I ask impatiently.

His expression one of bewilderment, Robert says, "A pool."

"Like... a pool of water? A puddle or a swimming pool?" Gabriel asks. "And which one?"

"I was looking directly down on an indoor swimming pool," Robert explains. "Black painted lane lines on the bottom. Filled with water. Nothing else, no surroundings, just blue water and black lane lines—Wait." Robert stops abruptly. And then his face blanches.

"What?" I demand.

But Robert shakes his head and regains composure. "Nevermind. It's not important. But I can tell you I've seen this vision before, only not so clearly."

"What am I supposed to do with a pool?" I ask.

Robert shrugs, but his excitement and enthusiasm about the pool vibrates in my own chest. "This is a very, *very* good vision. Purely informational."

A pool... What does it mean? Before Gabriel or I can speculate about it aloud, Robert stands up. "I think you've got it from here," he says brightly. "I should be getting back to the office."

I watch his back as he leaves, and though I don't yet know what to do with his vision, I do know that Robert is thrilled. I don't think I've ever felt him so elated in the time I've known him.

34

"*W*ater therapy or something?" I suggest, though it sounds really bizarre. "It's about relaxing, right? So maybe we're supposed to spend time in the pool to relax. What you do to the body, you do to the life force and vice-versa, right? A relaxed body means a relaxed life force? One that will let us look through it more easily?"

Gabriel paces slowly in front of my chair. "We can certainly try that. But we've been in the colorworld right after a shower before—something definitely relaxing—as well as other relaxing activities…" He grins at me. "And I didn't see anything odd in your life force. He said it was purely informational, not situational. I think we should assume it's not about the pool, but about water—a lot of it," says Gabriel. "So what are the qualities of water?"

"Um, it's wet," I offer, wanting to stop talking about it and actually *go* to a pool and then look in the colorworld there. Not that I have *any* idea what I'd see. Water is invisible in the colorworld, so why it would have *anything* to do with life forces is beyond me.

"It's made up of hydrogen and oxygen," says Gabriel. "*Hydrogen and oxygen. Hydrogen and oxygen…*" he mumbles as he paces.

"There's an awful lot of it," I say. "Kinda crazy since it's totally invisible in the colorworld."

"Indeed, over seventy percent of the surface of the earth is covered by it," says Gabriel.

"And our bodies are made up of seventy percent water also. At least, if we're well hydrated we are," I say.

"That's closer to what we're looking for," says Gabriel. "Let's see, chemical properties. It's the universal solvent—" Gabriel stops abruptly. He turns to face me, eyes wide. His train of thought leaps off of a cliff, exploding mid-air. I gasp and grip the sides of my chair. The surprise of the mental movement is just as jarring as if someone had shot a gun right next to my ear.

"It's a solvent!" exclaims Gabriel, clapping his hands in the air.

"Yeah but what does that have to do with—"

"Substances spread evenly throughout water because of it's properties as a universal solvent," Gabriel interrupts me excitedly, crouching in front of me, hands on the arms of my chair, his dark brown eyes gleaming. "What happens when you let your hair out in the water?"

I visualize what he's asking, and it clicks into place immediately. "It separates!" I shout, jumping up only to become immediately lightheaded. Gabriel catches me in his arms though and picks me up and swings me around.

"Woah. Dizzy," I say, clutching his arms.

"My apologies, Love. My excitement got the better of me. Are you alright?" he asks as he sets me gently back in the chair.

"Yeah," I say, closing my eyes and waiting for more oxygen to make it's way to my brain. "Moved too quickly."

"This is fabulous!" cheers Gabriel. "We have to test it out right away!"

"Okay," I mumble. "Just give me a minute."

"Water! I should have considered it before. It's genius! Hair separates in water because of dissociative properties. I never imagined that water would have the same effect in the colorworld. Like you said, it's invisible there."

Gabriel catches sight of me again and he crouches down to my level, suddenly very worried. "I'm so sorry, Love. Are you really alright? You look pale. Can you speak?"

"Yes," I say, opening my eyes as the dizziness fades. "Hold my hand, will you?"

Carefully, we make it down the hall and into the kitchen. Gabriel tries to sit me down in a chair but I resist. "No. Where is this experiment taking place?"

Gabriel gives me a once over and doesn't like what he sees. However, he says, "What do you think? Will the sink do?"

"It's a start. If it really is like hair, we should be able to tell in a little water," I answer, making my way to the large double sink and leaning my weight on the counter. "I'd guess that the reason Uncle Moby saw a pool was because that's the only body of water big enough and clean enough to fit a whole person in and see anything—the only way to unravel a *whole* life force, right?"

Gabriel lifts the lever on the sink, and we both wait in nervous expectation as it slowly fills. Gabriel keeps sneaking glances at me until I finally say, "What is it?"

"You look awfully pale. I'm waiting for you to pass out. I don't want to miss catching you," he says.

"Well forget that. I'm not fainting. What's up with the fancy dress today? Planning on celebrating your tumor shrinkage?"

He purses his lips in distaste. "Heavens no. I told you I wasn't exactly happy about that. It's Valentine's Day. I was planning to take you out. I was going to ask you as soon as I got back, but we got a little distracted as you know."

"Oh..." I say, having forgotten the day completely. Although I *would* say that Gabriel isn't telling me everything. There's something more to his plans than just a Valentine's outing. So I look at him expectantly. He knows he can't hide things from me.

"I wanted to... go over an alternative treatment plan with you," he confesses.

"That's a cause to be nervous?"

"If it's something you might not like, sure."

"Why wouldn't I like it? Could it possibly be any worse than what I've already been though?"

"Yes." He turns the water off and puts his hands on either side of the sink, guilty. "I was going to recommend an experimental transplant procedure. Transplants require the patient to be in remission—which you aren't—but this particular trial doesn't. It's new, and extremely risky—at least for normal individuals. The hope would be that because you don't succumb to infection as easily as a normal transplant patient, you would survive the procedure. The worry, however, is that you would be more likely to reject the transplant due to your sensitive body. There are so many unknown variables. We have no data to draw conclusions. But in the face of your cancer becoming resistant to treatments, it presents the only possibility."

My heart pounds, reminding me that my fear of dying is still in effect. "And you were dressed up to tell me that? To *convince* me of that? I doubt even *you* want me to do it if it's as risky as it sounds. Unless there's something you're not telling me."

"The sink is full," he replies, shutting the water off and putting a hand on mine to cue me into the colorworld.

I pull my hand away. "Uh uh. First you come clean. We're about to have what is probably a *major* breakthrough. Let's clear the air so we can properly celebrate when that happens."

He turns to face me, leaning one hip against the counter.

"I was also going to tell you about the surgery I'm going to have for my bone tumor. It has to come out. Depending on how invasive it is, I may lose my leg completely. It's a miracle it hasn't broken from the tumor growth already. Dr. Altman also recommends removing part of my left lung. He says we need to jump on my improvement and take out as much of the malignancy as possible. And I have to agree based on how long it's taken to get this far. My liver and kidney function is gradually decreasing due to all the chemo because they're not having a chance to recover. And I *can't* stop to recover. The lung tumor seems to grow as quickly as it shrinks. Based on Ezra's calculations and mine, I'll need a liver transplant before I reach remission—which I won't get in my state. Surgery on my lungs is the only way to give my other organs a break."

My face pales and I'm lightheaded again. Gabriel catches me as we sink down to a crouching position. "What else?" I say, picking up Gabriel's guilt clearly.

He groans quietly. "I was going to present all of these things and then ask again if you would consider the experimental strand insertion as an alternative."

I look at him through my eyelashes. I shake my head, irritated.

He looks down. "Emotional blackmail, like you said." Depressed, he puts his forehead in his hand. "I don't know why I don't see things the right way when I'm doing them. You were right. And I didn't see it that way until you went to see Robert about getting a vision. I realized it wasn't my pressure that motivated you to act. It was telling you how much I cared for you—how much I wanted you to live. It was... confessing my *own* weakness, not pointing out yours." He looks up with pleading eyes. "It wasn't until then that I saw how awful I'd been to you. And I was about to do more of it. I thought I was past this... this control thing after we reunited the last time. But I guess I'm not." He lifts his shoulders and lets them fall dejectedly.

"Why did I have to drag that out of you?" I ask. "You usually jump at the opportunity to clear the air."

He shakes his head. "Because I don't have a solution. I can't promise you I won't do it again, because if I do it, clearly I won't realize it. Apologies mean nothing if you can't fix it."

"That's not true," I say, reaching out to touch his cheek. "Apologies aren't meant to fix anything. They're a way to tell someone else that you know you aren't perfect, that if you knew how to do it right, you would. It's a way to be vulnerable."

I sit down on the tile floor completely, cross-legged. "I wish you'd do things differently sometimes, but it seems like no matter how you do things, it always works out." I smile at him. "Being married to you has taught me over and over that if I stick by you, even when I want to kill you, I'll come out on the other side a better, smarter person." I lean forward and pull him into a hug. "I'm already over it. So let's do something to celebrate now, okay?"

He kisses my forehead, his lips lingering. "I'm sorry, Wendy. I hope that's enough for now—until I can figure out how to change."

"Of course it is," I say, struggling to my feet. Gabriel helps me, and we stand over the sink of water as he unbuttons his cuff and rolls his sleeve up. Then we look at one another, full of nervous apprehension and blossoming hope.

"Let's do it," I say as I hold my bare hand to his neck and channel us into the colorworld.

We look down at the yellow-glowing sink that appears to be empty, but we know it's full to the brim. Gabriel plunges his arm as far in as it will go.

The effect is exactly like looking at hair as it's submerged in water. The strands spread out and separate more and more, moving with the flow of the subtle but invisible waves caused by Gabriel's disturbance of the water when he put his hand in. The strands look completely tangible... completely vulnerable. Completely at the mercy of the water. For once they are not mysterious. They're subject to the properties of water like everything else.

Gradually Gabriel's skin is revealed underneath, and the mystery of where the external strand ends are supposed to go is solved. They're attached to his skin exactly like hair attaches to the scalp. They root there somehow and the surrounding bulk of strands swirls around in the water, looping and spreading and moving with it as surely as seaweed in the ocean. And his skin... it looks exactly like it does in the visible world, except with a kind of gleam to it that isn't normally visible. It's not easy to see though, as densely packed as the strands are.

"Amazing!" I breathe.

"Look there," Gabriel says, pointing with his free hand. "There are several free ends floating around there. Do you think they are supposed to be attached to the skin or into the chest?"

"Or head," I add.

"Right, so there are evidently three places the ends could go. Either the head, the chest, or the skin's surface."

"Yeah," I agree.

"I'd love to see a whole body submerged," Gabriel says in wonder.

"That's probably what it's going to take," I say.

"Agreed, a pool ought to do it," says Gabriel, chuckling.

I shake my head, astounded. "A pool. A giant container full of the one thing that's not even visible in the colorworld. Who knew?"

"Indeed, who knew that the strands could be manipulated so easily by something like water?" Gabriel said. Then he shakes his head. "I should have guessed this, Wendy. I've been caught up in the movement of the strands lately, trying to discern what it is that makes them move to some kind of wind we can't see or hear or smell. There must be *something* that made them move that way. Perhaps some gas naturally found in the air, and I'd been talking to Robert about getting my hands on some of the more commonly found gases to experiment. The idea that it could be the *water* in the air didn't even occur to me."

My trip to the Monterey Aquarium comes to mind then. "The fish school was a hint," I say with certainty.

"The school of fish that operated like a life force when they were together?" he asks.

"Yeah, and separated as easily into smaller parts. Water really is the universal solvent. It has the power to separate everything, including the stuff that makes up life forces." I say, astonished by my own connection, but also remembering something else that was supposed to be a hint to me as well.

"The pier," I say, astounded, leaning heavily against the counter for support. "I met Robert at a pier that first time after you were admitted to the hospital. I overheard this couple talking about pollution. The woman, she reminded me of you. Her male companion was complaining about the pollution in the water and she was telling him about how pollution doesn't have much of an effect on the water if you consider how vast it is. She said water was a solvent and that meant that pollution would be dispersed evenly, mitigating the effect of anything put in the water." I laugh in incredulity. "She even talked about rivers and estuaries and streams above and below ground being a giant vascular network like a human body. My gosh! It was a hint, and I have totally forgotten about it until now."

"That's quite an epiphany, Love," Gabriel remarks. "A vascular network on earth mirroring our own... Fascinating! Cycles repeat at every level..." Gabriel's face moves into his familiar thinking pose.

"We need to get to a pool," I say. "And we need Kaylen." I sit on one of the kitchen chairs. "We need some normal subjects to observe. Ezra will do but we need others. How are we going to know which strands go where? There are billions of them. Isolating individual loose ends? Thank goodness my eyesight is so good or it would be like trying to split hairs, literally."

"One step at a time," says Gabriel, thinking intently. "We need to go about this with a precise plan."

"This is about to be the most unique Valentine's date ever."

35

Gabriel, Ezra, Kaylen, and I stand in our swimsuits on the edge of an Olympic-sized pool that Robert acquired for our private use this evening. As we look into its watery depths, the air is electric with anticipation.

"So, I guess I'm the first specimen, right?" says Ezra.

"You are the control," Gabriel replies.

"Okay, bombs away," says Ezra who then leaps into the pool cannon-ball style while the rest of us try to back away quickly enough to avoid getting wet.

"Nice Ezra," says Kaylen sarcastically. "We're not here for water sports. Can't you be a little serious?"

"Nope," says Ezra, backstroking in the water. "I've spent the last three months being serious. I'm sick of it."

"As we all are," says Gabriel. "Wendy? I think we're ready. Ezra, you're going to need to stay still while we get a good look."

Kaylen has pulled up a chair for me and I immediately sit down. I put my hand on Gabriel, Kaylen holds her hand on my arm, and then we are in the colorworld. We can all see instantly that Ezra's strands are spread out around him in the water. I still can't figure out what Ezra's body looks like beneath the strands very well, but it's radiant in its own way.

I remember Sam's body once his life force left, and it was green. But I can definitely say Ezra's is not. It's the same color as it is in the visible world. I guess a body changes immediately once the life force is no longer animating it.

The strands themselves are fascinating though. When Ezra moves, the strands pull behind him, reacting to the viscosity of the water exactly like hair. Just as we assumed, Ezra has no loose ends. Strands attach to his skin like hair, and it looks like the other ends loop out and lead to either his head or his chest. The flow of the life force makes it difficult to follow a single strand attached to the body on one end to where it inserts into the head or chest.

Because of how the strands spread in the water, a swirl is no longer visible. When Ezra's head comes up out of the water, however, the strands immediately twist themselves tight into the swirl on his head. I expect them to look wet after being in the water, but they look the same as they did before he jumped in.

"One end attaches to the skin, the other end goes to head or chest just like we thought, right?" I ask, hoping Gabriel can tell better than I can.

Gabriel nods and then says, "Can you submerge yourself again, Ezra? And spread out on your back for about five seconds and then turn to your front for about five seconds." He focuses intently on Ezra's strands.

Ezra dives back underwater, spreading his hands out beneath the surface and kicking his legs and hands to maintain his depth. As if I wasn't already daunted by the task of having to fix strands, their visible delicacy, small-size, and sheer number make it seem almost impossible. It could take hours to pick out all of the strands that are loose for Gabriel, Kaylen, and me—I have no idea how many *are* loose, but it's probably more than a few.

"29,535,358,333," says Gabriel a few seconds after Ezra surfaces.

"Wow," Kaylen says loudly, dumbfounded.

"Are you saying that's how many strands there are?" I ask, floored.

"Yes," replies Gabriel, "Ezra, is that number mathematically significant?"

"Not that I know of," replies Ezra.

"Can you submerge your head now? Let me take a second to count the ones going just into your head," says Gabriel, looking up from his intense concentration.

Ezra does so, and within a few seconds he comes to the surface and Gabriel says, "18,253,855,320 in your head and 11,281,503,013 in your chest."

Once again, Kaylen and I are stunned by Gabriel's ability. "Good night, Gabriel! How do you keep it all straight?" I ask.

He shrugs. "I don't know. To me, it's as easy as counting to ten."

"Kaylen, let me have my phone," Ezra demands suddenly, swimming over to us, and when he comes in range, we can tell he's excited.

Kaylen gets her cell phone from her purse and hands it over. Ezra clicks a few buttons, bites his lip and then looks up in astonishment. "Yep, that's the golden ratio."

"You were right," I say, amazed.

"Between the number in your head and the number in your chest?" asks Gabriel, giddy with our new discoveries.

"It's accurate to the ninth decimal place, so I'd say yeah, it's the golden ratio," Ezra says, grinning.

"Wendy, who cares about moving things with your mind and seeing invisible colors when you can count to billions in a matter of seconds, spot geometric significance in a swirl, and calculate ratios on sight? Why do I care if I can demolish a house if it won't help me pass chemistry?" huffs Kaylen.

"Agreed," I say, envious.

"That is so cool though!" Ezra says to Kaylen. "I'll trade you. And besides, I only estimated the ratio. I had to verify it with the calculator."

Kaylen throws up a hand. "Stop trying to downplay what you can do. It's patronizing."

But Ezra seems oblivious to what he just did. In the past few months I've seen my brother's ability in an entirely different light. His math skill is just as supernatural as my own ability.

"Well then, who's next?" asks Gabriel.

"I'm cold just *looking* at that water," I say, grimacing.

"I'll go," volunteers Kaylen, easing herself into the water. Her strands immediately fan out around her.

She pushes herself out and away from the edge and we immediately see the displaced strands spread out and separate. There are a lot of them; loose ends stretch out from beyond the looping mass of her healthy strands like they *want* to find a home.

"Wow, that was easy," I say, thinking it's almost *too* easy.

Gabriel sighs. "Water... I still can't believe we never thought to try it all this time. So *simple!*"

He then watches Kaylen intently as she turns under the water so we can get a good look at her strands—or rather, so Gabriel can. She repeats the same process that Ezra did, and I see Gabriel's eyes twitch as he counts at an otherworldly speed. What we are attempting would be impossible without his skill.

Finally, Kaylen surfaces and Gabriel announces, "You have 28,975,419,173 total. In your head are 17,907,771,350. But your chest has 11,067,200,532. And the ones that are displaced are 447,291. Furthermore, our theory has been fully confirmed. All displaced strands have been pulled either from the head or chest but remain attached to the skin."

"About half a million out of place then. How do we know how many are displaced from the head and how many are displaced from the chest?" asks Kaylen.

"Well, if we go based on the golden ratio, you should have..." says Ezra, biting the inside of his lip and typing some numbers in the calculator, "424,753 missing from your chest and

22,538 missing from your head. Looks like you have a head over chest ratio just like Uncle Rob and me."

"Ezra, your contribution has been irreplaceable," Gabriel says. "I don't know that we would have discovered the connection between head and chest so quickly without you."

"Math is life," replies Ezra. "It applies to everything."

Things are coming together so well. With Ezra and Gabriel around, the job might actually be do-able. The trick, I imagine, is going to be when it comes time to actually re-insert the things.

"Okay, well I think you guys need to look at a few more regular people before you act on this theory," I say.

"One other problem," says Ezra, worried. "How do we know whether a loose strand belongs in the head or in the chest?"

That stumps us all. It's one issue that came up when I refused to experiment with Gabriel's loose strands.

Gabriel looks intently at Ezra's strands again, his eyes darting from side to side, up and down over Ezra's life force. Then he looks at Kaylen who has gotten back in the pool so he can look at her life force.

After a moment, he sighs. "I can't make out a pattern, though that's not to say there *isn't* one. But I have no idea." He looks at me. "This is your call."

Propping my chin on my palm, I think about it long and hard. I obviously don't have time to wait around for more inspiration to come. There is no way that Gabriel is going under risky surgery and no way I'm taking on an iffy transplant. If I plan to act, the time is now, and I'm a little less afraid than I was all those months ago with Gabriel. I know that every action requires some kind of faith. Gabriel was right. I will likely never have all the facts on life forces and how they work.

"Strands act as one unit," I say, testing. "They give the body consciousness by working together..."

"Like a neural network," Gabriel says. "We create new paths in our brain all the time. Logically I think we can accept that the life force acts as one entity, therefore it's capable of adapting."

I nod, feeling the truthfulness of that. Life adapts. Always. And the colorworld has consistently proven that it follows the same logic as the visible world. It behaves predictably. Like now, surrendering itself to the properties of water and holding to a golden ratio pattern like so much of nature.

"Okay. Let's do it," I say, feeling even better now that I've made the decision officially. "We won't worry about which ones go where. We'll just get the ratio correct."

"So what do we do when we fix yours, Gabe? Get a mirror or something?" asks Ezra. "'Cuz none of us will be able to count them. Although I bet I can get you pretty close, just by looking for the golden spiral to start working right."

"That should do it," Gabriel says.

I'm up next, and Jeanelle comes in from where she's been waiting outside to disconnect my pump, my wrist monitor, and waterproof my tubes. Once I slip out of my towel, sharp little intakes of breath sound from all around as I bring my frail body into view. I should have said something to at least prepare them ahead of time, but I've been too excited to think about how awful I look.

In order to avoid our strands becoming too tangled, I only touch fingertips with Gabriel once I get in the pool. I hope it won't cause problems for his counting.

Curiosity overtakes Gabriel and me at the exact same moment. What does it look like when we touch when our strands are separated in the water?

"Let's see," I say excitedly, answering our shared question. And we lower our hands in the water slowly. It looks like a jumbled mess to me. I can't tell which strands are his and which strands are mine and whether something unusual is happening at all. They are utterly tangled. That's disappointing and also worrisome. How will Gabriel count my strands if he can't differentiate them from his own?

Gabriel observes where our fingertips touch for a few moments as strands loop out and mix together. He works through something before settling on astonishment. Finally he inhales sharply and says, "I think I know what's happening. Ezra, how about you reach for Wendy's other hand under the water so we can see the interaction as it occurs."

Ezra picks up quickly what we're after. So he crouches down and brings his life-force clad hand under the water. He reaches his fingertips out for mine slowly as Gabriel and I watch.

It's so quick I can't be sure I saw it, but as our hands come into contact, I could swear I can see my strands detach from my body at the points that they attach to the outside of my skin. It's like seeing hair strands get pulled out of someone's scalp. I'm only touching index fingers with Ezra, but it's clear to see that he now has more skin attachment points on his finger than he did before. His life force 'hair' is thicker in his finger region. I pull my finger away and then touch him again to be sure I see what I think I'm seeing.

"Are my strands… *attaching* to him?" I ask, flabberghasted. Gabriel's brain is in overdrive, and I can tell I'm right. "Incredible," he breathes, spellbound.

I keep touching Ezra and then letting go, trying to get a better look as the interaction happens. When I let go, my strands move back to adhere to my own skin. Kaylen, meanwhile, has grabbed on to my hand that holds Gabriel's so she can see what we're going on about.

"Freaky, Wen," Ezra says finally. "That's just plain freaky."

"I know," I reply. "Gabriel, how are you going to be able to count my strands if they're detaching from me like that?"

"Oh it should be no problem," Gabriel says. "I can see where your strands are crossing over to attach to me."

I shake my head in awe as I look at the jumbled mess where we touch. Now that I'm looking for it, I can tell that where my skin touches Ezra's or Gabriel's, a small area of surrounding skin becomes 'bald' as strands move to attach to them. It amazes me how easily my strands seem to detach and reattach as easily as… magnets. Excited, I realize that's what I've been feeling all this time when I touch Gabriel.

Gabriel finally gets to counting, and declares that the number of my displaced strands is quite a bit less than Kaylen's: about 350 thousand. Kaylen has been the subject of hypno-touch far more than I have, giving her more opportunity to have had strands yanked out, which worries me. She probably won't live as long as I have given how many more strands she's missing.

"You also have a head over chest ratio," Ezra observes.

"We need to test the other ingredient of this," Gabriel declares, and we all look at him. "We need to see how effectively Kaylen can grasp the loose strands and move them around."

Kaylen looks nervously between us, and suddenly I worry this is moving too fast. What we've learned today is huge, and I want to be cautious. So after some contemplation I say, "Fine. Kaylen, see if you can grasp the end of a strand and move it where you want it—as if you were going to thread it somewhere. But let's hold off on that actual insertion part. Once we know we can do it, we need to look at more people in the pool to confirm what we think we know. Then we can act on it."

Gabriel can't hide his disappointment, but he has the good judgment not to say anything. Kaylen turns her wide, nervous eyes to my mess of strands.

A lot is riding on her young shoulders, and I squeeze her hand. '*You can do this, Kaylen,*' I whisper mentally so everyone can 'hear.'

'*That's right, Kaylee. Take it slow. We'll work one strand at a time until you get the hang of it,*' agrees Gabriel.

'*We got your back, Kaylen,*' says Ezra.

'*Grab any loose one you see, Kaylen,*' thinks Gabriel.

Standing in the pool next to the side, head and shoulders out of the water, I hold on to Kaylen's hand as she sits down on the edge. Gabriel and Ezra are on either side of her, and both of them touch the skin of my arm so they can watch.

With bated breath we look into the water—which is invisible but for the particles floating in it—and watch my strands, none of us but Kaylen knowing which one will move first.

I sense confusion in our group when we don't see anything happen, and I am probably the only one that recognizes it as Kaylen's—I have felt her enough times to pick her emotions out. I glance at her, but her face scrunches in focus. I look back at my strands, but I still don't know which one she's concentrated on. But suddenly a strand comes up out of the water. Actually, it shoots up out of the water, surprising all of us, Kaylen included.

Kaylen is frantic for a millisecond as she gains control over it before it can zoom up to the ceiling—which is where it looks to be headed.

She pants a little to dispel her adrenaline that now courses through all of us. It's clear that the strand moving that far and that fast was not her intent. The strand itself now hovers in place about a foot over the water.

"What happened?" Ezra asks.

"I'm not sure," Kaylen gasps, taking calming breaths as she holds the wayward strand even closer to me as if she's afraid it's going to make an escape. And actually, it kind of does look like that, squirming and slithering in her mental grasp. I think it wants to go back to the water, or maybe just to the other strands. That's the impression that I get.

"It took a lot of effort to pick it up while it was in the water, but as soon as I got it to the surface, it was as light as I first expected it to be," Kaylen explains. "That's why it looked like it took off as soon as it got above water. But in the water, it's like lifting something really heavy. I'm just glad I caught myself before I ripped it right out of you."

That definitely gets Gabriel's thought processes going, but once Kaylen calms down, she is the first to offer an explanation,

"It must be the water. I've never been able to move water telepathically before. I've assumed that's why I can't move things that have high water content either—like people. It must be that the strands are in the water that makes them so hard to pick up. I swear it's like the water retards my ability."

All of us consider the implications of that. For one thing, Kaylen does get depleted. If it takes so much effort to lift a strand out of the water, she's going to get tired more quickly. She's got to do it for hundreds of thousands of strands. It's fortunate at least that she's got the three of us connected to her. With my channeling ability, Kaylen has access to not just her own energy, but to ours as well. Even so, it's clear that this is not quite as easy as we imagined. The water may be the key, but it's also complicating other things.

"It can be done," Gabriel finally says. "It will obviously be more tedious than expected though." He reaches out to me to help me out of the water where I wrap myself in an over-sized towel, freezing.

After waterproofing his chest tube and feeding tube, Gabriel gets in the water then, and while he can't see all of his strands at once to give an accurate count, he is able to estimate that the misplaced number is at least four million. That number gets gasps all around. But it's visually obvious. He looks like a porcupine and he's not even all the way under the water. It's no wonder he got sick so quickly.

The other thing I notice about Gabriel's strands—at least what I can see of them—is that they are really densely packed into his skin. I can't even see his skin beneath them. "Gabriel..." I say.

"You have a super hairy life force," Ezra says, finishing my thought—though not in the way I would have put it. "Can you estimate your strand total?"

"Yes. Perhaps thirty-five billion?" Gabriel offers. "But I can't say for sure. I can't see anything above my waist with any accuracy. I can spot the loose ones because they naturally separate."

"Good thing since I have to pick them out," Kaylen say.

"Your life force is so weird..." Ezra says. "You have got to be an anomaly. I'm just not sure why."

"We'll take a look at more people," Gabriel says, climbing carefully out of the pool, his life force springing back close to his body once he is completely out of the water. "And we'll forgo action until we've looked at some of Robert's men in the pool. We need to be absolutely sure that we act on the maximum amount of information available to us."

I smile at him, grateful that he's willing to be cautious. He's probably only doing it for me, but I appreciate it anyway.

Right then, Gabriel's phone rings and he snatches it up. "Hello?" he says.

I recognize the voice on the other end of the line as Mike's and I strain to hear.

"Where are you?" Mike demands.

"Business, brother. What's it to you?" Gabriel asks.

"I called Mamá just now. She said you'd disappeared and she didn't know where you went," Mike replies.

"We left in a bit of a hurry," Gabriel says.

"To do what? It's ten P.M."

Gabriel glances at me before saying, "Confidential."

Silence fills the line before Mike says, "You're kidding, right? Don't be an ass, Gabe. This isn't double-oh-seven. Did you meet with a new doctor?"

"Mike, it's confidential. Just know we've made progress."

When it becomes clear that Mike is planning to argue for a while, I stop listening and go to the locker room with Kaylen so I can change back into warm clothes.

"I think that's a good idea," Kaylen says once we're through the door.

"Yeah..." I say. "We've learned how to unravel a life force and how water can manipulate strands. That's something I bet Louise would have killed to know."

"She did," Kaylen says, frowning.

"True," I say, remembering all of Louise's awful deeds. "And I can't stand Mike anyway."

"That must be how hypno-touch works..." Kaylen says. "The water in our hands does the moving. That's why it takes so many sessions and repetitive hand movements. It basically uses water in order to ease the strands out."

I stare at her. "That's brilliant, Kaylen. I think you're totally right."

"So why do *your* hands move strands more?" Kaylen says. "Do you have more water in your body?" She wrinkles her nose. "That doesn't sound right. You got four million strands out of him in just twenty minutes. It must be something else."

"It is," I say. "It's not my hands that do the actual manipulation. It's my own strands."

"Really?" she says, plopping on the bench and toweling her hair. "I wonder why?"

"I think it's clear that my strands do things other strands don't. They disconnect from me and attach to the people I touch, for goodness sake." I shiver, both from cold and from how bizarre that sounds. I wrap the towel more tightly around me.

"I wonder if they can do anything else?" Kaylen muses.

"If they can, they sure don't tell me."

She chuckles. "You act like your strands have a will of their own."

"Well it's not me that makes them detach or grab on to other strands and yank them out or *kill* people."

"Hmm. Maybe *all* strands have a will of their own," Kaylen says. "And maybe your ability is actually that they can act on it."

"Fantastic. My superpower is letting my soul run amok." But then I remember the sound I heard when Louise was dying. Her strands, I could swear, were screaming. And in the colorworld I hear voices. Maybe it's life force strands... I shake my head at myself as I pull clothes out of my bag. That idea is so disturbing. I don't want to think about it. What I *want* to think about is what we just did and what it means for Gabriel, for Kaylen, and for me. Kaylen's telekinesis is invaluable to moving the strands around precisely. Ezra can check our work and make sure the finished product is right. Gabriel can count out strands... What other four people can do what we are about to do, even if they do have special abilities? I can't think of a single ability I encountered at Louise's compound and in Robert's old files who would have a hope of doing what we are about to try.

It seems too easy, too coincidental to be true. Doubt lurks in the background, stalking me, waiting for the opportunity to emerge once again. I desperately hope we have overcome the last roadblock, and everything will go as smoothly as it seems it should.

36

"*U*ncle Moby, do you have a way to contact Carl?" I ask first thing the next morning, still in my pajamas. I didn't sleep much last night and came out of my room as soon as I heard Robert exit his. With a possible fix on the table, I started thinking of all the people that are hypno-touch injured. We can help them now, and while I am thrilled with the possibility that Gabriel and I might see a cure, the idea that countless others can benefit as well has had me bouncing with excitement all night. I can undo this. I can fix what Carl broke. This can all be worth it.

Robert is equally lighthearted as he fills his mug with hot water and swirls his customary ginger teabag in it. "I do. He's been calling fairly frequently to check up on you. Would you like to call him now?"

I nod and smile, taking a seat next to him on a barstool. "I want to see if Carl will give me the names of all the people he and Louise worked on. Hopefully we can fix them."

Robert pulls out a cell phone, thumbs through it, and then hands it to me; Carl's contact information is on the screen.

I touch his number and hold the phone to my ear, my nerves bubbling up.

After three rings, Carl comes on the line with, "Rob. Is she alright?" An edge of fear has sharpened his voice.

"I'm still alive if that's what you're asking," I reply.

"Oh, Wendy," Carl says, and I can hear the panic in his voice ease. "Rob never calls. I expected horrible news."

"Not today," I say. "I have good news. And I need something from you."

"You do? What is it? Did you figure it out?"

"Maybe. And that's all you get to know. What I need from you are names. All the people you and Louise sentenced to an early death. On paper. Any contact info for them that you have as well."

Silence for several beats. And then, "You've got to give me more than that."

I snort. "You're kidding, right? I'm not dumb. I'm not giving you *any* information."

"Wendy," Carl says, reprimand in his voice, "Of course I don't think you unintelligent. I do, however, think you're ignorant to the implications of what you're saying you can do. Can you at least tell me what the problem is? You either tell me what's wrong or you get no names."

I think about it. I want those names... I have been dreaming about those people for months. I need to make this right. I glance at Robert who is watching me and sipping his tea. I put my hand over the phone. "He wants to know what's wrong with the life forces. Should I tell him?"

Robert nods without hesitation. "He needs to understand enough to get the implications of what he's done. The intricacy of the life force should be impressed upon him so he may perhaps stop pursuing this. As little as possible and enough to scare him. And nothing about the pool of course."

Taking my hand off the phone I say, "The life force doesn't just surround the body. It's inside it, too. Hypno-touch pulls it out of the body. That makes the body sick. The more of the life force you pull out, the quicker the person gets sick."

Robert nods approval, and Carl says, "You indicated to Louise once that it was made up of strands. Is it the strands that are wound through the body?"

"Uh, yeah," I say, having forgotten what I told Louise about life forces. "Tens of billions," I add, thinking if he already knows they are strands, I might as well add a daunting number to it to deter him from thinking he can experiment further.

"So strands are pulled out. And you think you can put them back in?"

Carl's no dunce. "Yes," I say.

Carl sighs a long sigh, and after several seconds of silence he says, "So if you put them back, do you think the subject will lose their ability?"

At first, Carl's words have no meaning. Why would re-inserting strands cause the person to lose their ability? Then the realization comes. Of course they'll lose their ability. That's how the ability came about isn't it? Pulling strands out? I stare unblinking at the mottled surface of the granite countertop in front of me, dumbfounded.

"Wh—what?" I stutter as I reel from what that means.

"Or do you think it's something else in the energy touch that gives the ability? If so, can't there be a way to manifest abilities without pulling the strands out? Or maybe a way to put them back in that will still allow for an ability...?" says Carl to himself, oblivious to my reaction.

I struggle to engage my brain. "Are you saying you think that re-inserting the strands will take away an ability that's already manifested?"

"I don't know. I was just asking the question," Carl replies. "If loose strands are the only indicator that someone's life force has been tampered with to give them a special ability, then maybe that's why hypno-touch works in the first place. Putting them back the way they were would essentially be a reversal of the original hypno-touch. At least, that's my line of thinking. You would know better than me."

I close my eyes. If people lose their ability when we fix them, so will I. That means that someone, probably me, will have to be cured last. I have to be last. No one else can see. Gabriel may retain some of his ability since part of it's natural, but he may not be able to count as high afterward. Kaylen won't be telekinetic, which will make it impossible to fix me, because I don't have the dexterity with them in the colorworld that's necessary. I lay my forehead on the counter. There is no other way around it. Gabriel and Kaylen can't be cured without me keeping my ability, and essentially my disease.

"I don't have anything more to say to you, Carl," I say. "I told you what I'm willing to tell you. It's your turn. I need those names."

Silence fills the line.

I lift my head to find Robert holding his mug near his mouth, concern wrinkling the corners of his eyes.

"Carl," I demand. "If you have any remorse for what you have done, for all the people you've killed, for killing my mom—both of them—for killing me, you will give me those names!"

"I'll be in touch," Carl says, and then the line goes dead. I stare at the phone, trying to decide if there was any commitment in his voice. I have no idea if he'll give me what I ask.

I can't get away from the thought of dying though. After all this, I'm going to die. It's funny how realizing that makes our findings at the pool all the more finite. There is no doubt in my mind that it's going to work now. It had all seemed so easy, like the solution was too blatantly there. But now the story will have a bitter-sweet ending, and that's more fitting. No wonder everyone so easily accepted not carrying out the procedure yesterday. We all knew some piece was missing. Thank goodness we didn't, or everyone would die, having no chance of cure.

I turn to Robert, my eyes filling with tears. "We have no way to fix my strands," I say blearily. "Because when we fix a life force, I'm almost positive that the person will lose their ability. And we need my sight for Kaylen to be able to see and fix strands. I... I don't even know if we can save Kaylen. I don't know at what point she'll lose her ability during the strand re-insertion."

Robert is stunned and confused, looking at the floor, trying to direct his thoughts. "You must be mistaken," he whispers.

"Uncle Moby," I plead through tears, "what do I say to them?!" I reach for his arm.

Robert takes several shaky breaths and closes his eyes. He forces himself into some kind of meditation and it upsets me further. Can't he see I need him? Why is he withdrawing?

"Every miracle has a price," I blubber. "That's what you said. It's me this time... What do I say to them?" Ezra... Kaylen... Gabriel... My heart is shearing into pieces for them. "I gave them hope. They all stuck by me and trusted me. And now I'm going to take it away!" I heave in a breath. "Gabriel... Gabriel will lose it."

Robert's eyes flash open and in a sudden movement he puts his arms around me. "Shh," he says, holding me tight.

"What's going to happen?" I plead, wetting his clean pressed white shirt that smells like ginger and laundry detergent.

"I don't know," he says, standing up now to hold me against him. "Wendy, it will be alright."

"No, it won't," I gasp, not wanting to remain upright.

Robert sits up and away, hands on my shoulders, forcing me to look him in the face. "Get it together, Wendy."

"But what do I do?" I cry. "They trusted me. I'm going to fail them!"

His eyes narrow and he frowns. "You haven't failed. Even if you die in a month, it will not be failure."

Twisting my fidgety hands, I say through my sniffling, "What is wrong with me, Uncle Moby? I've been terminal all this time but it wasn't even until yesterday that I actually accepted death as a possibility. And I'm afraid of it. It isn't supposed to be like this! I'm supposed to be brave. I should be able to accept my own death after all these months, but instead I'm acting like it's news. I'm stupid and immature and I'm totally freaked out about dying instead of excited about all the people I can save!"

Robert's expression softens further and softness overcomes him. He sits on the adjacent stool again, holding my hands in his. "You are not alone in your fear, Wendy. It is brought upon a person who knows their future. But do you realize that every person alive shares it? That every one of us knows our ultimate

305

future in mortality? It is death. We *know* the end point. So let me ask you, what would happen if we did *not* know this future?"

I expect the question to be rhetorical, that Robert will answer it, but he doesn't. He looks at me and waits. So I think about it, remembering how Robert said knowing the future was a burden. And he's right about death. It happens to everyone, yet we fight against it. We prolong life no matter the quality. We do not go quietly. We try to hide the indicators that we are moving closer to it even though we all know we're headed in the same direction. If we *didn't* know death was waiting, I have no idea what would happen. We'd be kind of like children, I guess. And kids are... carefree for the most part. That sounds blissful right about now...

"We'd be innocent," I say. "And ignorant."

"Is that what you want?"

I look up at Robert. "Sometimes."

He smiles. "Leaving innocence for good is not an easy thing. Why do we shy from death, Wendy?"

"I don't really want to be a child," I admit. "I want to be who I am now." My shoulders slump tiredly. "It's not really death I'm afraid of. It's the pain it will cause Gabriel and Kaylen and Ezra. I know what it's like to lose someone this way. I know what it can do to you. What if they don't bounce back?"

"Did you fail to bounce back?"

"Yes."

He tilts his head at me.

"I was an irresponsible, selfish, uncaring jerk. I caused people sorrow. I broke my mom's heart."

"And then?" Robert says.

I purse my lips, resistant, but Robert's eyes bore into me and I say, "And then I got Ezra. And here I am now. But Uncle Moby, some people fail. Lots of people do. I could have so easily."

He squeezes my hands. "And that is the answer," he says just above a whisper. "That's why we fear death. We fear the failure of those we leave behind. We fear being unable to help them. Though we rarely recognize it, we feel moment by moment the burden of responsibility toward those we will leave should we pass. We want to leave our mark, to ensure the success of those in our wake. As we approach death, whether by illness or age, the urgency of responsibility we feel increases. Once we are gone, there are no more opportunities. Isn't it beautiful? Humanity, at it's heart and soul, lives and dies for one another." Robert rubs his eyes, which are wet. "Life will remove their innocence with or without your help. Your loved ones approach death as you do, just under different circumstances. You can either show them how to move toward that death with grace, how to make the most of the few precious moments we get of life, how to not waste time, or you can lament a death that came before you were ready. You can cry together over lost moments and relive past ones. Both courses will have an impact on them. What do *you* desire that they do with their time in life? Whatever it is, you be the example of it."

It's hard not to think of my mom at a time like this, how she tried to protect my innocence for so long, and how that was what caused my greatest times of regret. But I also think of how she prepared Ezra for not only her departure, but mine. She had some losses, but she also had wins. And I can trace all of those wins back to times when she didn't let us mope, made Ezra face the things that were hard, forced me into changes I didn't want. And I have not failed. My mom, despite missteps, did not fail either.

"Okay, Uncle Moby," I say. "Let's save some people. Do you think Briona would let us dip her in the pool?"

***

"Dr. Altman flies in today," Gabriel says, changing out his fluid collection bag. He's not supposed to do that, but then Gabriel never listens to Jeanelle. "Now that I don't need his assistance with my illness, I've been racking my brain as to what it is we should have him do while here. I believe in always following through on a bet. What do you think?" He then starts replacing the hazardous waste trash bag—something else he isn't supposed to do—and starts chattering again. "Do you suppose Robert has contact information for Carl? Maybe we can go into the compound for the rest of the files there to start locating those poor people who are hypno-touch victims. It's going to be quite an adventure traveling around and knocking on doors. I wonder how many there are in actuality...? Can you imagine how they'll react when we tell them they'll die an early death if they don't take a dip in the pool?" Gabriel chuckles. "It'll be like that story in the Bible where the prophet tells the king to bathe seven times in that filthy river to cure his leprosy. My mother would have a hay-day. I don't plan on letting her come though. We've got to keep this as confidential as possible."

I suppress a long sigh. I've been waiting for an opening— one that will fit the giant bomb of crushing news I need to share. But of course, there's no good time to destroy someone's world. I've been going over Gabriel's possible reactions: denial, anguish, outrage, determination. I must admit I have no idea what to expect, and for that reason I am absolutely terrified. I can usually eat something in the morning before infusions, but today I couldn't stomach anything. Gabriel attributed it to my elevated white blood cell count, and I didn't argue any different. Pressure has been building in my chest since my conversation with Robert early this morning, and I can barely breathe now. I even turned my oxygen up, but it hasn't helped. I'm inhaling lead. Despite knowing the direction I want to take with the last bit of time I have left, following through and just... walking... It feels akin to climbing Mount Everest, and I halfway wish I would die right now so I don't have to endure the look on Gabriel's face when I tell him... and then Ezra... and then Kaylen.

Oh God, I can't do this...

When my attention comes back to the room, I'm startled to find Gabriel's eyes on me. Dread catches in my throat and I wonder what my face looks like. Smiling awkwardly, I say, "I'm sure if you start ordering Dr. Altman around like you do Jeanelle, that will be punishment enough."

His face doesn't shift a millimeter.

Flight instinct in full effect, I shuffle to my feet. "Speaking of Jeanelle, I need to go find her. A1c test today. What time did you want to do Mark and Farlen? Robert has the whole team on alert to be our pool specimens."

Pool... I don't ever want to see a pool again.

Gabriel strides toward me, but apprehension of the moment is so stifling that my automatic reaction is to jump away. Unfortunately, my oxygen tank is behind me and I trip over it, falling backward into the corner of the bed.

I expect to hit the floor, the bed, something, but I find myself in Gabriel's arms somewhat instantaneously. How did he get over here so fast?

"Careful, Love," he says, lifting me up and sitting me on the edge of the bed with excessive care. "I'll get your wheelchair," he says softly.

Watching his back as he goes out into the hall, I follow the trail of his emotion, thinking that maybe he's enduring some dread of his own. I'm not sure because my own is consuming me.

When he comes back, apprehension builds within me ever more as he helps me into my wheelchair, and though it ought to be easy to pick up on him, I can't. I'm frantic inside.

"We'll head over to the pool with Mark and Farlen in about an hour," Gabriel says, wheeling me next door to where Jeanelle is waiting for me. "I'll go alert them."

He stops me in front of Jeanelle, and then turns to leave.

The sight of his back to me, walking away, strikes unarticulated fear in me—different from the kind I've been experiencing all morning. "Gabriel!" I call out without meaning to, my hand stretching out with my voice. I pull it back, wondering what I'm doing, what I want to say, and why, after wishing all morning that there would be some way to leave Gabriel in the dark for as long as possible, I'm upset that he's *allowing* himself to be in the dark.

He stops, but doesn't turn. He lowers his bald head though, and his hand goes up to meet it. His shoulders slump. Those simple movements speak clearly: *he knows already.*

"I'm sorry," I whisper.

He whips around. "This is not your fault," he insists. "None of this is your fault, Wendy," he says loudly, waving his hand. His eyes turn red-rimmed and he digs his palms in there.

I bite my lip and glance at Jeanelle, who takes a clue and sneaks past us and out.

"How did you find out?" I ask, unable to manage more than a whisper still.

"Same way you did, I imagine. I thought about it long enough." He still can't face me.

I don't bother correcting him. "I'm sorry," I say again. "It wasn't supposed to be this way…"

"Stop saying that!" he says, his voice cracking, his eyes still avoiding me. "It's not your fault. I hate that you think everything is your fault, your responsibility, your job. As for how things are supposed to be…" He inhales through his nose two times, looking upward. "You don't need to worry about that." He looks at me finally. "For once promise me you won't worry about that?"

I look at him with confusion. I don't know what he means. "It doesn't matter," I say. "It is what it is. We can't do anything about the outcome. It has to be me. I have to be last."

"No," Gabriel says, holding up a hand. "We're not going to talk about it."

"How can we not talk about it?" I say, baffled and frightened by this direction. I guessed at a lot of different reactions from Gabriel, but not this one. "If this is what has to happen, we need to… we have to…"

"Help me," Gabriel interrupts, turning around finally. But his eyes won't meet mine. "That's what you mean. Right now, the only way you can help me is to not try to figure out how to… *soften the blow* for me. As you said, it is what it is—though I will say we still don't know how it will ultimately go, and I'd like to leave it at that. But there's no point in commiserating. We have people to help before we will know that outcome, and I want every moment with you. I want to make a difference with you. I don't want to be apart for even one second. Come what will, we face it together."

"Okay," I reply. "I can do that."

"Promise me," he says.

"What exactly?"

"That you won't concern yourself with how I will cope and how I will survive. That you will do nothing but *live* your moments by my side for however long you..." He chokes on a few breaths. "Have left," he finishes.

"Of course," I say, reaching toward him. "I promise." My jaw trembles as he comes to take my hand, kneeling in front of my wheelchair.

He takes my face in his hands, places his forehead against mine. "May I kiss you, Wendy?"

"Always," I whisper, reaching for his face, unable to contain my tears.

37

"Miss Briona," Gabriel says, bowing to the wiry Jamaican woman after he pushes my wheelchair into her office. "I-ney. Mi ave heard bout yuh. Ah ah pleasure to meet yuh."

I give Gabriel a look and then smile at Briona. Her hair is different today. It's combed out into an afro. Her office is also a lot more colorful, mostly because plants are everywhere, piled against the window and littering her desk. "This is my husband, Gabriel," I tell her. "How are you doing?"

Briona stares at Gabriel's outstretched hand, her own hand over her chest. She looks thoroughly at each of us; we're clearly ill with bald heads and ostensibly thin bodies—not to mention I'm in a wheelchair.

"Wa a gwaan?" she says, taking a step back, obviously frightened.

"Figive wi," Gabriel says, lowering his hand. "Wi figet ou sick wi appear. An mi know de lass time yuh saw Wendy, shi was de picture of health."

I turn my head slowly to look at Gabriel. "What are you doing?" I ask him.

"Practicing my Jamaican patois, Love," he replies. Then, to Briona, "Wi need to discuss sinting urgent."

"Stop it," I say. "You're freaking me out. And you're freaking Briona out. Talk normal."

He looks to Briona. "Am mi bodering yuh?"

"What are you *saying*?" I ask him, annoyed.

"I asked her if I was bothering her."

"You're bothering *me*. And I told you you're freaking her out. Emodar, remember?" I look at Briona whose eyes are the size of saucers. "I'm sorry, Briona. He gets excited about, uh, dialects. And languages. I know I look different, but that's what we're here to talk to you about."

Briona's mouth is open, and she looks at me, squinting. "Miss Wendy? Ah dat yuh?" She glances at Gabriel. "Dis mon ah fi yuh usband? Yuh play a card pon mi?"

"Nuh cards here," Gabriel replies. "Shi tol de trut."

I reach out and swat Gabriel's arm. "Stop it!" I turn back to Briona. "Yes, it's me, Wendy. I have Leukemia. Gabriel has lung cancer. That's why we look like wraiths."

"Wa mek yu galaan so, Wendy?" Gabriel says. "Mek it stay."

"I don't know what you're saying!" I hiss, wishing I'd left him behind.

All of a sudden, Briona starts laughing. "Oh Miss Wendy. Yuh dont fava yourself. Himma yuh usband, mos def. Hush. Yuh appearance..." She shakes her head. "Scared mi at first."

"See, Wendy?" Gabriel chides. "It had noting to du wid fi mi words."

"Yu eaz hard, Missa Mention," Briona says, looking at Gabriel now. "Listen to fi yuh wife. Fi yuh patios ah too heavy fah har to undastan. Yuh cum bak anudda time. Practice den."

Gabriel clicks his heels together and salutes her. "Excellent point, Miss Briona. Forgive my exuberance. It has been a while since I've had the pleasure of Jamaican conversation."

She smiles, moving forward and extending her hand finally. "Pleasure to meet yh, Missa Mention. Mi did nah know Miss Wendy was marrid. Suh young."

Gabriel shakes her hand. "Indeed she is. But I couldn't have anyone else snatching her up, see? Marriage was the only way to ensure that wouldn't happen."

Briona chuffs and smiles. "Yes. Mi see." She moves back around to the other side of her desk. "Now wa is all dis 'bout?" she says.

Gabriel wheels me forward and sits in the available chair.

"We're here about the Obeah that Louise did on you," I say. "The hypno-touch? We found out that it's lethal. That's why we look like this. And we want to fix your life force before you get sick like us."

"De spell?" Briona says, sitting up straighter. "Yuh want... to tek it off?"

"Yes," I reply.

"If yuh do dis..." Briona says tentatively, hopefully. "Den nuh mo seeing death?"

"Yes, there is a strong possibility that you'll lose your ability to sense death." I say, glancing at Gabriel.

"But we don't know for sure since you will be our first test subject," Gabriel adds.

"Som bly ah wut it," she says.

"Excuse me?" I say.

"She says she'll take the chance," Gabriel explains.

"Wah yuh need mi to du?" Briona asks eagerly. I guess seeing death is not something she enjoys even a little, but then, who would? Seeing my own is more than enough for me.

"Accompany us to a pool this afternoon," Gabriel says. "Wear a swimsuit and prepare to be in the water for a few hours. I can't say it will be an especially engaging experience, but when you come out of it, your life force should be right as rain."

Briona stands, eyes bright with excitement. I think she wishes she didn't have to wait for the afternoon. "Yuh ave ah deal," she says.

***

This past weekend we confirmed that Ezra's Golden Ratio theory is consistent, at least among Robert, four of his men, and Jeanelle. We also confirmed that they all have strand counts close to 30 billion. Strangely, though, everyone but Robert had a chest over head ratio. That makes Robert, Ezra, Kaylen, and myself the only ones so far to have the larger strand count in our head. Who knows what Gabriel has. But we took Ezra to a mall briefly to take a look and he said every one of the people he saw, based on their arc length or whatever he called it, had to have chest over head ratios.

Head over chest. Chest over head. What does it mean? All of us, without saying so, however, have decided to ignore that anomaly because the problem is loose strands. We know how the life force is supposed to look, regardless of head over chest or chest over head arrangement. The Golden Ratio is the key. And urgency is driving me to get this done soon. Each day that passes is another day closer to death. I just want to get on with the business of curing people. And I can't think of a more delightful person to start with than Briona. On the way to the pool, she schools Gabriel on regional differences in Jamaican dialects, which he listens to and practices with rapt attention.

I have not told Kaylen and Ezra about what I suspect about fixing life forces. I tell myself it's because it's just a suspicion, not fact, but it's probably more likely that I'm a wimp. Either way, they're going to know soon. All of us will.

Once we are at the pool that Robert had reserved for our sole use, sitting at the edge, Kaylen and Gabriel each take one of my hands, and Ezra sits behind me, his hand resting on the back of my neck. I channel us all into the colorworld and look at Briona who has stepped down into the water. The injured state of her life force is immediately obvious, loose strand ends reaching out past her mass of purple threads.

"Okay, Miss Briona, submerse yourself chest-side up," Gabriel says. "Count to five, then turn over under water for another five seconds. Understood?"

Briona nods curtly and does exactly what Gabriel asks without question.

As Gabriel counts, I once again try to wrap my head around how he manages it. The strands are so densely packed and constantly moving. Gabriel says if he can see it, he can count it, but even with my exceptional eyesight I still don't get it. It's much easier for me to fathom how it's possible to see something as fantastical as the colorworld than it is to imagine how he keeps track of billions of things at once when they move all the time.

Gabriel informs us telepathically that Briona has just over twenty-nine billion strands. He refers the exact head and chest counts to Ezra who tells us that Briona has over two hundred twenty thousand strands out of place. That's the easy part. The next part we have never tried and our nerves are palpable. Briona has her head out of the water, which we at first think is not going to work. But the strands seem to like the water, and all of the loose ends stay underwater where we can see them easily. That turns out to be a good thing since Briona can't stay completely submerged forever.

"Alright, Miss Briona," Gabriel says. "This next part is going to take quite a while. We're not sure how long since you are our first subject, but we'll let you know as soon as we do. For now I'd suggest holding as still as you can. We won't be talking and it's going to appear that all of us are staring at you the entire time, but just know that we're hard at work. It's going to be a tedious process."

I expect Briona to ask questions, but she doesn't. She seems set and determined as if she has some reason beyond our word to trust what we say.

And then it occurs to me that she probably does... *She sees when death is near.*

'*How far in?*' asks Kaylen nervously, interrupting my morbid ponderings, having already grasped the first loose strand out of the water.

'*I think maybe just hold the end to her head and see if it takes without actually pushing it in,*' thinks Gabriel, looking from me to Ezra. '*Agreed?*'

We nod in confirmation.

'*Okay, here goes nothin',*' thinks Kaylen determinedly.

We each hold our breath as the strand end approaches Briona's head swirl. Kaylen aims for the very center of the swirl and moves the strand closer millimeter by millimeter. When the loose strand touches the strands at the center of her swirl, the effect is instantaneous: it plunges in, and we all gasp. It's only perceptible to our heightened senses, but we can clearly see it submerge several inches there.

'*I didn't do that!*' thinks Kaylen in fright. '*It leapt out of my grip!*'

Gabriel is smiling in delight. '*I think that's perfect, Kaylee. Don't fret. That's exactly what we were hoping for.*'

I unfocus to look at Briona, who watches us with casual regard, looking completely unaffected.

'*Okay, Kaylee,*' Gabriel thinks. '*One down, 9,498 more to go in the head. You're doing fantastic.*'

I squeeze her hand.

Kaylen grabs another strand now, and this time I pay close attention to her mental state. I could swear that I can perceive the current of energy Kaylen is using just by monitoring the magnetism between our hands. The pull strengthens a great deal when she picks a strand from beneath the water's surface, but eases to pretty much imperceptible once she has it out. She doesn't stop though. She grabs several strands at the same time now, bringing them up out of the water with rigid concentration on what she's doing. She brings them all together, which seems to make them happier, although the thin thread of rope still squirms in her grasp. She doesn't hesitate. She grabs more from the water and brings them to join the others in her grasp. She does this a few more times, building up the tiny rope of life force strands outside of the water.

'*You lost two, Kaylee,*' Gabriel thinks, as she goes for several more in the water.

She stops and looks at the thread of rope. '*From the ones I already have out of the water?*' she asks.

'*Yes, they appear to slither downward out of the bunch—I guess they like the water as much as they like to be together,*' he replies.

That disappoints Kaylen and she thinks, '*I was hoping I could concentrate on holding the bunch as one thing. But if they slip out all the time, I have to concentrate on them separately. And if I have to concentrate on each one and exert more energy to get them out of the water without ripping them out of Briona, I won't be able to hold that many at once.*'

I have no idea why she's so flustered about it. Maybe because if she can't do a bunch at once, it will take a lot longer. '*Just put those in for now*,' I think. '*It'll get easier with practice.*'

Kaylen sighs and brings the small bunch to the top of Briona's head. Like the single strand, the bunch of twenty or so plunges in like they belong there and like they know exactly what they're doing. And that makes all of us happy,

Kaylen continues on and I can tell that she's trying to hold more and more with each bunch she assembles. And I can tell that Gabriel is hanging on her every strand. So is Ezra. Suddenly, Kaylen shouts, "I know, Ezra! But you are not helping!"

That startles all of us, especially Briona who has been standing in the water and enduring the silence patiently.

I can only imagine the reason for Kaylen's outburst, and though it takes a great deal of practice to speak to only one person telepathically while we are linked like this, it can be done. I look over at Ezra severely. "What did you say to her?" I demand.

"I didn't say anything!" he says defensively.

"Ezra," Gabriel says calmly. "You need to learn to control your emotions better." Then mentally he adds, '*Remember that we can all feel them. And translate them. And Kaylen needs to concentrate.*'

'*You all know, don't you?*' I say mentally. '*Gabriel, did you tell them?*'

Everyone starts 'speaking' at once. Gabriel says it wasn't him. Ezra didn't realize *I* knew, and Ezra told Kaylen. It sounds like everyone came to the same outcome concerning life force repair and tried to spare each other by not saying anything. Kaylen has been pushing herself to move more strands at once in hopes that she can insert all of her strands and mine together rather than strand by strand, believing this would stave off loss of ability until our life forces are both healthy. She and Ezra collaborated on this idea. And Gabriel apparently asked Kaylen at some point to see how many strands she could move at one time.

With everyone trying to make their point at once and the atmosphere getting more and more agitated, I release Gabriel and Kaylen's hands, holding both of mine up. "Alright, everyone," I say loudly, turning to look at each of them. "I want all of you to forget anything beyond this day. Right now, it's more important that we confirm we can do this at all. Stop getting ahead of yourselves." I twine my fingers with Gabriel's and Kaylen's again and rest my eyes on her now. '*One strand at a time*,' I whisper everyone mentally. '*One life force at a time. That's all you have to do. Right now this is about Briona. And with every strand you put back in, you are adding more time to her life. Don't think of anything but what you are accomplishing right here and right now. It's amazing all by itself.'* I squeeze Kaylen's hand.

She inhales and nods. "I know. You're right."

"I think I need to sit this out," Ezra says. "You don't really need me anyway."

"Yes, we do," I reply aloud sternly. Then I give him a look over my shoulder to indicate he touch me again. When he does, I say mentally, *'It is taking a lot of energy for Kaylen to do this and we're only a few hundred strands in or so. She's got a lot more to go. She's going to need energy from all of us to make it happen.'*

Ezra slumps, releasing his pent-up frustration, but he remains silent. It pains my heart. I want to talk to him about it, but we have a job to do.

Kaylen resumes the strand insertion, this time with more conservative bunches.

'I wasn't helping,' Gabriel thinks, and I can tell he has put in the effort to speak only to me so as not to distract Kaylen. *'Thank-you for putting our efforts back into perspective, Love.'*

'You can't occupy yourself with counting?' I ask, directing my words to Gabriel's mental wavelength.

'Not at this speed. She's moving quickly, but it doesn't take much effort for me to keep track of the number. I've too many leftover mental processes.'

I smile at him and roll my eyes. *'You and your ridiculous brain. So how many has she been able to gather up at once?'*

'Seventy-seven is her record so far. Her speed is quite astounding though. The longer she goes, the faster she gets and each bunch takes her about five seconds. I surmise she'll get closer to doing that many even faster if she gets really practiced at it. That is definitely a good thing or we'll be here all day.'

'I wonder how long it will take at that rate...' I reply.

'Ezra, given an approximate rate of 75 every four seconds, how long will it take to put back all 221,411 strands that are displaced?' Gabriel asks, now including Ezra in our telepathic exchange—he's getting really good at this mental direction thing.

After a moment of mental silence, Ezra thinks, *'Under three and a half hours.'*

'That's probably accurate,' Gabriel replies. *'She's getting quicker all the time—Oh she just upped her new record to eighty.'*

Ezra remains silent, and I watch Briona's strands weave back into place in her head.

'*Okay, Kaylen,*' Gabriel says, interrupting her work. '*Two more large bunches like you've been doing, and then we'll need a smaller one to make the final count for the head.*'

Kaylen completes two more large bunches, and Briona's head now looks similar to Ezra's.

'*Forty-one for the last bunch,*' Gabriel thinks.

Kaylen collects another smaller bunch and Gabriel verifies it and has her gather up ten or so more before declaring she has the exact number left to put in the head. She sends them in, and Briona's head now looks healthy and well.

Ezra is the first to respond to what we see, '*Yep, that's a perfect golden spiral.*'

"Briona…?" asks Gabriel carefully. "We're, ah, trying to ascertain the state of a person's ability as we repair their strands. Would you say there is any change in your ability? Is it something you can tell?"

Briona's eyes grow wide.

"No details though," I blurt, not wanting her to start telling us how close I am to death—or Kaylen. "Just… has it changed that you can tell?"

Briona blows air out of her pursed lips and shakes her head. "Nuh change."

"Well let's finish," I say, not daring to be hopeful, and not wanting to influence the others one way or another, and not wanting to wonder how it is Briona knows so well whether her ability is working.

"Finish?" asks Briona. "Yuh aren't don?"

"About three more hours," Ezra replies.

Briona's expression turns baffled but she stays silent.

Gabriel instructs her to move to another section of the pool where her chest is just above water. He then nods at Kaylen who focuses again on Briona. Just as before, she collects a small bundle of strands and aims them straight at the place over Briona's heart. And just as before, the strands seem eager to be there. And they insert themselves for a lot longer than the head ones did. Perhaps they have a lot longer to travel along the vascular system?

"Excellent," Gabriel says. Then mentally, '*Well, have at it, Kaylee. Obviously all the remaining loose ones go in the same place.*'

It's a long and meticulous process, and during the course of it, Gabriel reports telepathically to Ezra and me the time improvements, and the average bundle size which does increase little by little. After about an hour, Kaylen can move nearly ninety strands at once in about three seconds. Her focus is so intense that I'm in a little bit of disbelief that she can keep track of so many strands at the same time and that she can do it over and over without stopping. She hasn't broken concentration even once. I expect I should be getting tired after so much time being awake— Leukemia calls for multiple naps a day—but I remain alert. It must be because I'm connected to two other healthy people.

After two hours of this breakneck pace, it's clear that Kaylen has improved enough to cut the original estimated time considerably. Gabriel thinks, *'Only a few thousand left. You are breaking all of our time expectations, Kaylen.'*

Her focus moves back to us and she blinks her eyes blearily. *'Thank goodness. I'm going to be moving life force strands in my sleep after this.'*

So after a several more rounds, the last strand goes in. Gabriel has Briona move around to be sure none were missed and submerge herself so we can verify her ratio. And then we all stare at Briona in wonder. She's whole. She has a beautiful head swirl and a beautiful chest swirl to match.

"It's perfect," I breathe.

There is a flood of relief all around. None of us knew exactly what would happen at the outset. We did it. Probably not as quickly as we hoped, but that doesn't matter. We have found a cure. At least we've found one for Briona. I desperately want to take care of Gabriel's strands right now, but we have one more thing to check.

Does Briona still sense death?

38

"It's gaan," Briona says for the third time. Each time she has said it, it's been with more excitement for her and more resignation for us. She's out of the pool, a towel wrapped around her shoulders, breathing deeply as if death was once a smell all around her and now the air is clear.

"Altogether?" Gabriel asks.

Briona nods, inhaling again.

"Well that's that," Ezra says, sitting back in his chair and crossing his arms.

"Do you know when you lost it?" Gabriel says. "Was it gradual?"

"Mi tink it faded," Briona replies. "It was neva loud. But presen like de sound of appliances. Yuh don't noice it until de powa goes out."

"When did you first noice it start to fade?"

Briona ponders it. "Bout han owa ago? Mi don't know fah sure."

"So we know abilities go gradually," I say, wondering *how* gradual and whether or not inserting *some* of the strands can buy me more time... whether it will buy Kaylen more time. How many will she be able to insert before she can't move any more?

"Tenk yuh suh much," Briona says, her eyes filling with tears. "Tenk yuh. It's been suh hawd. All dis time..."

I look around me at all of the miserable faces, pulled between two extremes. They've barely heard Briona, lost in adjusting to what this discovery means. But Briona feels light, like she just dropped a thousand pounds.

"You're welcome," I say just above a whisper, wanting to cling to her happiness. Otherwise I'm probably going to cry.

Eventually though, Briona gets up to change, her white teeth showing brilliantly as she smiles like she'll never stop.

"Wheel me to the bathroom, would you, Kaylen?" I say after a silent moment among our group. Then, to Gabriel and Ezra, "I'll meet you out front."

Once we're in the bathroom, I say, "I don't know how you managed that, Kaylen, but that was amazing. How on earth did you control nearly a hundred strands at once?"

Kaylen leans against the sink counter. "I've never been able to control that many things at once before. It was pretty much like that time you touched me at the shopping mall. I think you don't just energize me, you boost my ability somehow."

I nod slowly, knowing that Kaylen is not as bright as Gabriel and me, which means we would naturally boost her ability. In fact, because Ezra is not as bright as us, she probably would have been able to do even more strands if he hadn't been connected to me at the same time as well. In fact... if I could get some of Robert's light Kaylen would be able to move even more. I shouldn't fixate on it though. We have a lot more people to help— if Carl comes through, which I'm starting to think he won't. Robert, however, has a short list of people he knows about. We can start there.

"You felt like you were getting pretty tired at the end," I say, imagining my remaining days filled with more of what we just did. "Are you going to be able to do more than one in a day?"

She shrugs disinterestedly. "I don't know. I'll do my best."

"You obviously have two different aspects to your ability... control and how much you can lift. Control is determined by light, but how much you can lift and for how long is determined by something else..." I tap my chin, thinking. "You talk about running out of energy. Maybe it has to do with the energy vapor I see in the colorworld."

"Wendy," Kaylen says.

"We know emotions make it increase, and you kissed Ezra that one time to power yourself... yeah I think that's it."

"Wendy."

"We can at least solve the issue with running out of energy by having me touch someone else... Mark or Farlen maybe," I say, thinking we need to keep this in-house as much as possible.

"Wendy!" Kaylen says loudly.

I look up to find her twisting her hair over her shoulder. "What?" I say, already knowing what. I have emodar for goodness sake.

"I'm not fixing myself."

I frown. "Yes you are. Don't be dumb."

"We fix you first. Maybe we can get you more time."

"No."

"It doesn't matter what you say. I'm not fixing myself. You can't make me."

Flustered, I have no idea how seriously to take Kaylen. I don't have enough experience with her. "Kaylen, you have to. We have no guarantee that reinserting any of my strands will make a difference. We *know* that the less strands you have pulled out, the more time you get. And you have *way* too many pulled out."

She pushes away from the counter and stands in front of me, arms crossed, jaw taut. "You don't get to decide. So you either let me try to fix you or neither of us gets a chance."

And then she leaves, almost running into Briona who has come in from the locker room.

"Miss Wendy, wat can mi du to help yuh? Mi ave ah debt."

I shake my head, sitting in my wheelchair, hands folded in my lap, resentful of Kaylen for making this harder. I'm going to die. Why can't she let me do it my way? "You don't have a debt, Briona. I'm just glad I got to help you. It makes all this worth it." I hold my hands up to indicate myself.

Her brow furrows and she tugs her bag higher onto her shoulder. "Death stalks yuh, dats fah sure. Yuh life ah inna fi yuh own hands, Miss Wendy."

I have to bite my tongue to keep from asking more. In fact, my head is bursting with questions, and for the solid minute while Briona is in a bathroom stall, I think of at least five excuses for why I should be able to ask Briona what she knows—not the least of which is the fact that she doesn't actually have the most up-to-date information because she no longer has her ability. So I should be able to ask as pure speculation, right? Once she comes out, I decide I'm allowed one question—a non-specific one.

"Briona?" I ask. "How did you know when death was near someone?"

She dries her hands with a paper towel slowly before looking at me and answering, "De closa dey ah to death, de hawda dey push on mi chest. Lacka pressure. Right yah suh." She pats her chest, right on her sternum. "Sometimes makes it hawd to breade."

"Oh… sorry," I say, thinking I must have been crushing her all that time.

She chuckles, throwing her paper towel out and coming behind me to push my chair. "Miss Wendy, yuh look like death, but yuh a surrounded. Death wants yuh. But so du de living."

She makes it sound like the living can keep me alive, but wishing has never helped anyone else. "Surrounded?" I ask, pushing the door open with my foot. "By what?"

"Mi don't know. Mi guess? De dead."

***

"I have twenty-one on file," Robert says when we arrive back from our pool session with Briona. "Most of them are up and down the coast. The others are east."

I prop my chin on my hand, thankful that at least one person isn't a drain. Gabriel, Ezra, and Kaylen all begged off the evening for various reasons. Gabriel and Kaylen are supposedly going to assemble a list of people they remember from the compound that we can track down and help. I'm just glad I don't have to be around them right now.

"Do you think Carl will come through?" I ask.

Robert stares off into space momentarily. "It is my sincere hope. I believe if Carl will do that, he will be on the road to recovery." He looks at me now. "Don't worry about that right now. Just do what you have to do. Twenty-one names will keep you plenty busy for now."

My phone rings from my bag on the counter at that moment, and I dig through it, surprised to find that the caller ID identifies it as Mike. I haven't spoken to him since he gave me 'permission to die already' a few days ago.

"Hi Mike," I say when I pick up.

"Hello, sis," he says with what I could swear is an edge of mocking—although I expect it so I'm not sure if I'm hearing things. "What's new?"

That was unexpected. I'm also not prepared to answer, so I pause for a good bit. "I can save Gabriel," I say. "But first we have a bunch of other people to save."

"Really?" Mike says, definitely suspicious that I'm joking with him. "How?"

"That's not your business," I reply. "Just know that I can. And I will."

"Why can't you tell me?" he asks, and for once I don't pick up animosity. But I'm starting to wonder if he called me for this information because Gabriel already told him no.

"Because we agreed that we were going to keep information about life forces confidential."

"You're saying you don't trust me," Mike replies, and I can tell he's struggling to keep belligerence out of his voice now—that's more like the Mike I know.

"I guess not," I say. "That surprises you?"

He snorts. "Why can't you fix Gabe now? Why other people first?"

"None of your business," I reply.

"What about you? If you can fix him, you can fix you, right?"

"Why do you care?"

"Because my brother does. And he's an annoying bastard when he's depressed. If you died, he would be unbearable to deal with."

"Why are you calling me, Mike?" I say, aggravated.

"I like pushing your buttons. It's so easy. And I get a kick out of it because I don't like you. My brother met you and all of a sudden his whole life is a secret. Gabe? *Secret?* That's not him. I don't like what you've done to him. I don't like that our relationship is completely messed up because he spends all his time keeping you locked away in a tower. You took my brother away from me. And I will never forgive you for that."

I sit up straight, incensed. "Know what, Mike? I'm done with you. I don't care that you are Gabriel's brother anymore. From now on, you are just some idiot that has my number and shows up uninvited. Know what I do to guys like that? I have my uncle's bodyguards toss them out if they show up. And I also hang up on them when they call me. So goodbye." I press 'end' on the call and slam the phone against the counter.

I catch my uncle's expression out of the corner of my eye. Eyebrows raised, he watches and waits for me to speak.

"That guy has serious issues," I explain.

"Gabe's brother? Has he threatened you?" Robert asks.

"No," I sigh. "I wouldn't be surprised if he did though. I swear I don't know what put the bee in his bonnet. Any omniscient advice concerning my brother-in-law, Uncle Moby?" I ask jokingly.

"Yes. Stay away from him," Robert says, surprising me with an immediate answer.

I turn in my chair to face him completely. "Why? What do you know?"

Robert chuckles and stands up from his stool, grabbing his satchel off of the counter. "I know he is a negative influence in your life that you don't need. Let Gabe handle it. You have other things to do. I'll have Lacey coordinate on arrangements for you all to get started. ASAP."

I watch Robert's back as he leaves, thinking he's probably right. Clearly the only thing that will make Mike happy is for me to disappear… It's looking like he's going to get his wish soon. My question now is how soon? My heart sprints into overdrive.

I'd rather argue with Mike and have him insult me than think about what's going to happen to me and when.

39

$\mathcal{W}$e plan to start with the names that are closest to our current location. Between Kaylen, Gabriel, and Robert's efforts, we have twenty-seven to work with. Kaylen, though she was on the compound most of her life, unfortuantely did not have or recall enough information about most people to track them down. But after speaking to my doctor this week, finding enough time to get even the twenty-seven done is going to be pushing it, so I can't find it in me to be disappointed that Carl hasn't come through. I've been continuing with the same drug cocktail this week, and my numbers, though they are far too elevated, have remained stable at least, and we're afraid to rock the boat. My spleen is starting to ache again, which means it's swelling again.

Two days after our success with Briona, and as we make preparations to see more people, Gabriel is analyzing my biological mother's file for probably the twentieth time. He has memorized it completely, but Gabriel is the kind of person that likes to hold paper in his hands if he gets the choice. And although he hasn't voiced it, something about that file continues to niggle at him—he just hasn't come out with it yet. I know he's looking for a hint, something that will save me, or maybe just buy me more time.

He has been pretty quiet the last few days, and we still haven't spoken much about... after all this. I am at a loss for what to do or say, and he made me promise not to try. But I am slowly drowning in fear for him, for Ezra, and especially for Kaylen whose life ticks excruciatingly close to death. That she refuses to even *try* to save herself makes that reality even harder to bear. It's suffocating, and I often find myself in the bathroom at least once a day, just getting the tears out so I can face them again. I want out. I want out of all of this. I want peace and laughter and even anger again. I want to feel something other than the paralysis of dread.

Putting on an oversized sweatshirt, I lay back on my bed and gaze at the chart across the room that catalogs the progress of my disease via blood counts. I used to avoid it. Now I look at it all the time. Familiar anxiety bubbles within me. That happens any time I spend too much time thinking past today. It's especially strong right now, and I can't sit still through it. Watching TV sounds about as entertaining as chewing on cardboard, and I'm too tired to get up and actually *do* anything. My chest throbs, and I know I'm going to have to go cry again soon if I don't do something.

"What is it, Gabriel?" I blurt. "That file's got you obsessed."

He swivels in his chair to face me, wearied features looking like death. That's another thing: Gabriel is fading too. I want to cure him right now because I worry he'll be too far gone to heal, not that we know whether healing is even possible. We only know we can repair life forces.

"There is a chunk of time unaccounted for in this file," he replies, rubbing the calf of his bad leg (the one with the bone tumor), up and down. He does that a lot lately, usually without realizing it. "Gina quit treatment four months prior to her death according to this. But her white blood cell counts were terrible prior. She couldn't have lived that long without treatment. No transfusions. No drugs. It makes me wonder if part of the file is missing. How did she live that long?"

"Ask Carl."

Gabriel snorts and turns back around. "Already tried. He hasn't returned any phone calls."

"Bastard," I mumble.

Gabriel lets out a strained sigh and extends his leg out and squeezes his shin in both hands now, wincing as he flexes and extends his calf.

"Getting worse?" I say even though it's a dumb question. Of course it's getting worse. It does every day. "You need to have it removed."

He pushes himself up out of his chair then. "I need to consult with Altman on this file. He's the only doctor that listens to me."

"It's not even remotely the same kind of cancer he's used to dealing with," I say. "And besides, we need to focus on the people we're going to be seeing, not my disease. We need to—"

A dull crack interrupts my sentence suddenly, followed by a loud roar of agony from Gabriel, who collapses on the floor, shin in his hand.

Leaping off of the bed toward him, I yell for Jeanelle at the top of my lungs and then to Gabriel, "Oh my gosh! Was it your leg? I told you! I told you you needed to get it taken care of. Dammit, Gabriel, why are you so stubborn?"

"Confound it, woman!" Gabriel says between gasping and grunting. "You really want to do this now?" And then he lets out another roar of pain.

I yank off a glove and put my bare hand on his arm, channeling us into the colorworld. Searing agony moves from my shin up to my pelvis. Holy crap, that hurts! But it equalizes between us until it's at least manageable.

"Don't do that!" Gabriel says, jerking away from me. "This was my mistake. I shall deal with it by myself."

"No you won't," I snap, grabbing on to him harder. "I'm done with you trying to deal with everything by yourself. It's making me *miserable!* Hold still and let me help or I will smack you!"

He relaxes just as Jeanelle rushes in.

"His leg?" she says, not really expecting an answer. She has bickered at him every day about it. "About time," she snorts, reaching for a wheelchair and then calling for Farlen who is on duty right now. "Maybe we can all rest a little easier now that we know it's not going to snap on your way down the stairs. Can't even use the damn hell elevator like you're supposed to." On and on she goes, taking the opportunity to complain about everything Gabriel does that makes her mad. And I could swear she's getting a lot of pleasure out of seeing him helpless and in pain. In her defense though, Gabriel does treat her like slave labor.

Farlen comes in to help Jeanelle get Gabriel into the chair and I have to let go of him momentarily. He howls the whole time until I grip his hand again. Weakened by all the excitement—and the pain—I lean heavily on him until Jeanelle says, "Wendy, we'll take care of him. You go lie down."

I shake my head. "He needs me for the pain. Get the extra chair. I'm coming."

Jeanelle rolls her eyes as she goes out to the hall. Poor woman. We put her through a lot of demands that she doesn't understand.

Ezra and Kaylen have showed up by now and I explain that Gabriel's finally getting the bone tumor taken care of. Ezra crosses his arms and shakes his head. "Idiot. We told him this would happen." And then he turns and leaves since it's obvious that no one is dying.

When we load up in the van to head to the hospital, I notice how minimal the discomfort is suddenly. I find Kaylen sitting behind me, touching my neck lightly, sharing a portion of the discomfort in the colorworld—basically rendering it nothing more than a sharp and penetrating ache. Thank goodness. Gabriel is on the edge of losing it. The extra pain may send him over the edge.

He grips my hand harder and puts his face closer to mine. "Don't let them take my leg, Wendy. Whatever they do, I don't want to lose my leg."

"Gabriel, a cancerous tumor is a lot more to worry about than your stupid leg."

"Promise me," he says in a low voice after they slam the door shut. "The leg stays."

"Since when are you caught up on something so silly? So what if you lose it? It's not like it's your brain—which would definitely be something to get upset over." I'm not sure what to make of Gabriel. He's absolutely desperate about not losing his leg.

"I just want to be whole."

"Whole? Look at us! We are anything *but* whole."

He reaches his free hand out for my face, cupping my cheek and then stroking the length of it. Tears fill his eyes, and then his shoulders start shaking as sobs rack his body. He pulls my face to him almost violently, holding me like he's afraid I will try to leave.

Frightened by the state of his emotions, I reach up, putting my hand on the back of his neck. "Shhh. I'm here," I say. "I won't let them take your leg. I promise. Don't get so upset. It will be okay." I have never seen Gabriel so distraught since he was having psychological side-effects from chemo. I don't think it's that though. He feels like himself, just a very distressed version of himself.

He cries, burying his face into my neck until it is slippery with tears.

"Gabriel, Gabriel," I plead, crying now because I am desperate to help him. "What's wrong? I told you the leg stays. I'll make sure of it!"

Gasping through the words, he says, "But we *are* whole, Wendy. We *are*. I want to stay that way."

I pull away just barely. Surely Gabriel has lost some sanity after all. "What are you *talking* about?"

"I'm keeping the leg," he chokes out. "I'm keeping it or nothing at all." He enfolds me in his arms possessively.

"Gabriel! I told you you can keep the stupid leg! No one is going to take it. Can you stop talking crazy?"

"He's talking about you," a quavery voice says from nearby.

I look over Gabriel's head to see Kaylen, leaning forward with her hand still touching my skin. Her face is wet, tears suspended on her eyelashes and her porcelain cheeks tinged with red.

"He's not talking about the leg," she whispers. "He's talking about *you.*" She looks away from my face, out the window. "He wants to die with you."

Blinking at nothing as Gabriel grasps on to me desperately, I recognize that Kaylen is absolutely right. Even Gabriel's emotions confirm it, and I cannot believe that I never once suspected that this is what he has been thinking all this time. This is why he made me promise that I would allow him to cope in his own way. He even asked me to promise that we would *face it together.* Apparently he meant even death.

I don't know what to say. I can't let Gabriel give up a chance at life.

But I promised.

I didn't promise with this in mind though…

I glance at Kaylen whose face is distant, she holds her emotions in check. Neither she nor Gabriel are going to let me help them.

Even though I am initially touched by Gabriel's sincere desire, this is not how this is supposed to go. You don't watch loved ones die and decide to kill yourself along with them. And for a moment I'm irritated. I shouldn't have to go through this right now. Isn't dying enough? It sure is hard enough. I have my brother to think about. And Robert. And Kaylen has a chance. A *real* chance. And Gabriel has talents and zeal that shouldn't be wasted. He can live again. And love again.

But the colorworld does not allow irritation for long. With Gabriel's life force intertwined with mine, his colorworld scent moving in and out of me, I cannot but love him in that helpless way that overcomes me here. We have shared the most intimate of experiences here. We have known each other more profoundly than probably anyone in the history of humanity. Our relationship is different. Sure, we argue about the same things as other couples. We struggle. We fight to come to common ground. We have pushed and pulled and nearly broken, but I cannot imagine my life without Gabriel. I get that most people say that in a situation like this. But Gabriel and I are bound too closely. I know his body *and* his soul. What we have gained through my abilties is a miracle, but as Robert says, miracles come with a price. What we gain, we also risk losing. So it's not so unreasonable that Gabriel should want this. He can never hope to find the same bond with someone else. The colorworld has brought us an unparalleled relationship.

Gabriel's cries have quieted, but his face remains tucked against my neck as he breathes me in.

The van stops at the emergency room entrance and the door opens.

"Gabriel," I say, lifting his head to look at me. "If it's what you want, we will stay whole. I will never leave you."

He squeezes my hand and kisses my forehead, and for once he remains wordless. But in the colorworld we speak more accurately than words. We love more precisely. We are not inhibited by the distracted nature of our bodies, and we are never misinterpreted here. It is here we find the purest kind of honesty.

40

Gabriel's surgery goes well, and he comes out of it with a rod to hold his leg together. He finally concedes to stop trying to get around on legs, but instead use a wheelchair. Now that I have agreed to let Gabriel see this to the bitter end with me, he is much less combative about medical procedures. He even allows Ezra, Kaylen, and I to bear the post-surgery pain without a single complaint.

Maris and Mike show up in post-op, and Mike stands nearby, his arms crossed like a night club bouncer as he glares at me. Even without the daggers he's sending my way, I feel guilty. I'm letting Gabriel die after all. He hasn't told them of his plans, but I could swear Mike knows it already. In fact, I think this is why our last phone encounter went the way it did. He must know Gabriel well enough to guess at what he'd do in a situation where I couldn't be cured and Gabriel had a choice not to be. I don't think Maris knows I even *have* a cure. I have a suspicion Gabriel didn't tell her because dying was his plan ever since he figured out I couldn't be cured—which wasn't long after we discovered the pool. So I say nothing, just grit my teeth through Maris' anguish and muttered prayers. I feel horrible. Maris is Gabriel's mother. As a mother—even if it was a short time—I can't bear the thought of what she is slated to endure. I swear, if it were my decision I'd make him live if only for her. I'd leave the room, but Gabriel needs the pain buffering. So I close my eyes and pretend I'm asleep.

After a couple of days in the hospital, we're all a bit stir crazy, and I for one am ready to get to work so I can stop *thinking* so much. Robert has a list and route compiled for us, and pool arrangements made. I grin when I see that the very first person on our list is someone I know from my stay at the compound: Jimmy, the thirty-something man with photographic memory who once asked me what it was like to kill someone with my touch.

I expect things to go well with Jimmy because both Gabriel and I know him, but I should have counted on Jimmy's analytical, invasive style of questioning, especially when he sees the state we're in and calculates the possibility of both of us being stricken at the same time with terminal illnesses. I can see and feel the wheels turning and am not surprised when he asks the one question we don't want to answer: "If you have a cure, why haven't you fixed yourselves?"

Gabriel clears his throat and replies, "Because, Jimmy, doing so will reverse your ability and we can't save anyone if we lose our abilities."

Jimmy then tries to probe for more information, but we don't give it. Even more important than saving these people is making sure that we leak as little information as possible. We agreed on this at the beginning.

Nevertheless, and somewhat enthusiastically, Jimmy agrees to let us work on him, and when we arrive at the pool we warn him what a boring process it will be, and how he will be standing in the pool for hours. That elicits more questions from him that we won't answer.

Like Briona, we work on Jimmy's head first, and like Briona, he does not seem to lose any ability when we finish inserting those strands. He has a similar number of missing strands, so we are able to give him an accurate guess on how much time it will take, and he waits through it patiently, sometimes asking us questions—which we don't answer. He then proceeds to tell us throughout the process how lucky we are that he is putting his blind trust in us like this.

When we are finally done, and Jimmy's life force looks like it was never tampered with, I give him the one piece of pictorial literature I have—a pamphlet on stem cell transplants that has been floating around in the bottom of my bag for months. A transplant is something I was told by doctors early on should be my goal. That's not happening.

We watch Jimmy's eyes scan the page. We watch him flip through the pamphlet to different pages, each time more frenzied. The incredulity on his face reveals the result: his ability is gone. He finally looks at us again. "Put me back," he demands.

I blink at Jimmy. Is he serious?

"Jimmy..." I say, "It worked. Your life force is perfect."

"I don't care. I want it back," he says firmly.

"Jimmy, why did you agree to let us do it if you just wanted your ability?" I ask, confused.

"I didn't believe you!" he yells. "I thought if you messed with my life force, it might increase my ability, not make it disappear!"

We are all stunned into silence.

"Dude, you're an idiot," Ezra says.

"I wasn't going to get sick," Jimmy snarls. "You're a liar. You took away my ability so you could charge me to get it back. Change me back, right now!" he demands.

"Jimmy—" starts Gabriel.

"No," I say firmly. "We're not touching your life force. You can go find someone who will. But we won't. Not for any price." I turn my wheelchair toward the door and Kaylen hops up to push me.

"Quite a show you've put on," Jimmy says mockingly. "But you are going to pay for this. You tricked me!"

"Nobody tricked you, man," says Ezra then, getting annoyed. "What is your problem? You worried you're actually going to have to work hard like the rest of humanity? You don't have an advantage over everyone else? That's what's bothering you, isn't it? You want to be special and all that crap? How about actually do something worthy of being special. All my sister did was help you, you sorry bastard. She's giving the rest of the days she has left to help you, and all you care about is trying to get ahead in life. You make me sick. We're done with you. Have a happy and long life. That's more than she can say you sorry son of a—"

"Enough Ezra," says Gabriel firmly, reaching up to touch Ezra's arm.

Ezra snorts and then storms out.

"Jimmy, I'm sorry we part on such bad terms. I hope one day you will realize what we've given you. Most likely not... but I hope so anyway," says Gabriel soberly, turning his chair to follow me

Kaylen, who is stunned, remains silent and pushes me out.

"Do you believe that guy?" Ezra asks once we are inside the van—a large handicap-accomodating vehicle that Robert provided for travel.

"Ezra, you ought to learn some self-control. He irked all of us. But that wasn't called for," says Gabriel sternly.

"Oh can it, Gabe. We shouldn't have even wasted our time on that guy. What an ungrateful moron," Ezra snarls. He is furious, and I can't believe this is upsetting him that much.

Gabriel looks at me for help.

Most likely Ezra is upset that we continue to prove that abilities disappear at some point along the course of strand repair. And we've also proven that Kaylen's ability is incredibly limited when working with the strands, (she didn't break any more records today). We've taken away more hope. It's going to take a miracle to fix Kaylen. To fix me really does seem impossible.

"You're right, Ezra," I say. "He *was* an ungrateful moron, but I didn't do this for him."

Grief pinches Ezra's brow. "Wen, that's not the only thing. I'm disappointed, yeah. But I'm pissed off that he thinks he has the right to react that way. You can't waste your time on people that could care less. I can't watch you laying yourself out like a doormat for them to walk all over. Please don't do this. After all you're probably going to end up giving up? Everything *I'm* giving up?"

Ezra's sadness tugs at me, and the walls close in as I look ahead to the hardship he will have to face if I die. He's going to have to grow up even more than he already has. He's losing everything and everyone. A person can't take that kind of loss without losing some part of themselves in the process. I just hope that whatever Ezra loses is something that Robert can help him cope with. What can I say now that he will remember later? That might get him through this?

"I'm doing this because I don't want to become Carl," I say. "When my mother got sick, he couldn't deal with it. He started using his death touch to kill people and watch them die in the colorworld so he could figure out the interaction of the life force and the body. He did it so he could find a way to fix her. But that was his turning point. You can love someone, but it's not love that makes you willing to sacrifice other people for them. I love you. I love Gabriel and Kaylen. I love Uncle Moby. But I can fix these people. *Not* helping them is the same as hurting them. And I can't do that. Not even for you. But in the end, what I do now is for you anyway."

"I'll be sure to write you a thank you card," Ezra says sourly. He leans forward and puts his elbows on his knees, his head in his hands. "But why help them if they don't *want* to be helped?"

"I'm not going to force anyone. But I'm not going to hold back either. These people need me whether they admit it or not. If I… can't live, I want *them* to. I want to give as many people more time as possible. My happiness and the time I have left is not dependent on whether or not Jimmy or people like him change their tune. They don't have that kind of power over me. And you shouldn't let him have that kind of power over you either."

Ezra eyes twitch with irritation, but acceptance is trying to blossom. His expression softens and he says, "Wen, you are a different person than you were a year ago."

I give him a half-smile. "I know. I'm a much happier person, and that's what I'm trying to show you. How to live through hurt, not how to avoid it."

***

The following weeks pass with insane quickness. I get chemo in the morning and spend the rest of the day either at the pool or meeting with new candidates, or both. Robert has them scheduled to arrive at intervals so we can meet with them and then handle their strand repair in the following two days. A few days we handle two repairs a day. Those are hard. We usually have one early in the morning, I get chemo while Kaylen recharges, and then we do another repair in the afternoon, sometimes with Farlen tacked on to our group to give Kaylen some extra juice. One day, after one of her midday breaks, she comes back with a thick lock of her hair dyed purple. I comment that it looks cute and she says she wants to keep her head in the right place so it's a reminder. Later that same day I notice a bracelet on Ezra's wrist made from purple embroidery thread—surely made by Kaylen. I ask her to find me a purple scarf for my head the next day, and she delivers. I wear it every day after that.

When Gabriel, Ezra, Kaylen and I are together, we are stuck like glue in the colorworld. We cling to one another physically via my skin, and mentally as well. I'm beginning to feel as if we are one entity. Being disconnected is weird. Despite their support, I have less and less energy each day. And I am forgetful. Sometimes I don't know what time it is, what we've already done that day, or whether I slept the previous night. I'm so tired all the time that I often argue with Gabriel that they didn't let me sleep the previous night and I shouldn't have to go out to the pool. Sometimes I tell Jeanelle in the evening that she forgot my infusion that day. Those moments are a little frightening. To have lost hours-worth of memories cannot mean anything good.

But we are successful. Except for two, all of the fifteen people that know Robert on our list allow us to cure them. It helps, I think, because Robert pays to have them brought to us in Monterey, which demonstrates the seriousness to them. The remaining twelve—those that Gabriel and Kaylen came up with that could be located—yields only eight takers. To my surprise, it's only a minor letdown. Maybe I'm too exhausted.

Gabriel is on oxygen constantly now, and Jeanelle frets over his oxygen saturation regularly. Dr. Altman has been in and out, making treatment suggestions, but taking his own notes, baffled and intrigued by our situations. He keeps telling Gabriel he needs a lung transplant, but there is no way he's getting one, especially now that he plans on dying anyway. I admit I still haven't fully accepted that. I want to fight back with him all the time on it, but I made a promise. Living and dying is in Gabriel's hands. And I'm not going to take his decision away.

I wish I could say I am fully prepared to die. I thought that's what happens when you get close to it, but that peace people describe has not come over me. I've become a bit bitter about it, almost refusing to accept it. Yet every day my numbers creep closer and closer to unsustainable. Pretty soon transfusions will be the only arsenal I have.

Three weeks after Gabriel's leg surgery, we complete our last name, and inevitability settles over me. With nothing else that needs doing, there is nothing but... dying. I rebel, bitter and confused that I can't find acceptance, that I can't go toward my end more peacefully.

So I do what I always do when life confuses me. I go see my uncle.

"Uncle Moby, I don't want to die," I say, wheeling myself to the kitchen on my own for once and cornering him.

"I don't want you to either," he says, sitting on a stool.

"I can't figure out how to do it," I say.

"How? I don't think it requires effort on your part," he says. I roll my eyes. "I'm talking about... psychologically."

"I think that's because you aren't ready yet."

"Of course I'm not ready!" I say, throwing my hands up. "That's what I'm saying."

"Wait until the end of the day," Robert says. "I think it will make more sense then."

I scowl. "Is this your omniscience talking?"

He chuckles, pulling his travel mug out from under the coffee maker, which he only uses for hot water for his tea. "I'll be home early today. Just after lunch. We'll talk then."

I'm left staring at his back, excited. Robert knows something that he's not saying. And I am so impatient to find out what it is that I forgo the opportunity for a nap. Instead I play cards with Ezra and Kaylen. Gabriel, on the other hand, takes a really long nap, which he deserves. He has been pushing himself way too hard. Kaylen and Ezra can tell my attitude has shifted but say nothing, probably afraid that I'm going to turn into a cheery dying person now that I don't have to think about which person I'm going to convince to let me save them next.

Robert returns just after lunch, as he promised. He immediately calls all of us together in the living room and hands me his phone.

"Am I calling someone?" I ask.

"No, someone is calling *you,*" he says.

I can't get a single question out before the phone rings in my hands and the caller ID shows that it's Carl.

"Carl," I answer, and everyone's curiosity peaks.

I put Carl on speakerphone as he says, "Wendy. I should have known. Rob's doing, I'm sure."

"What can I do for you?" I ask. "My time's limited you know."

"I know. I've been keeping tabs on you. What are you doing at pools?"

"What do you have for me, Carl?" I say. "Because I have nothing for you."

"I know what you're doing—curing people. With so little time left, why? It wasn't your doing. It was mine."

"You left a mess. I'm cleaning it up."

The line is silent for about five counts and then Carl says, "I am not supposed to do this, but I am for you and for Gina. She would want this. Rob's secretary should have a list of names, addresses, and phone numbers in her email now. And Gabe should have a copy of the missing portion of Gina's medical file in his email now. Good luck, Wendy." And then the line clicks into silence and the call ends.

We all look at each other in incredulity. Gabriel is the first to break the stunned silence. "I'm going to check my email." He wheels himself out.

"I'll have Lacey compile the names and a schedule," Robert says, standing.

"Wait, what?" I ask. "Schedule?"

Robert comes over to squeeze my arm. "Yes. Carl is buying you more time. And he's sending you more names to work on."

"My mom's file…" I say. "She did something to keep herself alive for four more months after she stopped treatment."

"Freaking great," Ezra says. "More ungrateful SOBs to see. This is going to be *amazing.* Rejection is just *the best.*" He stands up and walks out.

"More time?" Kaylen says. "And he just *now* tells you about it?" She shakes her head angrily. "Gosh I can't stand him. What kind of father holds your life over your head?"

I have no idea. Carl is a mystery, motivated by things I still don't quite understand. But I'll take it. I don't even know what this treatment entails, but I'll do it if it means more time.

41

"*A* transplant?" I say. "That's impossible."

"Not impossible. Just not advisable," Gabriel replies, not looking up from the pages in his hands.

"That's like... suicide. Can you imagine how my whacko immune system would react to foreign marrow? I'd die of transplant rejection within a week."

"An autograft..." Gabriel mumbles, his brows knit. I don't think he heard me.

"Autograft?" I say. "That's using my own marrow, right? How on earth would that help? My marrow is total crap."

"I'm not sure..." Gabriel mumbles.

"Maybe Carl lied. Maybe he's trying to kill me."

Gabriel shakes his head slowly, his attention still on the paper.

"You don't think he's trying to kill me?" I say, crossing my arms from where I sit.

Gabriel sits back in his chair finally, extending his good leg and propping the one in a cast up on an ottoman. "I daresay Carl is trying to help. I can't fathom why he would want you dead. Not when you are able to do what he's been hoping you'd do all along."

After blowing air out through pursed lips, I say, "Forget whether or not we'll go through with the treatment. What doctor in their right mind *will* do it?"

"Carl provided that information."

"Same person that did my biological mom?"

"I don't know. It doesn't say. I have no doubt it was a procedure that wasn't medically approved at the time. Carl must have bribed someone. Either way, we need to decide if we're going to do it."

I roll my eyes. "Do we actually have a choice? This sounds like our only chance. I might do it and die, or do it and live a little longer, or just don't do it and die anyway." I roll my eyes for a second time. "It's just so hard to pick..."

Gabriel chuckles and it's nice to see that we can finally have a sense of humor about death. "Sometimes, Wendy, it's nice to have no choices. It takes away the agony of indecision."

"So we're doing it."

"Looks that way."

I have met a lot of doctors and nurses in the last few months. Their feelings about my case have generally been the same hopeless pity, but with variations in personality. But Dr. Martinez is not like any of them. Like Dr. Altman, Dr. Martinez is extremely intelligent and curious about my case. But he is also confident, almost overly so, about how I'll hold up to an autograft marrow transplant when I meet with him at a small research hospital in Nevada. I will be staying here for the duration of my treatment, which will take two weeks.

Normally the preparation for transplants and the recovery is extensive and takes months. But because it will be my own marrow, Dr. Martinez says we will know right away if it's going to work or not. I'll also undergo blood irradiation at the same time. The treatment, which I have never read about in any leukemia literature, is basically a reset. Get my marrow and my blood back to normal levels even though my marrow is still cancerous. It will buy time before the cancer builds back up to its current state.

First, my marrow is harvested as well as my stem cells. Then I undergo hellish chemotherapy to purge the remaining cancer that might have harbored itself in my major organs. Gabriel consults with Martinez on chemo dosages, but supposedly the man has already seen my medical file and is aware of the treatment I've been getting and what I can handle. I'm amazed at how open-minded he is and how easily he goes along with Gabriel's instructions. Putting me 'under the knife' so to speak doesn't concern him at all. He's upbeat and positive and I worry a few times that this isn't a real hospital and is instead a black market surgery center. It checks out, but I don't have a choice. Robert showed me the list of names he acquired from Carl. There are one hundred and sixty-one people on it. Names, addresses, phone numbers, and even birthdates. If I die too soon, so do they.

The two weeks pass in a blur. I am so out of it once all my vital blood parts have been harvested that I can't think straight. I can't sit up for more than a few minutes let alone walk or carry on intelligent conversation. Gabriel remains by my side the whole time except for a few hours each day that Jeanelle administers his regular chemo. Kaylen and Ezra are with us, easing the discomforts, but I still feel sort of like Frankenstein, the way my blood and marrow are pulled out of me, irradiated, and then put back in after my body has been chemically purged. I feel half dead and sometimes I wonder if this is actually death, if it takes a while to transition out of life. Several times, someone, usually Gabriel, tries to talk to me about something and I become distracted by a sound or the angle of light through the window. I wouldn't call it an unpleasant experience, but I rarely feel that I am fully awake and aware.

It's not until I 'wake up' that I realize what a nerve-racking experience it has been for everyone else, because the drugs I was on even prevented me from fully-utilizing my emodar; my body wasn't capable of generating the physiological responses required to feel any range of emotion. I learn after the fact that I endured several bouts of extremely low blood pressure as well as anemia. My heart stopped at one point, but I don't recall that *at all.* In fact, I'm pretty sure I lost days-worth of memories surrounding the episode. Lucky me. Gabriel, on the other hand, looks even more frail, and lines of stress and worry crease his skin more deeply. It also has an ominous grey tinge.

On the morning before the day I am scheduled to leave, Dr. Martinez stops by my room and looks me over. I'm alone for once, Gabriel having gone to use a phone to arrange for our flight back to Monterey since cell phone signal within the hospital is nil.

"How long?" I ask Dr. Martinez, grateful that Gabriel isn't here to hear me ask such a question.

He looks at me from under extremely bushy eyebrows. "I understand you're in a hurry. But we'd like you to stick around until tomorrow."

"No, I mean, how long do I have to live?" I say.

"Ah," he says. Then he shrugs. "Anyone's guess. Your disease may come back slowly. Or it may come back even quicker than before. You're going to want to stay on a preventative therapy in order to slow it as much as possible, though. But you should be able to get it in shot form rather than an infusion."

"My mother got four months. Will I get four months?"

His brow wrinkles. "Your mother?"

"Yes. Regina Walden? I'm told she had the same treatment here and she lived four months after it."

"When was this?" he asks, preoccupied with note-taking.

"Uhhh, nineteen years ago."

He chuckles and says, "I wouldn't know of your mother's case. I've only been working here for a few years."

I roll my eyes. Even I can see that Dr. Martinez isn't old enough to have been my mother's doctor. That's not what I mean. "Well you have it, don't you? I mean, didn't you look at it before this procedure?"

"Oh sure, sure," he says, as if someone like me coming in is a daily occurrence. "I look at a lot of files. They are not named though. We work under an extremely strict privacy policy. Even your file is nameless."

"Really?" I say.

He nods. "This is a privately owned hospital. Strictly for research. You have to know someone to be seen here. We don't serve just anyone. You must know some very important people, Mrs. Dumas."

My eyes widen slightly. "I guess," I reply, wondering once more what it is Carl is up to, who he knows, and what his ultimate goal really is.

.

42

"To the Batmovan!" Ezra says when he sees me shake my head as Gabriel and I approach him.

I giggle as Kaylen comes forward to take my wheelchair from Farlen. That's what Ezra has dubbed our van—a sinister-looking, black monstrosity that has been hauling us, our wheelchairs, and emergency medical equipment from place to place. We're in San Jose, California, our list of names in-hand, trying to convince people to let us dip them in a pool for a few hours.

Once we are all loaded, Kaylen opens the notebook she keeps the names in and puts a big fat X next to a name: Elise Stepke. That's whose apartment we just visited. She turned down our offer. Two weeks ago when we started out after my transplant, we would get upset about rejection. But it has become so common that we move on pretty easily. Whereas most of the twenty-seven names we fit in prior to my transplant accepted our claims because most of them knew one of us, we have no rapport with these people. We've also decided not to have Kaylen and Ezra with us when we meet with people. It's too hard for people to take us seriously even *without* having two teenagers along—even if some of them remember Kaylen. Most of those would have known her when she was younger anyway.

Jeanelle makes her rounds, checking our vitals, and Ezra says, "What was the reason this time?"

"Didn't believe us," I say.

"Maybe I should go with you… show people my telekinesis," Kaylen offers. "That might make them at least believe we are who we say we are."

I shake my head. "No, she didn't believe that hypno-touch can cause cancer. She said if that was true, why would Louise be doing it, let alone pro-bono? I told her she was dead. She said she was sorry but it sounded like we were looking for something to blame our cancer on."

"Mister Dumas," Jeanelle says, and we all turn toward her. Jeanelle rarely talks so loudly, let alone interrupts our conversations. "Your heart rate has been gradually speeding up the last few days." She holds the nasal cannula Gabriel left behind in the van in her hand as evidence. "You *cannot* spend any time without your oxygen, especially when you've finished your infusion only a couple of hours ago."

We all look at Gabriel now. He shrugs. "The woman was a smoker. I didn't want to take chances with flammability." And then, as if on cue, he starts wheezing, but he has been doing that progressively more in the last week, so I don't think it was purposeful.

Ezra snorts. "Right. And she was going to light up right in front of your nose?"

"Perhaps," Gabriel says quietly to avoid coughing again. "Everyone calm down. I'll keep it in from now on."

Jeanelle looks like she wants to say something else, but she decides against it, as she does usually. She knows too much to not be curious, and too little to understand much of what's going on.

"Did she know Carl—Kevin?" Ezra asks. "Elise?"

I shake my head. "It seems that Carl was rarely personally involved in Louise's dealings. I'm not sure what he has been doing all these years."

"Pretending to be a CPA," Kaylen grumbles. "And it doesn't surprise me. I told you he was hardly ever on the compound."

"Thirty people..." Gabriel sighs. "Only four and a half repairs. And this started off so well originally."

"An invitation to spend hours standing still in a pool isn't exactly appealing," I say. "Last night I spoke to Robert about offering them money..."

"Not a good idea," Gabriel says.

I nod, and Kaylen says, "Why not?"

"First of all, Robert would have to handle the money part, and we don't want any of this linked to him since he has no relationship with these people. Secondly, if someone you weren't quite sure whether to trust offered you money to stand in a pool to do something they refused to give extensive information about, would you think it was safe?" I ask. "Especially if we had all your contact information and knew about a secret study you participated in years ago?"

"Oh," Kaylen says. "Yeah, that does sound shady."

"Yep, and knocking on their door multiple times a day until they answer doesn't sound like stalking at all," Ezra says.

"Actually, it sounds more like a proselyting effort," Gabriel says, smiling slightly. "It even includes baptism."

I have to laugh at that.

"Well even when we convert them and then dunk 'em, they act like idiots," Ezra says, opening a bag of chips and popping open a soda as the van starts to move again.

Ezra is referring to the fact that everyone, with the exception of one woman, was surprised that they lost their ability even though we told them it would happen. The first person, our 'half cure,' that we took to the pool didn't even let us finish the job. We planned to test her ability along the process to find out when it would start fading. She could basically summon energy and infuse it in herself or someone else. She demonstrated it on me, and it felt like a burst of life in my chest that pulsed outward. It was a neat little trick, and I could easily see how it could take the place of an energy drink or a morning coffee infusion. I think the source of the pulse is the space around her because she says she can't do it again in the same room for several hours, which makes me believe the space must need to recharge. In fact, I'm willing to bet people are the primary source of this 'energy' she pools, though I couldn't see any indication in the colorworld. Unfortunately, after about fifty thousand strands in, we took her into the hotel lobby that connected to the pool we were using, and it became clear that her ability had lost a bit of punch. And that's when she called it off. From that point we decided we'd no longer pause to test anyone's ability.

A few days later, another man even tried to rush Gabriel when he realized his ability was gone. Fortunately Farlen was nearby and was able to handle it. But when it was over, Ezra suggests we don't tell people at all that they'll lose their ability. Instead, he said, we should tell them that we fixed our life forces but it didn't cure our illnesses since they were already present. He thinks we'd get more takers that way. Gabriel vetoed that idea. First of all, he can't lie, and second of all, he thinks it's wrong to trick people. They should have the opportunity to choose whether a life force ability is worth a shortened life span.

Of the five that allowed us to work on them, only one was truly grateful. She thanked us all heartily and said she knew that Louise was up to something fishy. That one person made all of the other rejections worth it.

It's been a slow and brutal process. We have a rough quota of five people per day to visit as long as five can be found in the same area without too much driving in between. But the quota is always thrown off because of pool trips, driving, and our treatments, which are ongoing. We are pleased to find that most of them are up and down the western side of the country. There is a large speckling of about fifty up and down the east coast, and a few in Arizona and Nevada. Other than that, everyone else is along the west coast with the largest concentrations in San Diego and LA, which will be our next destination before flying to the east coast to finish up.

I am amazed that so many of them are young—early to mid-twenties. That is part of the problem. When you are that young, you don't see death as imminent. You feel immortal. To a twenty-three year old, ten to fifteen years of life is like a lifetime. (I should know. I'm twenty and would *love* to get fifteen more years). Falling deathly ill in fifteen years to *them* doesn't seem possible. It causes a roadblock on almost every occasion. Whenever we see that the next person on the list is under thirty, we all groan. But we do it anyway. We bite our tongues and knock on the door, prepared for any reception.

One girl—the twenty-fifth person on Carl's list—upon learning that she would lose her ability in the process, told us she believed us one hundred percent, but no thanks, she was good with it. She said in fifteen years they'll have a cure for cancer and she'll be fine.

She walked us to the door and said, "Thanks for the warning though, I'll be on my toes about it."

Turning my attention to Kaylen now, because growing confusion from her has gotten too strong to ignore, I see her leaning over her list, pen in hand.

"What is it?" I ask.

"It's just that there are a lot of people I remember from the compound who aren't on here at all," she replies, flipping through the pages.

"Carl didn't give us all the names then?"

Kaylen shrugs. "It doesn't look like it. But why wouldn't he?" She looks up at Gabriel and me like we have an answer.

"Is there a commonality you can draw from the people you remember who are missing?" Gabriel asks. "Something they all had in common?"

Kaylen thinks for several minutes as she scans the list. She grabs a scrap piece of paper and talks to herself as she writes, stopping at intervals to rack her brain, "Layla, Finn, Liam... Marty, Frederick... Sue Ellen, Brady, Cho, Liz... Faye... Joseph..." She writes a few more names and then counts them. Then she looks up. "I probably haven't got all of them because I can't remember, but I have fifteen here at least. And..." She looks down at her handwritten list again, thinking for several minutes, scribbling things on the paper next to the names. We watch her closely, impatient to learn what her conclusion is—if there is a conclusion at all.

Kaylen throws her hands up. "I don't know. The missing ones are from all over I think. I'm not sure… I really don't remember that much. A *lot* of people passed through the compound."

"Demographics?" Gabriel asks. "Ages? Races?"

Kaylen takes her hair in one hand and writes next to the names with her other—age ranges, I think.

"The only thing I can tell from this list is that none of these missing people are over the age of forty," she says as she begins to write their races.

Ezra leans forward to see. "And none of them younger than twenty-five."

"That's a pretty narrow age gap," I point out.

"If I'm even remembering their ages right," Kaylen says. "I'm just guessing based on what they looked like."

I look at Gabriel. "Ages twenty-five to forty are missing. What does that mean?"

"They're dead already," Ezra suggests.

"True," I say.

"Not *all* of them are missing," Gabriel says. "But clearly there is a correlation among the missing ones. We have seen an awful lot of individuals from Carl who are quite young. I suggest we give Kaylen's list to Robert and see if he can get the truth out of Carl in the meantime. That's all we can do at this point. We can't meet with people we don't know how to contact."

"Are the missing ones married?" Ezra asks.

Kaylen looks surprised by the suggestion but contemplates it. "I… I think so."

"That is an excellent idea," Gabriel says, leaning closer to Kaylen's list. "Twenty-five to forty is the prime age to be married. Beyond forty and many are divorced or perpetually single. I don't see how it will help us, but we ought to keep it in mind. Understanding the whys to it should help us better understand Carl."

Kaylen giggles and we look at her. "Well guess who our next one, number thirty-one is?" she says. "She's over forty. And single."

I lean forward to see her list.

"Miranda DeLange," she replies at the same time I read it. *Randy.*

We all look at each other.

"What do you think she'll say?" I ask lightly.

Nobody offers a guess.

I start laughing then at how silly it is that we're doing this. It's almost as bad as going to Louise herself and asking her if we can fix her.

"I know. It's awful isn't it?" jokes Gabriel. "I am ever so curious what she'll say though. She always came across as a practical sort. I kind of liked her actually. She was abrasive but very real. Who knows? She may surprise us."

"But be ready," I say to Farlen and Mark who are with us, sitting in the front. "We might need you for this one."

"She was always decent to me," says Kaylen. "I doubt she knew everything Louise was doing. She didn't really become important to Louise until Dina died."

We arrive at that moment, and, without a word, get out in front of a contemporary-looking ranch-style home. It's immaculately well-kept, just like I remember Randy's office was.

Farlen grabs my wheelchair, and I plop down, summoning my energy. "I think you and Ezra should come this time," I say to Kaylen, and she follows.

I hear a TV going inside and a person who sounds like they're sitting still. Gabriel rings the doorbell and we wait. It's a long time before we hear movement. I have Gabriel ring the doorbell three more times, assuring him that someone is indeed inside. They are probably just asleep.

Finally, I hear steps across a wooden floor and a person's breathing on the other side of the door as they look through their peephole at us. The person hesitates, and then finally the door opens a crack and Randy's face appears over the chain.

"Is this revenge? I swear I'll call the cops." But her eyes roam over me with a bit of confusion and shock.

Randy looks more disheveled than I have ever seen her. She isn't wearing any makeup, and her hair is tied back pell-mell. She looks like she's in a T-shirt. I barely recognize the woman who is ordinarily cognizant of every detail of her appearance.

"Randy," says Gabriel. "We're not here to threaten you, just to talk to you."

"Well talk then. I'm not opening the door for five people that would just as soon see me dead." says Randy sharply.

She'd probably be even more alarmed if she saw that Farlen was armed and if she knew Mark was scouting her perimeter.

349

"Wendy and I are ailing as you can probably tell," says Gabriel. "We have found that the work at the compound is making people ill. We've found a way to reverse the damage done to a life force and we want to offer that same thing to you. We desire no vengeance. We want to help."

Randy eyes both Gabriel and me. Her eyes rest on me for a long time, taking in my feeble appearance. Finally, she closes the door, unlatches the chain, and opens the door fully.

"Well, come in then," she says and turns, indicating that we follow her.

Gabriel and I glance at each other briefly before following. Ezra looks like he is going to jump out and attack someone. Farlen observes every corner of the inside of the house, which is just as immaculate as the outside. It's big and open and airy with vaulted ceilings and fresh colors. We make our way into a living room decorated in the contemporary style I know Randy likes. She turns off the TV and makes her way to an easy chair. It looks out of place in the room, like it's been added after the fact. I notice then that Randy moves with a bit of stiffness, like she's taking extreme care with her steps.

Once we are all settled with Farlen standing behind us on guard, Randy looks at me with a raised eyebrow. "You aren't looking too good, Wendy."

"Tell me about it," I say, smiling.

I don't find any resentment toward her. She lied to me and also helped Louise keep us captive, but I can't find it in me to dwell on that. I don't know how much she knows about what Louise has been up to—what she has caused to happen to people—so neither Gabriel nor I make any assumptions. We go into the tale in the same way that we have with everyone else.

When we're done, I see tears in Randy's eyes. She wipes them away quickly and looks at both Gabriel and me and says, "I'm so sorry for everything I've ever done to you. I was so horribly wrong. I didn't realize what was happening. Or maybe I didn't want to believe it. And then I got diagnosed and I knew what was happening. That was shortly after you left. I parted ways with Louise a couple of months later. I—I'm so sorry. But what you said... Is it true? You know how to reverse it? You can cure me? Wait... you can't," she says, taking in Gabriel's and my appearances again.

"You're sick?" I ask, seeing Randy's careful movement with new eyes.

"I was diagnosed with ALS one month ago," she says. "It's progressed at an alarming rate. I'm already experiencing significant lack of movement in my limbs. So you can only prevent it then, is that right?"

"We don't know," says Gabriel. "We've already repaired the life forces of five others. We know that part can be done. The one drawback is that you will lose your magnetic manipulation ability."

"We've never done it with someone who is already sick. We don't know yet if it reverses disease," I say.

Randy looks confused. "You haven't done it to yourselves yet? Why not?"

"Because we're the only ones who can do it," says Kaylen from behind me. "If we fix our own life forces, no one can be healed."

"You—you are going on like that just to fix other people's life forces? You both look like you could die next week. Why would you do this? I've only ever harmed you. I don't understand."

"Everyone has a chance to be healed, no matter what they've done," says Kaylen, and I can tell she is eager for Randy to say yes. I think it's partly kindness and partly driven by a need to know if saving Gabriel and me would be possible without the issue of losing our abilities. I try to not care; Gabriel is planning to die with me anyway. But I still want to save him, and if Randy can be cured, it will make that wish stronger. And at this point, I don't have the energy for battles with myself. I want to honor what Gabriel wants. I want to do that for him.

Randy seems to only just notice Kaylen, despite the fact that she's already spoken. "Kaylen, what is your part in all this?"

"We can't do this without Kaylen," I say. "We work together. Fixing life forces cannot be done by a single one of us working alone."

"I would think your propensity with hypno-touch would be enough," Randy says. "I heard... well, Louise said you were capable of *seeing* them. Is that true?"

I sigh and nod. "But we aren't sharing that bit of information when we meet with people. And if you could keep it to yourself, that would be great."

Randy nods in-turn. "I didn't do anything to deserve this. I... I don't know how to thank you, for offering in the very least. And if it cures me, I'll do anything you ask, anything you need."

"Good," says Kaylen, "Because we're having a heck of a time convincing people to let us fix them."

"People won't let you fix them?" asks Randy in astonishment.

Ezra rolls his eyes. "Yes, you can't imagine how many selfish self-centered jack—"

"Thank you, Ezra," Gabriel interrupts and then under his breath says, "Someone needs to teach that boy some manners."

"I guess I can see that... Hard to say how I would react if I weren't... ill," says Randy.

"Lucky you then," I say with a smile.

"Well we are in a hurry as you can imagine, Randy. Lots of people to see. Would you like a ride to where we're going or do you want to drive yourself?" Gabriel says.

"I can't drive. My motor control is too unpredictable. I would appreciate a ride. Can I offer you anything before we leave?" asks Randy, pushing herself up out of the chair with some difficulty.

I've never seen her so... weak-looking. "No thanks," I say as Kaylen rushes to help Randy to her feet, smiling at her, exultant.

We still haven't determined at what point people lose their ability entirely. Certain that Randy will allow us to document the process more precisely, I'm eager to test this out finally.

Our group drives to the designated pool in a few minutes. Robert has planned our trip carefully, reserving hotels and their pools for our sole use while we are there. He plans out the exact order of visits and we never have to think. We follow the schedule. I miss Robert, though, and his quiet presence. I often battle with how much to bug him. I want to ask him things about the future. But knowing the struggle he faces daily with his ability, I don't want to make it any harder. But I am still struggling with death, with mine *and* Gabriel's. I know there will eventually be an end to all this.

Unlike the three weeks prior to my transplant when we fixed twenty-two people, I have been more aware this time around. Relative health may be good for my body and for endurance, but it has taken it's toll on my mind. I've had too much time to think despite having plenty to do. Most of it doesn't require much of my participation, just my presence. My grip on staying the course is tenuous, and some days I wish in the depth of my soul that I could quit. I *want* to quit. Death creeps toward me, growing in size like a monolith on the horizon. Thank goodness I spend my time in a wheelchair, because all I have to do is keep my mouth shut and allow myself to be taken to the next destination. As long as I don't express how much I don't want to be here doing this, my life will continue moving in this direction, a direction devoid of meaning anymore, especially when we have found so little success. All I know is I decided some time back that it was right, and the more I acted on that belief, the more this direction has solidified as something that *must* be done rather than something I am deliberately choosing. At some point I lost part of my will. And I'm not sure if that's a good thing or a bad thing.

43

Gabriel, Kaylen, and I grip each other's hands tightly, and Ezra's hand rests more heavily on the back of my neck. The flurry of emotions is hard to endure, so it's a good thing I'm sitting down.

"I understand the swimsuit request now… But I still don't get what you're going to do," says Randy, crouching down carefully to put her feet in the water. Kaylen moves forward to help her down into the pool.

It's always entertaining to see the reaction when we tell someone they'll need a swimsuit for where we're going. During the whole time we're working, their expressions change from disbelief and confusion to boredom. They really have no indication that we're doing anything at all, so it's understandable that their reaction to losing their ability would be so violent.

When Randy is in the water, I channel us into that familiar world of swirling colors and focus on the scenery to calm myself. Kaylen told us early on that the calmer we are, the easier it is for her to concentrate and move more strands at once. This one is going to be a doozie.

"Good, Wendy," says Kaylen appreciatively. Then she turns to Ezra. "Maybe you should sit this one out until you can get a hold of yourself. You're wound tighter than a jack-in-the-box."

"Nu uh," protests Ezra. "I'll be calm, just watch."

He closes his eyes, taking cleansing breaths, and Kaylen rolls her eyes. We know each other so well by now. That Kaylen is able to pick out whose emotions are whose is telling of that fact. Gabriel is never a problem. He is always good at controlling his thoughts. It helps that he can spend his time counting and rechecking his counts though.

Randy observes with interest, clearly having a lot of questions—especially about my casualness in touching people—but is willing to let them go and let us do what we have to. That's refreshing. Of course, Randy is the first of the people we've met that knows what I can see.

"Okay, Randy. If you'll submerge yourself, first revealing your front, and then revealing your back—about five seconds for each side. Then you'll stand with your head as the only part of you above water—from the chin up, that's all," says Gabriel in a rehearsed voice.

I know inside he would be reeling with the possibilities of this experiment if he didn't have a cap on his emotions. Focusing only on the task is his way of staying calm.

Randy does exactly as Gabriel asks. In fact, she stays under a long time. A lot longer than I could. Ezra shifts in his seat in impatience.

"Ezra," says Kaylen sharply.

"Sorry."

Randy emerges, crouching in the water and keeping just her head above water. "Like this?" she asks from within her swirling purple mass.

Gabriel nods and rattles off the numbers telepathically to Ezra for double checking. Ezra gives the right count for head and chest and Gabriel thinks to the group, '*Okay, Kaylee, this is a lot. We're looking for just over thirteen thousand for the head. And around three hundred fifty thousand for the chest.*' Then he looks at Randy. "Your life force is quite a mess. How long have you been having hypno-touch?"

"On and off for probably ten years," she replies.

'*Wow,*' I think to the group. '*It's a miracle Kaylen and I are still alive if that's standard for life expectancy. Kaylen has half a million out. I have less out than Randy, but close. We should have been dead years ago.*'

'*Indeed,*' Gabriel thinks to us pensively. '*Perhaps it helps that you had it done so young? I have no idea.*' He looks at Randy. "This is going to take a little more than three hours. Would you like a chair?"

Randy's eyes widen in surprise but she says, "Yes, I think so."

Ezra grabs a plastic patio chair and hops in the pool to arrange it for Randy.

"It seems like a long time," Randy says then, "but on second thought I guess it's impressive that you can fix things so quickly bearing in mind how many hours I spent under hypno-touch having my life force rearranged."

'*I've never done a stint like this,*' Kaylen tells us. '*So everyone... try to stay happy or something so it will give me an energy boost to get through.*' Kaylen crosses her ankles and leans forward with her hands clasped across her lap—just as she's looked the twenty-seven other times she's done this—while I keep a hand on her arm. She doesn't wait for an answer and loose strands immediately rise out of the water. Gabriel focuses, counting as she goes so she doesn't have to stop, just as we're used to them doing.

Kaylen has averaged her strand control to somewhere around a hundred every three seconds. She completes Randy's head in about six minutes which is astounding. I know she's been disappointed in herself that she can't control more strands at once, and she's always pushing her control to its limit in order to improve. And to see a hundred life force hairs rise in the air at once and move into Randy's head within three seconds is mind-boggling. Without her ability to control so many at once, inserting hundreds of thousands of strands ought to take days. That Kaylen can fix a life force in a matter of hours means we can help more people before Gabriel and I deteriorate to the point of being unable to travel at all. It's a miracle, really. I wish I could find more than mild appreciation for it.

When Kaylen completes Randy's head, Gabriel says, "Randy, we'd like to determine at what point individuals lose their ability in this process. So would you mind? Could we give you a piece of metal to test?"

"Of course," says Randy.

"I'll get it," says Ezra, who lets go of my hand. Then he says, "Uh, what kind of metal? How big?"

"The most I've lifted is a set of about six keys. We can start there, I suppose," says Randy.

"Right," says Ezra. He turns to the bag I brought and mutters, "She's no Magneto."

I giggle at his comic book reference which makes Gabriel smile in turn. Ezra retrieves some keys and then hands them down to Randy. But instead of taking them from Ezra, she holds her palm up toward them about a foot away. The keys fly out of Ezra's fingers and into hers.

"It seems as strong as before," says Randy. "From what I can tell anyway."

'Let's do about fifty thousand in the chest, Kaylee,' thinks Gabriel.

"Okay," replies Kaylen as Ezra gets Randy situated in the shallow end so her chest is just out of water. Once we're all arranged again, Kaylen concentrates once more on Randy. On and on the strand insertion goes until Gabriel confirms that Kaylen has reached his desired count.

Ezra holds the keys up again. This time, the keys move toward Randy's hand but don't leave Ezra's fingers until she moves her hand a tad closer.

"Definitely weaker," confirms Randy. "The field doesn't extend as far."

A half hour later, we test again. Randy confirms her capability is ever weaker. So I ask, "How do you feel?"

Randy flexes her fingers with evident stiffness. "There doesn't seem to be any change," she says, disappointed.

"Well don't lose hope yet," points out Gabriel. "Expecting the body to heal instantaneously doesn't really go along with biological capability. So let's keep going. Obviously ability weakens as we work." Then, to the rest of us, *'Another fifty thousand, Kaylen.'*

"Got it," she says, bringing more strands into the air and plunging them in Randy's chest.

It's another half hour later that Gabriel confirms that Kaylen has reached the count. This time, the keys don't move at all and Randy has Ezra take one key off and hold it out.

The single key doesn't move until Randy's hand is at least six inches above it. But it flies upward into her palm and she catches it.

'Still some ability and she's only got a little under two hundred thousand remaining,' thinks Gabriel. *'Kaylen, a hundred thousand this time, if you will?'*

Kaylen gets to work. An hour later, we stop to test once more and discover that Randy can only make the key shift a little in Ezra's palm, even when her own hand is about four inches above his.

It's gratifying to know that even at less than a hundred thousand strands out, Randy still has some ability, even if it's so little. I want to get all of Kaylen's strands back in, but if I can't, I'll settle for most of them.

"Are you up for another hour or do you need a break?" Gabriel asks Kaylen. He's referring, of course, to the fact that Kaylen's rate has been slowing. We all feel her depletion.

Before Kaylen can answer, I say, *'Let's get Farlen. No need to prolong the job if we don't have to.'* I look at Ezra. "Will you go get him? He should be right outside."

"One of these days, instead of sending me after Farlen, you'll say, 'Ezra, can you please make out with Kaylen so we can speed this up?' and that is going to be so much more fun," Ezra says, hopping up, kissing her on the forehead, and heading for the door.

Kaylen giggles and then Randy says, "So I'm starting to understand that you are using telekinesis to fix my life force... I'm just wondering how exactly."

When none of us immediately answer, Randy raises her hands, "No need to answer. I get it. Information is powerful and I obviously lack judgment."

"If only everyone were so understanding," Gabriel sighs as Farlen comes in behind Ezra.

Farlen sits next to Ezra behind me and touches my skin. Liveliness moves over our group, and Kaylen sighs. "Yep, that ought to do it."

She continues her work on the remaining strands, focused and intent on her task. I'm so proud of her. She's a mere sixteen years old and handling the pressure with so much grace. I wonder what it is that moves the strands precisely. It seems like we ought to be able to see some indication of it in the colorworld. I remember the energy vapor I see on occasion when the lighting is right, and I wonder if there is some kind of barely visible manifestation of her ability.

"Kaylen?" I interrupt her mental concentration, and the strands she is grasping drop back in the water as she looks over at me.

'Sorry,' I think to everyone. '*I was thinking, well wondering actually, what it is that moves Kaylen's ability. Ezra, why don't we turn out the lights? It's dark outside so if it's possible to see, we should be able to see it in the dark. I'm curious...*'

Gabriel stares at me, stunned. "That's incredibly insightful!" Then he turns to Ezra, "Would you mind?"

Ezra jogs over to the light switch and says, "Just call me the gopher with occasional mathematical insight who would be happy to offer occasional making out for utilitarian purposes." Kaylen shakes her head at him, but with a hint of a smile.

When Ezra turns off the lights, it doesn't make the room darker—at least not how we can see it—but brighter.

"Wow," I say.

'*So bright!*' thinks Kaylen, squinting.

'*Indeed, the darkness does have an amazing effect on bringing out the light, doesn't it?*' thinks Gabriel.

Ezra jogs over and takes my free hand. He blinks at the lights as well. '*Why haven't we been doing this all along?*' he asks. '*You can actually see better this way... Although I wouldn't have thought that was possible.*'

Energy vapor is everywhere in the darkness-enhanced light of the colorworld. *'Kaylen,'* I think, *'how about pick up a few strands.'*

Kaylen turns her attention back to Randy and, so instantaneously that I don't really see exactly how it happens, a thin train of iridescent steam from Kaylen forms a bridge of connection between her life force and Randy's strands beneath the water.

Kaylen gasps at the sight but keeps her grip on the strands, heaving them out of the water. As soon as she does so, the tiny flow of vapor from her stills to near-imperceptible amounts. I think we only see it because we're looking for it.

'Well that explains that,' Kaylen thinks in wonder. *'It does literally take more energy to get them out of the water. I wonder why?'*

'Maybe water makes the strands heavier for some reason when they're submerged,' Gabriel offers. *'How about hold one under the water for a minute and we can get a better look at what that vapor is doing.'*

Kaylen does so, moving the strand out of the water more slowly, but it still looks like the vapor surrounds the strand somehow before it moves out of the water. The vapor dissipates quickly and we can't tell what's happening.

'Maybe the water makes it hard to see,' I offer. *'Try something else out of the water that's bigger. Like that table behind us.'*

Kaylen turns her attention to the table. The effect is so instantaneous that it's like a visible stream of thought from her appears out of nowhere, connecting her life force to the glowing yellow table. But now we can see that it's not really like the vapor grips the table; the table appears to absorb it before lifting up in the air of its own accord.

"Woah," Farlen says.

"Fascinating," breathes Gabriel, and we all stare in dumb wonder for at least a minute.

"Alright, well I'm sure we could experiment all night, but let's get back to it," I say, turning back to Randy's luminous purple life force. Kaylen begins working again and now that we can see it, the steam she emanates is a continuous stream between her and Randy's life force. It's really something to watch, almost like there's some kind of communion going on between her and Randy.

'*It's like... her thoughts are speaking to the strands,*' marvels Gabriel to me only.

'*I guess they'd have to...*' I reply. '*I mean, if everything is sentient somehow, seems like you can't just make the strands go where you want. You have to... ask them, I guess?*'

We continue to watch what Kaylen's doing with her vapor stream as she moves strands and it's so mesmerizing that the hour is up in no time. With the final bunch of strands that Kaylen releases into Randy's chest, the vapor or energy—whatever it is—dissipates into the surrounding air. The swirl at Randy's chest is now perfect.

I let out a great sigh. Gabriel has her go under the water once more to confirm with Ezra that her ratio is correct.

Once that's done, Ezra thinks, '*So... maybe not worth mentioning for the tenth time, but I still think it's weird that everyone has more strands in their chest than their head while us three and Robert have more in our head. Except you, Gabe. Who knows how your ratio is distributed.*'

"Yes," agrees Gabriel, "That did occur to me. Although, we hardly have enough to draw a conclusion about it still. And what conclusion we would draw, I have no idea."

Ezra shrugs. "Like I said. Probably not worth mentioning. But I figured I'd do it anyway."

"Well, Randy, let's see if you have any magnetic ability left," I say.

Ezra holds out the key again. Randy extends her hand above it, but nothing happens.

"I don't feel any of the gathering magnetic force. It's gone," marvels Randy.

"Still feeling stiff?" Gabriel asks Randy.

"Afraid so. But we'll see, won't we?" asks Randy, tentatively hopeful.

"No one's ever been cured of ALS before. Who knows how long it would take if they could be," points out Gabriel.

"Thanks for your willingness, Randy," I say. "We really learned a lot."

She climbs out of the water carefully. Kaylen hands her a towel and she wraps it around herself. She looks at me then and says, "I assume you'll want to know if I get better. How should I contact you?"

Gabriel writes the number down and hands the paper to her. "Let us know as soon as you experience any improvement."

Gabriel begins a fit of hacking after speaking then and has to sit down to recover himself.

Randy looks on in blank horror but finally turns to me again. "I'm so sorry... to all of you. I just... Well, I wanted to make things better. That's all."

"I know," I sigh, looking at Gabriel. I hear him struggling to breathe, and it has me worried. He's getting to the point where he can no longer endure his pain without us. I want to get him back to Jeanelle.

And I want Randy to get better so I can fix Gabriel... My heart catches momentarily and I suddenly feel on the verge of tears.

"If I do get well, I'm serious about accompanying you," Randy says, confidence returning to her voice. "I'll do everything in my power to help you gain cooperation from past clients."

44

Once we are in our hotel room, Jeanelle listens to Gabriel's breathing with her stethoscope and checks out his vitals. She sighs and looks at him. "I don't like your chest sounds, Mr. Dumas. We might be draining it, but that much fluid accumulating so quickly is a bad sign. I'm afraid to see your CT results on Friday. I give you another week and a half of this, and then you're going to be on a ventilator."

Fear grips me. It's happening, and much too quickly. I won't be able to hear Gabriel's reassuring voice. He'll lie still on a bed, dying, and dead in a matter of weeks. Tears come to my eyes and I cover my mouth so that maybe I won't start sobbing. Gabriel pulls me closer to him on the bed, but I kind of want to run away.

"I'm also going to up your oxygen," Jeanelle says, writing something down on the chart she keeps. "And get you back on cough suppressants." She looks up from under her thick eyelashes. "Is there any way you can have less outings each day? It's too much stress. You need to be resting more."

I look at Gabriel and he looks back at me for several beats before we both turn to Jeanelle. "No. We can't afford to take it easy," I say, though the words offend me and I don't want to say them. I only know I *have* to say them. I have to *do* them. And then, because Jeanelle has been so patient with us, and because I'd like less frustration in my emodar, I add, "What we've been doing is fixing damage that has been done to people so that they will not end up like us. Once we die, there is no hope for them. We count on you to keep us alive as long as possible, because we're running out of time to save them." I bite my lip with the bitterness that comes over me at my own words. It should sound beautiful. But it doesn't to me anymore. My stomach is hollow with dread and tormented with outrage.

Jeanelle stops writing and stares at me, surprised that for once I am answering her questions. "Understood," she says. "I give you my word I will do everything in my power to keep you alive as long as possible." She hops up. "I'll see you in a few hours."

I lay down next to Gabriel, and I wait, but he says nothing. I think we are both in shock over the future we have expected finally becoming reality. And Gabriel is exhausted, so I wait until he is asleep to truly think about it.

When he fades into slumber, I do something I have never done: I pray.

I have heard and felt Maris do it enough times that I know how it should go. I also know from her that the most important part is directing it. It's like my telepathy. I have to *direct* my thoughts to... God. I don't know God, what he or she looks like, acts like, or cares about. But I do my best to imagine a benevolent and powerful being that's got an ear directed my way. And maybe it is something built into me as a human being, but it doesn't feel as weird as I imagined it would.

And I pour my heart out. I let my tears and grief flow *toward* the creator of the universe rather than simply to the space outside of me. The more I do so, the smaller I feel, maybe because I now imagine how I must look to that being. If God sits in the heavens somewhere, I must be atom-sized compared to the surrounding vastness, which makes me feel utterly insignificant. How ridiculous it was that I supposed I could shoulder this job of saving people. So then is it truly that selfish to want out simply because I don't want to watch my husband die amid constant rejection? Is it selfish to want to give up this crazy nomadic quest in order to prolong his life? If it is, someone tell me how to do this in a way that's bearable. Because what I'm doing right now is not going to work. It's clear that both Gabriel and I can't really function while the other is close to death, let alone after death. We can't work in these conditions. It's too much to ask.

These are the things I tell God. And when I'm done I expect to feel better the way Maris does when she prays. But I don't. I even give it a minute to let it soak in. But nothing happens. I just feel angry. I am angry that no one answers in this most desperate moment when I need it most. My conviction and my will to continue on this ridiculous journey crumbles. If no one out there cares, then why do *I* care? Haven't I done enough? Where is my peace? I've been fed nothing but angst, uncertainty, and a death sentence. What is the point of trying so hard when no one is around to take notice and give me a little help? I can't do this anymore.

Though I have only worn it off and on since my transplant and am not wearing it now, I get up to find my purple scarf. And then I throw it in the trash.

***

I have become a mute. I think it was a choice. I'm not sure because I'm pretty sure I *can* talk, but every time I decide to open my mouth, it hurts. Not physically, but emotionally. It feels like I did last night when I pled with the unknown master of the universe for help and received no response. An aching desperation that has no outlet bubbles up into my throat. I'd rather not talk if communicating inflicts that on me. Plus, there's nothing I want to say that badly. I've used words for months now to try to talk my way through what is happening in my life and come to terms with it, but it has yielded nothing but torment. As it is, by avoiding the burden of words, I can actually face the burden of the one hundred and thirty names we have left on our list that have yet to be seen.

Jeanelle cried brain damage and wants to order a CT, but I shake my head at her. Gabriel asks me to go into the colorworld, and I do. He asks me questions there, but I don't answer mentally either. He begs me to speak, and I just squeeze his hand. In fact, the more I don't speak, the better I feel. I even stand up, get myself dressed in tights that are now slightly baggy on me, and cut-off shorts. Digging through my clothes, I see that Ezra's Superman shirt was mistakenly put in my pile of folded laundry, and I'm feeling a bit more empowered today so I put it on, followed by my gloves. I dig my purple scarf out of the trash and tie it on my head. I wait in my wheelchair next to the door, coat over my lap, and ready to meet my quota for the day. Gabriel and Jeanelle watch me with confusion and worry.

I taste the air, which feels a little more alive today than it did yesterday. I think briefly of Randy, but decide not to linger on that too long. I went to sleep last night, determined not to do even one more name on our list, but I woke up in silence, and for the moment I don't feel that way. I don't want to go thinking about things that might sway me.

Kaylen and Ezra appear at our door. Kaylen hands me a bottle of juice, and asks, "No word from Randy yet?"

I shake my head, uncap the juice, and take a swig.

She sighs. "Well maybe it will at least slow the progression, right?"

"Wendy isn't talking today," Gabriel says, hobbling over with crutches and sitting down in his wheelchair. The look on his face when he does that is always priceless. He acts like he's being asked to sit on a pile of dung.

The corner of my mouth turns upward and he raises his eyebrows as he catches it. "Apparently her sense of humor is still intact, however."

"She's not talking?" Ezra asks, and then, "Hey, I've been looking for that shirt."

"Not a word," Gabriel says. "Not even telepathically. She appears to be herself in every other respect—except for the shirt. I have no idea what possessed her to wear that." He starts coughing briefly. Jeanelle walks forward and hands him a paper cup with two pills in it and an open bottle of water.

"Why?" Kaylen asks, looking at me and then Gabriel and then Jeanelle who is gathering up her things behind us.

Gabriel shrugs. "Stubbornness perhaps." He throws the pills back, chasing them with the water and cringing as he closes his eyes for about five seconds—which he does every time he has to swallow through his sores. "Rebelling. I have no idea. Jeanelle thinks it's brain damage, but I can tell it's not."

Ezra leans to the side to put his face level with mine, observing me before he says, "She's done this once before."

"Really?" Gabriel exclaims, only to be rewarded with coughing.

"Yeah," Ezra says. "It was after the baby died, and it lasted through the first two months of her senior year."

I have totally forgotten about that...

Gabriel looks at me, this time with pity rather than annoyance. "I hope you don't plan on doing this for two months," he says softly. "I will miss your voice."

I hope I don't either. But I have a hole in my heart and I'm afraid that opening my mouth will cause me to bleed out. When I went silent after Elena died, my devastation was similar, but mostly I was quiet because I wanted to be left alone. I didn't want to go to school and be asked what happened over and over again. My silence told people clearly that I wasn't doing well, and that's all they needed to know. I didn't start speaking again until I found a way to mask the emotions that bubbled up when I spoke. I suppose people could assume I'm not properly dealing with my emotions now, but the reality is I can't deal with them *and* do what I need to. And right now what I need to do takes precedence. In fact, it occurs to me that I've found a way to answer my own prayer and I wonder if that's the point of prayer: voicing our honest feelings as a way to overcome them. Maybe that's why Maris prays so much: to get stuff off her chest so she can think again.

"Well let's get going," Kaylen sighs, but behind her sigh I've jarred her. She's clearly the most bothered by my behavior. But I can't do a thing to help her. If she can't endure my silence, she sure can't endure my death. And right now all I can do is work on fixing life forces while Gabriel's labored breaths stalk the background.

So we go about our day and the rest of the week. Kaylen starts coming along, doing most of the talking because Gabriel can't be long-winded anymore, and I won't. In fact, prior to my silence, I had stopped speaking when we met with people anyway, so my new silence doesn't require much adjustment.

Kaylen, I can tell, is desperate to make them see, to give them a chance at a life that we can't have. I am starting to think that the people we meet with are getting the impression that we are sales people, trying to convince them to partake in our services and we might decide to charge them later. This comes to me when we are asked for the fourth time if we have a naturopathy license, or if we have a certificate showing our completion of energy field training. Kaylen begins emphasizing the pro-bono part at Gabriel's instruction.

It doesn't help much though. Though we meet with twenty-six more possible candidates after Randy, only six allow us to work on them. But all six of them are polite and gracious. They don't lose it when they realize their abilities really are gone.

Seven days after fixing Randy, not having found anyone that will take our services today, we trudge to our rooms with a cloud of foreboding hanging over us. Having a fruitless day has become harder to bear as we approach the end of our list. It's compounded because we haven't heard from Randy. She is obviously not going to get better, and that's hard. We don't have a lot of hope for ourselves, but what we do have left is draining away each day that we don't hear from Randy. I have mixed feelings about it though, with my promise to Gabriel in mind.

Gabriel has deteriorated significantly in a week, and my silence has deepened. Words and death have never seemed compatible to me. And I can tell Gabriel more accurately of my love for him through my emotions in the colorworld. We can share more than anyone else even without being verbal anyway. Silence has been a comfort to me, and I have shared the peace it brings me with Gabriel through the week, and he has become quieter as well, partly out of choice, partly out of necessity. In the quiet we have found solidarity. We have met up on the same path at the same time finally on this journey, and it feels good just to be together. It has felt good to share his pains as well, to keep him from suffering alone. Kaylen and Ezra are often silent healthy forces in the background because most of our days have been so busy that the quiet is a welcome break, and we recuperate more easily in silence.

Today, however, when the two of us retreat to our hotel room at the end of the day, Gabriel breaks the quiet by whispering, "I never imagined silence could be so therapeutic, and I never imagined you could connect as thoroughly without words."

I'm content, and maybe even a little bit happy. Gabriel falls asleep, curled up next to me, and I listen to his breathing, which instantly removes even that meager slice of happiness. He sounds horrible, and for a moment, panic overcomes me. We are losing Gabriel. I don't want to think of how much time he has. His cancer has metastasized further, and it no longer shrinks. His chemo is strictly palliative now.

A quiet knock sounds at the door. I look to Jeanelle, who is nearby, and she gets up to answer it.

It's Kaylen dressed in flannel pajamas. And I can immediately tell she has been crying. I hold a hand out to her and she reaches for it, kneeling next to the bed.

She does not speak, only holds our hands to her face, her dark brown hair cascading down. The purple section has faded mostly. She is so beautiful and healthy. But I know what her life force looks like. I want to save her. I want to save at least one person I actually *know* in all this. It might not make the end so bitter if I can save Kaylen. After so much rejection, I wish she, of all people, would let me try to fix her. She isn't sick yet, so she still has a chance. In the hours we have spent next to a pool, I have formulated a lot of different ways that we might be able to save her. Besides asking Robert to be in our group, I've been thinking that maybe we could try different techniques of being able to assemble the strands into a rope out of the water and have them stay in a rope until Kaylen can insert them—like tying them in a loose knot for instance.

"Okay," Kaylen says quietly before looking up. "Okay, you can go last."

That was unexpected, and it takes me a second to recognize that she's giving me what I was just wishing for from her. Tears of happiness immediately come to my eyes. I hold her head to my chest, crying tears of gratitude.

"*Thank you,*" I mouth into her hair, though no sound comes out.

But now Kaylen is crying and telling me how sorry she is that she put me through this, that she knows about Gabriel's plans, how much it must hurt me not to be able to save any of us and how she wants to give me that if she can. But I don't care about the reasons. I am on cloud nine. Kaylen has brought a little hope back to me, and because I am so low, that tiny bit has a profound effect.

Right then, my phone rings. I almost don't get it, so caught up am I with Kaylen's news. But I remember it's always Robert, and I want him to know that Kaylen has changed her mind.

I reach for my phone on the nightstand and hand it to Kaylen with a smile.

She takes the phone, looks down at it, and her brow furrows before she picks it up.

"*Wendy! It's Randy!*" says the voice on the other end of the line.

"Randy?" Kaylen says in complete surprise. "Uh, it's not Wendy. It's Kaylen."

I sit up and shake Gabriel awake. I even turn on the lamp to get some light in his eyes which are blinking groggily. "What?" he says, slightly alarmed.

"*Is Wendy there?*" Randy is asking. "*Tell her she did it! I'm cured! I mean, I haven't been to the doctor or anything to confirm, but I know it. I feel 100%! I'm sorry I didn't call you all sooner but I've been asleep. It was so bizarre! I was sitting at home after we met and I got ravenous. It was like I was preparing for hibernation or something. I ate everything in sight. Then I went to sleep and woke up the next day starving as well. I spent all day eating and being depressed. I thought it was the side-effects of the lithium the doctor put me on. And then I fell asleep again that night. I woke up a few times to use the bathroom, but I was too tired to do anything but go straight back to bed.*

"*I finally woke up, about an hour ago, amazed that I had spent an entire week sleeping mostly. I didn't realize it at first because waking up after that time period had me disoriented. I saw the date and couldn't believe it, and then I remembered you all and then I felt my limbs... I couldn't detect stiffness or pain anywhere. I pulled on my running gear and ran a mile with no problems at all. It was so invigorating! Can you believe it? Oh my gosh! I'm so grateful. Where's Wendy? I need to thank her. It worked! I'm healthy, I'm whole, I'm—*"

"It worked?" Kaylen says, trying out the words.

I, on the other hand, am having trouble waking my brain up to the idea. Actually, I have no idea what to *do* with the information. Do I care?

Gabriel, I notice, has taken the phone from a stunned Kaylen, and Randy continues talking although I don't register any of it.

"Randy! That's incredible!" he says, trying not to wheeze.

"*I know! I can't believe it myself. Oh you have no idea. I'm so grateful. What can I do to help? Are you still in San Jose?*" asks Randy.

"No, we've moved on to LA as of two days ago, but we would still welcome your assistance and would be glad to fly you down here," says Gabriel, his voice uncharacteristically quiet so he can speak without wheezing.

The two of them continue to talk, but I am lost in a choppy sea of emotion stronger than I have felt in quite some time. It takes me a while to figure out what it all means. The conclusion is not one I welcome. I try to deny it. This is not something I can ask for. In fact, I'm not even sure why I want it so badly, but for months it has stayed like an aftertaste on my tongue:

I am desperate for Gabriel to live.

45

Ezra asked me a lot this past week what I was waiting for in order to speak again. Each time I shrugged because I really didn't know. I didn't know why it was working so well for Gabriel and me either, especially when prolonged silence between a couple is seen as a bad thing. I knew that if I spoke I would be hurting, and I couldn't afford it until I figured out how to deal with it. And the reason I was hurting was because of Gabriel and the promise he asked me to make. I don't resent him for that, especially when it drew us closer, but it was clearly a much bigger deal to me than I could see at the time. I didn't see it, but some muted part of my soul did, and that's why speaking hurt. My soul ached for words that I didn't want to believe and didn't want to say.

But now Randy is well. And Gabriel can be also, so I am forced to face the question. I need to speak to him about it, but a week of silence has taught me it's power. So as we go back to bed, exhausted after the excitement in my room over Randy's recovery dies down, I pull the two of us into the colorworld, which gets Gabriel's attention despite his need for sleep.

'*What is it?*' he asks telepathically.

I give him my reply by feeling. I close my eyes and imagine what Gabriel will look like on a respirator. I imagine the death pallor his skin will take on. I imagine what it will feel like to see him helpless and immobile. I imagine the coma that will follow, except this time he will not come out of it. The nurse will pull his eyelids back and shine a light in his eyes to see if he reacts. He won't. I will grip his hand and he will not respond, even emotionally. I will call his name telepathically but face only emptiness. Before I know it, tears rush forward, pushing their way out of my closed eyes.

Letting it flow, I find solidity again, and I fight to remember what I felt that day Gabriel cornered me on the path at the compound, when the intensity of his presence magnetized me yet held me in place. I was changed that day. Gabriel changed my expectations not only for myself but for other people. And then he proceeded to change *me*. Through hardship. Through love. Through never giving up on me or us, Gabriel taught me about commitment, and it is that commitment that has guided my actions in the five months since Gabriel's diagnosis. I owe everything that

I now am to him. The people we have saved so far owe their lives to him.

As I think of him with so much gratitude, I search for a memory that will impress upon him his importance, and it comes to me almost immediately: the life force lights I saw from the plane window in the colorworld once; life forces feed everything around them. I replay the wonder I felt that day when humanity became inexplicably significant, when something in me knew that their purpose was real. *That* is what Gabriel is to the rest of humanity. A light of rare proportions. And I want him to light the world for as long as possible.

Gabriel has been following along, and as I approach this conclusion with my emotions, his heart begins racing. "No," he whispers. "You promised."

I turn over to look at him in the colorworld, the colors somewhat blended and hazy because I am still crying.

'*Please don't make me do this,*' Gabriel thinks to me with tears in his own eyes. '*I will give you everything and anything, Wendy. Just please not this.*'

It tears me in two to have him plead with me. It twists the remaining shards to have to ask him for the one thing he does not want to give. I take his hand and hold it to me.

'*Please, Wendy,*' he begs, his breathing getting louder and louder. '*I can't live without you. I don't want to.*'

Emotion overcomes me and I cry for his agony. It's mine, too. It's the agony of separation, and I'm not even sure why I am asking this of him, why I feel I need it so badly. But I know he will survive, and even thrive. That's what Gabriel is best at. I say nothing, only kiss his hand as he continues to petition me. I picture a happy and healthy Gabriel in my head. I cling to that image so his desperate pleas won't break my resolve. Because now that the words are out there, and now that my soul has said what it has been holding in, I can't take it back even though I want to. I want to give him what he wants. What is wrong with me? I am a walking contradiction!

"Wendy, I can't," he heaves. "Please don't make me. Why are you doing this to me? Can't you feel it? It's tearing me up inside. I'd rather die, Wendy. I'd rather die than live without you. Can't you feel that? I know you can. Please," he moans, barely above a whisper, covering his face with his hands.

Tears blur my vision, thankfully, so I can't make out his stricken features. I can't speak; I can only cling to my conviction, and it takes every ounce of energy I have. Because Gabriel's agony is real. It cuts me like a knife, and my throat aches with longing. He longs for me. He sees every dream he ever had for us turned inside out and the contents tossed to the wind.

Gabriel is hooked up to several monitors at night, and one of the alarms starts to beep. Jeanelle appears in moments from the adjoining room. "What is going on?" she asks, rushing over to him, checking his monitors for placement, but she can hear him. He can hardly breathe.

She opens a bag and grabs a face mask out.

"Please, Wendy," Gabriel pants. "Don't do this. I won't survive it. I hope I don't. The wound is too much. Why do you want me to live without you? Don't you love me? Don't you want me in death also?"

His torment is unbearable. I should be breaking. It might be better if I do. I can't even see his healthy and lively face in my mind now. I have nothing to cling to. I can't do this to him. I should give him what makes him happy. I promised that, didn't I? I've said it's all I want, to make him happy. This is my Gabriel, the man I love, who loves me, who has been by my side all these months. And if there is a life after this one, I want him still beside me.

I look upward without knowing why. All I see is the textured ceiling of our hotel room, so I hang my head instead.

Haven't I already given up everything else? Now you want me to scar the one person that matters? How dare you make me do this!

I don't know who I'm talking to.

God, I realize. Funny that the two times I seriously try communication with God, it results in anger. But really, can't God step in with a miracle or something? Isn't that what God is known for?

But I remember Gabriel's claim: that God abides by rules. I scoff. I'm pretty sure, being the ultimate rule-maker, God could find a way. I'm pretty sure God *should* find a way. I'm not even asking much. I'm asking that we die together. I'm not trying to change the future with a vision. I'm not asking for long life or eternal youth. All I want is that our shared end-point—death—be at the same time. How does that harm anyone?

"What happened?" a familiar voice says next to me. I glance over to find Kaylen in pajamas. Jeanelle must have gone through Mark or Farlen to call an ambulance and the word spread. Ezra comes up behind Kaylen, wide-eyes, unsure of what to do with himself. He is so much older both in age and maturity than the last time he watched someone die. But in his eyes is the same vulnerable youth. The two of them will have Robert, thank goodness. If they didn't, I would ask Gabriel to stay alive just for them.

So why *am* I asking him to stay alive?

"Wendy, he's not getting enough oxygen," Jeanelle says from somewhere to my right. "I need to intubate him."

Alarm almost moves me, but my legs have gone heavy at the visual conjured by the word 'intubate.' It is a huge step closer to death, not life. I cannot think of it as life-saving because I have only ever seen it as people move toward the end, which is exactly what it will be for Gabriel.

"Wendy, you either calm him or I am taking over," Jeanelle says firmly and I know she means it. Jeanelle is good at her job of navigating our demands with her own expertise, and without my direct order, she will have Mark or Farlen move me out of the way.

Gabriel's hands are now scrambling under mine as he fights for air. I squeeze his hands flat against my chest, looking into his face as I take slow and deliberate breaths for him to follow. Tears are brimming from my eyes, but I fight to look into his as I breathe and beg another silent prayer.

Please God, can't you intervene this once? Can't you make this right? I've only ever wanted to do the right thing. But it's never enough for you. You always want me to give up more. And more. And more again. Will it ever end? You make me kill Gabriel inside by forcing him to live. And then what? Watch Kaylen die for real?

No answer comes, but I know, holding Gabriel's trembling hands as he haltingly mimics my breathing with great effort, that he will do whatever I ask despite the depths of his despair. This is who he is. He fights for life because I have told him I want him to. Gabriel gave me his will a long time ago. I knew it on our bathroom floor at my Uncle's house as he suffered but held on, and I know it again now. And I know that I will keep him alive, even though I don't want to.

I inhale and exhale, letting him follow the rise and fall of my own chest. He struggles to copy me, concentrating on my eyes and the feel of his hand over my ribcage. It is a long time, but he finally calms his breathing enough that it's no longer a wheezing, and the beeping in the background changes. Jeanelle is fussing with Gabriel's IV line, but I get no relief. Instead I let out a great sob of fury as I squeeze his hands tighter.

I don't want this! I shout toward that being that ignores me over and over. *I don't want him like this.*

But that is what it requires. I am giving him up. I am sending him into life as I descend further toward death, and the separation of our one path into two separate ones feels like it's ripping apart my insides.

I drop my head to his chest, clinging to him, ignoring Jeanelle's aggravation at my being in her way and possibly obstructing his breathing. Gabriel puts his arms around me, curing her of that concern. *'Why?'* he asks, confused by my insistence that he live but my reaction that he has agreed to. *'I don't understand why.'*

I have no answer to that. I don't know why, but either way I will pay. If I let him die my soul will whither. I have felt that this past week. But to force him to live means a broken promise. Right now I have no idea which is worse. Except for one thing:

To preserve his life is right.

Why? I ask the ever Silent Being.

Treated with more silence, I stare blearily at the room, strewn with bags and medical equipment—at least from where I lay against Gabriel's chest—and my eye catches on one thing: Kaylen's notebook. It has a neon yellow cover—which Kaylen insisted on so that it would be easy to spot if we misplaced it. Kaylen has organized it with color-coded tabs. I still don't know what they mean, but I don't have to. In that notebook are the names of people we have not only seen already, but that remain to be seen. They are the people that will have a chance at longer life if they take it. They are the people whose lives we can change if they let us.

But of course, most of them will not let us. It's silly, really, what we're doing. The book represents nothing more than an attempt to make more out of ourselves, so we can die with some kind of purpose, but we can't even do that right.

Except that some let us. And that's when a shaft of light peaks its way into my dark and somber state, slowly illuminating things I have forgotten.

Lifting my head, I put my hands on Gabriel's oxygen-mask-clad face. And with my mind, I show him the image of Kaylen's notebook.

Surprised for a moment, he draws the wrong conclusion. *'You don't need me to fix them. Ezra can make sure they're right,'* Gabriel pleads mentally now. *'I know you might not get the exact number, but you can get close. They'll probably never notice if we get a few strands out of place. But Ezra's good. He can tell if they are the slightest bit off.'*

Gabriel is right. He is the fastest way to accomplish the job, but Ezra is the failsafe and can make sure the swirls look right. But it's not that notebook of names I'm referring to. It's the *idea* of the notebook that I want to convey.

"Imagine," I say softly, uttering the first words that I have spoken in a week, "that I gave you a new notebook, many times bigger than the one that Kaylen carries. In it are the names of the people whose lives you will touch if you choose to live. Some of them will hate you. Many you will inspire. Others will fall in love with you." I smile and stroke his face. "And some I know you will save. You will be a force gusting through their lives, changing their course and altering their beliefs.

"Uncle Moby says that our futures are intertwined not just with each other but with every other person that has, does, or will ever live. I believe that. I have seen it. And I *know*, Gabriel, that you are a force that the world needs desperately. I am not asking you to find another me and live happily ever after. I'm asking you to live like only you know how to do so that you can find all the names in your notebook and help them just as you have the ones in Kaylen's notebook, and just as you have *me*. They are waiting for you. They are penciled into the future, but only you can choose to meet them.

"Uncle Moby also says that knowing the future is a burden because we always do one of two things: we either try to avoid a future or we try to make it. In both cases, it never goes right. It always does more harm than good. You know only one thing about your future: that you will die one day. And because of the circumstances at this moment you are trying to choose the terms of it. Regardless of your best intentions, you don't know enough about your future to decide what's best and..." I grip his hands tightly. "I love you, Gabriel Dumas. I want to give you what you want so badly. But some part of me knows it's not right. And when I tried to keep my promise, my body... it wouldn't work right. I couldn't feel without being overwhelmed. I couldn't speak without leaking out of my eyes. I couldn't do anything but exist with you—which was wonderful—but eventually life catches up. Circumstances catch up. And you have to do something. I'm sorry. I'm so sorry, Gabriel..." I lay my head back on him gently as my tears have gathered a new supply again.

"Wen—" he wheezes.

"I know," I quaver, horribly guilty over the misery I'm inflicting on him. He should not feel badly for having wished for death with me.

"No," he gasps, pushing me so I will sit up and look at him. "You... right...... always... right..." He wheezes between each word from behind his mask.

I hold his hands to my mouth, breathing in his scent, not begrudging the tears intent on falling. After a minute, I look up to see that we are surrounded by people. I spot Ezra next to Farlen.

"Get his wheelchair, please. We're going down right now," I say.

"Wendy, he's barely stable," Jeanelle complains. "And the paramedics will be here any moment."

"Tell them it's a false alarm. He'll hold on," I tell her, my eyes not leaving Gabriel. If anyone knows how to fight with solid will against lungs that don't want to work, Gabriel does. His commitment to me has never failed. The strength of it now builds an iron barge amid a tumultuous sea of anguish. He pulls the barge in closer, foot by foot, until he climbs aboard and I can tell he is prepared to fight for his life. He will die one day. But not today.

I barely hear the sounds of the mumbling people around me. I see and feel his admiration for me. His pride that I belong to him and he to me is infused in his touch as he moves his hand across my cheek. It does not matter that we are most surely going to be separated, him in life, and me in death; we will always belong to each other. If there is one thing I know about life forces, that was impressed upon me that day I saw them from the plane window sprinkled over the earth below like beacons, it is that they are meant to endure. I have no idea what happens to a life force after a person dies, but light cannot be destroyed, and light that bright cannot truly be lost. We will be together again. And if there is a god, I will not be denied.

46

'*One-eight-nine-two-six-eight-six-one-two-three-four*   in   the *chest, Ezra,*' Gabriel thinks to all of us.

There is a collective sigh among our small group. It took a lot of time and brainstorming to figure out how to get Gabriel in the water and able to see all of his strands. Jeanelle fussed over waterproofing his tubes for thirty minutes, as well as checking and re-checking his vitals. Mark and Farlen had to get in the water to position the mirrors in just the right way so that Gabriel could see all of his strands. It involved moving up and down the length of the pool to get the right depth.

I've spent the time in the water during the adjustment, holding Gabriel's hand to keep him in the colorworld, and marveling over the water and the mirrors. They are probably the two most unusual things in the colorworld. Water is invisible, which is good because it would be impossible to see the strands well enough if the water were anything but completely transparent. But mirrors appear exactly as they are. I'd think they ought to have the same kind of fluctuating colors like other inanimate objects, rendering them useless in the colorworld. Even glass is something I have to focus on in precisely the right way to see through in the colorworld. But the combination of the glass and the reflective surface reflects the colorworld lights just as they do visible world lights.

Once they had the mirrors positioned and it was time to actually count, I sat on the edge of the pool, touching just fingers with Gabriel so that we could keep our strands tangling to a minimum, and it worked.

Eighteen billion... That's close to the number we've been seeing in all the others who have a chest over head ratio.

Ezra voices the same observation, "I guess Gabe's the first of us to have a chest over head ratio."

Gabriel doesn't respond, only looks at the mirror that has been positioned above him and held in place with ropes that Farlen and Mark have had to rig up. His eyes focus intently as he sinks down into the water until most of his head is covered. He motions at Mark who now moves another mirror behind Gabriel so that he can get a good look at the top of his own head. A couple of times he motions for Mark to move that one around to different positions. He even requests an additional mirror be placed on the floor of the pool. Gabriel twists and turns over and over with effort for a long time and I worry he isn't going to be able to do it. He's full of disbelief, agitating me with every moment that passes. After at least forty-five minutes of this I am tired, cold, and about to lose it, but before I can say something, he preempts me and thinks, '*Four-nine-five-six-two-four-two-eight-oh-oh-two total.*"

"Did you say forty-nine billion?" I ask, staring in astonishment, thinking he must have said it wrong.

"We've never had anyone with over thirty billion before," says Ezra, bewildered. "And I take it back. With that number, you are definitely head over chest like the rest of us."

'*I know. I counted several times,*' Gabriel thinks. '*But I've gotten the same count each time so I know it has to be accurate.*'

So that's why he took so long. He couldn't believe the number himself.

"So how many stray ones?" I ask.

'*Four-three-oh-one-six-eight-four.*"

"Wow, dude. Four point three million. No wonder you look like crap," says Ezra, smiling as he punches numbers on his calculator.

Gabriel rolls his eyes.

"Hey man," Ezra says, biting his lower lip, "As if your strand count isn't weird enough, I'm almost positive that you aren't missing any from your head."

Gabriel's lips purse in consternation and we all look at Ezra.

He punches some more numbers again. "Yep," he says, looking up. "For starters, your head swirl is a perfect golden spiral. We've worked on enough people for me to know that when someone's head swirl is a perfect spiral like that, it's intact. When it's missing even one strand, the spiral's not perfect. I guess it needs all of them to flow exactly right. And secondly, if you take the chest number and the displaced number and you add them, you get 18,931,162,918. Subtract that from your total count and you get 30,631,265,084 as your head count which gives you the closest number to the golden ratio possible given your total number of strands. Head number on top and chest number on bottom, of course. A little too coincidental if you ask me. But I'd say, yeah, you definitely aren't missing any from your head."

Gabriel shrugs. '*Definitely odd, but perhaps it explains my natural ability.*'

"That's what I was thinking," says Ezra. "Plus, I told you that head swirl of yours is big. More arcs than any I've seen before. I don't think it's possible to actually pull any out, let alone put any more in. Of course, who knows. But it very clearly supports why you are so weird."

Gabriel rolls his eyes again and thinks, *'Four point three million is easily seventeen times the usual number we deal with. We're used to around two hour stints. There's no way Kaylen will be able to hang on that long without reenergizing—or sleeping in the very least. Farlen and Mark aren't going to cut it for one sitting. So what's the plan?'*

"I'll go until I'm tapped out, sleep, and go again. Rinse and repeat," Kaylen replies stalwartly.

I squeeze her hand. Gabriel and I may be the ailing ones, but when it comes to perseverance, Kaylen wins the medal. Each time we have fixed someone, she has had to go for hours concentrating intently on her task, no breaks. No silent, telepathic conversations like the rest of us can have. I can even sleep if it suits me. But I can do the math on this one. It's going to take over thirty-two hours to get this done. Of course, we won't be able to go without stopping, but Kaylen will have to endure long and tedious hours anyway. But from her emotions, I don't sense a bit of hesitation or complaint about the upcoming task. I plead again with that Silent Being to let me save her.

"Alright," Kaylen says in a take-charge voice. "Since all the strands go in the same place, I assume you don't need to count, Gabe? So all of us can be out of the water then. You may be able to count with all these strands everywhere, but I'm afraid I'm going to tangle yours with someone else's or insert some of Wendy's loose strands into you. I don't even want to think of what would happen if I did that."

Gabriel considers that possibility and then shrugs and mouths, "Okay." Then he settles into his plastic chair in the water, prepared, I guess, for a long stint of being in the pool. Thankful to be completely out of the water, I get wrapped up in a bunch of towels and a blanket Ezra brings me. I lie on a lounge chair, but Kaylen chooses a straight-backed chair next to me like she always does and begins working. Gabriel, meanwhile, lays his head back and closes his eyes to rest. I watch him for a little while, still wondering how he managed to count his strands like that without being able to see them all at once. It's beyond my comprehension. As I think about it, I honestly believe that Gabriel's ability to count is the most impressive feat of human intellect I've ever encountered. And in my time exposed to the world of superhuman abilities, that's saying something. And his ability is natural to boot… well, most likely.

I fade in and out of consciousness as the night—which started extremely late—wears on, but every time I wake up enough to notice, I can tell that Kaylen is entirely focused still. Mark and Farlen have both put their hands on me at some point. Jeanelle takes our vitals a few times during the night, checks that Gabriel's chest tube is still airtight, and generally hovers. She's bewildered by our setup in the pool. We have never let her in on one of our pool sessions before, but her presence is necessary this time.

It's morning when Kaylen finally stops. I look at the clock on the wall and realize she's been going for eight hours straight. I look over at her and her eyes are a bit bloodshot. All of us feel like we've been flattened with a steamroller; Kaylen has sucked us all dry.

Without much fuss, all of us go back upstairs to our rooms, ready for a good long sleep before going again. Jeanelle checks our vitals once more and leaves our room. I put my arms around Gabriel then and whisper, "I'm so sorry. I want—"

He places his fingers over my mouth. "I understand," he whispers back. "I'm sorry I made it so hard for you to do what you knew was right."

"You didn't," I say. "It still would have been that decision whether you had protested or not. At least you told me how you felt—what you wanted. I wouldn't have wanted to find out later how strongly you felt. If the situation were reversed, I'd feel the same as you." I blink back a few tears, experiencing Gabriel's gut-wrenching sadness.

He realizes the vibe he's sending me and whispers, "Apologies."

"Don't be. You shouldn't have to apologize for being sad. I'm sad too. I can't help it. That's emotion, it's terrible and it's awful, but it's also more wonderful. I have enough wonderful memories of you and our happiness together that my sadness won't win. I'll always be happy knowing that you love me, no matter where I am."

"Me too," whispers Gabriel. "But I shall never have enough happy memories. I want to gild the lily with you… Always."

I tuck my face closer to his chest as our mutual sadness of imminent separation entwines, and we became one soul, lamenting the same lament, remembering the same joy. We hold each other for a long while and I channel us into the colorworld so

I can share my mind with him, too. We send our favorite memories back and forth to each other that way, reliving so many moments with one another that were so full of joy: our first meeting, the time he told me I was head over heels for him and then walked away laughing, the moment I gave him the trigger-phrase and he held me for the first time. And there are tumultuous memories, too. Our relationship has been like a roller-coaster, but it has only served to tighten our bond. So many memories so full of life and experience together: the escapes from Louise, the separation after we were married, the first touch, the first kiss, the many touches since that have never ceased to thrill me. We have a past with so many sad moments, but so much more joy. We have fit more into a year of life than most people manage in a lifetime. And that's perfect, I think.

If I am going to die, and we must be separated, at least I will die knowing that our life together has been lived to its fullest. I regret none of the time since meeting Gabriel. I'm a new person, a better person, a person the old me wouldn't recognize or fathom could be real. It warms my chest to think of what I have become. For the first time in my life I am proud of it. While the transition will be hard for Gabriel, he will not ultimately regret our decision to keep him alive. For the first time in months, I am finally at peace with the idea of dying.

* * *

Kaylen is the strand-repair Gestapo. She allows us about six hours of sleep and then is at our door again, insisting that we get back to the pool. Ezra appears next to her as well, looking and feeling in such a way that has me sure that Kaylen must have accosted him for an additional reboot.

When we get to the pool and our hands are joined again in the colorworld, energy hums between us again. I don't know how Kaylen managed to recharge so much so quickly, but I've barely wondered when she answers my question, "The excitement of possibly seeing Gabe well is giving me a boost—that's why I was able to go so long last night. Anticipation kept recharging me enough to keep going."

And with that, we continue again. Gabriel is still exhausted though. As soon as she starts working, he's asleep again in his chair reclined in the shallow end. I realize I'm more energized as well and I wonder if maybe it was Gabriel and I spending so much time this morning reliving happy memories together that filled my own energy stores. Thinking that must be it, I decide to spend the time daydreaming. Happy memories ought to help replenish the tank. Mark brings us a late lunch while Kaylen works, and the sunlight streaming into the windows seems to give Kaylen even more drive.

I marvel at the power of light. A little goes a long way, especially in the darkest of times. There was a moment last night with Gabriel that I felt a great weight of guilt over making him live. I thought I would carry it for the rest of my life—as short as that is bound to be. I had accepted it as the price I was going to have to pay. But instead, now that we've made the decision to heal him and we're doing it, I get the innate impression that things are going to be okay. I don't know what 'okay' means for us, but I don't jostle with indecision and I haven't sensed that Gabriel does either. The right choice, I realize, will always be ultimately easier than the wrong one. It only seems harder at the outset.

As I lay pondering this and being more and more grateful for the peace it brings, the room grows brighter and brighter until I am seeing things with almost the same clarity I do when I am touching Robert in the colorworld. Life is dancing around me. The facets of every object blaze with dazzling color and movement. I feel like the entire room is bathed in rainbows that dance to the rhythm of my insides, which feel lighter than air. My mind is as buoyant as sunshine. High is the only word to describe it, and it washes through every part of me. My clarity is as crisp as the colorworld itself.

I think that Kaylen and Ezra are experiencing the same thing but they attribute it to the fact that we are all in high spirits, looking forward to seeing Gabriel whole again. Kaylen doesn't notice in the least, as intent as she is on her task. But I know better. The detail I am seeing now, the way the colorworld itself is more solid than ever before, can only be a result of someone's light improving. And my guess is that it's me. The realization brings tears to my eyes. Happy tears. My soul has gown two sizes and my heart seems like it might burst. The colorworld regains newness, and wave after wave of gratitude engulfs me at the miracle that it is, the beauty and secrets it offers. It's a wonder to me that nobody else notices enough to say something, but I don't care. I couldn't properly describe why I feel the way I do, why it permeates me in a way no other emotion has. I simply bask in it, not thinking, just experiencing.

Around dinner time, the strand-Gestapo begrudgingly allows us to break for twenty-minutes to eat and it's mostly because Jeanelle insists on it. I haven't been hungry since my transplant; Jeanelle has to remind me all the time.

"I'm in a zone," Kaylen says when Ezra tells her to take it easy. "I don't want to fall out of my groove."

Kaylen's in a zone alright. The girl has some kind of determined fire burning in her that has kept her going for the last four hours without needing Farlen or Mark in our group.

Gabriel, on the other hand, seems partially aware and partially comatose when we get him out of the pool. I can tell he's completely exhausted, although from what I've seen, he's been sleeping on and off. Gabriel normally has no appetite either. In fact, along with his chest tube, he also has a feeding tube to supplement his diet when he can't get food down. But to everyone's surprise, he wakes up completely when the food arrives. Without an explanation, he devours all of the fruit and yogurt that was brought for him. As soon as Gabriel finishes his own food, Ezra holds out half of his sub, which Gabriel takes immediately. The only sound he makes is an annoyed grunt as he eyes the sandwich after the first bite as if it has offended him. Gabriel hasn't been able to eat anything that solid for quite some time. It hurts too much, so I can only assume the look he gives the sandwich is because it scraped his raw throat going down. But he finishes it without another sound and then sits back in his chair and closes his eyes.

A corner of Kaylen's mouth turns up in a smile. We all know what Randy described of her own recovery, and that looked exactly like it, and we aren't even halfway through.

"Well dang," Ezra says softly. "I guess we'll make sure to have more food on hand next time we stop."

At that moment the door to the pool room opens and someone appears—the one person I didn't realize I wanted to see more than anyone right now: Robert.

I'm the first one to see him and I jump up—probably faster than I've done in months—startling everyone. I sprint to him, practically falling into him really. But he catches me despite his surprise and says, "Well hello to you, too." Then he chuckles and I can tell I've pleased him immensely.

"Uncle Moby!" I say exuberantly. I may be able to accomplish an energized voice, but my quick movements have cost me. My head spins and I have to hold on to Robert to recover. "Sorry," I say. "I got ahead of myself. Hold me up a minute so I don't fall over."

Kaylen comes up behind me then and hugs the side of Robert I'm not clinging to. "Uncle Robert, it is so good to see you," she says. I can tell she shares my relief and contentment at his presence.

It's clear that Robert is surprised by our reception, but in a good way. Once I finally recover I pull away and look at him, smiling. "How did you know we needed you?"

He raises his eyebrows. "I didn't. But you do?"

"Always," I say, leading him over to a chair and finding my own again. And then I launch into an explanation of the last twenty-four hours. We haven't had a chance to call him with Kaylen around pushing us to work every waking minute.

"You caught us in the middle of Gabriel's procedure," I finish, glancing at Gabriel who looks like he's fast asleep. I'd like to say he looks healthier, but he doesn't. He looks just as frail as ever, but his vitals are stable at least.

"That's fantastic news," Robert says, smiling widely as he leads me to a chair so I can sit down. "I imagine if he gets healthy, you'll be able to work more quickly. You at least look like you're holding your own."

"For now," I sigh. "I'm trying to enjoy relative health while I can. I swear I don't know what it's like to feel normal anymore, so I figure this ought to be considered 'good.'"

Ezra snorts. "She feels like crap, Uncle Rob. The whole time we're working, my insides throb constantly and my legs and arms ache like the circulation is cut off. I think that's why Kaylen works like a boss. She focuses on it so hard so she doesn't have to pay attention to the aches and pains these two put out together usually."

"In this case, it's anticipating one of them not feeling that way that keeps me going," Kaylen corrects. "Which reminds me, we need to get back to it."

"Are you up for joining our group?" I ask, thinking this is the perfect opportunity to see how much Robert can boost Kaylen's capability.

"Join your group?" Robert asks.

"Yeah," I say. "Remember how your light boosted my ability before? Well it should help Kaylen, too. Maybe help her move more strands at once. And right now, we are twelve hours into a thirty-two hour strand repair. And Gabriel is kind of critical right now. The faster the better."

"Okay…" Robert says. "Anything to help."

"That's interesting," Kaylen says hopefully. "Actually, I think I've been moving more than usual this past session. I can't count them or anything, but I could swear they are not only easier to see but easier to move. You think Uncle Rob will make it improve even more?"

I can't believe I totally forgot about increasing my own light. So Kaylen noticed too—by way of her ability improving.

"Yeah," I reply. "It should definitely improve it a good bit."

So we get dinner cleared up and we move back to our respective places. We have to rouse Gabriel to get him back to the pool and he groans for a moment before coming around. Then he realizes Robert is here and he reaches for his hand to shake it. He tries to give Robert a hello but starts hacking and heaving again. I have to help him focus on his breathing again for a couple minutes before we can get him back into the pool. Jeanelle, concerned about his oxygen saturation, insists on keeping his nasal cannula in for the pool, so we have to figure that out as well.

We finally start working once more. It's just Kaylen, Robert, and me this time, because my guess is that the less people to feed on Robert's light, the better. For a minute, Kaylen is surprised by all of the visible energy vapor but she opts to work instead of comment. It's evident right away that Robert is helping her more than I was. It takes less effort for Kaylen to get the strands out of the water. The channel of energy vapor that she uses to control the strands is thinner than what I remember from the time we worked on Randy in the dark. I can only to take this to mean that Robert's light is making Kaylen's mental commands more efficient. This frees up a bit of Kaylen's focus and I can now see that she's gathering a lot more strands than before. It will take Gabriel to get a definite count, but even Kaylen can tell. My estimate is that if she was consistently controlling a hundred and ten before, she's now moving closer to two hundred.

Her excitement over accomplishing so many more at a time energizes her and she's able to work for three more hours before I notice her slowing. Jeanelle starts putting up a fuss to check on Gabriel and so we decide to call it a night and continue tomorrow. Kaylen looks like a zombie and Ezra leads her back up to her room while I wait for Farlen and Mark to get Gabriel out.

Robert pushes my wheelchair while Jeanelle pushes Gabriel who has still not really come around other than to acknowledge gratefully that he's going to be able to sleep in a real bed and not a pool. I can't decide whether to be worried by his grogginess or excited. I opt to at least not worry because if it's bad, we're doing all we can to fix things. And if it's going to work, we'll know soon enough.

"So you're holding up?" Robert asks as he wheels me into the elevator.

"As good as can be expected," I reply. "But I'm so glad to see you. What brought you down here?"

"I knew you all were struggling after thinking Randy hadn't been healed so I came to offer moral support for a while. It looks like you don't need it after all though."

I reach up and squeeze his arm as the elevator dings at our floor. "Thanks, Uncle Moby. But that's not entirely true. There's still the problem with Kaylen and me, so we aren't out of the woods. But at least Gabriel isn't about to be intubated and we've got a little more time to work if he gets better."

"Kaylen also brought me," Robert says with a sigh. "I've been communicating with her in the past week quite a bit, and as you can imagine she's fairly stressed over this whole thing with you. I'm heartsick for her. The way she's been orphaned this way and continues to be faced with losing people that are important in her life... Ezra's in the same boat, but Kaylen is having a hard time feeling like she belongs in our family whereas Ezra seems to make himself at home wherever he is. Kaylen feels her adopted status strongly. And she has felt it her duty to preserve your family by trying to save you rather than herself. She sees you as vital to the family and herself as merely a bystander. I want to let her know that not only does she deserve life as much as you, but she's as much a part of my family as you and Ezra are."

"Oh Kaylen," I say, my shoulders slumping. Kaylen admitted as much to me months ago, but I'd forgotten. "Just before Randy's call, she finally told me she'd let us fix as much of her life force as we could. But I'm afraid she did it out of guilt rather than actually believing she *should* live. I'm glad she has you, Uncle Moby. I'll do my best to show her she belongs, but she couldn't have a better father-figure than you. I wish I knew how to save her. *All* of her."

"Me too," Robert says. "In the meantime I've been hoping I can find out her biological parents in hopes that it will give her some connection to her past, but I haven't had much luck. Carl is reluctant to give me any information on her adoption and I'm trying to use visions sparingly. But I'm getting the impression that her biological parents are no longer living."

"Speaking of Carl, did you ask him about the names we suspect are missing from the list?"

Robert is silent for a moment as he pushes me before saying, "Yes. He claims the missing individuals are people he hasn't been able to locate. Yet he refuses to give me any more information on them. I am sure there's more to the story."

With my emodar fully intact, and possibly functioning at a higher capacity than ever before, I take pause at what I pick up from Robert. He is holding something back, but Robert must know I know that. He hasn't attempted to hide it from me.

"Uncle Moby, is this one of those scenarios where you know more than you're saying. Only you can't say because it might violate the future?"

Robert stops in front of my door and comes around to face me. Jeanelle wheels Gabriel inside and works on coaxing him to get up and get out of his wet clothes. "I always know more than I say," Robert says. "I know too many things. But in this particular instance, I can tell you that I have purposely shielded myself from trying to learn more about Carl and what he's doing and his motives. Therefore as far as the individuals he has left out, I haven't spent any more time on it than to simply ask him."

I nod in understanding. "It's hard to watch him only do part of the right thing."

Robert smiles but it's strained. I know I'm on the right track, but I think I'm missing part of the story. After the last twenty-four hours I've had though, I swear I don't want to know.

So I change topic, sort of. "Do you think that Kaylen was maybe not adopted?"

More comfortable, Robert says. "I honestly would not put anything past Carl. Abduction seems to be the only reason I can think of that he wouldn't want to give me info on Kaylen's parentage." Robert smiles. "But don't you worry about it. You have plenty of other things to concern yourself with."

"Well I won't, but about Carl..." I say. "I can't help but notice you have guys still staked out all hours of the day to look out for us. I don't know if it's habit for you to be overprotective or if there still is a threat from him."

Robert strokes his goatee for a moment. "There still seems to be some activity. Mark tells me you've been followed on several occasions no matter what locale you're in. Carl certainly has an interest in keeping up with your progress. I'm sure he hopes you'll figure out a way to get well, and if you do he can solicit you for help in his cause—whatever that may be at this point. Either way, I'm committed to being on my toes about it."

I tilt my head for a moment, thinking about my last encounter with Carl. I've mulled over it from time to time, and something about it still seems off to me—like I missed something concerning his motives while I was there. Well obviously I did since he has withheld names from our efforts.

"Robert, do you think Carl works for someone else? Someone bigger?"

Robert holds his emotions in reserve enough that I know I've hit a nerve. "Why would you think that?"

"It's just that last time at the compound when those six people were sneaking up on our camp... And then how they all retreated once we started shooting... And then Sam and I ended up outside the research building because it sounded abandoned. The three that didn't get shot fled into the woods. They didn't go to the compound—the logical place for them to retreat to. It was weird. I didn't hear anyone there. And Carl just had that one bodyguard with him. And one of the first questions Carl asked me was, 'Do you have any idea what's going on here?' At the time I assumed he was being evasive and stupid, but I've been going over that day so much in my head, especially since my transplant at that weird hospital in Nevada. It doesn't feel right, you know?"

"I'll admit that the kind of force you've told me you encountered in the times you've come in contact with threats has surprised me. It does seem beyond Carl and Louise's pool of assets. But it's not entirely impossible. He could have billions stashed somewhere that I don't know about. And as for the compound, maybe he was planning on staging it differently and it didn't work out. And it was clear that day that you were ill, so maybe he changed his plans. Furthermore, he was around Louise for many years. Making you paranoid and confused about her purposes was her MO. Carl surely picked some of those skills up."

"You're probably right," I say. "In fact, I'm pretty sure the timeline on the vision was what it was so that I would be sick enough for him to notice and finally have the guts to kill Louise. That and the necklace pretty much sealed the deal for him. He definitely could have had a different outcome for that night planned out and then completely dropped those plans when they didn't work. Carl's no dummy."

"Whether it's Carl, or some threat merely related to him, don't you worry about it. Just focus on the task. Let me handle the rest."

"I fully intend to," I reply. "But I have one more question."

He tilts his head questioningly.

"Do you believe that there is life after death?"

That takes him completely by surprise, and he's undecided about how to answer at first. He reaches out and squeezes the top of my hand though and says, "Yes, I do." I can tell he has more he wants to say, but resists, closing his eyes and fighting back words riddled with indignation and desperation. When he can't control his mind to his liking, he turns and walks away, and I am left holding my hands rigidly in my lap so I don't chase after him. How does Robert do this? Know things and keep from wanting to know more? How does he keep from chasing visions to know more of the future? It takes great effort for me to turn my wheelchair toward my room and go in.

47

$\mathcal{T}$wo more six-hour sessions is all it takes with Robert in our colorworld group to get all of Gabriel's strands back in, and we do both sessions the next day. Kaylen is unstoppable. And when she sits back in her chair after the last strand goes in and she and I see the perfect swirl at Gabriel's chest, we squeeze each other's hands and I can see tears coming from her eyes. There's a bit of sadness there as she looks over at me, but mostly she's so relieved to see Gabriel whole. So am I. More than I want to admit since I am still a bit sore over practically forcing him to live.

Gabriel barely acknowledges the reflection we show him in the mirror. He just grunts approval and demands to never have to endure sleeping in a pool again. He falls asleep promptly after his strand repair, following a similar pattern to what Randy described. He wakes the next morning with a ravenous appetite. He eats everything brought to him—usually smoothies and softer foods that go down more quickly and easily—asks for more, and then sleeps again. He barely talks and his intellect seems to be shut down or shifted down several gears into eating and sleeping zombie mode. After a few days of this, he comes around a little more when he wakes up, but it lasts only an hour or so before he goes back to sleep.

I pay close attention to his chest sounds and his smell and determine that he is not only sounding better, but smelling better. I forgot how good Gabriel smells while healthy. It brings back memories of more amorous activities we did together while we were both well, and I keep having to remind myself that he is a recovering cancer patient, and I am a dying leukemia patient with little to no energy for physical activity. But the smell is intoxicating, and more telling to me than any other sign that Gabriel is getting well. Joy swells within me, and it's hard not to be hopeful although I have no idea what I am hopeful for exactly. Saving more people, I guess?

In the interim we take a fully-recovered Randy with us on our visits in LA and San Diego, meeting with some forty people. It becomes Randy and I that tell the story since Gabriel is asleep eighty percent of the time. And we are having far more success. Since Jimmy, we haven't met with anyone else Gabriel and I knew from the compound, but in LA we meet with Celine, Will, Gina, Davis, and Corinne—all people we know. All of them, including Celine who detested me, agree to allow us to reverse their energy work. Randy's testimony helps immensely since she was an authority figure at the compound for all of them. We've had to schedule them all for a later pool date because we need to wait for Gabriel to recover. His counting is still the fastest and most accurate way to tell if we've inserted the right number of strands into the right places. Robert stays with us for about a week, but then heads back to Monterey where his work is piling up without him. I know that he's helped Kaylen. She's more positive about the outlook of things—not positive about my fate but positive that life is going to be okay for her and less guilty about letting me work on her rather than myself. She comes to accept in some small way that she can only do what she can do. She's a bit less maniacal in her task and smiles more and a little of her bouncy innocence reemerges from behind her eyes and in her voice. I'm glad to see it there again.

I do my part, but I'm preoccupied. With death mostly. I am resigned to the reality of my death approaching swiftly. To confirm it, I begin to decline just as Gabriel starts waking up. It has been two weeks since we fixed his life force strands and when we wake up that morning, Gabriel is livelier than I've seen him in months. He has quite a bit of stubble, both on his face and his head, and he has put on at least twenty pounds. The transformation is amazing. And he smells delicious.

"Morning, Love. Might I say, you're looking especially pulchritudinous this morning. You have me so smitten with you I'm starting to think baldness becomes you more than hair."

"Pulchri-what?" I ask, hoping he'll keep talking so I can close my eyes and listen to the liquid cadence of it that falls so effortlessly from his mouth. It has been a *long* time since he has said anything without it being extremely labored.

"It means stunning, lovely, dazzling, beautiful, and what have you," he explains.

"Oh please," I scoff. "Blindness must have been a side-effect of fixing your strands. Although your vocabulary seems to be in working order."

"This is blindness?" asks Gabriel looking pensive. "I'll take it. Everything is so much more beautiful this way."

I smile at him and say, "So the hibernation is over?"

"I could climb the stairs of this hotel twenty times and not feel tired. I'd forgotten what it was like to be so physically capable. But..." he says, looking at me with sadness in his magnetic, fiery eyes, "I can't help but feel mentally lower than I think I have ever been. Maybe this is what they call manic depression."

"Don't be sad," I say, reaching out as he sits on the bed next to me. "I love to see you happy, and so healthy. It does my heart good."

"Wendy, I have to say, I have not given up hope yet," he says, and then hits the floor and starts doing push-ups as he talks, and it's clear that while he does look better, he's going to have to put more effort in if he's going to be as physically fit as he was before. "There has to be a way. With the help of Robert's light maybe your sight will fade slowly enough to get most of your strands back in. Furthermore, I still suspect that perhaps some portion of your ability must be natural. Carl and Robert both having a natural ability seems a bit coincidental. Furthermore, we know Ezra must have inherited his ability from his mother. There is something to genetic predisposition for natural abilities. There is also the question of the head over chest ratio among those that we know have natural abilities—although it doesn't explain Kaylen, does it... unless there is a natural portion to her talent... That would solve everything then, wouldn't it? In any case, lots of possibilities. Maybe we can prolong your life."

"Kaylen is my priority," I say. "We try to fix hers first. You know as well as I do that she can't handle both of our strands simultaneously. Poor girl's been pushing herself so hard these past months, trying to grasp as many as possible. I can't stand for her to feel guilty. I can't make her think I expect anything of her. This is how it is. I've had a year of the most wonderful life that anyone could ask for. Kaylen needs her wonderful life, too."

Gabriel does five more push-ups and then hops up. He sits down, pulling me onto his healthful sounding chest where I lose myself in the beat of his accelerated heart. I love the feel of it.

I have missed his body. I love his soul, but I am convinced that a life force, while it makes up a person's most essential parts, does not constitute the whole person. There is something about a body. My body responds to Gabriel's, and his to mine. Our bodies are programmed to each other. I touch his bare chest with my hands.

"What are you thinking?" he asks.

"How much I like your body," I reply.

"That is a statement rife with so many possibilities that it distresses me not to be able to carry any of them out," he answers with a lamenting sigh.

"I'm not completely broken you know," I say, calculating. "I'm sure you would be careful. Just because I am too exhausted to do anything, doesn't mean I'm too tired to receive it."

Gabriel mulls it over briefly and then he looks at me. "I don't think so. I'm not interested in self-gratification. And you look so fragile."

"Then gratify *me*. I want you close. We've both had to be so careful, especially you with getting your breathing too labored. But we don't have to worry about that now. I'm tired, not brittle," I say, deciding I want it very much.

Gabriel thinks again and then begins to kiss my neck so carefully. It's hard to remember what his kisses felt like when I was healthy but they feel very nice currently, even in the face of fatigue and the throbbing that has increased in my side in the last week. I tug him closer to me, wanting him ever nearer, wanting to forget what lies ahead.

And Gabriel responds, taking care of his every move, hardly taxing me at all. I want to respond with fire, but my body won't let me. This is all it can give me, but as Gabriel and I know, intimacy is more than physical pleasure. It's closeness and honesty. It's touching our souls together and listening to the sound. We have learned to do all of those things very well.

***

"Well this is bizarre," Gabriel says as he comes into our hotel room several nights later. I'm busy trying to talk myself into eating the food Jeanelle brought. But I'm so exhausted that the thought of swallowing that many times nearly has me in tears. We have fixed ten life forces in the last three days—all the people whose pool date has been waiting on Gabriel to recover. Robert even flew in to help us. It's not like I've had to do anything, but I'm still wiped, and I cried this morning when I saw Kaylen had taken the time to re-dye the purple section of her hair. I've needed any support I can get because we have six more in the next two days.

"What's bizarre?" I ask, setting my fork down because Gabriel's boggled emotions have hit me. Whatever it is he thinks is so odd has shot him with a dose of hopefulness. But just as quickly, his logic raises some serious doubts in whatever he finds so interesting.

He sits on the edge of the bed, a book in his hands that he's thumbing through, becoming more and more incredulous with every page he turns.

I lean over to get a look at the title: *The Republic*, by Plato.

Plato... that's philosophy, I guess. Gabriel has had a philosophical epiphany?

"Well I—" he starts and then flips through a few more pages slowly. Then he looks up at me. "I haven't lost my memorization capability."

I raise my brow. "You can still memorize books?"

He nods, moving through possibility after possibility but hitting a dead end. "I can't fathom how or why..." he says. He looks at me like I might have some explanation.

"But every other person we've worked on has lost their ability, Gabriel," I point out. "Are you sure you have it at full strength? You said you've always had a good memory..." I know it's a dumb question, but I have to put it out there because Gabriel having kept his hypno-touch manifested ability despite fixing his strands doesn't seem possible.

"Of course I'm sure. I might have noticed sooner but I haven't picked up a book since before my recovery. But after such a long bout of unconsciousness, I was warming up my brain a bit with some light reading. I had planned to devote some time to... your problem." He sighs, knowing I won't like that he is still convinced there is a loophole that will allow for mine and Kaylen's survival together. "Anyway, I could tell right away. It's like the page imprinted itself on my brain in the same way it has ever since you did hypno-touch on me. Do you think...?" he says, tilting his head at me.

My heart aches for him. "Gabriel," I say quietly, knowing exactly what he's asking, "you know the likely explanation has to do with your natural ability and your unusual strand count, right?"

"Well yes but..." he says, and I can tell that his logic is leading him in the same direction as me, only he wants to cling to hope.

"I know it's easy to take it as some kind of sign. But you know as well as I do that the logic doesn't line up. I have just as many strands as any other person. My strands are mussed in the same way as any other hypno-touch victim. You are obviously a special case. I have no idea why you still have your ability; I wish I did so you didn't have to live with what ifs."

"But Wendy, you aren't the same as everyone else. Your ratio and Kaylen's ratio are head over chest. No one we've worked on has had a ratio like that other than myself. Remember we even counted Robert's strands? He has a head over chest ratio, too. There must be something to that... like the sign of a natural ability."

"If there's some loophole there, Gabriel, then Kaylen has it, too," I point out. "It would definitely be a welcome miracle if it turns out we don't lose our abilities for some reason. But we have to do our best to save Kaylen first." I reach for his hand. "If we try to fix me before Kaylen and my ability diminishes like everyone else's, I'll never forgive myself. And neither will you."

He groans, putting his face in his free hand. "I know," he says, trembling. "You're right." And then he becomes vulnerable and agitated. It troubles my overworked heart, but I pull on his hand weakly so he'll come sit closer to me. He lays his head on my lap and sighs. "There has to be a way," he says. "I won't give up. If Kaylen keeps her ability, then you both can be saved. I'm holding out for that."

I bite my lip and look up at the ceiling to hold back tears. The likelihood of Kaylen keeping her ability is slim to none, even with the difference in our ratios. Despite my assertion not so long ago that having hope is never a bad thing, I can't help wishing that Gabriel would just accept what is. Maybe because I feel like I'll be letting him down by dying, as if I have any control over it. It's silly and illogical, but I start to beat myself up for making Gabriel stay alive. He is so harrowed and desperate. Because I share his feelings so regularly, I have to endure the throbbing of uncertainty and impending loss with him. It would be nice, as the dying person, to have more time to ponder things without so much agonizing worry going on around me that doesn't belong to me. But out of the necessity of our task, anxiety is ground into me so much that I have been working really hard to foist it off of me. When I do, peace and acceptance surface. But they are fading under the weight of so much negativity.

So I say nothing to Gabriel, only stroke his head and practice pulling myself out from underneath his heavy emotions.

Part III

48

San Diego to Washington. Arizona. Las Vegas. Florida to New York. Two days will mark eight months since Gabriel's diagnosis in November. It has been not quite five months since we first cured Briona in February, our very first hypno-touch repair. It has been almost three months since my transplant in April. And two months since Gabriel's strand repair in May. We have totaled one hundred and fifty-nine contacts from Carl's list. The other two couldn't be found. Forty-five and a half allowed us to manipulate their life forces. And today is the fourth of July, *my* independence day. Because today I finally get to return home and stop knocking on doors and being rejected. We have finished our notebook of names. It's time to save Kaylen, and right now that's all I want to think about.

Waiting in the terminal, however, for Robert's plane to be prepped, we learn that our scheduled flight is canceled because a huge hurricane that has made landfall just south of where we are and they have grounded all planes until it passes, which could be two days or more. It was probably foolish to come to the airport, considering how ugly it looks outside already, but I wanted to try, hoping against hope that we could beat the storm. We had plans to fly low over cities on our way so we could see fireworks displays from above, and I was looking forward to my first leisure activity in months. But all the money in the world, evidently, is not going to get us in the air any time soon. It shouldn't upset me; I've been away from home and shuttled from place to place for months. But it does. Massively. I want to go home. And save Kaylen. That is the last thing on my checklist—*the* thing. But I want my whole family around. And Robert is part of that family.

Seeing the look on my face, and knowing how desperately I want to be on the move, Gabriel says, "Do you want to rent a car? We can head west until we get out of the no-fly zone."

I lay my head back in my wheelchair, offended by the weather. I am no expert, but I am pretty sure it is *not* hurricane season. *What the hell, God?*

Oh yeah, I talk to the Silent Being sometimes. Maris was right. It's a great way to get stuff off your chest, and it's sort of become my habit to whine at the Silent Being whenever I'm irritated. Maris probably wouldn't approve of my language choice though.

"No," I sigh. "We'll just… wait it out… in a hotel."

Ugh. If I never see a hotel or a hospital room again it will be too soon. I try to adjust my expectations, to not be upset at this setback, but I had hoped, once I had done my duty, extended help to everyone that would take it, that I could have things my way. I could have the moments of closure I've needed to have with each of my family members one-on-one. I could do it in the familiarity of home and not in one of a string of hotels. Because I can tell they each need it. They need me to tell them it's okay, that *I'm* okay with dying and they should be, too. And I think I am. I'm most upset at not being able to give my family the time with me that they need. But I've spoken to Robert multiple times about it, needing his assurance that holding their emotional needs at bay until we push through our list is the best thing.

But it's been so hard to hang on to the reasons as we've been doing this. I've spent so much time being bitter, and that is not how I had hoped this mission would go. It's not how I've wanted to spend my last days. But I think the problem isn't me as much as it is the others. I feel what they feel so it makes it hard for me to really know where my own mind is most of the time. And I resent myself for preferring to have people outside of my emodar now. Even Gabriel is a hardship to endure. He's so depressed and anxious all the time. Despite the storm going on in his head, he has been pretty silent. He's at a loss for what to say, wanting to say a million things but wanting more to say the one right thing. He's still holding out hope, but he has slowly come to accept the most likely scenario: my death. But he doesn't know what to do with it.

Mark leaves us to make new arrangements for a flight out as well as a hotel, and Farlen walks up next to me to take Mark's place, tucking his phone in his pocket. I've come to know Mark and Farlen pretty well in the last eight months. Mark is a short, balding, old guy with a bulldog attitude that makes him perfect to lead Robert's security detail. Farlen is tall and lean and is usually expressionless. He's also exceptionally quiet most of the time, but he is always scanning the perimeter. I've never asked, but I am sure that Farlen used to do really high profile security. He has that look and professionalism about him. Ezra calls him Spock all the time, and it kind of suits him. Farlen has dark hair and slim eyebrows. Currently, Spock—I mean Farlen—has a rare half-smile on his face, his hands folded behind his back as he scans the crowd.

"What?" I say, trying not to let surliness come out in my voice, but I think my mood is going further south by the minute. My side is throbbing, and my neck is beginning to ache.

Farlen looks down at me, his perfect eyebrows arching charismatically and I wonder for a fleeting moment if he plucks them. "Did you need something, Mrs. Dumas?"

"Yeah, for you to stop smiling like that unless you're going to tell me *why* you're smiling."

He nods curtly and commences his expressionless stare once more as his head moves slowly from side to side like an oscillating fan. Despite his blank face though, I can tell something's got him at least mildly excited and he is clearly not going to share it.

I slump more in my chair and frown, fingering the frayed edge of my shorts. I even dressed for the trip home today: red tights, denim shorts, a white t-shirt, and navy gloves. I seriously want to go into a closet and cry for myself. I woke up so content, and now everything I envisioned is ruined. This sucks so bad. I spot Ezra and Kaylen huddled together nearby. I catch the words 'strands' and 'water' and I don't need to listen to any more to know they are again discussing ways to get more strands into Kaylen at once. They try to make it seem like these discussions are for Kaylen's benefit, but they always carry a lot of stress for everyone, which is a clear indicator that they all hope such talks will lead to saving me. I can't take the stress and anxiety when they discuss that stuff. My body, which is almost completely useless to me at this point, reacts poorly to high emotion. I have passed out twice because of it. I've received two transfusions in the last week just to keep me functioning, and aside from palliative drugs, I've not received chemo. We tried it a few times when my white blood cell counts started rising again, but I couldn't tolerate any dosage level. I've needed to be at least conscious in order to bring us into the colorworld, but chemo knocks me out.

I am so tired. I lay my head back because I can't hold it upright.

I smell Gabriel and open my eyes to find him on the other side of me. He puts his phone in my lap and gives me an apologetic look before going to where Kaylen and Ezra are.

I look down at the phone to see that it shows *Mike Dumas* as the caller. I haven't spoken to Mike since I told him to kiss off and leave me alone months ago, but today is not the day to start our dysfunctional relationship back up.

I hold it to my ear, but all I can muster the energy to say is, "What?"

"Hello Sunshine," he says.

I roll my eyes and lay my head back, my arm tired just holding the phone up. "What do you want, Mike?"

"Oh just some civility," he replies in his low tone tinged with the barest amount of mocking. "Are you drunk?"

"I am not drunk," I snap, though I think my words really are beginning to slur. That's not a good sign. "And I reserve civility for people I don't dislike."

"Fair enough," he says casually. "So I have a question."

"And I'm on pins and needles to answer it," I reply dryly.

"I bet. Look, I need it straight, and for once Gabe won't be. Are you dying? Honestly?"

"Yes."

Silence pervades for several moments. I prop my arm on the side of the wheelchair, thinking I would give anything to be lying down right now. My eyes won't stay open.

"Wendy?" he says, and for the first time I don't hear antagonism.

"What?"

He takes a deep breath. "Thank you. For saving my brother. I know it... can't have been easy. To convince him to stay alive."

I wouldn't have predicted that Mike's words would touch me so much. Why I should care about Mike at all is a mystery to me. But if I had to guess, I'd say that Mike's attitude has all been a show. If I hadn't been dealing with huge, life-altering decisions and suffering daily for them ever since I met Mike, I might have invested more effort in blowing a hole in his well-fortified exterior. But at the moment I can only return the favour of courtesy. "You're welcome, Mike," I say just above a whisper.

The line clicks off, and I think I should spend more time thinking about the conversation, how it might be the last I ever have with Mike, but my brain is spinning it's wheels. I'm too tired to think. I'm about to ask Farlen to adjust my chair so I can sleep when Jeanelle rushes up, her bag flapping behind her and her black hair coming out of her customary bun. "We need to admit you to a hospital," she says. "I got your CBC back, and you need a transfusion this minute." She looks at Farlen. "I didn't call an ambulance this time like you asked, but you need to get her to a hospital, and quickly."

Farlen moves into action, Gabriel has already asked to see the CBC report. Kaylen and Ezra are moving closer, their faces used to the worry they now wear. So many voices surround me, each of their accompanying emotions building to a fever pitch. *What the hell, why not? I said I wanted a nap, didn't I?*

Just before I drift off, however, I see Robert come into the terminal through the double glass doors. The instantaneous joy I experience at seeing him sends a jolt of energy into me. "Uncle Moby!" I squeal, sitting up too abruptly. This has to be what Farlen was smiling about; he must have spoken to Robert. And Robert must have used his omniscient skills to know we wouldn't make it back to him, so he came out our way instead to surprise us.

I reach out for him and he beams at me. As he closes the distance between us, my vision spins and I no longer know which way is up. Everything goes black and I'm falling.

***

"Please get me out of here," I whimper softly, because the last thing I wanted to see upon waking was the white ceiling tiles that adorn a typical hospital room. And I certainly didn't want to smell sanitized surfaces and the rubber tubing of IV lines. As if that's not bad enough, I remember that I am still in Florida, nowhere near Monterey, so I start crying.

"Wendy," says a voice, and I turn my head toward it, cringing because it hurts my neck to do so. But I grin when I see that it's Robert. Worry lines crease his eyes, but Robert's emotions are as steady as the sun. Though he harbors a vein of worry, the primary force behind his will is confidence and steadfastness that soothes my soul that has been tormented by the anguish of others for the past few months. Robert understands things that the others don't. He is burdened by things we know nothing about, just as I carry the weight of emotions of those around me, so he gets it. It is hard for me to imagine that I have only known him a year. I feel like he has always been with me, that he has always been aware of me—and he probably has.

"I love you so much, Uncle Moby," I whisper, tears springing to my eyes because my heart isn't big enough to contain my feelings for him.

"I love you too, Wendy," he says, smiling gently and squeezing my outstretched hand. "And don't worry. They fought me on it because you just finished your transfusion, but you should be out of here within the hour so we can take care of Kaylen. A hurricane won't stop us. We've got a few hours yet before the winds get too strong to drive in."

"You read my mind, and you are a miracle-worker," I reply, surprised at first that Robert is in as much of a rush as I am to save Kaylen. But then, Robert must know something I don't, as usual. He's here after all, knowing I would need him. I try not to imagine the possibility that he knows how soon I'm going to die and that's why he's in a hurry to help. "They've made me stay overnight the last two times. The way I see it though, I don't have the time to waste worrying whether a transfusion will kill me. I'm going to die soon and Kaylen is the most important thing for me to do. Nobody else has the same urgency." I frown.

"I'm guessing the past few weeks have been difficult," Robert says, scooting his chair a little closer to my bed. "With the others?"

I swallow a few times to keep from crying—this time for a different reason. "I think my emodar improved along with my vision a month ago while we were fixing Gabriel. It works from further away. I don't know what my range is anymore—especially with the three of them. They try to spare me their emotions but they still bleed into me if they're in the same room. I think it's also worse because they're usually negative emotions and negativity sucks at the space around it. Plus they have to touch me to go into the colorworld, and I think that puts me even more in tune with them." My heart hurts just thinking about the dread I now experience when I have to touch them. "I wish I could not hate being around them," I whisper.

"And how do *you* feel?" Robert asks.

"I'm not sure anymore," I reply. "I know what I *want* to feel. Happy. At peace. I used to feel that. But I'm losing my grip on it even when I'm alone. I'm too tired to fight to remember what I want, even in my own head, so I end up being angry because it's the easiest way to cover their emotions."

"So you're saying they are always down? No moments of positivity?" Robert asks. "I wouldn't have expected that from those three. They are all highly self-aware and for the individual seeking understanding, watching the death of a loved one is full of both lows and highs."

I think about it a moment and then say, "Honestly I'd expect that, too. But I think it's the colorworld. It heightens connection, deepens empathy. Now, even when we aren't in it, we are more in-tune with one another, and when someone is having a down day—which someone almost always is—it infects the rest of the group until everyone assumes they felt that way from the get-go."

"It sounds like the colorworld offers a connection that requires skill to balance."

I nod just barely, thinking, glad to be around someone whose emotions are *letting* me think. "It offers the highest of highs and the lowest of lows," I say, remembering that day we discovered Kaylen's telekinetic ability in the colorworld and how our positivity elevated with every passing second, bouncing off of each of us like we were mirrors, magnifying the joy of the moment to levels one wouldn't normally experience.

"Perhaps, Wendy," Robert says, "you need to stop trying to escape their emotions and instead guide them. If one person can bring everyone down, then one person can bring everyone up."

"Guess I better learn that skill quick," I say. "I don't have much time."

Robert does not respond to that, but I feel the effect of my words on him. I can't be sure, but I could swear Robert also harbors doubt about my death. Hope, I decide, is something that can never be fully lost, no matter how much you know about the future. And hope is dynamic. When hope in one thing is lost, it moves to a new thing. I should stop fighting against Gabriel and Kaylen and Ezra's hope, because it will never go away. But I should start using it, moving it in a direction so it can take root and blossom in the right place.

49

*O*ne would think I was leading these people on a death-march. Kaylen cries silently the entire trip to the pool. Ezra sits rigidly, stone-faced. Gabriel... he has his head in his hands, drowning in misery. Jeanelle, her movements abrupt and agitated, checks my vitals every five minutes; her opinion on having me taken out of the hospital so soon after my transfusion is clear.

The atmosphere outside this car is no different. The sky is nearly black and it's pouring rain for one thing. Traffic lights are swinging dangerously in the wind and trees are bending to it's force. We're driving through one of the most powerful forces of nature to get to a pool so I can try to save Kaylen. Why are the elements fighting against me? I wish Robert were beside me. But there are no extra seats in this van so he's riding in a separate car behind us.

We pass a billboard that's advertising a Fourth of July celebration that is to take place at a nearby city park. *That* won't be happening. In fact, I'd forgotten it was still the Fourth of July. I guess I'm not the only one whose plans have been ruined. It sure would be nice if it was sunny though. I close my eyes and imagine that instead of grey skies and boarded up windows, people are everywhere, gearing up their Fourth of July celebrations. The smell of charcoal and barbecue wafts into the van as we drive by a park, and some people haven't been able to wait to break out the sparklers and the poppers... I imagine hearing their small explosions from miles away and smelling the heady scent of sulfur mixed with the twang of metal. Freshly cut lawns and automotive exhaust from all of the traffic... The air would be full of the scents of people embracing life.

Jeanelle is checking my blood pressure again so I open my eyes and find the van exactly the way I left it. This killjoy atmosphere is exactly what I told Robert about, and I wonder what I can do to turn it around, to make these people excited about saving one of our own finally. We should be celebrating, and all I can find within me is anger at them for making this so hard, for literally sucking out any happiness I might get from looking forward to seeing at least some of Kaylen's life force repaired.

I close my eyes again, desperate for escape once more, but I start crying instead. Dammit, why does the weather have to be so dreary? I need the energy of thousands of people around me casting their eyes upward simultaneously, full of wonderment at exactly the same time. With my heightened ability, I just know I could feel it, even from a mile away. That kind of emotion doesn't have bounds. I need the sound of exploding gunpowder reverberating through my bones and filling the masses with excitement. I need their fervor. I need to not go quietly. I need celebration to push us all forward, to give us hope.

Instead there is silence, and I rack my brain for something to say to get these few loved ones of mine out of their funk. I don't think I have ever felt so mentally low. Kaylen, I've noticed, has kept the section of her hair bright purple since Gabriel was cured, but I can't find appreciation for it when her emotions don't match this show of support.

When we arrive at the pool, our driver gets within a few feet of the door and Gabriel carries me out and into the building— a closed country club. I anxiously await my wheelchair, and when it hits the carpet, Gabriel does not seem inclined put me in it, instead clutching me closer and fighting back irrationality as if I'm going to die the second he lets go of me. At that moment I am so hurt and furious that they are all working against me that I am ready to drop the whole thing. As immature as I know it is, I want to tell Kaylen, nevermind. She can keep her screwed up strands if that will make her happy. I'm done.

"Put me down," I say through gritted teeth.

Gabriel flinches at my rebuff, and relinquishes me to my chair, hurt as he backs away. But I'm too resentful to care.

I look between Gabriel, Kaylen, and Ezra. "Don't come near me again until you can find it in yourselves to not make my final days so torturous. Gosh! You three don't see what you're doing to each other and to me. It's like you—" I stop because Robert has come through the door and I am immediately ashamed of what I have just said and I can't stand the idea that Robert should witness me acting like a selfish child.

I pinch my eyes. "I'm sorry," I whisper. "I didn't mean that. I just... am out of ways to help the situation. And I'm tired. It's very difficult for me to endure your emotions constantly. I've never wished so hard that I could shut off my emodar, but that's really selfish too, to want to escape your sadness because it's not my problem. Please, tell me what I can do differently? How can I make this easier? I want to be happy today."

They stare back at me, stunned for several awkward moments. Then Ezra buries his palms in his eyes. "Crap, Wen. I'm sorry. I didn't realize..."

"That you were suffering so much," Kaylen finishes, her eyes filling with tears. Again. "We've been trying to keep our distance…"

Gabriel is crouching, elbows on knees, hands behind his neck. He says nothing, and he's not close enough to read precisely, but I still pick up guilt. I am a piece of crap.

"If I'd realized what was happening sooner, I might have saved us all a lot of grief," I say, feeling like dirt. "But I think sharing my emodar has made this so much harder for all of us. And it affects us even when we're apart. The colorworld has put us more in-tune. I've been trying to hide from it the whole time because I wanted to push on and get the names done. But I think you were feeding each others' grief. That's why it's been so hard to dig yourselves out of it."

"It's still inexcusable," Gabriel says, lifting his head. "Even when we've been around you, we've never offered relief. Only guarded heartache."

I sigh, hating myself more for making them feel so badly. "I don't want to do this. What's happened has already been done. And I don't have the time to go back and hash out every wrong. I want to move forward differently. Now, I want to say something to each of you before I go dying on you and I don't want you to get sad when it sounds like deathbed words. I need to do it. Is that okay?"

"Actually," Ezra says, stepping forward. "I think we all feel like jerks and we'd like to redeem ourselves before you get sappy on us. So let's do what we came here to do because we know you want it more than anything else. Am I right?" He looks around.

Gabriel looks up. "Of course," he says.

Kaylen's face is stricken, but she steps forward purposefully and pulls something from her jeans pocket. My purple scarf. I thought I'd lost it after I fainted earlier. She ties it carefully on my head and steps back. "One more to do and you'll never have to wear purple again." I squeeze her hand before she can back away.

I suspect that Ezra isn't going to let go of the possibility of my survival until we prove that it's not going to happen, and that means fixing Kaylen's life force first and watching her lose her ability slowly. Hopefully when we're done, everyone will have closure, and they can move to a new level of acceptance.

"Well let's go," I say. "Gabriel, will you help me get my suit on?"

He comes behind my chair to push me. I reach up and touch his wrist. "Will you carry me? Kaylen can get my chair."

He hesitates, but picks me up gingerly, and his heart catches on a barb of sorrow—which he immediately feels guilty for experiencing. I don't have a lot of strength, so I rest my head against his chest as a sort of embrace, hoping it conveys that it's okay for him to feel what he does. It's not his fault that I can pick up his every emotion. As he carries me down the hall and toward the locker rooms, my bag over his shoulder, he says, barely more than a whisper, "I'm sorry, Wendy. I don't know how to do this."

"Do what?" I ask.

"Let you go," he says, trembling over the words, and I can tell his throat is thick with unshed tears. We reach one of the changing rooms, and once we are inside the door, he leans against the wall. "I keep expecting some kind of acceptance to come. But I only become more desperate, like I'm drowning and I have no idea how to swim." He sinks down to the floor with me. "Help me," he whispers, looking into my eyes.

For the first time in a long time, I look back, facing the harrowing emotions that hide behind his eyes: the clenched despair, the suffocating fear of the future that makes even moving painful. It's a paralysis I'm familiar with. The mire Gabriel is stuck in is one I have been in before. And I have turned away from it violently these past few weeks because the last time I faced it, I ran away from it and into destruction. This time, with running not an option, anger became the coping method. I could have done it right this time. I could have been helping Gabriel, but instead I left him to fend for himself.

With no time to dwell on what I should have done, I think of what to say, and I do it by taking Gabriel's emotions into me and letting the familiarity dust off the memories of my past. I remember my mom and what it felt like to face her impending death. She was my rock, always around for me to turn to when I got in trouble or when life confused me. She was the grounding force that I took for granted, so much so that the thought of losing her was about as fathomable as losing the force of gravity. It immobilized me because I didn't know what direction would give me sure footing.

"I truly think I shall die of heartbreak when you leave me," Gabriel says, tears now falling from his eyes. "How do I live? You are my heaven. How can I ever be happy again when I've tasted heaven and then lost it?"

His arms about me tremble and I reach for his face. "Oh Gabriel," I whisper. "Wounds always heal. But the longer you stay in the desert, the longer it takes."

"Without you, the desert is everywhere."

"Only if you don't move," I say. "You just put one foot in front of the other. You make the choice to live each day, and one day you'll look up and realize how far you've traveled and that the ocean is right in front of you. And the ocean heals wounds faster, you know."

"Wendy," he whispers, aching, longing, reaching out to me with his thoughts. "I love you. I love you so much. When you die it's going to cut me so deep that even the ocean won't fix it. I'll never be the same without you. I'll never be whole. You're too much a part of me. You make everything more lovely."

"We're not meant to stay the same," I say. "I wasn't the same after my daughter or my mom died. I wasn't the same after taking care of my brother, after I left you, or after I was diagnosed with Leukemia. Everything I've been through that I thought I could never handle changed me. And it made me better. You will be, too. So promise me you'll change. If you don't you'll be stuck in the desert forever."

He tucks his face next to mine, kissing my cheek before taking my hand, kissing my palm and letting his lips linger there. "If I can't live with you, I'll live *for* you. I'll do anything for you, and if you believe I can, so do I."

"I do," I reply. "Just head for water, Gabriel. I'll even point you the right way. It starts with saving Kaylen, okay?"

"I trust you," he says. "You tell me what to do, and I will do it. I promise."

"Be you," I say. "Move forward and be you, and remember how much I love every part of you, how I want you to live so more people can know you and see what I see." I pull the purple scarf from my head and clumsily tie it to his left arm, unable to do it tightly with the excessive weakness in my hands.

"I trust you," he says again, looking at the scarf on his arm before standing up with me once more. As he helps me put my swimsuit on, his tender and lingering movements speak of reverence for me that I always feel is undeserved. I am a twenty year-old girl. I have made more than my fair share of mistakes. I was a pretty average student and a below average daughter. I am impatient and cynical. I don't possess mind-blowing skills other than those given to me by Carl through hypno-touch. I did not grow up aspiring to do anything that would change the world.

But here I am. I hardly recognize myself. How did I get here to this moment with a man crouched at my feet, putting my socks on with such care as if it is a priviledge?

"Gabriel, why do you love me?" I ask, as he tucks a blanket around me.

He stops and looks up at me, tilting his head slightly. "This could take a while," he replies.

"No, I didn't ask what you love *about* me. Everyone has qualities that are worth loving. What I want to know is why me?"

He doesn't consider it long as he puts my footrests down, placing my feet in them one by one. "Because you chose me."

50

"*W*e're looking for around twenty-two thousand for the head, Kaylee," says Gabriel, placing a hand on me to channel into the colorworld. I'm impressed with his clarity after our conversation. But I have always been able to count on Gabriel to jump into the task at hand with dedication. I focus on Kaylen now, as if my will alone can make her successful at this. I'm laying on an inflatable raft right next to the water's edge, wrapped in several towels and also covered with a blanket while touching fingers with Kaylen to avoid getting our strands confused. But I'm prepared to get into the water if need be.

Strands start rising into the air until Kaylen is straining under the burden of keeping her grip on them all. It is, by far, the largest bundle I have seen her manage.

'*Two hundred seventy-seven*,' Gabriel whispers to my mind alone.

I smile at her effort. She promised me she would try her hardest to save herself, and I'm thankful she's following through. In the past few weeks, she has tried different methods of holding the strand bundle together, like twisting it or tying a knot. But the strands appear to be entirely frictionless, and their draw toward the water below them is stronger than their draw toward each other. They don't stay in any configuration without Kaylen holding each strand in place.

A few strands drop off now and Kaylen struggles to pick them up, to keep control, and with one swift movement she shoves them to the top of her head, watching in the mirror held by Ezra in front of her on the edge of the pool. She almost loses them all then, by switching her viewpoint to the image in the mirror, but she catches them, and picks up a few that have dropped back into the water.

She grabs more strands hectically with her mind, bunch by bunch, and puts them into her head. Gabriel watches intently, keeping count.

She finishes her head without much problem, other than her frayed nerves. Gabriel lets go of me since his part is done. The rest of the strands all go into the same place now. Our plan is to have only Robert and Kaylen touching me so as to maximize on Robert's light, therefore keeping Kaylen's ability at maximum capacity. With Gabriel no longer touching me, I catch the slightest improvement in my vision, verifying that light truly does get spread evenly among the people I touch. Robert, I think, must be practicing some kind of meditation behind me. His mental presence is barely there, and his hand rests lightly on the back of my neck.

Before starting on her chest, Kaylen closes her eyes and gathers her nerves back in. Then she concentrates on the loose strands in the water, and we wait for the process to start once more. With Robert's light, the energy vapor, representing her stream of consciousness, extends out from her life force and toward her strands like an intricate spider web. She is definitely moving a record number. I have no idea how many without Gabriel to tell.

She brings them to her chest and they leap in. Kaylen lets out a small gasp, and confusion overcomes her. She lets go of me momentarily and bends her arms and legs as if to test them.

"What is it?" I ask.

"Did you feel that?" she asks. "It's like... my brain went fuzzy or something. Like waking up in the morning and not being able to make sense of things right away. I'm not sure how to describe it. My body feels numb somehow." Testing her arms again, she shakes her head.

"Well you still look the same," I offer.

She shrugs. "Let me get back to it then." She touches my fingers again, her focus moving back to her strands.

But something is wrong. With Robert touching me, I should see the energy vapor between Kaylen and her loose strands, but I don't. I can certainly feel her trying, and I look closer, seeing that there is, in fact, a bit of energy vapor moving away from her, but it's not getting far and nothing is happening. Kaylen becomes flustered.

"What's wrong?" I ask.

But she doesn't answer. Instead she's concentrating harder than ever. She stares into the water, her eyes unmoving. She does this for about a minute and then gasps for the breath she was holding. "I can't move anything!" she says, looking from me to Gabriel.

Gabriel steps forward and touches my skin to come into the colorworld. "Try again?" he asks, his pulse accelerating and panic driving a hole into his usually composed mental state.

Kaylen does, and the same fleeting stream of energy vapor moves from her chest and funnels outward, but it dissipates before it ever reaches the water. She shakes her head. "It's not working!"

She lets go of me and puts her arms on the side of the pool, concentrating on a nearby plastic chair. The energy vapor moves a little further away from her this time, but it loses direction before it reaches the chair.

"Ezra, get me something smaller," Kaylen demands.

"Smaller how?" he asks, frenzied and in search of something that matches Kaylen's criteria.

"Smaller!" Kaylen shouts.

Ezra bounds over to his bag and yanks out a shirt. "Is this small enough?"

Kaylen doesn't answer; she focuses on it. The same thing happens.

"Bring it closer," Kaylen says, struggling to keep calm.

Ezra walks forward until he's a couple feet away from her. Kaylen concentrates again and this time her energy vapor stream connects with the shirt, which then flutters in Ezra's hands. But it doesn't leave his fingers.

"I don't understand!" says Kaylen. "Why did it go so suddenly?" She looks at me and then Gabriel for an answer. But we're both as stunned as she is.

When we don't reply, tears spring to her eyes.

"I take it that abilities usually wane more gradually?" Robert says.

"Yes," I reply softly. "She had all of her ability after she put in her head strands. And she only put in a few hundred to her chest. That shouldn't have made her ability diminish so quickly. I... I have no idea why it would do that."

Gabriel's composure is crumbling, but he says nothing.

Kaylen, meanwhile, lets out an impassioned growl and pounds the surface of the water.

To have watched Kaylen lose her ability as gradually as the others would have been disappointment enough. But this is beyond anything we expected. It's much, much worse.

"I told you we should have fixed you first," Kaylen sobs. "This was pointless."

I hate to admit it, but she is kind of right. We might as well not have fixed any at all considering how few we managed to get in. But we could not have guessed at this outcome.

Not knowing what to do or say, I stare at Kaylen's strands in the water in dumb confusion. This is not how this was supposed to go at all. I can't even save her *a little*?

Loose strands shift with the current of Kaylen's movements. Her head is in her arms that are folded on the side of the pool as she releases a dam of emotion. I watch the strands just... float there. How can something so small and vulnerable defeat me like this? And how is this an ending? I try to imagine accepting it, leaving this place and going back to the hospital, most likely, as I wait to die, thwarted in my final efforts to make things right.

It doesn't compute. This isn't just unfair. It's unjust. It's... not even logical. Fixing Kaylen has been the finale that I was sure would make everything better, that would allow my family to get some kind of victory. How does something feel so right but end up going so wrong?

I feel betrayed by my own faith, and I didn't realize what a huge deal that would be, how frightening it would be.

Kaylen lifts her head finally, her red cheeks streaked with tears. "I'm sorry," she whispers.

That Kaylen would apologize to me for not being able to save her own life clenches my heart. She just wants to give me my dying wish and it's killing her that she can't. I just want to save her. Why can't I save her? Tears come to my eyes finally to see her so sad and to know that she could fall ill next week and no one would be able to do anything about it.

Distress leads to anger. Anger over everything I've been put through yet being unable to have a single thing work in my favor. In fact, everything has gone precisely *not* my way, exactly as if there are powers combined against me. And now this. The epitome of injustice. A slap in the face.

Someone's hand rests on my head and a voice says to my mind, '*Life disappoints us in order to get our attention, Wendy.*'

It's Robert, but he releases me, stands up, and heads for the door.

"Uncle Moby," I cry after him, struggling to sit. "What do I do?"

He doesn't answer, but pushes through the door, disappearing from my sight.

"Damn you, Uncle Robert, this is not the time for being cryptic," I mumble, my arms shaking as I try to hold myself up. Gabriel catches me before I collapse back on the mat.

Despite my irritation at Robert, his words stick. This feeling. It was the same feeling I had over Gabriel when we were separated. All creation seemed to be working against me. But at the end of it, when I finally stopped trying to force things my way, I saw that all those things were moving me somewhere. And I was almost too late in seeing the message then.

And I am missing the message now.

That realization slams into me, knocking the frantic anger right out of me. I even feel short of breath because of it.

I try several deep breaths but the feeling doesn't go away. In fact, it kind of hurts to breathe. Instead, I close my eyes, and think about Kaylen's life force, about how I need to fix it. I become discouraged quickly because if there's a message written in the fact that Kaylen lost the bulk of her ability so quickly, I have no idea what it's supposed to be. Maybe nothing. Maybe it was meant to get my attention and nothing more.

Well that's doesn't sound right... And nothing else about the last few weeks grabs my attention other than Gabriel mysteriously keeping his ability... And today with the dumb hurricane keeping me trapped here. Last time, when I touched Gabriel for the first time on that balcony, it was the weather that grabbed my attention, made me think.

Extra strands... sudden zapping of an ability... reversed ratios... hurricanes.

I groan, fighting to not let frustration overcome me. But I have no conclusions, and I am out of time.

I think of the Silent Being then, AKA God. Because what else does a person do when in a helpless situation? Gabriel said once that God is knowable because he goes by the same rules as the rest of us. I was thinking more about scientific laws and stuff at the time. But I've seen a lot of things that are outside of our current scientific understanding. If God can do things like those of us with life force abilities, he ought to be capable of telekinetically putting Kaylen's strands back where they go.

But capability and rules are two different things. But they are interdependent. Robert taught me that. In fact, it is Robert's rules that make his ability so effective. He follows those rules so that he doesn't force someone to unwittingly pay the price for the miracles he's able to render. Robert tries not to disturb the natural progression of events unless he can be comfortable with the price, and somehow he manages to come out on top and is actually able to see more of the future than one would guess, simply because he is so strict with himself. I bet God does the same thing. Except He knows even more than Uncle Rob. So there must be a price for God's direct intervention. I'm not going to try and guess what that might be. I do know, however, that Robert says that information is almost always a safe bet. So I can ask God for information, can't I? If there is a way for me to fix Kaylen, then surely he can tell me.

Okay, you, I think to the Silent Being who I hope, for once, will not be silent. *How do I fix Kaylen? Let me be the price if there is one. I'm listening. I'm trying. I need to do this. Help me.*

Kaylen has been looking at me and becoming more and more resigned. Gabriel is holding on to me tightly, and it seems like he's hanging on for dear life, like he expects me to die right now. It kind of hurts my chest, but it keeps my breathing under control.

I look down at Kaylen's loose strands again, searching for inspiration, begging to know what to do, but the Silent Being doesn't answer, or He must not exist. Or He must not care. Or maybe the answer is right under my nose and I'm too much of an idiot to see it.

One of Kaylen's strands is floating near the surface, the same one that looked so vulnerable, but now it's mocking.

And then... inviting.

I reach out, simply because it feels like the right gesture. We've tried to manipulate the strands with our hands in the water before and they've always gotten tangled with our own. I don't expect that reaching out now will do much other than possibly move the water, which might make the strand shift position a little with the current. But that's not what happens at all.

I'm holding Kaylen's strand, but my hands aren't doing it. My own life force strand—one of the loose ones—has grabbed a hold of her strand, seemingly as I will it. One thread of silk wrapping around another. My eyes widen in shock. I perceive nothing with a tactile sensation, but with awareness that resides outside of touch.

I am in complete disbelief. Maybe hallucinating is a symptom of approaching death. I go along with it though, moving the strand toward her chest where it leaps from my grasp and plunges into her chest.

Gabriel gasps.

"Did you just grab her strand with yours?" asks Ezra. He must have grabbed on to me at some point. I don't pause to discuss it though. I plunge my hand into the water again, and several of my strands reach toward the next closest silken thread, grabbing it like tiny tentacles. I plunge it toward Kaylen's chest where it quickly embeds itself. I need to move more. Grateful that I have my swimsuit on, I push away from Gabriel and into the water, fighting the weakness in my body, my chest now throbbing as I breathe more heavily. Gabriel comes in behind me though, holding me upright.

We are in a section that is only about four feet deep, so I don't have to reach far to find more strands. I don't even have to move my fingers. I reach my arm out because it's instinctual, but it's my strands that do the work. I just will it and my own misplaced strands grab hold of hers. Again and again I reach out under the water. Sometimes my strands grab several of hers at a time, and I lift them out and hold them to Kaylen's chest.

As time wears on, I feel my body weakening. I'm lightheaded and short of breath in the worst way. But I ignore it, consumed with what I am seeing with my eyes and what I now sense with my own life force. I don't move now. I just let Gabriel hold me up in the water. My displaced strands feel like extra appendages the longer I work. Kaylen is no longer in the colorworld with me, but she knows what I'm doing, Ezra having explained it to her along the way, because he got in the water with us at some point so he could touch me and see.

Getting better and better at controlling my own strands, I'm eventually able to grasp some hundred of hers with some hundred of mine. I've even managed to use my strands to hold my life force away from hers so they don't tangle. With every 'strandful' that I grab, I search out every single one of my displaced strands, willing them forward so they can get more of Kaylen's strands into her at once. The only thing that slows me down is searching for all of Kaylen's loose strands from her bulk of billions.

Soon, I can't see any more of her wayward strands. I look from side to side to spot any I missed.

"You got them all," Gabriel says quietly, awestruck.

Relief overcomes me, counteracting the adrenaline I've felt coursing through me this whole time. And now that I'm finally paying attention to my body, I realize I am gulping for air. And it hurts. A lot.

"Ga—" I try to say, falling back into his arms, but panic engulfs me as I recognize that I can't breathe.

"Wendy!" Gabriel says, holding me close to him.

He says something else but I can't hear him over the sound of my own panting. My vision fades also, and within seconds I lose consciousness.

51

A wind is beating at my back. It hasn't let up since I came here. I've retreated as far away as I can to escape it, and I'm so tired that I can ignore it for a while, but eventually the relentlessness of it keeps me from the quietude I crave. I want to find somewhere darker where the wind won't find me, so I burrow further into my head, curling up tightly. But it's as loud as ever, and it's empty here. In fact, I'm not quite sure where I am.

My instinct, which comes rather suddenly and out of nowhere, is to yell at the wind to shut up, but I'm not sure how to do that. There is just the wind. So I move toward it, intending to push it away.

That tiny movement shifts the wind into better focus: it's not wind.

It's whispering.

But it's so quiet I can't make out the words. I reach for the sound, straining toward it, intending to tell whoever is speaking that they need to be quiet.

'*There is an underground chamber like a cave,*' says the voice, '*with a long pathway that reaches the light outside. In the chamber are men who have been prisoners in that place since birth. Their legs and necks are fastened in such a way that they can only look straight ahead of them and cannot turn their heads. Behind them further up the cave, a fire is burning.*'

The whispering voice continues but I don't know what it's talking about. It seems like it might be a story, but I can't visualize what the words mean. I'm more interested in *who* is saying them though, so I move closer to it, and though I couldn't say why, I think the words are directed at me.

'*...A curtain has been built between the backs of prisoners and the fire...*'

Why is the voice not making any sense?

'*The puppeteers are carrying all sorts of figures including men and animals along behind the curtain so that they cast shadows over the heads of the prisoners and onto the wall they face...*'

I search for my mouth again so I can speak to the voice, but I don't know where it is. I can only listen. I'm so tired. I wish they would be quiet.

'*Would the prisoners see anything of themselves or their fellows except the shadows thrown by the fire on the wall of the cave? How could they see anything else if they were prevented from moving their heads all their lives? They would suppose that the shadows they saw were the only reality there was.*'

The longer I listen, the more aware I become that the voice carries with it more than merely sound. It also carries an inkling of feeling. Liveliness and interest. Both of these things bring me more awareness, and I begin to wonder why it is I can't really move and why I can't speak.

'*Imagine one of the prisoners was unbound and told to stand up and turn around. What if he were to walk toward the fire and the curtain and the puppeteers? Looking at them would be painful, would it not? He would be too astonished to look upon the objects that he used to see as only shadows.*'

Though the voice is just a whisper, its delivery is familiar. I become intrigued, something I had forgotten I could feel. And as it warms me over, the voice becomes even more clear.

'*What if he were told that what he used to see was purely nonsense and that what he was now seeing was truer and more real? What if he were asked to name the objects which passed in front of him? Would he know them? Wouldn't he think the shadows were truer than what he now sees? But then what if he were pulled up and out of the cave entirely? It would be unbearable, wouldn't it? He would be blinded by the glare, unable to perceive any of the objects until he grew accustomed.*'

The whisper pauses and sighs then, remaining silent for a moment. And I'm trying to figure out how to talk to it, becoming flustered that I can't. Something is wrong with me, and I wonder why I'm only just now becoming upset by it.

'*This story reminds me of you,*' it continues. '*You are like that person who was pulled up out of the cave and into the light. The colorworld, of course, being the blinding light. The rest of us live in mere shadows, incapable of seeing the true nature of things.*'

The voice must really be talking to me. But then it continues, as if referring back to the story.

'*At first he could endure only shadows, then reflections. Then perhaps he'd be able to observe the objects themselves. Eventually he would be able to look at the sky—the stars and the moon. And lastly he would be able to look at the sun itself without a medium.*'

I know this voice. I know it but I can't remember from where or when, but it excites me nevertheless.

It stops again for a brief interval before saying, '*Mi encantadora doncella, you have brought me out of Plato's cave with you, and without you I cannot see a thing. And I fear that nothing will make sense again. Your life force is still here, so you must be, too. Please, won't you speak to me?*'

I know those words, *mi encantadora doncella*. It awakens something in me, a little embarrassment, a little pride, but mostly familiarity so strong that I'm sure I must know the voice very well. And I like… connecting to something. It's new. And it's so wonderful that imagining going back to where I was before is terrifying. That was… alone. I don't want to be alone again. With these feelings I am… here. Afraid of losing the sensation, I cling to the feelings, thirsting for more. And they come as if simply wanting them turned on the faucet. Growing more forceful, the emotions release in one great torrent that's overpowering at first.

I try to shut it off, thrashing out with unseen hands to dam them back up. *Too much,* I think, surprising myself that these are *my* words, and not the illusive but familiar whisper.

'*Wendy? Wendy! Was that you? Are you here?*' says the voice.

My name. That is my name. A wash of hopefulness invigorates me, the most intense emotion yet, and it tastes delicious coupled with the relief at finding out that there is more to me. I have a name! *Wendy. My name is Wendy.* I want to say it over and over. *Wendy. Wendy. Wendy.*

'*Yes!*' the voice says, interrupting my chanting, full of glee. It's louder now. '*Your name is Wendy. Do you know who I am?*'

Joy encompasses me now, stealing every bit of my attention. I can't find the wherewithal to speak now. I can only find enough to feel. The joy is like sunbeams radiating through my whole being… sunbeams. I know what those are! As I think it, I see it. Yellow light cutting through puffy white clouds, like hope filtering from above.

Like feeling for the first time when the voice said encantadora doncella, the visual of sunbeams now release a tidal wave of images. At first I only see them as colors rushing by too quickly to process, and each one comes with its own thread of emotion. I'm having a hard time wrapping my ever-growing awareness around it all. Eventually though, I find the ability to grab on to images as they pass and look at them more closely. I see faces first. I know all of them, but I can't put a name to them right away. But then one appears with a tanned complexion; a soul patch; a wide, mischievous grin; and probing eyes. I know that this is the person whose voice has been speaking to me. And I know his name.

Gabriel.

'*Yes!*' says Gabriel's voice now. '*I'm Gabriel. And I'm here, right beside you, holding your hand and waiting for you to wake up.*'

'*Wake up?*' I ask him, purposely now. Speaking to Gabriel like this is also familiar. And I'm confused, because something is still not right. If I can see images and people, where am I? Why can't I feel me? Why can I only hear Gabriel and not see him?

'*You've been in a coma for five days,*' Gabriel answers. '*I've been trying to reach you day and night. This is the first time you have spoken back to me. And I need you to wake up. If you don't, you are going to die and I will never hear your voice again.*'

It takes me a moment to process what his words mean. More images come to mind, more understanding lights me up, and for the first time, an edge of fear creeps in. '*Don't lose me,*' I say firmly, because I'm not sure how to wake up. Gabriel found *me,* so clearly he has some power that I don't. Every time he speaks, it moves something within me that makes me feel more alive, more aware. '*I don't know where I am,*' I say, frightened that I will be stuck right here, or worse, back to that place I was earlier when I was alone and didn't realize it. '*I need you,*' I say, disappointment welling up in me over my helplessness. '*I can't do it by myself.*'

'*I'm here,*' Gabriel says soothingly. And then, with a bit of affront, '*Heavens, woman, do you know what I've been through just to get you speaking to me now? I have no intention of leaving you. So how about you wake up already so we can get on with the business of fixing you?*'

I have no idea what he's talking about, but he sure sounds and feels confident. '*Then wake me up,*' I command.

'*I told you, I've been trying,*' he says with some amusement. '*But unfortunately, Love, I don't have control of your body or your mind. You have to do your part.*'

My body. I was thinking I had one, but I don't know where it is. '*I can't find my body,*' I tell him. '*Where is it?*'

'*Right beside me. And your life force is still with it. Mostly. You need to search for it with your mind. It will help you wake up.*'

Frustrated that he won't help me, I say, '*How?*'

He doesn't speak for a moment, and I think I can feel him pondering it. *'The first words you said were "too much." Why did you say that?'*

'I felt... things. It was hard to feel them and I didn't like it,' I reply. *'It brought me out of... where I was. You did it. Not me.'*

He considers that, and then says, *'So you're saying I made you feel things you didn't like, so I need to do that again?'*

'I don't know. You said you have my body. Why don't you wake it up?'

'Okay, okay,' he says. *'I get it. You aren't fully yourself because you aren't awake. Let me think about it... Oh! Got it. My brother came by earlier.'*

'Your brother?'

'Mike. You know. You can't stand him.' And then he chuckles. *'I see you've wiped him from memory at the first opportunity.'*

'Mike,' I seethe, having finally pictured the burly man with a compression shirt and a bad attitude. He's got a self-satisfied look on his face in my memory, filling me with distaste.

'Yes. Mike,' Gabriel says. *'I've been in perhaps the lowest spirits of my life the last few days and he came by to get a look at you and... Well let's just say he tried to persuade me to stop keeping you alive in what started off as a seeming well-intentioned way, but it evolved into demoralizing and insulting. I swear to you, Wendy, I do not understand what that man has against you. It is beyond my comprehension. Something has taken him over in the past year and I simply won't stand for it anymore. I chased him outside where we proceeded to have a fist fight over it like a couple of rough and tumble boys. I have to admit it felt good to release some stress even if he did pin me in the end. I'm not in as good a shape as I was before cancer. Anyway, when it was over, I told him I didn't want him in my life ever again. He didn't say a word. Just walked away.'*

'This is supposed to help me find my body?' I ask, stretching out to find it again, imagining arms and legs, but I'm wondering if they've been amputated.

'No, it's supposed to help you find the rest of your mind. Plus, it was only two hours ago that this happened. When I came back into your room, your heart rate was bouncing all over the place like you knew what was happening. I almost darted out to get Mike to come back and insult you more, but I couldn't bear to leave you any longer. I tried calling him. Nothing. That's when I started reading to you again in the colorworld. And now here we

are. In a roundabout way, I have Mike to thank that you are now at least partially aware, and I was hoping the excitement of the story would invigorate you somehow. I'm still a bit high from it myself. Now, I'm trying not to nag too much, but I really do need you to try harder to wake up.'

'*Gabriel, I don't know how,*' I protest somewhat angrily.

'*Mike said you'd never wake up,*' Gabriel replies.

'*I don't care about Mike.*'

'*He said your ability to sense emotions was the only thing that held us together. Without it, we never would have lasted.*'

Memories of Gabriel flood me, all of the things we have shared and been through. How would Mike know *anything* about what holds us together? '*That's a lie!*'

'*Prove it to him, Wendy. Wake up and let's fix your life force. You'll lose your ability, but I know our commitment is deeper than life force abilities.*'

'*I don't know how!*' I plead, struggling against the bonds around my arms and legs, and even my mind.

'*He said you were just another stupid girl I got obsessed over.*'

'*He's an ass!*' I reply, outraged, heaving my nonexistent chest.

'*"Gabe," he told me, "you've only known the girl for one year, not ten. You'll get over it, and God willing, we can all forget about the hell she brought into our lives."*'

"Wha—" I shout, my voice cut off my throat explodes with pain. Before I can recover, lights flash into existence before me. What's happening?

"Wendy!" Gabriel says, his voice choked with emotion as I feel him exultantly touching my face and squeezing my hand.

My hand. I can feel my hand! I squeeze back and he lets out a whoop of joy.

I blink my eyes, trying to make sense of the lights. I start to turn my face away from them, but my neck spasms, stealing my breath.

"Don't move!" Gabriel says. "Your lymph nodes are too swollen. Don't try to speak aloud either. It will be too painful."

Obeying, I blink again, searching for his face, but it's far too bright.

'*Can you see me?*' his voice whispers in my head.

'*No,*' I think back. '*Maybe if you got that damn light out of my face.*'

He laughs out loud and relief floods me in never-ending waves—his relief. "I have never liked potty mouths, but at the moment it's adorable," he says. "And the light you're seeing is my life force."

I hesitate in confusion for only a moment; I guess my memory is still not one hundred percent. *'When did I go into the colorworld?'* I ask.

"You didn't. I did," he replies as I practice opening my eyes for brief periods of time to adjust my vision. "I discovered I could use you to go into the colorworld. It takes me quite a bit longer than you though. I learned to use my 'energy senses' at the compound, but I'm as deficient at it as everyone else. It also takes quite a bit of focus to stay here on my own—unlike you. But in the last few days I've gotten fairly good at it. But unfortunately I can't do a thing with your life force—that was the reason I wanted to come here in the first place."

'Do what with it?' I ask as the lights finally fade enough to reveal shapes.

"Do you remember what happened with Kaylen?"

Kaylen. It takes about five seconds for me to remember. I would probably jump up if I could move. But I open my eyes wide instead, resisting the urge to turn my head so I don't experience that stabbing pain again. This time I refuse to shirk away from the lights. The purple of Gabriel's life force is on one side of me. The fluctuating yellow of the ceiling is on the other.

'Kaylen!' I shout to Gabriel's mind. *'Her strands are put back? Her strands are put back!'* I want to shout, to jump, but I content myself to reach up for Gabriel. He catches my hand to his face.

"Yes! You moved them with your own," he says, kissing my palm, anticipation shooting through him and into me, making it harder for me to lie still. "Now you get why I've been trying so hard to get you to come around?"

'I can move my own strands back into place!' And then I unfocus to see his face, which is covered in thick stubble, and beaming at me. Tears have filled his eyes, and one of them is red, puffy, and bloodshot. It looks like it's going to develop a pretty ugly bruise.

"Exactly!" he says excitedly. "Can you find them or do you have to be in the water to do it?"

Struggling to calm down so I can dig in my memory for the last time I was awake and trying to fix Kaylen's life force. I reached for her strands then, and it wasn't just my hand that moved. It was my own strands. Eventually they began to feel like arms. Hundreds of thousands of them.

I try to recapture that sensation, willing my strands to spread out. And I feel them obey—at least some of them. I don't remember questioning it the last time, but this time I wonder why it is I can only control certain of my strands. I know I can perceive them all. When I close my eyes they feel like tiny wisps of air gusting through me, and it reminds me of the time Louise had me hypnotized and I went into the colorworld at the same time. I had forgotten about that feeling until now, but I recognize now what I didn't then: I can distinguish my life force from my body.

'*I can only control the ones that are loose,*' I tell Gabriel with my mind as he watches my strands with astonishment.

'*Incredible!*' he replies. '*Fortunately, the loose ones are the only ones that need to be controlled.*'

He's right, of course. I remember that Gabriel said I have some three hundred thousand loose ones, but I know them because I perceive them. I have suspended them above me for Gabriel to count out the right number.

"Separate them into two groups. One for the head and one for the chest," Gabriel says. "Then I can tell you how many to move around to get the right number in each." He's still in shock at how readily my life force strands bend to my will. So am I.

I do exactly what he asks. I keep the large majority of them over my chest. The rest I send over my head. I find I don't have to actually see them to know they are there.

"Not quite enough for the head," Gabriel says. "Move this whole bunch over." He circles a life force-clad finger around the top of a group of strands. I think exactly that and the strands move instantly. I'm still not sure how. But it's just as easy as moving my hands.

Wowed, Gabriel says, "Seventeen more to the head."

I count out the ones I want and they move over to join the others at my head.

Gabriel stares at the two groups of strands, their ends pointed upward like candles on a cake—a cake with hundreds of thousands of candles, all thinner than spider silk. I can tell they would like to move toward one another in their respective bunches like a rope, but I will them to stay separated where they are so Gabriel can count them.

"Well, ready when you are," Gabriel says, enthralled. "It should go without saying but I'll say it anyway: try to insert them simultaneously."

I don't hesitate. I plunge them in to their respective locations without effort because I know exactly where they all are. As soon as I do, the lights go out.

52

$\mathcal{I}$'m blind. And I feel... isolated and empty. My skin is cold all of a sudden. I blink my eyes to see, but not even a shadow finds its way into my view. And it's silent. Deathly so. Have I gone back into a coma? I cry out in panic and then pain, only partially relieved to hear the sound of my own voice.

'Gabriel! I can't see!' I think, reaching out for him. One hand hits cold metal and the other is held in place by something warm.

"Calm down, Love," a voice whispers softly from far away. "That was instant, wasn't it? It must seem quite dark after that. Don't worry. I'm here."

I think it's Gabriel, but he doesn't sound the same. His voice is... flatter. And quiet. The whole room is. Chest heaving, I remember what he just said and I connect the dots. I don't know how I forgot that I would, but I lost all of my abilities when my strands went back in. He can't hear my thoughts. I can't hear his. The emptiness in my head is the absence of his emotions—or anyone else's. I have been alone before, with no one within my emodar range, but I never realized that I was still picking up an ambiance, the sensation of emotions that were once in the space I was.

I take a deep breath, which hurts because of my neck, and I blink my eyes again, looking for any change. Nothing.

I consider enduring the pain so I can tell Gabriel I can't see, but even opening my mouth hurts.

I flit my eyes everywhere, praying that some light will find its way into my vision.

"Shhh," Gabriel says. "I'm right here." Warm pressure surrounds my hand and I have to assume it's his skin. *Oh please no.* It's warm, but dead. My chest feels odd and I recognize that my heart is pounding. I just can't hear it.

I squeeze his hand back, hard. Over and over.

Something brushes my face. Is it his hand? It doesn't feel right. It could be a prosthetic hand for as much as my skin reacts to his. I search for his emotions then—an automatic response. But it's met with stillness, and I realize I am blind in much more than my sight. I begin to cry, struggling not to sob because any sound I make hurts so badly, but it stabs my neck anyway. I choke as I try to hold back tears.

"Oh, Wendy," he says, his voice gentle but faraway. "It must be so different." To hear but not feel his accompanying tenderness only opens my wounds wider. I search in earnest for the colorworld. I know I can't access it but I look for it anyway, desperate for some kind of familiarity. No sight or sound or feeling comes to me though. Tears fall in earnest, but I hold my mouth shut tight so I don't hurt myself with sound, hoping and praying that the barest hint of Gabriel's emotions will ease their way into my head so I won't be so alone.

Gabriel is stroking my face with a hand, but it brings no comfort. "I admit, I took for granted what it would be like for you after you lost your abilities—I have been too intent on figuring out how to bring you around. But I cannot imagine... Please, won't you look at me?"

I try. I shift my eyes up, down, back and forth, pleading for at least a shadow. But it's completely dark. I blink profusely to convey that something is wrong.

"You can't see me?" he asks.

How does he expect me to answer? I guess he remembers that and he says, "Two blinks for yes. One blink for no."

I blink once.

"Nothing at all? Shadows?"

I blink once.

He is silent for a moment. Then he says, "Your eyes must be far too accustomed to seeing more, so the world as the rest of us see it is too dark to perceive. I suppose it really is like Plato's cave. Can you feel my hand on your face?"

I'm not sure how to answer that because a yes isn't really accurate. I settle for blinking twice and then once.

"Yes and no?" he asks.

I blink twice.

"Well that's a relief. And apparently you can hear me so that's also a good thing."

I want to ask him if this is permanent. Maybe my diabetes has caught up to me. If I hadn't had colorworld vision all this time, maybe I would have been blind from escalating diabetes.

"I think it likely your eyesight may return more slowly," Gabriel says.

What about everything else? This world is so silent and still and empty of feeling. Maybe I am still partially asleep, and I look for some way to wake up, like moving. But the resulting pain convinces me that I am definitely awake.

"I am so sorry, Love. I can only imagine what you must be feeling. Is there something I can do?"

I don't know if there is an answer to that, but I blink twice anyway.

"I suppose I have to guess what it is," he says. "Hmm, well if you can only feel me—sort of—and hear me, then that narrows my choices... I know you're upset, but it's highly likely now that you are going to recover. I know you can't feel it, but I am positively bursting inside with that probability. I think my heart wants to leap out of my chest, and I am crying tears of joy. See?" He moves my hand across the rough stubble of his face and over the curve of his cheekbone to below his eye. It is indeed wet.

I smile, leaving my hand to rest there. He's right. I have been far too upset with the nothingness around me to recognize the implications. I'm going to live and my chest makes a little jump of anticipation.

"Oh the soaring joy at seeing you smile. For a moment I thought you would have preferred that I let you die so you wouldn't have to endure this comparatively dark and dreary world with me."

I blink once, decidedly. Although I'd like to add the word lonely. It's a lonely world, too. I would embrace blindness if I could just feel Gabriel connected to me like he used to be.

"Oh thank heavens! So tell me, do you know why you evolved the ability to control your strands? I've been stumped. Three blinks for 'I don't know.'"

Good question. I guess I could have improved my ability... but that's such a drastic improvement. Sharing somatosense was pretty drastic as well, but it was a more natural progression from the magnetism of my skin and the telepathy. But Kaylen did jokingly say once that my ability might actually be controlling my strands; I just wasn't good enough at it yet. Maye I *got* good at it? I blink three times.

"Your ability was a wellspring of possibility that delivered something new all the time. The combination of emodar and colorworld sight and channeling made for quite a fertile environment for so many talents to emerge. My only guess is you improved your ability somehow there at the end and that's what emerged." He sighs. "But I admit it doesn't align as well with your past improvements."

I'll probably never know now, and I probably shouldn't think about it either. It will only make me miss what I don't have. Acclimating is going to be hard.

428

I move my hand over Gabriel's face again because I need some way to connect. I linger my hand on his scruff and smile. I've never seen Gabriel with more than a five o'clock shadow. This is different.

"Do you like it?" he asks.

I blink three times. I strain to see his direction, hoping it conveys that I don't know if I like it because I can't see it, but when I do, an outline of his shadow moves out of the surrounding darkness. I blink again, trying to bring out the edges of it more clearly, but it remains obscure. I focus on it with all my might, afraid if I look elsewhere, this small bit of vision will disappear.

"Wendy, are you looking at me?" Gabriel asks.

I blink twice.

"Can you see shadows now?"

I blink twice.

"Excellent! I think it's going to come back—well somewhat. I doubt that if your vision returns that you are going to feel it's adequate enough."

Small victories. I try not to be discouraged, but I'm terrified of a future with this kind of loneliness. So I grip Gabriel's hand with the little strength I have, and I hang on for dear life.

53

"*Wh*y are you looking at me like that?" I ask Kaylen as I sit on the end of the couch opposite her. It was added to my room in Robert's Monterey home recently, taking up a space that was entirely occupied by medical equipment before. I've been staring a lot at the the chart that's still on the wall. An extension has been added to it to accommodate all of my cell counts the past few months, even my counts from yesterday, which were normal. I had a marrow biopsy three days ago, which came up squeaky clean. I'm cancer-free, and I'm trying to be thrilled about it.

Kaylen shakes her head and leans against the couch arm. "I don't think you get how miraculous your recovery is."

"Of course I know it's miraculous," I reply, drawing my knees up and looking up at the decorative clock on the wall across the room, straining my eyes to see the hands. I become frustrated *again* that I can't make them out. It's just like Gabriel said. My vision came back slowly, but it's still awful and I'm giving it two more weeks and then I'm getting glasses. Normal people can read a clock on the wall, right? I turn back at Kaylen who looks... aggravated? I don't know. I'm not used to depending on facial expressions to decipher people's moods.

Ezra walks into the room, grinning at me. "Look out, Kaylen. She's not blubbering or sleeping. Which means she's about to bite your head off."

I glare at him.

"Ezra, don't be a jerk," Kaylen chides. "You'd blubber all the time too if you woke up and felt like someone had lobotomized you. And you'd yell at people who told you to get over it and be happy about not dying."

Ezra's right. For the past three weeks I have either been a sobbing mess, a sleeping zombie, or a hibernating grizzly eating everything in sight. It's only been two days ago that I started being awake more than asleep and keeping a more normal sleep and meal schedule. The blubbering has been a result of what it's like to be awake: alone. Despite having so many people around me, I feel completely alone and I absolutely hate it. It's frustrating and frightening. And dark. All the time. I obsessively turn on lights. I even sleep with them on.

"Hey, someone's gotta snap her out of it," Ezra says. "I have the luxury of being related to her so I know no matter how mad she gets at me, she's not actually going anywhere. And one day she's going to stop whining about what she doesn't have and taking it out on people."

He doesn't get it. He never will. Nobody will. And one day he'll get tired of taking jabs at me. Or he'll go back to school in a month and be out of my face most of the day.

"Are we going to tell her now?" Ezra whines. "Gabe's finally gone."

Kaylen huffs and says, "I was *trying* to. And then you had to walk in and be all obnoxious and annoying."

"What!" Ezra says, dragging the desk chair over. "You were going to do it without me? You suck, Kaylen."

"Tell me what?" I demand.

"About what happened during your coma," Ezra says excitedly.

"It was a miracle you woke up long enough to fix your strands at all," Kaylen says. "Your lungs failed that day at the pool because of a complication with the transfusion you had earlier. You stopped breathing, and CPR wasn't working. If Jeanelle hadn't been nearby with a vent bag you would have died right there. Then on the way to the hospital your heart stopped. Once they got it started again, Gabe was fighting with the hospital staff to give you something to wake you up, because you know, he wanted you to fix your own life force. They wanted to keep you on sedatives to keep you out of pain and not messing with your vent. As he was arguing with them and trying to get a hold of Robert to swing his weight around, you had a seizure. And that's what put you in the coma. In the next three days, your kidneys failed, one lung collapsed, and your heart stopped again. This time because of fluid around it."

Seeing my eyes wide and my mouth agape, Ezra nods and says, "That's just the *beginning* of the story. In all that time Gabe was looking for some way to wake you up. For a while we were all with him about bringing you around. Nothing worked, and brain scan showed you weren't responding to stimuli at all. The only way to keep you alive another day was giving you transfusions, dialysis, IVs, and keeping you intubated. The doctors were convinced we were in denial about you dying. They tried to send in counselors and stuff so we would let you go."

"What was Robert doing?" I ask. I've talked to my uncle a few times the last few weeks, but mostly about my adjustment and how distressing it's turning out to be.

"Paid for it. But stayed far away. I have no idea where." Ezra says. "He wouldn't take our calls, and Mark wouldn't tell us anything. And that's when Kaylen and I turned. We figured Robert was just paying for it to appease Gabe and that he figured you weren't going to wake up and he couldn't take watching. We thought if you were going to live, Robert wouldn't have left that day by the pool. He would have been right there, trying to wake you up. It was really hard to watch you."

Ezra's expression turns somber, and Kaylen's eyes are red. "Gabe didn't ever give up," she says. "He was relentless, staying by your bed every single moment of the day and night, talking to you, coaxing you, squeezing your hand, wanting you to twitch or something. After two days he figured out how to go into the colorworld using you. That was a big victory for him since he remembered you woke him from a coma that way before. When that didn't immediately work, he started trying to figure out how to fix your strands himself." She raises her eyebrows expectantly.

I look between them with confusion. "How?"

"How do you think?" Ezra asks. "Gabe is a crazy S.O.B. that would do anything for you. Take a guess."

It takes me a few moments because my brain doesn't work like Gabriel's. There are two ways that I know of to fix strands: telekinesis and my loose strands. We no longer know anyone capable of telekinesis, and nobody has any loose strands— "Oh my gosh," I say. "He was going to have someone yank his strands out, wasn't he?"

Ezra nods vigorously. "Yep. He figured since you could channel your abilities, and one of them was now moving your own loose strands, all it would take was him being able to move yours with his own."

I close my eyes, familiar dread seeping into me at the possibility that Gabriel may have a messed up life force again due to a failed attempt to repair mine. "Please tell me he didn't end up trying that. Please."

"Nope," Ezra says. "We might have given up on you living, but Kaylen was *not* going to do something she knew you would never allow. She was the only one of us that knew enough about hypno-touch to be able to do it on him, so of course he tried to badger her into it. You should have seen her back him down on it. Literally. Backed him right into a wall and yelled at him to stop trying to desecrate something you died to save."

"He didn't take it well," Kaylen says, wincing. "He said you weren't dead yet. Then he started walking away, but he stopped, turned around, and said, 'Wendy is going to live. I promise you that.'" She stares at me knowingly.

I get the significance. Gabriel doesn't make promises he can't keep. That he would make such a promise with so much stacked against him boggles my mind. If I had been Kaylen, I would have been seriously worried about him at that point.

"What did you do?" I ask, leaning forward.

"I ran for the notebook in the van," she replies. "I was totally freaked out, so I wasn't thinking of the other ways he could get his hands on the names. He could have memorized them. He also had the e-mail from Carl with the names."

I nod. "Names of people who had had hypno-touch and probably knew how to do it, too. What did he do?"

"Ignored Kaylen and started packing an overnight bag at the hotel of course," Ezra says. "That dude is like... crazy, Wen. I have never in my life seen someone so determined. Honestly, he scared me."

"But who stopped him?" I ask, dying to know what person actually deterred Gabriel from something he was obviously so set on.

Kaylen and Ezra look at each other.

Ezra leans forward in his chair and looks at me. "Have you ever seen Uncle Rob yell?"

I think my face blanches. "He did?" I squeak.

Ezra laughs and leans back, clasping his hands behind his head. "No."

I lean forward and slap his leg. "Stop it and tell me what happened."

"Kaylen and I were in the lobby, trying to convince Mark that if he didn't handcuff Gabe he was going to kill himself. We were like, desperate. Mark wouldn't do it, but agreed to at least not *drive* Gabe anywhere. Just then Gabe came down and Kaylen and I were desperate for a new way to stall him before he could call a cab or something. But right then a cab pulled up anyway and we figured he must have called it from the room. Except then the door of the cab opened and Uncle Rob stepped out! Kaylen and I were like, *floored*, because Uncle Rob had been MIA for days. Uncle Rob walked right in through the front door all causal-like, as if he just *coincidentally* decided to drop by to check on us. He met Gabe right there in the lobby, stopped in front of him and said, 'Well hello, Gabe. Is everything alright at the hospital?'

"Gabe lit into him for like five minutes about where Uncle Rob had been all that time and what had been happening in the meantime. Robert stood there and took it, didn't try to fit a word in, even after Gabe got everything off his chest that he wanted to say. Gabe ended with the same promise he'd made to Kaylen— that you would live. The only thing Gabe *didn't* mention was finding someone for hypno-touch. I was about to run forward and tell Uncle Rob, hoping he could talk some sense into him. But oh my gosh, Wen, Uncle Rob looked right at me before I could even shift my foot, and I knew I shouldn't move. And I knew that he *knew* what Gabe was planning."

Ezra comes up for air, the words having rushed out of him. I'm sitting stock-still as if I was him, standing there in the lobby with Robert's knowing eyes on me.

"It was like ten seconds of silence between them," Kaylen says. "Then Robert reached out and put his hand on Gabe's arm. And then Robert said so quietly we could barely hear him, 'You are good at keeping promises, Gabe. No matter the circumstance. It's something I greatly admire about you.'"

"He lets go of Gabe's arm and then asked if he needed his cab," Ezra says. "Gabe stood there staring at him for a few seconds and then shook his head."

I stare at them, frozen in wonder. Kaylen and Ezra wouldn't know this, but Gabriel promised me that last day at the pool that he would live for me. Live. Not die. Robert was not there to hear it either, but somehow he knew to remind Gabriel of promises. Such a simple thing and it made all the difference. I'm sure now that Robert had to have known I would live. He made himself scarce so he wouldn't mess up that future, stepping in only when really needed. I love that man.

"From that point, Gabe went back to trying to wake you up, and strangely he was even more dedicated than ever," Kaylen says. "He started wearing your scarf on his arm everyday. We didn't come around because it was too heartbreaking."

The scarf... I tied it on his arm when he made that promise to me.

"So what about the intubation?" I ask. "When I woke up I wasn't intubated."

"Oh yeah!" Kaylen says, her eyes brightening. "It was like... the second day in? Yeah, I think so. Well Gabe noticed you were breathing over the ventilator. They hadn't been checking your lung function because they figured you were going to die before you ever recovered from the transfusion-related lung damage. But you did. Just like all the other side-effects you and

Gabe went through during chemo. Hypno-touch bodies heal quicker, remember? Even on your death-bed, apparently."

"Weird," I say.

"Yeah, but it was right after your heart stopped that second time. Gabe was probably at his worst. I think he wasn't even sure you were going to live. It was really hard for any of us to imagine that you could come back from your sickness if we did manage to wake you up and fix your strands. But when you recovered from that as sick as you were, Gabe was renewed and he didn't let go of any hope after that."

I stare at them in dumb wonder. Kaylen is right. My recovery is miraculous in more ways than I realized. Gabriel managed to find the one way to bring me out of a coma that was supposed to end in my death. He found me where I was in my own head. I told him a few days ago, after learning that it was Plato he had been reading to me, that the only reason I came around was because his voice in my head wouldn't shut up. He was boring me to death with thousand year old texts. But thank goodness for Plato. I suppose even Plato's philosophies have had a hand in the Gabriel I know and love so I can't dislike it even a little.

"Scary or not, Gabe kept you alive," Ezra says, hanging his head. "The two of us have been feeling beyond stupid for doubting him."

"Ezra," I say, "I am pretty sure I would have done the same thing. Apparently I married a man who doesn't know how to give up. So his persistence shouldn't make either of you feel bad. He's a superhuman, remember?"

"Oh yeah, I remember alright," Ezra says, nodding emphatically. "And I am positive that I will never be on the side he's not. Clearly, *that* is the losing side."

I laugh then, partly because Gabriel's tenacity is so appalling it's funny and partly because laughing makes things less surreal. I am alive by not one miracle, but many, not the least of which is Gabriel's persistent presence in my life. *I'm supposed to be alive.* I haven't admitted it to myself until now, but I've begun to wonder if I've cheated death and that's why living is now so hard. But after hearing all that, this sounds not only silly, but offensive to the efforts that went into keeping me here. Ezra's right. I needed this story.

"Why hasn't he told me this?" I ask.

Ezra shrugs. "He said he's ashamed that he almost broke a promise to you and that he tried to intimidate Kaylen. He said he'd tell you eventually, but 'A story like that doesn't inspire confidence in someone who is struggling to find her footing.'"

Ezra rolls his eyes. "Whatever."

Gabriel, who left earlier today on a mysterious mission he wouldn't tell me about, bounds into the room right then with a grin on his face, which is clean-shaven again but for the soul patch below his lip. "I bought you an anniversary gift." He holds up a set of keys. I can't tell what kind of keys.

"It's not our anniversary yet," I say. "You're ten days early."

"I can't help it. I'm terrible at withholding surprises. Besides, it's never too early to celebrate one's marriage to the most amazing woman on the planet."

I can't help but smile at his exuberance even though I feel anything but amazing. I've been pretty hard to live with the last few weeks. "Is it a car?"

"No. I bought you a home!"

"You bought a house?" I ask, wondering how he ever fit in the time for such a thing.

He tilts his head and purses his lips. "More or less."

"Is it a house or isn't it?" I ask, unsure about the idea of moving somewhere new right now.

"You'll see. Let me show you." He reaches for my hand, pulling me to my feet.

"Did you get the one I liked?" Kaylen asks, bouncing in place.

"Yes," Gabriel says to her, putting a finger over his lips.

"Oh my gosh, Wendy, you are going to *love* it," Kaylen says, beaming.

I look at Ezra because he's more likely to know what I'd actually love. He holds his hands up. "Wen. I can honestly say I have no idea how you're going to react to this one."

Now I'm curious.

"You two stay here," Gabriel commands. "I want the look on her face all to myself." And then he leads me out the door.

"So… you bought something that is more or less a house," I say skeptically. "If neither of us has a job, how is that possible?"

He gives me a look over his shoulder before opening my car door. "Because I am Gabriel Dumas, and I am determined to give you everything, no matter the obstacles."

I hold up my free hand in acquiescence. After the story I heard, I can't argue with that. But I can't help missing his emotions, which I'm sure would elevate my level of anticipation right now. I think I don't know how to feel strong emotions on my own—except fear.

***

We drive to the harbor—not at all where I expected—filling me with greater curiosity. Waterfront property is nowhere near affordable, unless Robert's paying. But I don't think Gabriel is the type to lean on Robert for the sake of extravagance.

Instead of a neighborhood though, we leave the car in a public parking lot, and Gabriel tucks my hand under his arm as we set off toward the wharf. It's a hot day, made hotter by the cloudless sky and the uncharacteristic lack of air movement that allows heat waves to linger above the asphalt. My hand under Gabriel's arm starts sweating by the time we reach the boardwalk. I look around, not knowing what I'm looking for, and fighting to not become upset that the people, sand, and water look like one blur. Gabriel leads me to the marina, and down one of the docks lined with moored boats.

"No way. Did you buy a boat?" I ask.

He doesn't answer, just leads me on while I entertain the idea of owning a boat. What kind of boat? He said it was a home, so a yacht? Houseboat? Holy crap. He wants me to live on a boat?

We stop directly in front of one boat, an older-looking sailboat.

"A sailboat?" I ask him. "Do you know how to sail?"

"Nope," he says, hopping on deck and holding out a hand to me. "But I've read plenty."

"Of course you have," I say, taking his hand and stepping aboard, a little thrill running through me over the fact that Gabriel has managed to surprise me completely. Again. Smiling, I check out the length of it. It's big. Not huge, but I bet there's a nice little apartment below.

He stops me before I can inspect below-deck. "She's seaworthy, but the interior is going to take some work. I was hoping we could do it together. Robert will allow us to live with him while we get it ready. I think it will be fun for a first home. I felt like we needed something simpler."

I look at him, baffled that buying a boat would occur to Gabriel at all. I've never heard him talk about sailing, let alone boats. "What made you think a boat would be simpler?"

His brow crinkles in worry at my interrogation, but he answers, "I didn't want to give you the familiarity of an apartment or something *normal*. Being in places you've already been and doing things you've already done after having lost what you've

437

lost won't bring you healing. I wanted you to adapt to your new life with something you've never experienced. Something neither of us has. We're starting over, Wendy. It's taken me a while to accept that, but we are. We are both so very different now. And the things that tied us together so easily are no longer there. We have to find new things to bind us. I want to build something with you. Both literally and metaphorically. This is the literal thing. The metaphorical thing, I hope, will come as we bring our efforts together."

My shoulders slump and my throat catches. Tears fill my eyes and I throw my arms around him. Guilt consumes me. Gabriel thinks I don't love him like I did before. He has felt my distance and seen my unhappiness. I don't blame him. I have not been intimate with him since his own recovery. I have not even kissed him beyond a peck on the cheek because I have been afraid for the same reasons that Gabriel bought a boat instead of an apartment: familiar acts will be nothing like what they were before. I will not be able to duplicate the connection we once shared. No feelings will move from him to me. Every touch will be less than it could be. What will be left? A one-sided act of self-gratification that yearns for more... The disappointment could tear us apart. I can't *un-know* what it's like to share every part of yourself, not merely your body parts—though I wish I could.

"I am so sorry," I whisper. I cling to him harder, remembering Kaylen and Ezra's story that evidenced how much Gabriel loves me and always has and will fight for me. I have taken him for granted and I've rejected him without explaining why. "You don't deserve this."

"Don't deserve what?" he says, pulling away to look at me and holding my hands in his next to his chest.

"The way I've treated you," I reply. "I..." I can't speak through my tears, which he is now wiping away with a hand. I look at him directly, something I have not done in a long time. "I want you," I whisper. "I just... want *all* of you. I want what we shared before. And I don't know how to teach myself to be satisfied with less. I'm afraid..."

He exhales deeply, and I'm not sure what it means. I watch his face closely, looking for an indication of what he feels, but he holds me gently to himself, tentatively, because in the past few weeks I have pulled away from him, uncomfortable with where it might lead. Even now I have to fight against my frenzied thoughts.

But he holds me softly, putting his cheek to my forehead. "You don't have to apologize. I have been prepared to wait as long as it takes."

My worry eases and I wrap my arms around his waist. "You shouldn't have to."

"But I too am afraid, Wendy. I don't want to... disappoint you either."

Gabriel is worried about disappointing me? Gabriel goes above and beyond in everything he does. I'm standing on the deck of our new boat for goodness' sake, because Gabriel didn't want a mundane apartment to *disappoint* me. I'm *alive* because Gabriel took on what everyone else thought was impossible.

Then what are you afraid of, Wendy?

I lift my head and look at him directly. "Disappoint me? You and I both know you don't know how to merely satisfy, Mister Dumas. You won't be satisfied until you are blowing my mind in every way." I lean in and put my lips on his, holding them there to fully-appreciate the sensation, determined to take this slow not out of fear, but to be sure I don't miss a single detail. His lips are hot from the heat, and I bet if I could feel his emotions, he would be completely taken by surprise. He also doesn't move, so I think he doesn't know what's okay to do, so I reach for his face, kissing him more firmly to indicate I want something with a little more fire.

He kisses me back finally, and I am surprised at how that simple movement increases my passion, and I'm too consumed by it to wonder why. I respond, because for once anxiety does not accompany the sensation of his skin on mine. I decide this is a lot like a dream, lacking the clarity and quality of real life, but still capable of eliciting strong emotions, which, I realize, is the form happiness comes in. I focus on the shape of him against the shape of me, reminding myself that everything we had before is still there. I'm just going to have to work harder to find it.

He is kissing a trail from the corner of my mouth to my ear, and I say, "I am ready for my mind-blowing normal life to begin."

"Mind-blowing and normal... Let me think on that," he says, pausing, and I think he is content to just hold me. "I'm not sure I know how to do normal."

"Me neither," I sigh, putting my cheek to his. "We're going to have to find someone normal to get some pointers on that."

He chuckles. "Something tells me, Wendy, that you and I will never be normal no matter what we do."

Epilogue

$\mathcal{M}$aris looks like she wants to ask me a question, although I can't be sure because I can't read her emotions. I know I have got to stop referring back to that particular deprivation, but I can't help it. How does one get used to being blind to the emotions of others?

Well I had better not make any assumptions. That has gotten me in trouble before. Most people don't analyze faces as much as I do, but I can't stand unspoken thoughts. That's why Gabriel and I get on so well. He says whatever is on his mind ninety-nine percent of the time.

His mother is starting to irritate me though with her sidelong glances. It makes me self-conscious. I am about to tell her to spit it out when Gabriel walks into the kitchen where Maris is teaching me how to make tamales.

"Su esposa está embarazada, Gabriel," Maris says.

The woman knows I don't understand Spanish, yet she tends to fluctuate between Spanish and English regularly. I think I recognize the word 'esposa' though. 'Spouse.' Is she talking about me behind my back?

I ignore her and turn back to peeling the onion in front of me.

"Estás loca, Mamá?" Gabriel replies.

I look over my shoulder to see him stopped dead in his tracks with a look of pure incredulity. I think he told his mother she's crazy.

"Les puedo decir," Maris replies.

Gabriel shrugs off his surprise and then says, "Es ridículo supersticioso mujer."

"Will you two please speak English?" I say. "It's bad enough I can't hear your emotions. Now I don't even understand the words that come out of your mouths." I hate being in the dark.

"Sorry, Love," Gabriel says, coming up behind me and putting his arms around my waist. "My mother thinks you're pregnant and I told her she was off her rocker."

I look at Maris, startled. Why would she think that? She must be trying to plant ideas in Gabriel's head. It's only been a month since Gabriel woke me out of my deathbed coma, and she already wants grandchildren?

"I am not superstitious, Gabe," Maris says. "You'll see. She is pregnant. Look at her. She's radiant."

Yeah, radiant. I call that miraculous life force strand insertion leukemia cure at work.

"Of course she's radiant, Mamá. She always looks that way. It's her natural essence," Gabriel says, nuzzling my neck and sending chills down my arms.

Maris rolls her eyes as she comes over to take the onions from me. She puts them in a large pot of water.

"I like this," Gabriel says, tugging at my head kerchief.

I smile, thinking of the red, green, and white silk I have tied on my nearly-bald head. "I figured you would. I got it just for you."

"Mmmm, it's quite bewitching. Were you intending to seduce me? Because it's working," Gabriel says quietly into my neck as he places kisses there in a way he knows I can never resist.

I can't believe he's doing this in front of his mother knowing how it will affect me. Of course, that's probably the point. He likes to push her buttons. Pushing mine is probably just a bonus.

I hear a loud smack and open my eyes to see Maris standing with a towel in hand, having just swatted Gabriel with it.

"Ouch, Mamá! What was that for?" Gabriel says, looking like a naughty school boy. It's hilarious how much he reverts to a mischievous child when he's around his mom.

"You know," Maris says, wagging a finger at him. "And I would say that if this is what you do out in public, it's no wonder Wendy is pregnant."

"I am not pregnant, Maris," I say.

She crosses her arms. "Oh? What makes you so sure?"

"Months of chemo, unrecognizable toxins in my blood, killing my bone marrow to reset my system, anemia, kidney failure, lung failure, you know, just to name a few," I say. "In fact, it was only six weeks ago that I went into cardiac arrest. For the *second* time." I won't add it to my verbal list, but Gabriel and I only started being intimate again yesterday—hence his exceptionally good mood today. "Pregnant," I mumble. "Impossible."

Maris gives me another sideways glance. "Have you had your cycle?"

Why is she bringing up my menstruation cycle? She is as probingly honest as Gabriel. Well, at least I know where he gets it from.

"No," I say. "But like I said, chemicals, toxins and stuff." *And no sex.* "Doesn't really do the ovaries good. Besides, the doctor said it would probably be a while before it came back."

"Furthermore, Mamá," Gabriel says. "Wendy and I had not engaged in intercourse post-illness until yesterday."

My mouth opens and my face turns red. I hide it behind the cutting board as I take it over to the sink to wash. I should have known Gabriel would just out with it like that.

"It only takes once," Maris says, unbothered by receiving details about Gabriel's and my sex life as she digs out several cannisters from a cabinet.

Gabriel comes to stand next to me by the sink. "You do realize that your recovery was not 'normal' right? There's no reason to expect that you shouldn't be fertile now. You're on birth control, right?"

I look up, and I think my cheeks grow red again. "Uh no," I say, feeling awkward—and naive. Do we really have to have this conversation *now*? The chances of me having gotten pregnant yesterday and then Maris being able to tell by looking at me are slim to none.

Gabriel raises an amused eyebrow at me while speaking to his mom, "You might be right, Mamá."

"Of course I'm right," Maris says offhand, clunking a large heavy steamer pot onto the stove.

***

I catch my breath as I watch the image on the screen. It's a baby. Despite the grainy resolution, there is no mistaking it because of the development. Nose, forehead, chin. Backbone with arms and legs... Fingers and toes. If I hadn't seen an ultrasound before, I might second-guess myself, but that is *not* a baby that was conceived only a week ago.

Anxiety overwhelms me. How is this possible? "How far along?" I croak, my mouth dry. Please let me be mistaken, because this is nuts.

Dr. Novak clicks a few keys and moves his mouse around, taking measurements as he looks at the monitor. Then he says, "I would say you are about seventeen weeks along."

I feel lightheaded.

"That cannot possibly be correct, my good sir," Gabriel says, his face a mixture of both doubt and absolute wonder.

Dr. Novak gives him a questioning look. "Why not?"

Gabriel and I look at each other, trying to figure out how we'll explain that seventeen weeks ago I was nearly dead and surely not capable of getting pregnant. Yet here I sit quite recovered from being on my deathbed so short a time ago.

Gabriel turns back to the doctor. "Because we've only had intercourse in the last seven days. Prior to that we had not engaged for at least seven months."

Dr. Novak looks uncomfortable, probably thinking I've been two-timing Gabriel and not wanting to be here when he figures it out. He looks back at the screen. "Well I would say maybe sixteen weeks on the conservative side, but certainly not less than that. Typically fetal age is calculated from the time of the last cycle, which means that based on my measurements, you conceived anytime between fourteen and fifteen weeks ago. No sooner. I'm sure of that."

"How is that possible?" Gabriel says, though I don't think he's speaking to the doctor now.

"Mr. Dumas, I assure you, I've done this for many years, and that," he says, pointing at the screen, "is at least a sixteen week-old fetus. Perhaps you'd like some time to discuss it with your wife?" He gets up from his chair, looking like he's ready to flee.

Not having considered the possibility that I might have been running around on him fifteen weeks ago, Gabriel looks in confusion at the doctor, then at my white face before realization comes over him. His brows turn into questioning arches, because really, infidelity is the only reasonable explanation, and Gabriel is logic-driven.

"Are you kidding?" I hiss, and then glancing at the doctor I say, struggling to contain my confusion as well as my fear. "Is it healthy?"

Dr. Novak nods. "Everything looks good so far. Did you want to know the gender?"

Oh my gosh. It's big enough to know the gender. My head spins again and I feel Gabriel's hand find mine, squeezing tightly. "Not at this time. Thank you, Dr. Novak," Gabriel says.

"You're welcome," Dr. Novak replies, wiping off my abdomen with a towel. "I'd like to see you again in one month. You can schedule it with the receptionist on your way out." Turning the screen off, he holds out a strip of ultrasound pictures. I didn't even know he'd printed them. "But take your time," he says, standing and pushing his stool out of the way before exiting the room.

Gabriel is holding the ultrasound pictures, scrutinizing them.

"Gabriel," I say. "I have never cheated on you."

He shakes his head as he continues to look down at the pictures. "I don't believe you were unfaithful, Wendy. I'm simply trying to figure out how—" Gabriel stops abruptly and assumes the intense thought expression I know so well. I wish I could experience the emotional version of his mental whir in my head. Ugh. I'm so empty up there.

"Oh my," Gabriel says, dubious.

"What?" I demand, knowing he has surely figured out an explanation for this immaculate conception.

"Well there was that one time..." Gabriel says, his tone giving away his skepticism.

"What time?" I ask. What is he saying? We never had sex fourteen weeks ago...

Oh, wait.

I pull out my phone to look at the calender, racking my memory for dates, but honestly the days were all blended into one back then. I count back fourteen weeks, then fifteen...

"Gabriel, is that even possible?" I ask, recalling the one and only time that coincides with the window the doctor gave us. Gabriel had barely recovered from lung cancer and I was starting to decline again after my autograft transplant. "I was dying! I had countless rounds of chemo after that."

"It's the only explanation," Gabriel says, still consumed with thought.

I lay back on the exam table, struggling past shock to actually think about what a huge curve ball this is. When Maris insisted I was pregnant, I kept beating myself up over not having taken precautions with Gabriel. I don't want to be pregnant. I am barely hanging on to living my everyday life as just me, a married woman with no superpowers. Emotionally, I think I'm no better off than I was when I did this at sixteen years old. I was a basket case then. I'm a basket case now. Why now? I'm not fit to be a mother right now. I can't even sleep with the light off.

I bought pregnancy tests as an obsessed precaution. And I only took the one two days ago because with the possibility of pregnancy on the table, I began to see signs of it everywhere. I needed an answer and I was determined to take one a day until I menstruated, just for peace of mind. When the first one came up positive I got an appointment as soon as possible, demanding a blood test. Dr. Novak felt my abdomen as part of the exam and then moved immediately to an ultrasound.

And now I find out I'm not *barely* pregnant. I'm nearly halfway done!

How on earth was I growing a person all that time?

"Gabriel? I may have been stupid to assume that I couldn't get pregnant right after my recovery but that does not explain how I got pregnant while on my deathbed."

"I know," Gabriel says, still thinking. After a moment he says, "I suppose it's possible... and your illness was unusual in every sense of the word. Hypno-touch-affected bodies were somewhat miraculous at times, as you know. Were you menstruating during that time I was recovering?"

I think back. "I was spotting. All the time. Couldn't tell you when it started or when it ended. I figured it was my insides trying to fall out," I say, annoyed for a reason I can't pinpoint.

Gabriel throws his hands up. "It's possible, Wendy. You did go off quite a few medications after receiving the marrow-graft. Your preventative chemo was light." Gabriel's face indicates that he has moved into thought once more.

I sigh heavily, zipping my shorts. "I think we've seen enough crazy stuff to know that crazy stuff can happen," I say, wanting to move on from the impossibility of the whole thing and into how to deal with it.

"So true." Gabriel looks at the ultrasound photos with a new expression: lips parted, eyes wide. The corners of his mouth are on their way upward, and it doesn't take emodar to see that he's a man lost in a moment of wonder. After a moment, he turns to me with excitement. "What do you think about the prospect of us becoming parents?"

I hop up to head for the door, looking back at him, unsure how I really do feel. A blanket of calm moves over me just looking at him. This isn't like the last time. I am married, not in high school. My child has a father who doesn't even know how to back out of a commitment, let alone want to. And I am many years and experiences wiser. I know how to take care of other people now. I might be relatively blind, but I am not alone this time. Not by a long shot. But I'm still getting used to the fact that I am alive, not dead, and have been learning to enjoy my new life with Gabriel. And learning it has been. It's been like being newlyweds again, full of insecurity and miscommunication. And due to my past, pregnancy has a turmoil of dread attached to it that's difficult to shake.

I bite my lip. "I'm kind of in shock. I... have a lot of reminiscing going on in my head and it's not all that pleasant if you know what I mean. And I'm still... recovering. I'm overwhelmed."

Gabriel pulls me into an embrace. "It's going to be different this time, you know," he says into my almost pixie-length hair.

I sigh into him. "I know. The past few months have been insane. The last few weeks have been a mixture of bliss and depression. I think I might be at my limit with this one. I need some time to process it. You?"

He lets go to smile at me. "Well I've thought about it a great deal in the last week since you showed me the test, and while it is probably not the ideal time, I must admit I'm quite thrilled."

I chuckle. "I wouldn't expect anything less from the man who lives for his next challenge," I say, squeezing his hand.

Look for book 3 of the Colorworld series:

Shadoworld

Visit the official site at:
http://colorworldbooks.com